BROADCHURCH

BROADCHURCH

ERIN KELLY

Based on the TV series by Chris Chibnall

MINOTAUR BOOKS

NEW YORK

BROADCHURCH. Copyright © 2014 by Erin Kelly and Chris Chibnall. All rights reserved. Printed in the United States of America. For information, address St. Martin's Press, 175 Fifth Avenue, New York, N.Y. 10010.

Based on the television series *Broadchurch* produced by Kudos and Imaginary Friends Productions.

www.minotaurbooks.com

The Library of Congress has cataloged the hardcover edition as follows:

Kelly, Erin, 1976– author.
  Broadchurch / Erin Kelly and Chris Chibnall. — First U.S. Edition.
    p. cm.
  ISBN 978-1-250-05550-7 (hardcover)
  ISBN 978-1-4668-5851-0 (e-book)
  1. Policewomen—England—Fiction. 2. Murder—Investigation—Fiction.
3. Mystery fiction. I. Chibnall, Chris, author. II. Title.
  PR6111.E498B76 2014
  823'.92—dc23

                                                                2014019562

ISBN 978-1-250-06797-5 (trade paperback)

Minotaur books may be purchased for educational, business, or promotional use. For information on bulk purchases, please contact the Macmillan Corporate and Premium Sales Department at 1-800-221-7945, extension 5442, or write to specialmarkets@macmillan.com.

First published in Great Britain by Sphere, an imprint of Little, Brown Book Group, an Hachette UK company

First Minotaur Books Paperback Edition: February 2015

10 9 8 7 6 5 4 3 2 1

There is a condition worse than blindness, and that is seeing something that isn't there.

THOMAS HARDY

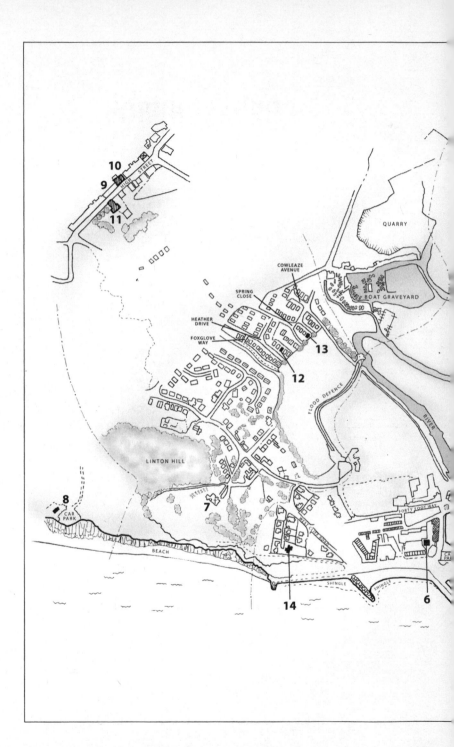

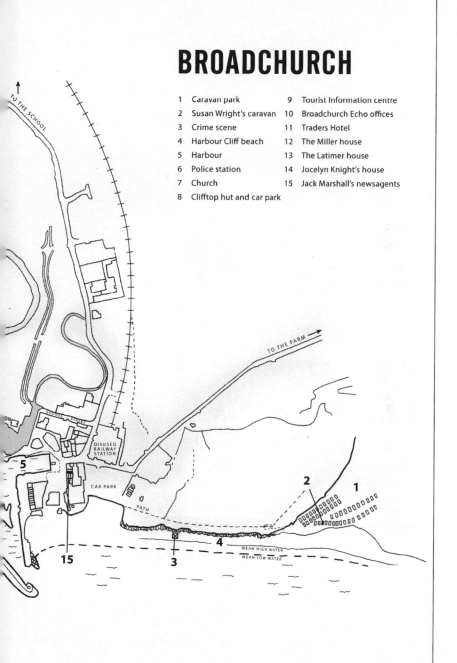

BROADCHURCH

1 Caravan park
2 Susan Wright's caravan
3 Crime scene
4 Harbour Cliff beach
5 Harbour
6 Police station
7 Church
8 Clifftop hut and car park
9 Tourist Information centre
10 Broadchurch Echo offices
11 Traders Hotel
12 The Miller house
13 The Latimer house
14 Jocelyn Knight's house
15 Jack Marshall's newsagents

BROADCHURCH

PROLOGUE

One road in, one road out. Broadchurch isn't on the way to anywhere and you don't go there by accident.

This sleepy coastal town is preparing to wake up for the summer season, but tonight nothing stirs. It is the crisp, clean night that follows a hot, cloudless day. There is a full moon and stars prickle the sky. Waves drag and crash as the petrol-black sea retreats from the beach. The Jurassic cliffs above glow amber, as though still radiating the heat they absorbed during the day.

On the deserted High Street, few shops bother to keep their lights on overnight. A single page of newsprint – yesterday's news – tumbles noiselessly down the middle of the road. The *Broadchurch Echo* headquarters and the neighbouring tourist office are in shadow, save for the occasional blink of computer equipment on standby.

In the harbour, boats bob and masts clank in the shadows. Overlooking the cobbles and jetties is the modern police station, its round steel keep clad in blond wood. The blue light outside flickers. Even a sleepy town keeps one eye open at night.

The church on the hill is unlit, the rich jewel colours of its stained-glass windows dulled to a uniform satin black. A weathered poster reading LOVE THY NEIGHBOUR AS THYSELF flaps uselessly from the parish noticeboard.

At the other end of town, the Latimer house is in darkness too. Their semi in Spring Close is like all the others on their estate; their estate is like all the others in the country. Moonlight shines through eleven-year-old Danny's half-open bedroom window, silvering posters, toys and an empty single bed. The side gate is ajar and the latch bangs slightly in the breeze but the sound does not wake his parents Beth and Mark, who sleep back-to-back underneath a BHS duvet. A bedside clock ticks off the seconds. It is 3.16 in the morning.

Danny is a mile and a half away, shivering in his thin grey T-shirt and black jeans. He is sixty feet above the sea, his toes inches from the cliff edge. A sharp gust whips his hair into little needles that jab at his face. Tears chase blood down his cheeks and the wind rips the cries from his lips. Below him is a sheer drop. He is afraid to look down. He is even more afraid to look back.

The sea breeze snakes through the town until it reaches his home and bangs the latch more insistently. Beth and Mark sleep on. The bedside clock jumps to 3.19, then stops.

On the clifftop, Danny closes his eyes.

One road in, one road out. Tonight, no engine fills the silence and the sweep of the coast road is unbroken by headlights. Nobody comes in to Broadchurch and nobody leaves.

PART ONE

1

Beth Latimer jerks upright in bed. This is the way she used to wake up when her children were babies, some sixth sense flooding her veins with adrenalin and shaking her wide awake seconds before they started to cry. But her children aren't babies any more, and no one is crying. She has overslept, that's all. The space beside her is empty and the bedside clock is dead. She gropes for her watch. It's gone eight.

The others are awake: she can hear them downstairs. She's in and out of the shower in under a minute. A glance out of the window tells her it's going to be another hot one, and she pulls on a red sundress. You're not supposed to wear red with auburn hair, but she loves this dress; it's cool, comfortable and flattering too, showing off the flat (for now, at least) belly that is one of the few benefits of having kids so young. It still smells vaguely of last year's sun lotion.

Passing Danny's bedroom, she notices with a shock that he has made his bed. The Manchester City duvet cover that his dad hates so much – he has taken Danny's sudden defection from Bournemouth FC as a terrible betrayal – is smooth and straight. She can hardly believe it; eleven years of nagging have finally paid off. She wonders fondly what he wants. Probably that smartphone that his paper-round wages won't quite stretch to.

She can tell by the trail of destruction in the kitchen that Mark is making himself lunch. The fridge door hangs open. The milk is on the counter, lid off, and the knife is sticking out of the butter.

'Why didn't you wake me?' she asks him.

'I did,' he grins. He hasn't shaved; she likes him this way and he knows it. 'You told me to piss off.'

'I don't remember,' says Beth, although it sounds like her MO. She drops a teabag into a mug, knowing even as she does that she won't have time to finish drinking it. A jumping electric pulse snags her attention; the clock on the oven is flashing zeros. Same with the microwave. The radio is stuck on 3.19.

'All the clocks have stopped,' she says. 'In the whole house.'

'Probably just a fuse or something,' says Mark, wrapping his sandwich. He hasn't made anything for Beth, but she wouldn't have time to eat it anyway.

Chloe is eating cereal and flicking through a magazine. 'Mum, I've got a temperature,' she says.

'No, you haven't,' says Beth, without bothering to check.

'I'm. Not. Going,' Chloe whinges, but her hair, an immaculate blonde plait, and the perfectly applied make-up tell Beth that she knew this battle was a losing one from the off. You can't kid a kidder. She remembers herself at this age – exactly this age, almost to the day – missing school to

6

meet Mark. There's no way she's letting history repeat itself.

Before Chloe can come up with a counter-argument, Beth's mum bustles through the back door, calling hellos and carrying a bowlful of eggs. She sets it down on the worktop next to – oh, for God's sake, thinks Beth – Danny's lunchbox. It's not like him to forget his packed lunch. Perhaps the effort of making his bed was too much for him. She'll have to drop it off on her way into work. Like she's not going to be late enough already.

'Love you zillions, babe,' says Mark, kissing Chloe on the top of her head. It must be the millionth – the zillionth? – time Chloe has heard this family phrase, and she rolls her eyes, but when Mark turns to leave and she thinks no one is looking, she allows herself a small, secret smile. Then she tries on the temperature trick with her grandmother, who puts her hand on Chloe's smooth brow, but it's just for show. Liz has been through all this twice now and is even less likely to fall for it than Beth.

Mark's out of the door, to catch his usual lift with Nigel, and his goodbye kiss is quick. He tastes of tea and cereal.

'Did you see Danny?' Beth shouts at his back.

'He'd already gone!' he throws over his shoulder. 'I'm late!'

He leaves Beth standing in the kitchen, Danny's lunchbox in her hand.

Detective Sergeant Ellie Miller's work suit feels weird and stiff after three weeks in a bikini and sarong, but they've brought the Florida sunshine back home with them.

Broadchurch High Street shimmers in the early morning haze and everyone's in a good mood. The sky is cloudless and people are feeling brave enough to put out signs and set up stalls in the street.

She's glad to be back, and not only because she knows that good news awaits her in the station. It feels right to be here, to be home again. This is Ellie's street, her old beat, although it's a long time since she's been in uniform.

She pushes Fred in the buggy, a bag of duty-free goodies for the gang slung over one handle. At the end of the road, she'll hand the buggy over to Joe, who'll walk Tom the rest of the way to school. For now, Joe has Tom in a loose head-lock and they're both laughing. They are reflected, Ellie and her boys, in the plate-glass window of the tourist office. Her sons are so different; Fred's got her dark curly hair while Tom's got choirboy looks. His blond hair is just like Joe's was before his hairline started to recede and he did the dignified thing and buzzed it all off.

It's one of those rare, unplanned moments when she sees her little family from the outside and recognises happiness, captured as in an unposed snapshot. She knows she's lucky. She refocuses her gaze to look through the window and nod a hello to Beth, but she's not at her desk yet.

Mark's there, though, at the other end of the High Street, plumber's bag over his shoulder, charming his way down the street. Ellie watches him flirt with a couple of girls in summer dresses and then Becca from the hotel, and trade banter with Paul, the vicar who's younger than she is. Mark almost bumps into a jowly, unsmiling woman whom Ellie doesn't know – a tourist? Doesn't look like it – out walking her dog. She alone seems impervious to the Latimer charm.

Tom opens his mouth to frame a question. 'No,' says Ellie, before he can make his usual request for a dog.

When their paths cross, Mark wishes Tom good luck for sports day and he beams.

'We should get the lads together,' says Joe.

'Good idea,' says Mark, without breaking his stride. 'I'll text you later.'

Ellie takes comfort from this small exchange. She and Joe both know that their set-up works – that it plays to both their strengths for her to be the breadwinner while he stays at home with Fred – but she still worries. She worries that people might think Joe is emasculated. She worries that he might *become* emasculated. So while the other wives are on the phone begging their husbands to come home in time to put the kids to bed, she's virtually throwing Joe out of the house and into the pub.

'Look!' says Tom, pointing across the street at a familiar figure with cherry-red hair. 'It's Auntie Lucy!' He lifts his arm to wave but Ellie pulls it down by the wrist. Three weeks have done nothing to take the edge off her anger at her sister. Lucy's lies and excuses have no place on a morning like this. Ellie glances back: Lucy hasn't seen them. Her eyes are on the pavement and she's dragging her hair-dresser's kit behind her in a wheeled suitcase, probably off to give some old dears their weekly shampoo and set. Ellie hopes they've locked up their valuables. The last thing she wants is to nick her own sister.

Tom pulls his arm away and rubs it, hurt and confused.

'Sorry, darling,' says Ellie. 'We don't want to be late.' It's true: they're in enough trouble as it is for taking Tom out of school in term time. They don't want to give the head even more ammunition against them.

Nigel Carter pulls up in the blue van with *Mark Latimer Plumbing* in white letters on the paintwork.

'You're late!' says Mark, swinging himself up into the passenger seat. Ellie lip-reads Nige say something about the traffic and then they both laugh. Whatever it is that Nige says next clouds Mark's expression. He snaps at Nige, wiping the smile off his face, like he's been put in his place, although Mark's not the kind of boss to bully or pull rank.

If her suit feels strange, the station feels stranger. The strip lighting inside is a harsh neon shock after weeks basking in real sunshine. She still can't get used to this building with its curved corridors of polished concrete. It's clean and comfortable and all that, but it's just not very *Broadchurch*.

Wolf whistles and clapping herald her return, turning to gasps of appreciation as they realise that she has come bearing gifts. No one is left out and everyone seems pleased with their souvenirs. She knows her team all too well. Just as she's settling in for the gossip, Chief Superintendent Jenkinson calls her in for a word. Ellie, knowing what this is all about, can't resist grinning at her team on the way in.

Jenkinson isn't grinning, but then that's not her style. While Ellie's already sweaty and frizzy from the walk into work, the Chief Super is her usual pristine self, her short blonde hair sleek, her shirt and cravat crisp. A bubble of anticipation swells inside Ellie. But instead of the expected congratulations, Jenkinson drops a bomb:

'We've given the job to someone else.'

The bubble bursts and Ellie feels the smile slide down her face.

'The situation changed. I know it's a disappointment.'

Disappointment doesn't begin to cover it. The tears press behind Ellie's eyes but there's anger too and that gives her voice attack. 'You said it would wait till I got back from leave,' she says, her post-holiday high well and truly punctured. 'You said I was a shoo-in! That's why I took three weeks. Who got it?'

'DI Alec Hardy. He started last week.' The name rings a distant bell but it's his sex that really annoys Ellie. 'A *man*! What happened to "This area needs a female DI", what happened to "You've got my backing"?'

Is it Ellie's imagination or does Jenkinson look shamefaced? It's gone before she can pin it down. 'Alec Hardy has a lot of experience . . .'

And then Ellie knows how she knows that name. Every police officer in the country knows that name. Christ, to be passed over at all, to be passed over for a bloke, but *him*?

She holds it together until she gets to the toilet, sits on the closed seat and slides the bolt across the door. She's actually shaking with rage, her feet doing a little tap dance to expel the nervous energy. She calls home and cries hot, angry tears down the phone to Joe. He feels it as bitterly as she does. This was his promotion as much as hers; they'd already mentally spent her pay rise on finishing the house. 'Shall I just clear out my desk and go?' she asks him, and although they both know she doesn't mean it, it feels good to vent. She's gearing up to tell him about the salt in the wound – he won't *believe* it when he hears who got the job – when there's a knock on the cubicle door. Can't she even rant in peace?

'I'm *in here*!' She throws the full force of her frustration behind her words.

'Ellie?' It's one of the female PCs. 'You've got a shout.'

2

Two miles down the coast, a man stares at the dissolving blue horizon. His rumpled suit hangs off his wiry frame; his top button is undone beneath his tie. A barbed-wire fence, rows of tiny devil's horns, has been severed between two posts. It's a clean and confident cut, done with a (professional?) tool.

With the fence breached, nothing stands between him and a seventy-foot drop. He could look over the edge, but he doesn't want to get too close and tempt the vertigo.

'You want to see this or not?' says the farmer.

Reluctantly, Detective Inspector Alec Hardy turns towards the crime scene, although it hardly seems to warrant the term. 'Siphoned the whole bloody tank,' says the farmer, pointing at the fuel cap that dangles open. Bob Daniels, the PC who called it in, shakes his head in commiseration and Hardy sighs inwardly. Is this the best use this force can make of a detective inspector? What next? Calling out a chief super for a cat stuck up a tree? He knows he wanted a change of pace after Sandbrook, but this is ridiculous.

'We'll be in touch,' says Hardy, turning back to the squad car, even as the farmer starts asking why they haven't got forensics involved.

'You called me at seven in the morning, for that?' he says to Bob when the farmer's out of earshot.

'Too good for it, are you?' sneers Bob. Hardy doesn't rise to the bait. It's not the first little dig his new team have made and it won't be the last. They resent the way he was brought in from outside. And of course, his history goes before him. Then Bob's tone changes. 'Just got a call. Coastguard reported something down by the shore.'

By the time Beth gets into school, sports day is in full swing and the playing field is alive with children wearing PE kits in house colours. The starting pistol goes off and the Year 3 sack race begins. It's hot – the teachers are walking around handing out water – and the colours are vivid. Beth scans the green for Danny. She can usually pick him out in a crowd within seconds. It's not so much the look of him as the way he moves that catches her eye. His pre-teen spideriness has recently given way to a rolling swagger that's pure Mark. Where *is* he? She squints into the sunshine and recognises Danny's teacher, Miss Sherez. A row of parents clap and cheer on a bench beside her. Beth marches towards it, lunch-box in hand.

She's distracted for a moment by Olly Stevens. He's there in his capacity as reporter for the *Echo*, persuading egg-and-spoon racers to strike a Usain Bolt pose for a photograph. Olly's been doing the job for over a year now and makes no secret of his ambitions to write for the nationals, but Beth still can't quite take him seriously as a journalist. Perhaps it's because she's known him since he was a teenager and always gets a shock when she sees him in a shirt and tie rather than his South Wessex Secondary uniform. She watches him swap his phone for an old-fashioned notebook and pen as he takes their names and ages.

Beth has barely sat down when Miss Sherez says, 'No Danny?'

Beth's cheeks burn. *Please* don't say he's bunking off. 'I thought he was here,' she says. Miss Sherez's face creases with concern.

'No, we haven't seen him since yesterday.' *Neither have we*, thinks Beth and her mind's eye presents her with two sharp images: the perfectly made bed and the lunchbox on the worktop.

Her pulse doubles its pace as the first cold trickle of panic begins.

She tells herself to stay calm, that it's probably nothing, but her fingers slip on the keypad when she pulls up Danny's number on her phone. Even as it goes straight to voicemail she resolves to keep it breezy because she doesn't want him to think he's in trouble, although if she finds out he's bunking off, God help her, she'll – 'Danny, it's Mum,' she says after the beep. 'So you're not at school, can you give me a call straight away, sweetheart, just want to know where you are.'

But even while she's talking her mind is running ahead of her and her next call, one second after ringing off, is to Jack Marshall at the paper shop to check that Danny did his round earlier in the morning. Jack tells her that Danny didn't turn up. He didn't call. This has never happened before. Beth cannot conceive a situation that would make Danny miss his paper round.

She keeps the next call short to free up the line for Danny. 'Mark, it's me, ring me *now*.'

And then what? She has tasted a diluted version of this quicksand terror before. All mothers have, when a little hand slips from yours in the supermarket or at the funfair. It's the speed of it that gets you; the way everything goes from happiness to hell in the gap between two heartbeats. Your breathing grows fast and shallow and your heartbeat speeds to a whirr and then a few seconds later they appear and you hug them tight enough to crush them, before holding them at arm's length and giving them a telling-off they'll never forget. The panic drains away as quickly as it arrived but you still feel its after-effects hours later, the flash-flood of adrenalin and the terror of 'what if'.

Beth tries to slow her breathing. She needs to keep a clear head.

She sees Danny's best friend, Tom Miller, with a plastic medal around his neck. She forces herself to walk, not run, towards him, to speak, not shout.

'Danny didn't say he was going anywhere this morning, did he, Tom? It's all right. He's not in trouble.' Tom shakes his head and Beth has no reason not to believe him. With a calmness she doesn't feel inside, she asks Miss Sherez to call her if Danny shows up. She starts to retrace her steps; she can feel the teacher's eyes boring into her back.

From the corner of her eye she can see Olly Stevens watching her, his antennae twitching. She spins uselessly around on the grass and sweeps the field one more time, but panic is making her half-blind and her gut tells her Danny's not here. Where then? In town? On the beach? She runs to her car and fumbles for her keys.

The road into Broadchurch shimmers in the heat. Exhaust fumes mix with the haze, making number plates blur. Beth's phone is on the passenger seat beside her. She keeps checking it, refreshing it, checking the volume, and the signal. It's still term time but the traffic is gridlocked, like August bank holiday in a heatwave. Horns toot in frustration. A few years ago there was talk of widening the road or building a bypass. Beth's was one of the voices of opposition, but now she regrets it. Let them pave over the whole fucking countryside if it gets her into town quicker.

Nobody likes traffic jams but Beth *really* hates them. She has nightmares about them. She can't bear being confined at the best of times, let alone now, when she needs motion, action. She feels as though she's in a sealed glass box that is quickly filling with cold water. She can't breathe. She lasts maybe five seconds before she has to throw open the door and escape. She asks the woman in the car in front what's going on.

'Someone said the police are at the beach,' she says. 'Might've found a body.'

Body. Police. Beach. Body. Police. Beach.

Danny.

Beth has the feeling of all her blood plummeting through her body, landing with an electric shock at her toes. Leaving the key in the ignition and the radio on, she runs. A police van overtakes her, going the wrong way down the dual carriageway, the pitch of its siren shifting in a Doppler effect as it passes. Beth just has time to read the side: Forensic Investigations. She lengthens her stride. She feels that she could outrun it.

3

Hardy hates walking on the beach. You never know where you are with sand. It shifts and tricks you, slows you down. And *this* beach, of all beaches, still seems to hate him as much as he hates it, coarse sand sucking at his feet.

The uniforms are just about holding back a growing crowd of early-morning rubberneckers, beach mats rolled up in their bags. There's a helicopter overhead: its blades drown out their murmurs. Hardy watches a PC unspool a line of crime scene tape but that's all until he rounds the promontory and there on the shore is—

The world seems to tilt on its axis and Hardy grabs uselessly at the air for support.

The tape forms a three-sided square that frames a little boy's body. He lies face down in the sand, one cheek visible. He's wearing jeans and a long-sleeved T-shirt, blue trainers with a yellow flash. His brown hair is damp and matted.

Hardy feels in his pocket for the pills – he learned to swallow them dry a long time ago – and remembers too late that they're on the bedside table in his hotel room. He breathes evenly, the way he's been taught to, and the panic attack begins to subside. 'Don't do this to me,' he says under his breath. He wants to close his eyes, lie down and go to sleep, but his training kicks in and somehow he keeps putting one foot in front of the other. 'Come on,' he says, and forces himself to take in every detail of the scene that's too much to bear. He looks up at the cliff, the grass fringe at the top, the sheer golden face and the rocks that surround the body. He tries to picture the trajectory.

'Oh God,' says a female voice behind him. 'No, no, no—'

There's a mumsy woman in a suit with mad curly hair staggering towards him. Automatically Hardy puts himself between her and the body as he tries to guess who she might be. Is she the kid's mother? How the *hell* did she get past the tape? Bob'll get it in the neck for this.

'I know him, he lives here, he has tea at my house, he's my boy's best friend,' she's saying.

A mother but not *the* mother. And she's given them an ID. They need to calm her down, get the facts from her. Hardy orders her off the beach, but with shaking hands she pulls a police badge from her handbag. He gets her name and rank in a flash but it takes him a further moment to absorb that this tearful woman is job.

'Oh God – Beth, does Beth know?'

'Calm down, DS Miller,' says Hardy, although he finds that her hysteria is fuelling his own calm. The more out of control she becomes, the more professional he feels.

'No, you don't understand – I *know* that boy – Oh God, Danny.'

'Shut it off,' snaps Hardy. 'Be professional. You're working a case now.'

'Shut it off?' Miller looks stricken and he knows how he's coming across, but it's either this or a slap to the face. It works. She stops crying.

'Alec Hardy,' he offers her his hand.

'I know. You've got my job,' she says.

'Really?' says Hardy. 'You want to do that *now*?' Behind his bluntness, he's encouraged. At least now she's talking like a copper. It doesn't last long.

'You don't even know who he is,' Miller accuses, like it's Hardy's fault for not growing up in this one-horse town, like it's bad policing not to be on first-name terms with all the locals after one week.

'Tell me!' he shouts over the crashing surf.

'Danny, Daniel Latimer.' Hardy hears the full name for the first time and knows that within hours it will have a terrible celebrity attached to it. 'Eleven years old. Goes to school with my son Tom. Family lives here, Dad's a local plumber.'

'Is this a suicide spot?'

'He wouldn't do that.'

Christ, he's got his work cut out with this one. No wonder he got the job if this was his competition.

'Answer the question.'

'No. There are other spots, one about three miles west, another inland.' She's on the defensive again. 'He's not that sort of kid.'

Hardy's heard enough from DS Miller and tells her to find out where the scene of crime officers are. Something about the neat way the boy has fallen doesn't make sense and he needs Forensics to capture what he can see. There's a cigarette butt by his feet that needs bagging up. No way he's letting evidence get away this time, not if he has to pick through every grain of sand on this beach himself.

As Miller makes the call, he wonders whether her relationship to the dead boy will make her an asset to the investigation or a liability.

The tide inches closer.

Beth is a runner but she has never moved like this. Her flimsy pumps hit the ground without absorbing the shock but she doesn't register the jarring in her joints. She clears the High Street in seconds flat and rounds the bend into the harbour. People huddle in groups of three and four, whispering and nodding towards the beach. Only Jack Marshall is on his own, standing sad sentry outside his shop.

Beth has no time to process this. She keeps moving, powered by a formidable internal force. She's breathing heavily but there seems to be an endless supply of energy. Her world has shrunk to this: the need to get to the beach and confirm that whatever they have found there is not Danny so that she can get on with looking for him. All the while, the freezing cold water of fear rises around her, lapping at her chin.

Squad cars and vans crowd the seafront car park. Their primary yellow-and-blue livery looks garish and wrong against the soft blues and golds of the coast. Beth is forced to calm her pace as she slaloms through manoeuvring cars, elbows the bucket-and-spade brigade out of her way and then she's on the beach. The sand threatens to slow her down so she kicks off her shoes, snatches them up and carries them. It's coarse beneath her feet. At the foot of the cliff, police tape flutters white and blue in the breeze. The officers on duty are trying to persuade the gawkers that there's nothing to see. It's easy for Beth to dodge to one side and slip under the cordon.

Halfway to the horizon a dark dash breaks the sand. If she hadn't been told that it was a body, would she know what it was? A few steps closer and she sees that it's too small to be a man, but it could be a woman. The nightmare reels her in and she keeps going.

A familiar silhouette steps between Beth and ... *it*, and Ellie turns slowly towards her. Beth recoils for a second because something is horribly wrong with Ellie's face. She looks like she's had a stroke. When she sees Beth it gets worse.

'Beth!' she says, running towards her. 'Get off the beach!'

'What is it?' says Beth. 'What've you found?' She's giving Ellie one last chance to tell her that everything's OK.

Ellie blocks her. 'You can't be here.' Beth almost wants to laugh. This is her beach as much as anyone's. How *dare* they tell her where she can and can't be? She keeps putting one foot in front of the other. She's fitter than Ellie and it's easy to give her the slip. The police behind her are close enough now that she can see their long shadows chasing hers across the rippled sand but still she keeps going, running towards the heart of her nightmare and then she sees the same too-bright colours flash before her again. Blue suede with a yellow flash. Danny's shoes, shoes that she bought herself, are not quite covered by the makeshift shroud. What is left of Beth's controlled facade crumbles to powder.

'Those are Danny's trainers!' Her voices bounces off the cliffs. *'Those are Danny's trainers!'*

She repeats this phrase over and over even as the police catch up with her and grip her upper arms. The black-and-white police uniforms flash in and out of focus. Sounds and voices come and go. Beth bucks and flexes but she can't escape them. She can't leave him there with his feet sticking out like that. He gets cold feet when he's asleep. She needs to tuck him in properly. She twists her body one last time in a futile effort to break free. As they drag her away, her heels carve gullies in the sand.

The rising tide of panic closes over Beth's head. The horror rushes like dirty water into her lungs. It floods her heart. She doesn't care if she drowns. She would welcome it.

4

The *Broadchurch Echo* newsroom is in its customary state of chaos. The paperless office is but a dream here, desks buried under reams of loose pages. The sleek new monitors on the desks are attached to a creaking computer system that hasn't been properly upgraded for years. Here comes Maggie Radcliffe, the editor: she's never been upgraded either. She's been in local news since cut-and-paste meant scissors and glue, and smoking at your desk was de rigueur. Now, an electronic cigarette twirls between her fingers as she squints at an Excel spreadsheet of falling revenues.

Olly Stevens, Maggie's latest protégé, comes in, dark hair tousled in a way that only the very young can get away with. He's looking pleased with himself. 'Reg didn't make it,' says Olly, referring to the veteran photographer who spends more time in the Red Lion these days than behind his lens. But Maggie still uses him; she sees him in the supermarket every weekend, and they look after their own in Broadchurch. 'So I did it myself with my camera phone.' Olly transfers the pictures of Tom Miller wearing his 'gold' medal with pride from his phone to the screen on his computer. There's enough here for a double-page spread.

'Aw, look at their little faces!' says Maggie. 'You've almost got an eye.'

She's still looking over Olly's shoulder when an email beeps its way into his inbox. 'Oh my God,' he says, fingers hovering over the mouse. '*Daily Mail*. My application.'

'Open it!' says Maggie.

He processes what's on screen in half a second and his face falls. '*Bastards.*'

'Oh, sweetheart,' she soothes. 'There's plenty of other newspapers.'

'I've tried them all now,' he replies glumly.

'You're good, petal. Your time will come.'

Further encouragement is interrupted by a text alert on Maggie's phone. She glances down. 'Yvonne says the beach is closed for some reason. Go down and check it out, will you?'

Hardy is back at the clifftop for the second time that morning, this time with DS Miller at his side. They climbed the steep coastal path to get here. Now police tape keeps the ramblers and rubberneckers out of the way. It's the closest thing there is to a fence. Hardy can't believe that people are allowed to walk up here without a safety barrier. Everything about the countryside is a deathtrap. He gets as close to the edge as he dares. A couple of feet below the grass verge is a shallow ledge, a place for people to think twice before jumping.

The Scene of Crime Officers crouch and crawl in their white suits, fingertips searching for clues, overseen by Brian

Young. His hood is down and his mask off to denote his authority; the breeze runs its fingers through his puff of black hair.

'How's it going?' Hardy asks him.

'It's looking like the fall was faked,' says Brian. There's a question in his voice; he's not doubting the evidence, more asking why. 'Angle of the body was wrong, too arranged. And up here there's no flattened grass or slippage, no loose rocks. No fibres, no handmarks, no sense of a downward trajectory.'

'You mean he didn't fall?' asks Hardy. 'Could he have jumped?'

'Unlikely, given where he was found, and the trajectory of the cliffs.' Brian motions the fall with two hands. 'Ask me, someone tried to make it look like an accident. I don't think he was up here at all.'

'See?' says Miller. 'Not Danny. He wouldn't *do* that.'

'Get on to the pathologist, tell him to hurry up, even if it's just preliminary,' he replies.

They go on foot back down to the beach. Miller talks Hardy through the different ways to access the cliffs from the town and he listens attentively. He still can't quite get his bearings, although he is starting to slot the different parts of the town together and to internalise his sense of direction, so that the place is slowly replacing the one frozen image from his past.

The mobile homes in the caravan park have a toytown look about them from above that is not lessened by proximity. Outside number 3, an unsmiling woman leans with a large brown dog at her feet, mug in her hands. Hardy takes a mental snapshot of her.

A battered red Nissan crunches to a halt behind them. A brown-eyed manchild jumps from the driver's seat and walks towards them, smiling. Miller quickens her pace towards her own car.

'He seems to know you,' says Hardy, seconds before the kid calls out, 'Auntie Ellie!' Miller glows bright red, to Hardy's amusement. She needn't be embarrassed; she's quite capable of looking foolish all on her own.

'Olly Stevens, *Broadchurch Echo*,' he says, and it's not funny any more.

'No statements now,' says Hardy automatically. He slams the car door on Olly but his voice comes through the window. 'I heard there was a body. Has it been ID'd? Please?' he says in the wheedling tone of a kid asking for an ice cream.

'There'll be a statement, Oliver,' says Miller. She drives away, leaving Olly in a cloud of sand.

Ellie can't remember the last time she drove to Spring Close: it's quicker to walk across the playing field that connects both their homes. She tries to focus on the mirror, signal, manoeuvre of the journey rather than what's at the end of it.

Then they pull up outside the Latimer house and reality bites down hard. She knows this place almost as well as her own. She can see it across the field from her kitchen window: they've spent more boozy Sunday afternoons here than she can count. And yet it looks strange, unfamiliar, as though she's never been here before. She feels the double responsibility of a friend and a police officer, in that order, and suggests to Hardy, as they get out of the car, that she leads because she knows them.

'How many deaths like this have you worked?' asks Hardy. She feels about an inch tall. 'This is my first.'

'You can't make it better. Don't try.'

'You don't know how I work!' He's treating her strength – finding the calm in the chaos – like it's some kind of Achilles' heel.

Hardy speaks in bullet points, his rolling Scottish Rs giving his words punch. 'Most likely premise is abduction. Was he taken, if so who by? Watch them. Every movement. Anything that doesn't make sense, tell me. The closer the relationship, the greater the likelihood of guilt. Don't look at me like that.'

Ellie didn't realise she was.

Inside, the Latimers line up on the sofa, Beth and Mark, Chloe – still in her school uniform – and Liz. Beth is shaking, hands fluttering from her belly to her mouth and back again. Mark is so still he barely seems to be breathing.

Hardy pulls up a chair from the dining table and faces them. Ellie feels a fierce protective urge that takes her by surprise: she doesn't want him anywhere near them.

'The body of a young boy was found on the beach this morning.' Ellie hears the stock phrase from the outside for the first time. The euphemism, designed with such care, serves now only to insult and delay.

'It's Danny, isn't it?' cries Beth. 'I saw his shoes.'

Liz makes the sign of the cross.

'Plenty of kids have those shoes,' says Mark, and then to Hardy. 'I'm sorry, you talk.'

'We believe it's Danny's body,' says Hardy. Ellie waits for the condolence, but no, that's it, the bare and brutal fact.

'Was it him, Ellie?' asks Beth. At Ellie's nod, Beth collapses as though her spine has been unstrung, her mouth stretched around a silent scream. Chloe makes a choking sound and turns wide frightened eyes up to her father. Mark hooks his right arm around his wife and she leans in to his chest. His left arm reaches round to include Chloe and Liz and he mutters over and over the wretched little lie that everything's all right.

Ellie is rooted and helpless as she watches them grasp at each other, raw in their grief, a terrible family portrait that will never be complete again. Her own tears are hot in her skull. She wonders how she will ever contain them and, as the picture before her blurs, she realises she has failed.

A cup of tea. It's all she can think of to do. Ellie feels like a WPC from the seventies as she rootles through Beth's cupboards, looking for the sugar.

The tears give way to mute shock surprisingly quickly. Beth and Chloe hold hands so tightly that their fingertips are purple with trapped blood.

'Was it an accident?' Beth asks. 'Did he fall?'

She addresses the question to Ellie but Hardy responds. 'We don't know yet,' he says. 'Can you think why he might've been up on the cliffs last night or this morning?'

'He *wouldn't* have been,' says Beth.

'Well, he obviously was,' snaps Mark. Hardy's eyebrows shoot up. Ellie resolves to explain how Mark's bark is worse than his bite. Then she remembers the way he shouted at Nigel in the van that morning, and feels a chill in the pit of her belly.

'How was Danny these past few days?' says Hardy. 'Was anything bothering him?'

'He didn't kill himself, if that's what you're suggesting,' says Mark. 'He wouldn't. He knows he can talk to us about anything.'

'He's been just . . . normal,' says Beth. The word sounds funny, as though she knows that normal is a word that will never apply to her again.

'And you last saw him, when?' presses Hardy.

'I looked in on him about nine o'clock last night,' says Beth. 'He was in bed reading. And this morning . . . ' Beth falters, and it breaks Ellie's heart to see the self-blame begin to take hold. 'He's up and out before anyone else, on his paper round. But he didn't turn up for that.'

She opens her face up to Hardy: Ellie reads her blind faith and her spirits plummet further. Now obviously isn't the time, but at some point soon she will have to learn about Hardy's last case. Ellie hates him for putting her in this position.

Hardy pencils something in his notebook. 'Any signs of forced entry or disturbance around the house?'

'Nothing.' Mark acts like it's a stupid question. Silence hangs. 'I want to see the body.'

Five pairs of eyes swivel in his direction. 'You might be wrong.' He shrugs. 'So I want to be sure. I want to see.'

5

Ellie drives Mark Latimer to the cottage hospital. It's a low
flint building with shiny NHS plaques and signs tacked on
to the old stone. Trees rustle overhead as they walk through
the tiny car park. Mark's expression is blank. The only sign
of what he's going through is a slight hesitation on the
threshold.

'How many times have you done this, El?' he asks her.

'I haven't,' she admits. Naturally she's been in the mortuary before, for traffic accidents, a couple of drownings and
an overdose. But never murder, never a child and, dear God,
never a friend. They trained her for this particular crime, of
course they did, but that was years ago and this is rural
Dorset. She had more or less accepted that she would never
have to deal with something like this. Beneath the shock and
grief, she's panicking. She can barely remember the procedure, let alone the right way to talk to the violently bereaved.

The viewing room has a churchy hush to it. The curtain is
pulled slowly back to reveal Danny on the other side of the
window. His face is still dirty: earth dulls his baby complexion

while grains of sand glow like sequins. He looks younger than she has seen him in years. He looks *alive*. She half-expects him to jump up and shout 'Surprise!' A few years ago he and Tom played a game of hide-and-seek that covered both their homes and the playing field. Tom once got stuck in the Latimers' wheelie bin and Danny sprained an ankle jumping from a tree to surprise his friend. The memory makes the room swim before her.

She looks at Mark instead and it's almost worse. That face she has seen in laughter and song, drunk and happy, is contorted with grief.

'All this way I thought it wouldn't be him,' whispers Mark. 'My Danny.'

Copper's intuition or maybe a parent's instinct tells Ellie what's coming next. 'Can I touch him?' Mark asks, and she has to shake her head.

'Why him?' says Mark, turning his anger on Ellie. 'He's only little. He's just my little boy.' He kneels by Danny's face and although it's Ellie's job to supervise she feels a sense of trespass. 'Listen, boy. I'm sorry I wasn't there for you. You're my boy and I let you down. And I'm so, so sorry, Danny. I love you zillions, superstar. I always will.' Mark gives in to noisy crying and his words roll into one another. They stay like that for thirty minutes.

Ellie says nothing. Tears soak her collar.

DI Hardy, looking down at the latex gloves on his hands and the plastic shoe covers on his feet, is transported against his will to another child's bedroom, another crime scene. He wants – *needs* – to sweep this room himself before SOCO get here.

He pushes open the door to Danny's room, childish stickers peeling under his gloved fingertips. Inside, an alarm clock flashes the wrong time. The window is ajar, key still in the lock. From it he can see kids kicking a football in the playing field out the back. Children run in and out of the gardens that line the field's edge. How long will that last, once word is out?

A school tie describes an S on top of the chest of drawers. A battered laptop computer and games console lie next to a telescope and a flip video camera. Sporting trophies jostle for space on shelves and the windowsill, and photographs of Danny in the pool or on the football pitch breathe life into the body on the beach. There are traces of his early childhood everywhere: an old, well-thumbed Pokémon sticker album is close to the top of the pile of magazines, and a cuddly toy chimp waits patiently on the pillow.

To one side of the door frame Danny's height has been recorded through the years, inked on the wall from his fourth birthday to a couple of months ago. The first few dates and measurements are in adult handwriting but most are in Danny's own, a round childish scrawl slowly evolving into a distinct hand. The lines come to an abrupt halt somewhere near Hardy's elbow. Heavy sadness pierces his professional armour and he sinks on to the bed and lets his head drop into his hands. For some people tears dam behind the eyeballs but when Hardy wants to cry he has to hold them in using the back of his throat. He sometimes feels it's the only strong muscle in his body.

When he looks up again, Beth is on the landing, staring right at him. He's seen that expression before, on another mother, and he has to turn his face away. It's not the grief he can't handle. It's the trust, the unquestioning trust she has already put in him.

Later, Hardy's on the quayside waiting for his boss. The conversation with Chief Superintendent Jenkinson is inevitable and he can predict her lines as well as his own. To his left is the beach where Danny was found, so he keeps his gaze dead ahead. Little dinghies swerve to avoid the motorboats that cleave their way through the still waters of the harbour. In front of him, jagged black rocks have been piled into sea breaks.

When Jenkinson comes his way she's carrying – Christ on a bike – two ice creams with flakes sticking out of them. One is clearly intended for him.

'Given the nature of this case, it probably makes sense for you to hand it on to another lead officer,' she says, handing him the cone. He tries not to let his boss see his distaste.

'No.' He's been preparing the one-word response since he first saw the body.

'It's not a question of your ability,' she says, pushing her expensive sunglasses up on to her head. 'We just don't want Sandbrook to become a thing.'

'I was completely exonerated.' If only he'd had a fiver for every time he's had to say that.

She licks her ice cream. 'Alec, you came here to lie low.'

She couldn't be more wrong. 'I *came* to do whatever the job requires.'

'But in terms of public perception, you may be vulnerable. I'm giving you the chance to step back. Nobody would blame you. This happened a stone's throw from your station.'

'I've met your team. There's no one as qualified as me.'
She doesn't contradict him. She can't. 'Sandbrook doesn't
make me vulnerable. It makes me the best man for the job.
You want to stop me, you're welcome to try.' He holds her
gaze to call her bluff. Nothing. 'Thanks for the ninety-nine.'

He turns back to the station. When he rounds the corner
out of Jenkinson's sight, he throws the cone into the harbour,
where it lands with a splash before melting away to nothing.

6

Ellie watches the team gather for the briefing, notebooks on laps. She's never known an atmosphere like this in the station and it's not only because one of the town's children has been murdered. Hardy's history charges the room with tension. Despite that, there's something compelling, almost inspiring, about him as he paces in front of them, firing out lists.

'Was Danny Latimer abducted? Did someone gain access to the house; if so, how?' His accent becomes more pronounced as he warms to his theme. 'And if it wasn't forced entry, who has a key? We need to collect any CCTV from a mile radius around the house. Miller: the family, where were they?'

Ellie doesn't like addressing the whole team at the best of times, let alone being thrust into the limelight without notice. 'Mother and daughter were in, watching telly.' She hears the stammer in her voice and cringes inwardly. DCs Frank Williams and Nish Patel, both keen – they've only been out of uniform for a couple of months, and this is their first big case – take detailed notes, piling on the pressure;

Ellie feels as though every word out of her mouth has to be precise, useful, motivating. 'They say that they didn't leave the house till school the next morning. Dad was out on an emergency call-out – he's a plumber; he got in around three. Neither parent thought to check on Danny. Grandma lives nearby, she was in all night . . . '

Hardy glares at his team. 'Until we're ready, all this remains confidential, *no gossip*. Understand? Right, go on.' He flicks his hand as though shooing chickens. 'You – Miller, come with me.'

They pass Bob Daniels coming out of the Gents. Bob's an old-fashioned copper, big and blunt. He plays on the same five-a-side team as Joe and Mark Latimer and his boy Jayden is part of Tom and Danny's gang. The thought of the boys reminds Ellie – she's been pushing the knowledge away all morning – that tonight, when she gets in, she'll have to tell Tom that his friend is dead. She has never dreaded a conversation more.

Bob's eyes are pink and he gives the involuntary jagged in-breath of someone who has been sobbing his heart out. The ripples this casts will be as wide as they are deep. In Broadchurch there are only ever one or two degrees of separation. Big men will cry tonight.

They need to control how the word gets out. Speculation will already be rife, but the statement isn't scheduled until this evening. Ellie feels strongly that local people, especially Danny's classmates, should be given the news early and without equivocation. She'll need to ask the press office how they do this. There is no precedent. Should they ring the school? And if so, then what? Urgent information is usually disseminated to parents by text message, but that would be an insult to everyone. If she could, she'd knock on every door, do it face-to-face, mother-to-mother, family by family. But she can't. She is needed here.

On the short walk to Jack Marshall's newsagent's, Hardy is deep in glum silence. After all her attempts at small talk miss the mark, Ellie gives up and lets her own thoughts brew.

She is trying very hard to persuade herself that this was done by a random opportunist, an out-of-towner, a passing care-in-the-community case. But with that theory comes an immediate counter-argument. For a start, you don't just pass through Broadchurch. And there are no lights on Harbour Cliff Beach at night. You'd need to know the place pretty well to find your footing, let alone leave a body behind and cover your tracks.

Who, then? Hardy, who has made no secret of his dislike of Broadchurch, is working on the theory it's someone local. The only person in the town on the sex offenders register is some old lech who's been bedbound in a nursing home for the past year. Like any town, Broadchurch has a handful of troublesome families but there is nothing in their history of infighting and petty drug-dealing to suggest progression to a child murder. That must mean it's someone respectable, or at least someone with no previous.

Ellie looks around. With the sun high overhead, the quayside is as pretty as ever, but suspicion is a filter placed over the paintbox cottages and picture-book boats, distorting and darkening everyone in the frame. Danny's killer could be any one of the men in sight. That middle-aged man balancing a crate of fish on his shoulder; the young bloke up a ladder cleaning windows. A vaguely familiar man in a suit drinking coffee from a styrofoam cup walks towards them. Does he look capable of strangling a little boy? He nods hello; Ellie's cheeks burn as if he's read her mind, and she looks down at the cobbles. At the time when she most needs to be observant, it seems that she can't look anyone in the eye.

She realises with a sinking sensation that it's probably someone she knows. Not well, not by name, but it could be someone like Mr Styrofoam there, someone she sees every week, someone she is on nodding terms with, someone who's never given them any trouble until now. And if she knows the killer, then so will half the town. The residents of Broadchurch are not so much close-knit as enmeshed.

But *who*?

Hardy breaks into Ellie's thought process at the moment it begins to repeat itself.

'Your son, Miller,' he says. 'He and Danny were friends. I'll need to talk to him.'

We'll see about *that*, thinks Ellie, although she doesn't say anything. There must be someone else who can interview Tom; maybe one of the female DCs. There's no way this brittle, surly man who can't even use anyone's first name will be able to communicate gently or effectively with a bereaved child.

If he stopped talking like a sergeant major, that would be a good start. It's worth a try. Ellie gathers her nerve.

'Sir, d'you mind not calling me Miller? I don't really go for the surname thing. I prefer Ellie.' The pause lasts so long that she wonders if he heard her at all.

40

'Ellie.' Hardy pronounces it with caution, like it's his first go at speaking a new language. '*Ellie.*' He wrinkles his nose. 'No.'

He makes her feel like a probationer. She bites her tongue until it hurts.

Jack Marshall runs the Sea Brigade as well as the local newsagent's and though he's technically an outsider, he's been here for so many years that he's a Broadchurch institution. Adults find him dour, but kids love him: there's a fairness about him that they warm to. Outside his shop, bucket-and-spade sets and postcards are for sale along with old-fashioned shrimping nets and pinwheels. Inside, jars of sweets are stacked floor-to-ceiling behind the counter. Jack thinks that self-service pick-'n'-mix is a haven for bacteria, so he weighs the sweets out himself, like they used to in shops when Ellie was little. He continues to display the old imperial measurements alongside the metric. Tom still loves coming here, asking Jack for his treats by name and hearing the clatter of boiled sugar as they hit the scales.

Their entry sends a breeze through the shop, rippling the plastic curtain of rainbow ribbons that separates the floor from the storeroom out the back. Jack is in the shirt, tie and cardigan he wears all year round. He looks like he's been expecting them; his seventies throwback shoulder-length hair has been brushed for once.

'Danny didn't turn up for his paper round this morning,' begins Ellie.

'I assumed he was sick.' His face and voice are utterly without expression.

'Did he often miss his round?'

41

'They all do, one time or another.' He seems determined to use as few words as possible. Ellie looks to Hardy for help, but he's browsing magazines, seemingly not listening.

'But you didn't ring to check?'

'I don't have time, only me here.'

It occurs to her that Jack hasn't asked what this is all about yet. 'How was Danny yesterday?'

Jack puts his hands in his pockets. 'No different from usual.'

'Did you notice anything on his mind in the last couple of weeks?'

'He was only in here fifteen minutes, first thing. I'm not a psychiatrist.' Jack has never been the life and soul but this chippiness is new.

Hardy looks up. 'You married?' The way he says it, it's a question with no right answer. Jack returns his stare.

'No. Are you?'

Hardy doesn't answer. Ellie glances down at his left hand. Bare.

'They brought him in here, Mark and Beth,' says Jack, unprompted. 'Three days old, he was … ' His tone has barely changed, but his eyes have lost their focus. He's staring into the distance, as though at a ghost.

7

Danny lies on a slab in the pathology lab, a white sheet pulled up to his little round shoulders. He seems to have shrunk since Ellie saw him in the chapel of rest. Whether it's the size of his body in relation to the slab, the fact that he's naked, or the first diminishments of death, she can't say. Now, there is no mistaking death for sleep and that sense she had before, that he might jump up and surprise her, is gone.

She has never met the pathologist, James Lovegood, before. There's a sour, aseptic smell in here and she wonders if it clings to his clothes and his hair when he goes home. She can feel it seeping into her pores.

'Seven weeks I've got left,' he says. 'They asked me to stay on an extra three months, while they find a new chap. I thought seven weeks, round here, should be fine.' He wipes his eyes. 'It's the children that upset me. Always have.'

'What've you got?' Hardy cuts in. There's a corresponding shift in Lovegood's tone.

'Superficial cuts and bruises to the face. No injuries consistent with a fall. Cause of death was asphyxiation. He was strangled. Bruising around the neck and the windpipe, and at the top of the spine. Pattern of bruises suggests large hands, I'd suggest male assailant. It would've been brutal. The angle suggests he would've been facing his attacker. He would've known.' He takes a deep breath. 'Sorry. Mercifully, there was no sexual violence.'

Beneath the relief of this, Ellie's mind whirrs. What does this mean for other children? Terrible things rarely happen in a vacuum. Patterns, that's what you've got to look for. Repetition and parallel. What if another little boy is out there now, holding close the knowledge that Danny can no longer share? The thought of a child keeping such a big, dark secret makes Ellie want to bawl.

'Time of death?' says Hardy, as though they're discussing bus timetables.

'I'd put it between 10 p.m. Thursday night and 4 a.m. Friday morning.' He sighs from his boots. 'We don't get these around here. Make sure you find him.'

'We will,' vows Ellie. SOCO are combing the beach, all leave has been cancelled and every officer is either on house-to-house or the phones. Who knows what's come to light while she and Hardy have been out? With luck, they will have made an arrest by nightfall.

Chloe has changed from her school uniform into her other uniform of jeans and a hoody. 'We're out of milk,' she says, head in the fridge. 'I'll go down the shop—'

Mark's off his feet and into the kitchen before she can finish her sentence. 'You're not going anywhere.'

Chloe's gentle response shows that she understands.

44

'Dad, nothing's going to happen to me. *Please*. I need some air.' She holds up her phone to show she's taking it with her. 'I won't be too long, I promise.'

She lets herself out of the back door. In the alleyway at the side of the house, she opens her bag and checks inside. Big Chimp, kidnapped from the crime scene of Danny's bedroom, looks up at her with button eyes. She keeps one hand in her bag, holding on to the toy's little paw, as she walks past the corner shop. Streets give way to lanes and lanes thin to alleyways as Chloe climbs the gentle slope that takes her to the top of the town.

Dean is waiting for her, leaning against an upturned boat. His motorbike is parked next to him, the helmet he customised for her hanging on the back. He opens his mouth to speak but nothing comes out, so he kisses her instead.

'I know,' she says. 'Doesn't feel real.' They stay where they are for a while, the town they both grew up in spread before them. Dean brushes fair hair from Chloe's eyes.

'Are the police round?' he asks, an edge to his voice. 'Do they know about us? You ain't sixteen yet.'

'Nobody knows,' says Chloe. She slings one leg over his bike. 'Let's go.'

'Are you sure?'

She brings her visor down over her face in reply.

Down on the beach, nothing looks the same and it's all too real. A crowd shifts at the edge of the police tape. On the other side of the divide, at the foot of the bluff, a large white evidence tent has been set up where Danny's body was found. People in white suits move in and out of it.

Chloe gets as close as she can without being noticed and stops by a lifebelt. She lays Big Chimp underneath it and kneels there. Her face is smooth for a few seconds and then the effort of holding back the tears is too much. Dean kneels beside her. She collapses into him and he half-carries her back to the bike. Big Chimp stays put, his mouth in a patient half-smile.

Somebody sees them go.

Olly Stevens is part of the crowd, his *Broadchurch Echo* lanyard swinging around his neck. His mouth falls open in horror. He gets his phone from his pocket without taking his eyes off the young couple and calls his contact on the Wessex Police force, who also happens to be his mum's sister.

Ellie answers in that terse way she has when she's on duty, so he goes straight into reporter mode.

'I've just seen Chloe at the beach,' he says. 'Is it Danny Latimer?'

'I can't talk to you. This isn't appropriate, Oliver.' *Oliver.* Not one professional to another but an aunt telling off a naughty nephew. Olly bristles. 'This is not confirmation, I am not confirming that!' she says. It's all the confirmation he needs. He ends the call. Seconds later, Ellie calls him back but he switches the ringer off.

Dean's bike roars off, Chloe's head buried in his shoulder. The tyres send sand billowing in their wake. Olly looks the other way, at the tent beneath the cliffs. He shakes his head. He stares at his phone for a while, then so slowly it's almost furtive, he pulls up the *Broadchurch Echo* Twitter account.

@broadchurchecho sources suggest body found on Harbour Cliff Beach is 11-year-old Daniel Latimer. Cause of death unexplained. More to follow.

His finger hovers over the glowing tweet button for half a minute before he presses send. He makes eye contact with Danny's toy chimp and his expression changes from triumphant to guilt-stricken. Staff reporter Oliver Stevens has got his first big scoop, but the cost is written all over his face.

Beth's home is a crime scene, Danny's bedroom door barred with a crossbones of police tape. She watches it all through a haze as Scene of Crime Officers in white suits traipse up and down their stairs.

They ask for a recent photograph and, as she flicks through the pictures on her phone, she realises it's been a while since they took any formal photographs of Danny. When did they stop documenting their children's every move? Even pictures from six months ago are unreliable likenesses. He was changing so fast.

In the end, she hands over the school photo. In it, Danny's hair is smoothed down. She remembers brushing it into a parting on the morning of the shoot and making him promise he wouldn't muss it up until after the photograph was taken. Her delight when he obeyed turned into dismay when they got the picture back; the smiling, tidy child in the picture bore no resemblance to her scruffy, cheeky Danny. But it's only a month old and it's the cleanest, the highest resolution. And it feels appropriate. That's what they always have, isn't it, a school photo?

Liz is making tea and toast, channelling everything she's feeling into feeding and mothering. They have all stopped asking her to stop. DI Hardy accepts the cup she gives him without thanks and sets it down on the side. He steeples his fingers and looks Beth and Mark in the eye.

'We have some preliminary findings,' he says. 'We're treating Danny's death as suspicious. We think he may have been killed.'

It's like Hardy's reading from a script. Perhaps he is, in a way: saying the things you have to say to people in her position. Beth doesn't know how to react so she just stands there. She wishes that someone would hand *her* a script so that she could say the right things, act like a grieving mother is supposed to, and then they might all leave her alone.

'My *boy*,' cries Mark beside her, and Beth envies him his tears.

'What happens now?' she says. She means the rest of her life, but Hardy takes it more literally.

'Well, we'll have to announce it to the public soon, but we won't do that without your permission,' says Hardy. He knows the ropes, Beth thinks. This once-in-a-lifetime tragedy is all in a day's work for him. The thought is as comforting as it is shocking. 'For now, we need to gather as much evidence as we can. I'm going back to the station, give Brian space to work.' He gestures to one of the men in white suits, who pulls down his face mask and becomes a human being. 'We'll be in touch soon. Soon. I promise, we'll find the person responsible. You have my word.'

Beth clings to DI Hardy's word. She almost likes the cold,

detached way he speaks to them all. It's reassuringly professional.

When Hardy goes, Liz pours his untouched tea down the sink and immediately refills the kettle, then saws at a fresh loaf with a bread knife. Beth watches the long, serrated blade flash under the kitchen light and thinks about turning it on herself. She wonders, if she plunged it into her – for a second she thinks belly but remembers and settles on thigh – would she feel anything. The warm yeasty smell of toast fills the room. Another plate is put in front of Beth and pushed gently away.

Brian Young comes down the stairs so quietly that Beth doesn't notice him until he clears his throat. 'We're going to take Danny's computer away for examination,' he says softly. His gloved hands hold a battered old laptop, covered in Man City stickers.

'Will they get it back?' says Liz.

'Once we've finished examining it.'

Uneasiness steals over Beth as Brian slides the laptop into a clear evidence bag. Headlines flash through her mind about cyber-bullying, trolls and chatrooms, grooming. She and Mark never really go through the kids' computers, partly to respect their privacy and partly because they don't know what to look for or how to look for it. Danny is the tech-head in the family.

Danny is.

Danny *was.*

The pain of the shifting tense makes her cry out. It is the first sense of the numbness starting to lift and she suddenly, desperately, wants it back.

Chloe is in the lounge, smartphone in her hand, eyes blazing.

'Why've you released his name?' she shouts at Brian, shoving the screen under his nose. 'It's on Twitter. From the *Broadchurch Echo*.' All four of them round on Brian. He flounders.

'You need to talk to the officer in charge,' he says.

8

The *Daily Herald* office is seven storeys above the sticky pavements of London. Senior Reporter Karen White sits under a noisy air-conditioning unit, breathing in the recycled yawns of her fellow employees, picking at a muffin and trying to sex up a press release about wind farm subsidies.

She's checking her emails, more to keep herself awake than because anything important is happening, when an alert hits her inbox that sends a shot of adrenalin through her veins. In a few keystrokes she's found a local newsfeed from Dorset and there he is. Her marked man, Detective Inspector Alec Hardy, looking, if anything, even rougher than the last time she saw him.

'This is a short statement to confirm that this morning the body of an eleven-year-old child was found on Harbour Cliff Beach at Broadchurch,' he says to the camera. 'The body was subsequently identified as Daniel Latimer, who lived in the town. We are treating the death as suspicious. Our investigations are continuing, and there'll be a full briefing later this evening.'

It takes Karen a second or two to digest the news that he got another job after Sandbrook and then she's off, fingers flying, tracing the story back to its source. The earliest mention is a tweet from the local newspaper, but the fuller story is not on their website yet, and none of the other nationals seem to have picked up on it. Good. There is still time to make the story hers. Her editor's door is open: Karen checks her reflection in a window, smooths her long dark hair into a ponytail, and pops the collar on the tailored jacket that means business, even if it is a decade too old for her. She doesn't bother to knock. Len Danvers cut his teeth on Fleet Street back when print was king; he thinks manners get in the way of a deadline.

'Are you taking the piss?' he says, when she's given him a précis of the situation. 'Let the agencies cover it, and you can polish it up later. Eleven-year-old boys get into trouble all the time.'

'But it's *Alec Hardy*,' she says. '*He*'s the story.'

'Only if he fucks up again.' Danvers waves a hand at a ledger on his desk. 'You know what the budget's like at the moment. I'm sorry, Karen. The answer's no.'

She returns to her desk, sits heavily down in her swivel chair. The press release about wind farm subsidies has not sexed itself up in her absence. She spends another ten minutes tinkering with it, then goes back to the *Broadchurch Echo* Twitter account. The journalist's name is Olly Stevens and his bio reads, 'Fearless reporter with thrusting local paper, *Broadchurch Echo*.' She googles his name: he's posted his CV and samples of his work online and states that his ambition is to be a lead reporter on a national. She punches in his number and is gratified by the admiration in his voice when she introduces herself.

'I saw you broke the story about Danny Latimer,' she says. 'I might be coming down to cover it. I wonder if you'd let me buy you a drink, find out more.'

Of course he says yes. Karen files her wind farm story, then puts in a call to the HR department. She's worked hard this year, and hasn't taken a day's annual leave yet. They owe her.

The street outside shimmers in the heat: the woozy outline of a black cab pulls into sharp focus as it draws near. She hails it and asks the driver to go to Waterloo.

Bloody *Twitter*. Hardy's heart sinks at the thought of the work they'll have to do to rebuild the trust of the Latimer family now. As he leaves the station, DS Miller is still trying to apologise for her nephew. Hardy's not interested. At least after this morning's bollocking he's confident she won't let that happen again. What a day. What a fucking day.

The fresh air outside doesn't clear his head: if anything, he feels worse. The shallow breathing and blurred vision that herald an attack set in and all Hardy wants is to collapse on to his bed before it happens in public.

It's an effort to push open the heavy oak door at the Traders Hotel. It was his choice to stay in a hotel – to look for somewhere more permanent would be to acknowledge that he is here permanently – but he wishes he was staying at the anonymous chain hotel on the ring road. It's very lovely here – all original flagstone floors, modern art and a Farrow & Ball colour scheme – but the room keys hang on pegs behind the desk and that means making conversation every time he leaves or enters the building.

'Long day, huh?' says Becca Fisher when he holds out his hand for the key. She's nice enough, with a beachy blonde glamour that marks her out as Australian before she even speaks. He quite likes Becca, likes looking at her, anyway, but he doesn't want her to make his day any longer. 'Really tragic,' she continues, blind to Hardy's impatience. 'Can't think what that family are going through. We're all in shock. Chloe's got a Saturday job here, you know. I don't suppose I'll see her tomorrow. Not that I'll need her. I've had two cancellations already today.'

Hardy mentally files the detail about Chloe but only nods in reply to Becca. He has one foot on the bottom stair when he hears his name behind him. He turns slowly, to keep his balance.

Great. It's Miller's roving reporter nephew standing next to a middle-aged blonde woman who might as well have him by the scruff of the neck. 'Maggie, editor of the *Echo*,' she says, extending her hand. Hardy shakes it limply. At Maggie's prompt, Olly says, 'I was wrong to post that news. I'm sorry.'

'I should hang him by the bollocks from the town hall spire,' says Maggie. 'All reporting on this will come through me now. The *Echo* works *with* the police. I'll talk to the Latimer family, give them our apologies.'

Hardy blinks slowly. 'Stay out my way,' he says to Olly.

It seems that there is to be one more obstacle to freedom. Becca Fisher follows him up to the landing. 'Do you think the beach'll be open tomorrow? Only so I know what to tell guests.'

54

'I'm going up,' says Hardy, one hand on the banister to support himself as well as signal intent.

The effort of climbing two flights has him perspiring and struggling for breath.

In his room at last, he empties his jacket: his wallet lands on the bedside table and falls open at the picture of the face that continues to haunt him. The little girl is backlit, her hair a white aureole. It hurts to look at her. All the more reason for him to see it every time he opens his wallet. Before he can loosen his tie or his shoelaces, his legs begin to give way and he collapses into the armchair. His focus switches to a canvas print of Harbour Cliff on the far wall. Even here, he can't escape the bloody place. Of all the beaches in all the world . . .

As the sweat cools on his back, he realises his pills are on the other side of the room. It takes everything he's got to get up and swallow them.

9

Ellie and Beth stand with their backs to the cliffs, looking to the water. A pink sun hangs low in a golden sky. The place is almost deserted, out of fear or respect. Even the sea is discreet, the tide on the turn. Ellie, terrified of saying the wrong thing, is relieved when Beth speaks first.

'I used to bring him down here when he was a baby,' she says. 'Middle of the day, just me and him. I'd pick him up and dip him in the waves, then whoosh him up, his little fat legs all wet. God he loved it, he used to laugh like mad.' She smiles, and it's the saddest thing Ellie's ever seen. Without warning, Beth punches herself hard in the chest. 'There's nothing *there*, Ell. Like, I know it's happened, but I can't feel anything.'

'I think it's shock.'

'Promise me, Ellie, 'cause I don't know your boss from Adam . . . ' Ellie's stomach flips as she realises that Beth still hasn't made the connection between Hardy and Sandbrook. 'But you and me go back. The *boys* go back. I'm counting on you to get them caught.'

'I swear,' says Ellie. Should she tell Beth now? Better she finds out from Ellie, from a friend, than she makes the connection on her own or she finds out from the press. Ellie draws a deep breath, but Beth's eyes are on her, pleading.

'He did know, didn't he? That I love him.'

The moment is gone. How can Ellie answer a question like that with the truth about Sandbrook? She can't kick her friend while she's this far down. She'll give Beth another day for things to sink in. Nothing will come out between now and the media briefing. 'Of course he did,' she tells Beth. 'He was a *beautiful* boy. You don't deserve this.'

Beth turns her head away. 'I just feel like I'm very far away from myself.'

The sun hits the horizon and seems to linger there for ever.

Ellie parks outside her house in Lime Avenue. Instead of getting out of the car, she stares through the windscreen at her home. Taking five minutes here usually helps her to make the gear shift between work and home, but today those boundaries were broken and she can't switch off. The light in Tom's bedroom is on: Fred's curtains are closed, meaning he's asleep already. Gratitude that her two children are still here gives way to a sickening guilt. Ellie has survivor's guilt by proxy: she wonders if Tom feels the real thing.

Joe must have heard Ellie's key in the door because he's waiting in the hall to hold her. He looks hollowed out. Ellie wraps herself in him: he smells of yoghurt and baby wipes and the familiar solid shape of him is exactly what she needs.

'Are you all right?' he whispers into her hair. She nods a lie into his shoulder.

'I'm just here for a shower, then I have to get back. Does Tom know?'

Joe breaks off the hug and shakes his head. 'He's upstairs. I kept him away from it all.' He covers his mouth with his hand, afraid to ask the next question. 'Should *we* be worried? For other kids?'

'I don't know,' she says honestly. 'I mean, we'll watch Tom like a hawk, but whether it's a one-off or . . . ' She can't finish her sentence: that there might be more is too horrific to contemplate.

Joe strokes her cheek. 'I'm sorry about the job,' he says. The contrast between the morning's happiness and this evening's despair is the trigger Ellie needs to break down and cry.

'I saw him lying there,' she says. 'I don't know if I can do this.'

Joe murmurs reassurances and rocks her gently.

'Hey,' he says, after a while. 'Actually, no, it doesn't matter.'

'What?'

Joe shakes his head. 'It can wait. You need to get on with your job.' He's always done this: he *knows* how much it infuriates her.

'I won't be able to concentrate on the job if I'm wondering what you're not telling me.'

'Lucy was round earlier.' Joe cowers in a pantomime of fear that is only partly feigned. He's always been slightly afraid of Lucy and that situation wasn't helped by the last time he saw her, the two sisters in a stand-up, screaming row over the missing cash. Mind you, he was probably quite scared of Ellie as well after that. She can't remember the last time she was so angry. 'She banged on the door really loudly,' says Joe. 'Woke Fred up from his nap.'

That doesn't sound like someone come to offer an apology, which is the only thing Ellie wants from Lucy now. 'That's all I fucking need. Did you tell her?'

'I couldn't find the words.'

She takes the stairs slowly, nursing a cowardly hope that Tom's already asleep and that she can put this off until the morning. But he's up, playing a game on his phone, tongue lolling in concentration. She seizes a moment to watch this version of her son, to savour the last few seconds of his childhood. Softly she creeps in and sits on the edge of his bed.

'You know Danny wasn't at school today?' she says.

Instantly he picks up on her mood. Fear leaks into his voice. 'Yeah?'

Ellie puts her son's little hand in hers. 'Tom, sweetheart. Danny died.' He doesn't react. 'I'm sorry.'

He blinks. Ellie knows that tears are on their way and sees the effort it takes him to hold them back. 'How?' he eventually manages.

'We're not sure yet. He was found on the beach, early this morning.'

'Do his mum and dad know?' The solipsistic innocence of the question, the idea that she would, or could, tell Tom before Mark and Beth, breaks Ellie's heart.

'Yes. So ... look ... When someone dies unexpectedly, it

leaves a big hole. It's all right to feel sad or have a cry.' She sounds even to herself like a pamphlet on bereavement.

'OK. Will you ... I mean, will the police want to ask me questions?'

'Yes. Is there anything you want to tell me now?' She walks the fine tightrope between gentle and vague. 'Was Danny all right?'

'Yeah. 'Course.' He picks at the duvet. 'Can I have a bit of time on my own now?' he asks.

Ellie wonders when he became ashamed to cry in front of her.

'Of course.'

By the time she's showered and changed, Tom's asleep. It's dark outside. So much for making an arrest by nightfall.

Joe presses a sandwich into her hand on her way out of the door. She eats it one-handed on the drive to the station, chases it with a cup of weak tea back at her desk and goes through the list that one of the DCs has left for her of belongings recovered from Danny's body and bedroom. Something – the lack of something – jumps out at her, making her heartbeat spike. She reads it again. No mobile phone. He definitely had one. It was the same model as Tom's. She looks for someone to tell, but she's alone in the office.

She sets that to one side, then starts to go through the previous night's CCTV footage from the town centre. She makes screen grabs of the few figures who appear. Then, at 10.47, she sees an image that steals her breath. The picture is grainy but there's no doubt that the boy whizzing down Broadchurch High Street on his skateboard is Danny

Latimer. What the *hell* is he doing out on his own? She replays it twice.

'Have a look at this!' she calls. This time Hardy materialises at her shoulder, new suit on. Ellie can feel a list coming on.

'He wasn't abducted. He snuck out. Why? Where was he going? Who was he meeting?'

He pauses to knot his tie. Ellie beats him to the next point.

'And where's the skateboard?'

10

Chloe is crying in her bedroom, soft ladylike sobs – even her crying is grown-up now – occasionally punctuated by the ping of texts hitting her phone.

'Do you want a cuddle?' Beth whispers through the keyhole. 'You know I'm here when you need me.'

The crying stops for a second. 'I'll come down in a bit,' says Chloe. In the next instant, her phone rings out and she answers it, speaking so quietly that Beth can't even pick up her tone, let alone her words. Who's she talking to? What's she saying? It guts Beth to know that Chloe's friends, who are good girls, but only children themselves, are giving consolation when Beth is not allowed to. Still, she respects the closed door. She wants more than anything to hold her daughter, to receive comfort as well as to give it, but she mustn't let Chloe see this. She's only fifteen. Her brother has died. That's enough to cope with, without knowing how much responsibility she now bears for her mother's state of mind. So Beth backs away and goes downstairs, her arms heavy and useless at her sides; at the same time she carries an unbearable surplus of love.

Mark is in the hall, staring at his phone.

'Every time it goes, I think it's Danny.' He has it set up so that every number in his phone book has a different alert. A klaxon for Nige, jingle bells for Beth. Danny's number the cheer of a crowd. They'll never hear it again. 'I keep thinking he's going to walk back in,' says Mark.

They've been having this conversation, or a circular version of it, all day, batting denial back and forth between them.

'Did you touch him? At the ...' She can't finish. Mark shakes his head.

'They wouldn't let me.'

They wouldn't have been able to stop *her*. Now that one terrible question is out there, the next follows almost without her permission. 'Why didn't you look in on him last night?'

'*Beth*,' says Mark, but she's started now.

'You always look in on him, when you come to bed.' As the words spill, she realises that she didn't actually hear Mark come to bed. Not that that's unusual; she rushes past the thought on the way to the accusation. 'Why didn't you see he was gone?'

'Why didn't you?' says Mark. It cuts her between the ribs.

Neither of them has an answer. Blame and counter-blame. Is this really what they are going to do to each other? Silently she vows not to let her marriage be destroyed by this. They owe it to Danny to stay strong and stay together. She needs Mark by her side and on her side if she is to survive this.

Karen White stands on the beach, shakes loose her ponytail and lets the salt wind blow London from her hair. The sun is a semi-circle on the horizon. A shrine has sprung up, as she knew it would. Cellophane rustles around supermarket flowers and tea lights gutter in jam jars. At the centre of it all sits a little toy chimp. A couple of kids tape a card to the lifebelt and leave, arm in arm, one crying into the other's shoulder, then Karen is alone. She approaches the sad memorial and drops to her knees as though in prayer. Glancing over her shoulder to make sure that nobody is watching, she picks up the chimp and puts it in her handbag. She uses the map on her phone to find her way to the media briefing at the school hall.

The place looks tiny, as primaries always do. Hardy sits behind a microphone, his Chief Super beside him in dress uniform. Behind them is a board bearing the insignia of Hardy's new force, the Wessex Police. Behind that, a jumble of PE apparatus.

Hardy stares past the assembled press to the far side of the room where paper fish swim across the wall. It's not a full house. There's a single camera crew and a handful of print journalists. It looks like the rest of Fleet Street concurs with Len Danvers. Good, thinks Karen. Less competition for the story. She'll show him. She sticks to the back of the hall, taking care not to be seen.

She recognises Olly Stevens from his website and guesses that the tall blonde woman next to him, matching *Broadchurch Echo* lanyard hanging around her neck, must be a colleague. She's on her feet with a question as soon as Hardy has been introduced.

'Maggie Radcliffe, editor of the *Broadchurch Echo*,' she says. The name rings a bell although Karen can't place it.

'What advice do you have for people in the town, particularly parents?'

Hardy addresses his reply to the camera. 'The crime rate in this area is one of the lowest in the country. This is a terrible anomaly. We're in the early moments of what may be a complex investigation.' He breaks eye contact with the lens for a few seconds and scans the room. The little flinch he gives when he spots Karen is not picked up by the camera, but she notices it with satisfaction. He blinks and continues. 'Danny's life touched many people. We'll be looking at all those connections. If you or someone you know has any information, has noticed anything unusual, please come forward now. I'd urge everyone: don't hide anything.' The cameraman goes in close so that Hardy's face fills the monitor. 'Because we will find out. We will catch whoever did this.'

Night finally falls on Harbour Cliff bay. The colours of day have faded but the evidence tents are lit from within, turning the white canvas a pale pink. They glow like jellyfish as SOCO work into the night.

Danny's death is the lead item on the ten o'clock news. The Latimers watch from the sofa, all three faces wearing the same stupid, stunned expression.

Up at the farm, cows graze in peaceful bovine ignorance as Dean watches on his phone.

Becca Fisher has the news on the computer at hotel reception. She takes a large tug on a neat whisky and checks her phone for text messages for the third time in five minutes.

Olly Stevens and Maggie Radcliffe, finalising the front page layout in the *Echo* office, down tools and watch in silence.

Nige Carter, working through the night to cover Mark's absence, sees the news in someone else's house, some woman who didn't even know Danny. She is crying but Nige is dry-eyed.

Jack Marshall, alone on the empty shop floor, listens to the radio, hands in his cardigan pockets, mouth set.

Paul Coates watches on his iPad in the vestry where the stone walls hang with photographs of his frocked predecessors.

Susan Wright watches on the portable television in her static caravan, the dog's head on her lap and a cigarette in her hand. She shakes her head, then exhales a long slow thread of smoke.

Joe Miller, clearing up the sitting room, is frozen to the screen, a stuffed toy in each hand.

Upstairs in his bedroom, Tom Miller stares at his phone for a long, long time. He chews his lip in deliberation, then his expression hardens. He checks behind him to make sure that Joe isn't lurking on the landing. All clear. Now he has made his decision he acts quickly. First he deletes all Danny's text messages, a record of friendship that goes back years. Then he's on his laptop, hitting the keys in a series of actions reserved only for emergencies. The warning message fills the screen: 'Are you sure you want to reformat the hard disk? You will lose all your data.' Tom clicks yes.

He looks over his shoulder again. That's not grief on his face. That's fear.

11

At first light, DI Hardy walks the route of Danny's paper round, a pencilled map as his guide. The kid covered a lot of ground: coastal footpaths as well as residential streets. He climbs a shallow hill that brings him out on a huge greensward high above the beach, a timeless green landscape. Cow parsley blooms in white foam at waist height. In the grassy dunes and hummocks Hardy sees only hiding places for those inclined to hide. The ground is booby-trapped with rabbit holes and their droppings squish like raisins under his soles.

On the clifftop trail that looks like a road to nowhere Hardy spots a CCTV camera attached to a telegraph pole. It points to a lone hut, something between a trailer and a chalet. It is out of place here: it could have been dropped there by a typhoon, like the house in *The Wizard of Oz*. He gets the impression a bad storm could send it tumbling down the cliff. He follows the sandy track that cuts through the gorse.

Up close, he cups his hands around his eyes to see in. It's

a holiday let, by the look of it: uninhabited but well-kept, tastefully kitted out in seashell art and a nice cloth on the table. It's Hardy's idea of hell – fresh air, isolation, grass, never-ending sky – but he knows that the world's full of idiots who love this sort of thing.

He needs to get in.

There's a shadow on the grass and then that woman and her brown dog come into view. She doesn't have the aimless walk of the tourist rambler; she knows this place. Hardy takes one step towards her but on seeing him she turns on her heel and breaks into a trot to get away from him. He's too tired and too far from his medication to attempt pursuit. But she is on his radar now.

Ellie's the first one downstairs, tiptoeing in her slippers around the silver slug trails that appear on their carpet every night. Joe insists that one day he'll catch the culprit and return it to the garden. He's big on the humane treatment and rescue of creepy-crawlies, a hangover from his former life as a paramedic. Ellie scrapes off the worst of the trails with a tissue. If she ever catches the slimy little bastard she'll salt it, but it's clever; it knows when they're asleep.

She suddenly sees herself as though from the outside. How pathetic is that, how *offensive*, getting wound up about slug trails when a little boy has been murdered? She feels sadness like a great pressure from above: she has to rest her head on the floor for a while. Ellie stays like that for a long time, crying softly for Danny, until footsteps overhead tell her that the boys are waking up.

She pours orange juice into a glass and takes it up to Tom.

Joe's waiting for her at his bedside. He looks exhausted, like his jet lag's finally kicked in.

'How're you doing, lovely?' She hands Tom the juice. 'You had nightmares. You were shouting in your sleep.'

'What was I saying?' His fingers trace the rim of the glass but he doesn't drink.

'We couldn't make it out,' says Joe. 'Heard you say Danny at one point.'

Tom drops his eyes to his lap. Ellie tries to remember what it's like to be eleven, how innocent secrets assume giant proportions.

'Are you going in to work?' he asks.

'Yes. Dad's got a quiet day planned for you.'

'We'll go down the DVD shop, rent whatever you like, get some popcorn,' says Joe, much too brightly. 'Duvets on the sofa. What do you think?'

Tom isn't fooled for a second. 'Will I have to talk to the police?'

'At some point,' says Ellie. 'Not today, I don't think. Unless there's anything you can think of that might help us?'

'When I have to talk to them, can it be you?'

Ellie shakes her head. She wonders who they'll get to question Tom. It'll have to be someone he doesn't already know, but he's been coming in to the station since he was a toddler. Her heart sinks to realise that there's only one officer in Broadchurch who fits the bill.

Karen White's joy at learning that she is staying in the same hotel as Alec Hardy has only been marginally reduced by missing him at breakfast. She's been waiting outside the police station since half-past seven, regretting the double refill of coffee at breakfast time. She needs a toilet break, soon, but can't risk leaving her post. It might be her only chance of the day.

He shows up at a quarter past eight, city shoes caked in mud and sand, like he's been for a long, ill-judged walk. When she calls him by rank and name he ignores her, so she puts her hand on his arm. He removes it like it's contaminated.

'Karen White, *Daily Herald*,' she says, as though he could possibly have forgotten who she is. Long after the rest of the press pack had moved on, she was still demanding answers. She's proud of that. But Hardy just looks right at her, hazel eyes unblinking.

'I wondered if I could buy you a cup of tea?' She smiles even as he turns his back on her: it's a trick that keeps her voice friendly when she's angry on the inside. 'You know there's going to be attention on you. You need someone to put your side of this across. Don't rule it out. If you need me, I'll be at the Traders. You know what, you can give me a knock—'

He rounds on her then. 'You are *astonishing*,' he spits, before swinging through the station door. It slams in her face.

Too right, thinks Karen. I *am* astonishing. You don't know the half of it.

Minutes later, she's at the *Echo* office. She pauses with her hand on the door, stopped in her tracks by a picture of Danny Latimer, grinning in a yellow T-shirt. It's different to the formal school photograph that the police have released.

He looks like the kind of kid she likes. Cheeky. Funny. For the first time it hits Karen, really hits her, that Broadchurch is not a spin-off of Sandbrook but a story – a tragedy – in its own right. She swallows the lump in her throat.

Inside, people are lining up to sign a condolence book that Maggie Radcliffe has set up.

Karen has remembered, with a little help from Google, how she knows Maggie's name. They studied her work on the Yorkshire Ripper at journalism college. She was one of the first to question the police operation. She was at Greenham Common too, taking part in the women-only peace camp as well as covering it for the tabloids. She's old-school, part of Len Danvers' generation. Karen has a lot of respect for her and knows that she won't be as easy to manipulate as Olly Stevens.

Luckily, Maggie's deep in conversation with a guy who looks much too young for the dog collar he's wearing. Karen's never seen such a young priest. She looks him up and down; his clothes are new, on-trend, not bought round here, and his fair hair, combed and slicked down in a side parting, is so old-fashioned it's cool again.

'The church should've done this,' he says, pen poised over the book.

'It's not a competition,' replies Maggie coolly. 'It's new to all of us.'

'I'd like to write a column,' suggests the vicar. 'Something like *Thought for the Day* on Radio 4. To remind people why the Church is important at a time like this, what it can offer them.'

Maggie snorts. 'Me and your boss had a parting of the

ways long before you popped up here. I was made to feel very unwelcome in your church.'

'Not by me,' says the vicar earnestly. 'You and Lil are both always welcome in my church.'

'I should think so too,' says Maggie, only slightly appeased. 'Look, thanks for the offer, but I don't want for editorial. What I need right now is advertisers. And that's not you.'

The vicar drums neat fingers on the countertop. 'OK then, I'll buy the space. My personal money. I'll write a piece, I'll pay whatever your rate card is. If I have to pay to get words of comfort out there, I'll do it.'

'I'll give you 10 per cent discount,' Maggie flashes back.

Karen smirks. Two minutes in and she's already seen corruption. So much for local news being the last bastion of good old-fashioned reporting.

Next up is Becca from the hotel in the kind of dress that showcases a flawless figure. You can tell she doesn't spend all day sitting on her arse in front of a screen, thinks Karen. Becca flicks her hair at the vicar, then at Maggie, as though out of habit. Some women don't even know they're doing it, and it's always the ones that don't have to try that hard.

'What do you write that doesn't sound glib?' asks Becca. Maggie's all smiles now, and it's easy for Karen to slip past her to the office.

It takes her eyes a few seconds to adjust to the darkness in here. How do they work like this? She's used to pale-grey ergonomic furniture, plate windows and strip lighting. This place ... there's more wood than in a sauna. An air vent in the tiny window is held together by masking tape and on the sill are some dried flowers in a wobbly clay pot and a wooden cat. A health-and-safety notice clings to the wall for dear life.

Olly Stevens is hunched before his monitor. He looks up at her with a spark of recognition that shows Karen that she's not the only one who's been on Google. She sits on the edge of his desk. He's cute, this cub reporter, even if he is a year or two younger than she first thought. Buttering him up won't be a hardship.

'So, d'you think you might have a spare desk or corner of the office I can squirrel myself away in while I'm here? We *are* part of the same newspaper group, after all.'

Olly's virtually set up a workstation for Karen before Maggie can stop him.

'Karen White, *Daily Herald*,' Karen introduces herself. Maggie takes the hand she offers and the two women size each other up.

'No,' says Maggie, in answer to the question. 'We're a very busy operation here.' Karen looks round the empty office and bites down hard on a smirk. 'And if I give you a desk, what happens if others start showing up?'

Karen goes to argue, but then thinks better of it. Less is more. It's what sets her apart from the rest, this ability to back off from a subject and give them room to think. Journalism is like showbiz – always leave them wanting more. It's the approach that got her in with the Sandbrook families. It might even work with Hardy one day.

Back on the High Street she weighs up her options. She reminds herself that she's the only national newspaper journalist chasing this story so far. She glances back at the *Broadchurch Echo* office on her way out. These people aren't her competition. If she plays them right, they could end up working for her. She thinks hard about the best way to get Olly Stevens onside without burning any bridges with Maggie. She sends him a text asking whether he'd like to show her the sights instead.

She opens the *Echo* website on her phone and runs the word Sandbrook through its search facility. It doesn't look like they've made the connection. Maggie Radcliffe was famous for having an encyclopaedic mind, but who uses encyclopaedias any more? And it doesn't look like anyone at the paper has thought to do background on the Senior Investigation Officer. Karen White is pleased. She likes to have the advantage.

12

The solvent smell of whiteboard markers always makes Hardy feel woozy, but with concentration he can print with a steady hand.

OPERATION COGDEN
SIO: DI Alec Hardy
Victim: Danny Latimer
Age: 11 years
Height: 4' 8" 142 cm
Loc: Harbour Cliff Beach, Broadchurch
Time of Death: Thurs 18 July 2200–0400h (est.)

CID is a mess. Everyone has been called into work at once, meaning they've got more officers than desks. Floor panels are being lifted to access power sockets and install new phone lines. A network of live tripwires criss-crosses the office.

The phone engineer, a burly bloke in gold-rimmed glasses, keeps flicking Hardy nervous glances. Hardy squints to read his name badge – Steve Connolly – and stares back with all the hostility he can muster. The more uncomfortable he makes this Steve Connolly feel, the sooner he'll get the job done and piss off out of Hardy's incident room. Hardy's not happy about having a civilian in here, moving desks about, toppling files that should be under lock and key. Do these people think he has a clean-desk policy for fun?

Miller's brought him a latte. He salivates at the creamy, nutty smell of it, but even a cup of instant could send him over the edge, and those café blends are like rocket fuel. Of course, she takes the refusal personally.

'There's a hut on Briar Cliff,' he says, ignoring her wounded fawn expression. 'Mile and a half along the coast from where Danny's body was found. Find out who owns it. And the car park below. Collect the CCTV from the camera there. How're we doing on house-to-house?'

'We've got five uniform allocated, two probationers, one who can't drive and one who'd never taken a statement before last night.' She grins an apology. 'It's a summer weekend. Three festivals and two sporting events within a hundred miles, all other officers attached to those until Monday.'

He hates this place. He hates the stupid people and the way they work, their smiley fucking faces. He turns his attention back to the whiteboard.

'Danny's skateboard, Danny's mobile. Priorities. Also, main suspects. You know this town – who's most likely?' Miller, not realising he's only halfway through, tries to interrupt but he bowls on: 'If the boy was killed before being left on the beach, where's the murder scene? What're you doing today?'

'We've managed to get a Family Liaison Officer, I'm taking

him over to the Latimers. And Jack Marshall who runs the paper shop rang in. He said he'd remembered something.'

From nowhere, Hardy feels his fingertips tingle, a sure sign that an attack is on its way. Miller's voice sounds as though it's coming from far away. There's a constriction in his lungs and suddenly there are two Millers standing in front of him, blurring in and out of focus.

'In a minute,' Hardy says.

He makes it to the toilet without incident. Mercifully alone, he pops two huge tablets from the blister pack in his pocket and washes them down with tap water. He studies his pale sweaty face in the mirror above the sink and wills it to return to normal.

On the way back, he almost falls over Steve Connolly, who's unrolling a long white cable. His face is ashen, and it takes Hardy the briefest inspection of the office to realise why. DC Frank Williams's desk is a mess. A list of questions that still need answering has been pinned to a screen, for fuck's sake. A picture of Danny's skateboard, yellow laminate with a jagged navy print, lies across a keyboard and visible under that is – oh, for fuck's *sake* – autopsy photographs peeking from the file. There's a blown-up picture of Danny's neck, huge red handprints on the white skin. Hardy sends Connolly away, then gives Williams a bollocking that silences the room. The talking doesn't start up again until he is halfway down the corridor.

It's business as usual at the newsagent's. Jack Marshall heaves a stack of papers up on to the counter. The effort leaves him slightly breathless.

'I couldn't stop thinking about him all last night,' he says. 'I run the Sea Brigade. Danny'd been coming about eighteen months, on and off. Cheeky lad, but a good heart. It matters, a good heart.'

You don't have to tell me that, thinks Hardy. 'You said you remembered something about seeing him.'

Jack gives a curt nod, as though he's speaking under duress. 'Must've been end of last month. Around a quarter to eight, on a Wednesday morning. Up past Jocelyn Knight's house. On the road leading up to the clifftops, near Linton Hill. I saw him.'

'What was he doing?'

'Talking to the postman.' Jack slices through the twine that binds the stack of newspapers with a sharp bright Stanley knife. 'Well, not talking. More like arguing. I was quite far off. But the body language was pretty clear. Then Danny got on his bike and stormed off. The postman was calling after him.'

'You're *certain* it was a postman?' says Hardy. Jack isn't wearing glasses, and doesn't look like the contact lens type.

'Who else is going to be out that time in the morning? Anyway, he had a bag. And one of those high-visibility jackets.'

'Describe him to me.'

'He was a long way off. Medium height, short brown hair, I think. It was only after you were in yesterday that I remembered. I should've mentioned it.'

Yes, thinks Hardy. You should have. So why didn't you?

The Latimer house smells stale, like a bedroom that needs airing. It's the wrong time of year to keep the windows

78

closed but the press have started to arrive outside and they need shutting out; if they're not pointing their cameras, they're making phone calls or bantering loudly.

'This is DC Pete Lawson,' Ellie introduces the gangly young man at her side. 'He'll be your Family Liaison Officer, keep you up to date with the investigation, answer your questions, talk to you about any questions we might have. It's a specialised job. Pete's just completed his training.'

'You're my first!' says Pete cheerily, his smile fading as he catches Ellie's fury. Of all the inappropriate things . . .

'But you *know* us,' says Beth, echoing Ellie's thoughts.

'The best thing I can do for you is find who killed Danny, and I will.'

Ellie lets Pete take charge of the elimination prints, willing him not to fuck it up.

Only Mark kicks up a fuss. 'Is this really necessary?' he says, as Liz rocks an inked thumb from side to side on the paper. He's insulted, Ellie can see that, and she understands. Even burglary victims give their prints indignantly. It's human nature: intellectually, people know that they're making a positive contribution to the investigation, but some people feel they're being processed like a suspect. Ellie cannot begin to imagine how much worse it must be after losing a child. Mark gives his prints, but reluctantly, shaking his head throughout. When the whole family has been done, he asks, 'When can we start arranging the funeral?' His voice catches on the word.

Knowing this question was coming doesn't make the answer any easier. 'That has to wait,' says Ellie. 'Until we have the person responsible in custody, Danny's – his body –

is the . . . look, I have to talk about it this way, I'm sorry – it's the most valuable piece of evidence we have. We can't allow him to be buried until we're sure we have the right person, and the right evidence to convict them.'

'We can't have him back?' says Beth, horrified.

'Not yet. Sorry.'

'He's not evidence,' says Chloe. 'He's my *brother*.'

'I know. Really I do,' says Ellie, well aware that she hasn't got a clue.

Beth raises her eyebrows in a silent query to Mark. He nods, and brings out a piece of paper which he hands to Ellie.

'We made a list,' he says. 'Of people who might have done it.'

Ellie unfolds it and reads in dismay. She knows most of the names on it. They have included any male with the slightest prominence in the community, and there is naturally some overlap with Wessex Police's own suspect list. And when they ran out of strangers, Beth and Mark looked closer to home. 'These are all your *friends*.' The couple look at her like lost children, like the teen parents they used to be. Ellie is reminded for the first time in years that Beth is still only thirty.

'We know,' they say.

Ellie is almost grateful when SOCO Brian calls her out of the room. Upstairs, he hands over an evidence bag.

'Five hundred pounds in cash. Taped to the underside of the bed frame in Danny's room.'

13

Karen asked Olly to show her the sights and he's given her a bird's-eye view. This clifftop bench is the perfect place for her to get her bearings. Down below, it's easy to see how the quaint, touristy part of town near the harbour gives way to a cluster of ugly municipal buildings that lower into the sprawl of the estate. The sea stretches before them. And then of course there are the cliffs, the steep mute witnesses to Danny Latimer's murder. They are mesmerising, with that unearthly golden colour. It's an effort for Karen to draw her eyes away from them and look at Olly.

'Tell me about Broadchurch,' she asks him. 'Who *lives* here?'

He ponders. 'Lot've been here all their lives, generations, some of them have never been fifty miles outside town. Then there's the incomers. Young families, left cities when they had babies, came here 'cause they fancied the schools and the sea. We get tourists for six weeks in the summer, but we're a working town mainly.'

'Crime?'

'Mostly thefts from lock-ups, odd bit of drug use, drink driving.' Karen can't hide her smirk in time. 'Seriously. I do the weekly crime report in the paper with one of the uniforms. About thirty offences a week, pretty much all minor. We've never had a murder.' His expression turns grave.

'And that's the sort of story you do at the *Echo*?'

He shrugs. 'Clubs, schools, council meetings. Maggie says we celebrate the everyday.' Karen shudders internally. She wouldn't work on a regional for a hundred grand a year. Mind you, Olly will be lucky to earn a tenth of that. She wonders if he still lives with his mum. Then she finds herself wondering what his bedroom looks like.

'What about you?' she asks. 'What do *you* want?'

Olly looks bashful for a moment. 'Work on a national. I want to be you, basically.'

'Careful what you wish for.' She smiles.

'How come you were here so quick?'

It still isn't time to let him know about her one-woman mission to find out where Alec Hardy has been or how he got here. She deploys distraction.

'If I report on this, I need to understand the town, the people. You help me with that, I might be able to help you. What d'you think?'

Olly beams. 'I think, good.' Karen notices his white, even teeth. It will be no hardship spending time with this one.

Ellie Miller takes a breather, going for a slow walk along the seafront. It's a glorious day but there are only a handful of people out. It looks bare without its usual milling crowd of kids and without the cover of chatter, the gulls and waves seem exaggeratedly loud, like someone's turned up the volume on a soundtrack of seaside noises. The few children around are hand in hand with their parents, even the older ones. She can't see anyone local letting their kids out alone for a long time. Tom's old carefree life of coming and going as he pleases is on hold until this case is solved.

Something catches Ellie's eye and she looks up at the bench on the hillside. A young woman in expensive-looking clothes and inappropriate shoes is picking her way down the sandy path. Ellie does a double take to see Olly up on the bench, mooning after the woman. She climbs the hill to join him.

'Who's your new friend?' asks Ellie, sitting down heavily next to him. Sweat dampens her hairline.

'She's a colleague,' says Olly importantly. 'A reporter from the *Herald*. I'm helping her get a feel for the town, give her a bit of local colour. She reckons the story won't be picked up by the nationals the way things stand.'

Ellie interprets it as a slight, although she's got nothing to do with the press. Maybe she's being paranoid.

Olly squirms. 'Did Mum talk to you before she went?'

'Went where?' she asks with a sense of foreboding.

'Bournemouth.'

Bournemouth, where the big casinos on the seafront welcome people like Lucy with open arms and chips stacked high on the baize. Ellie can't help the plunge of disappointment in her belly, even though she should know better by now. She really needs to lower her expectations of Lucy, but she can't seem to reprogramme their relationship. Part of her is still a little girl in thrall to her glamorous big sister.

'She told me she was skint,' says Olly miserably. They both know how Lucy can afford a trip to the bright lights. Her sister lives from win to win, the freak incidents of good luck that she uses to justify her behaviour on the other 364 days of the year. Ellie wonders how many thousands of other people's money Lucy squandered before a bet came good. Her debt to the Millers currently stands at over five grand, and that's just the stuff she'll admit to. The last time Lucy came to her for big money was when she pleaded for Ellie to pay for her rehab. In the relief of Lucy finally admitting to her problem, Ellie wrote a cheque without even asking Joe. She would have paid double for Lucy to get proper, professional help. The whole lot was gone in three days, pissed away in online poker rooms.

'When's she going to learn?' Ellie asks, but it's a rhetorical question.

'I thought you'd made it up about the rehab thing,' says Olly. Ellie can only shake her head. She doesn't have the heart to tell him about the most recent aberration, the worst one yet.

'I'd better go,' he says. 'See if anything fresh has come in to the newsroom.'

She watches him shuffle off, kicking a cloud of sand behind him. There's a hole in one of his shoes that rekindles a deep fondness in Ellie. It's a mercy that he earns as little as he does; he has nothing for Lucy to take.

Anger boils inside Ellie. She shouldn't have to deal with Lucy's shit on top of all the rest of it. Danny Latimer's death has put everything into sharp perspective. She fires off a sarcastic text.

Have a great time in Bournemouth! Didn't realise hairdress-
ing paid so well.

Looking forward to getting my children's money back on
your return.

There is no reply, but that's Lucy for you when she's off on
a bender. Ellie won't hear from her now until the money runs
out and she comes crawling back to Broadchurch, cap in hand.

There are reporters outside Beth's house and a policeman
inside. She can't get away from people and she can't have
the only person she wants. She is desperate to spend time in
Danny's room, curl up in his bed and breathe in the scent on
his pillow but the police tape across the door makes her a
stranger in her own home as well as a prisoner in it. The closest she can get is sorting the laundry that's in a pile in her
own bedroom and she goes through the pointless motions of
turning down the collar on his shirts, pairing his socks and
folding his T-shirts. The deflated outfits taunt her.

Her thoughts swirl with guilt; guilt at not having protected him, guilt at taking him for granted because she
thought she had him for ever.

The crying is constant now. The red rings around her eyes
are permanent, where the skin has been seared by salt. She
drifts in and out of it, only realising the tears are coming
when the stinging starts up again.

The metallic taste in her mouth, though, the copper-coin
tang that comes and goes, she can't attribute that to tears.
Every time it happens she craves – whether by hormones or
Pavlovian association – cheese-and-onion crisps. In fact, it's

the only thing she can imagine eating. It is the first sense of purpose she has had since it happened. She thuds downstairs and starts opening the kitchen cupboards.

'Where are the crisps?' she asks Liz, who's ironing creases into Mark's jeans.

'You don't need crisps,' says Liz. But by now the craving for cheese-and-onion crisps is inseparable from the craving for freedom. Liz looks at Beth again, and recognises her determination. 'OK,' she says, setting the iron down. 'Let me go for you.'

'Mum, will you STOP SMOTHERING ME?'

'I'm sorry,' says Liz through a cloud of steam. 'I want to help you.' Her own eyes start to shine.

'You can't,' says Beth, pocketing her car keys. She doesn't look back.

It feels good to be behind the wheel again, but the problem with driving somewhere is that sooner or later you have to arrive.

In the supermarket car park, Beth observes an unwelcome phenomenon; people staring, then looking away when she notices. Their glances cross for a split second and then bounce off each other like two marbles colliding. Just when she thinks she can't tolerate it happening one more time, a woman, protected by her own windscreen, gawps and forgets to lower her gaze, and that is worse. It is worse.

She tries to act normally. She has been coming to this supermarket since she was Danny's age. What could be more normal, more everyday, than shopping here? She picks up a basket and sets one foot in front of the other. A young couple do the supermarket trolley equivalent of a handbrake turn, steering abruptly down a different aisle. Shoppers cast their eyes down, or suddenly start studying labels with real intent. And here's the one that really hurts: a mother pulls a child out of her way as if loss is catching. Beth is radioactive.

Somehow she finds the crisps and pays. As she puts them in the boot of her car, an old man comes up and takes her hand.

'We're all so sorry,' he says. Beth knows that she should thank him but now *he* feels radioactive, his pity a toxin. She pulls her hand away and locks herself in the car. Blind with tears, she over-revs the engine as she prepares to reverse.

Bang. The seat belt cuts into her belly as she reverses hard into a concrete post. The boot flies open. She gets out of the car and kicks it where the metal has crumpled, not caring if she breaks half the bones in her foot. She can feel the eyes on her again as she screams and swears. Come on then, she thinks, hold my hand now, tell me you're sorry now, go on, I fucking dare you. But she hasn't got the strength to continue for long. She sinks down against the car, breathing hard, not knowing what to do.

Someone above is speaking her name. 'Beth.' It's Paul Coates, the vicar from her mum's church, although Beth isn't a believer and knows him more from Mark's five-a-side league. If he tells her that Jesus takes the ones he loves the best, she will hit him. 'You all right?'

She doesn't mean to tell him: it comes spilling out. 'I'm pregnant,' she says. Paul helps her to her feet, as though she's about to drop and not just a few weeks gone. They sit side by side in the boot, with the hatch up to make a little shade. It's weirdly intimate. 'Only found out two weeks ago,' she says. 'Haven't even told Mark.'

'Do you have anyone you can talk to?' There is something practised and professional about Paul's understanding face, but it is no less comforting for that. 'Your mum, maybe?'

'Not now. And don't you tell her either.' He has to keep secrets, doesn't he, or is that Catholics? She's a bit rusty with Church. She realises that she'll have to get reacquainted with it. The image of candlelight and a half-sized coffin imprints itself before she can censor it.

'What're you going to do?' asks Paul.

'Can you stop asking me bloody questions?'

'Sorry. I do that. Apparently.'

Beth gets a surprising glimpse of the man behind the dog collar; she gives the first genuine smile in days and he returns it. 'I'll leave you alone,' he says. 'You can come and see me. If you need to talk.'

'I don't know if I believe in God.' She needs to get that out there.

'It's not compulsory,' he says, like it's what he was expecting. 'I've been praying for you. Ever since I heard. And for Danny, too.'

'Thank you,' she says, and means it.

Her eyes are dry as she drives her broken car home. Back in Spring Close, she waits for the metallic wash to flood her mouth again but it doesn't come and she feels foolish. She has a cupboard full of cheese-and-onion crisps for no reason. The only other person who liked them was Danny. Now that the craving has subsided, the sight of them makes her feel sick.

Nobody in her house makes the connection.

14

They've found the postman who was on shift the day that Jack Marshall says he saw Danny. Ellie and Hardy catch Kevin Green on his round, up on the far edge of town, where the new-build houses abruptly give way to the countryside. He'd be hard to miss against this backdrop of muted greens with his fluorescent yellow tabard and the scarlet bag over his shoulder.

'Did you ever see Danny Latimer?' she asks. Kevin doesn't seem surprised by the question. What else could it be about?

'Yeah, all the time. He did paper deliveries to a few houses up here, including the hut. When I heard, I thought, I'd only seen him a couple of days previous.' He's not the first person to have this reaction: Ellie's learning that people are astonished that someone could die so soon after their last sighting, as though every encounter bestows some kind of immortality.

'Did you ever talk to him? I'm thinking particularly about the last week in June.'

Kevin thinks. 'I might've waved and said hello. I didn't really know him to talk to.'

'You didn't ever have an argument?' Hardy cuts in.

'What'm I gonna be arguing with a paper lad about?'

Ellie employs her new catchphrase. 'Where were you Thursday night?'

'Thursday, I'd've been with the boys. We had a golf championship on the PS3 and got hammered. Six of us, there was. We didn't finish till gone four. My missus had to wake me at seven, I was out cold.'

'We'll need the names of who you were with,' says Hardy.

Finally Kevin looks rattled. 'You don't think I had anything to do with it?'

'We just need to rule things out,' soothes Ellie. 'No need to worry.'

They begin the short walk back to the station.

'Don't say, "no need to worry,"' says Hardy when they are out of Kevin's earshot. 'Don't reassure people. Let them talk.'

She's had enough. 'Can I just say: you aren't going to rock up here and try to mould me! I know how to handle people. Keep your broody bullshit shtick to yourself.' She remembers who she's talking to. 'Sir.'

Ellie doesn't know him well enough to guess whether his silence is a sulk or genuine indifference, but she is shaken. She has never lost her temper like that with a colleague, let alone a superior, before. She works twice as hard on the phones when she gets back to the station. Four friends confirm Kevin's alibi: he was with them all night. She presents her findings to Hardy.

'So did Jack Marshall get it wrong?' she asks.

Hardy pushes smeared glasses back up a sweaty nose. 'Do we have any reason to disbelieve this postman?' he asks. 'How's Marshall's eyesight? Would he have any reason to lie? And do we think the money found at the house is connected?'

'You know you do this incessant question list? Like bam bam bam' – she chops the air with her hands – 'no space for anyone to reply? It's like you really enjoy it.'

'Do I?' Hardy shuts up for all of five seconds, and seems to recalibrate.

'First murder,' he says, in a convincing impression of a normal human being. 'How are you finding it?'

'Grim.'

'What did you make of Mark and Beth's list?'

'It made me want to cry,' she admits. 'Some of their best friends, Danny's teachers, babysitters, neighbours. They're traumatised. Not thinking straight.'

'Or they're smart. We didn't ask for a list. They may be trying to direct where we look. Taking focus away from their household.'

Ellie is aghast. 'They didn't kill Danny.'

'You have to learn not to trust.'

'I have to *what*?' Anger shoots from her core out to her extremities, making her hands twitch. There's a large hole-punch on her desk and she finds herself wondering if it would make a good weapon. 'That's what you've been sent here to teach me, is it? The benefit of your experience. Fantastic.'

It's as though the more emotion he's faced with, the less

91

Hardy displays himself. 'You have to look at your community from the outside now,' he says.

'I can't be outside it! I don't want to be.' He has missed the point, the point of *her*, by miles. Why can't he acknowledge that empathy is an asset? God knows they all need it more than ever, now Hardy's here. Smoothing the feathers he has managed to ruffle is a full-time job in itself.

'If you can't be objective, you're not the right fit,' says Hardy. Ellie snorts. It's almost funny. How can *she* not be the right fit? This is her turf! It's him who isn't, swanning in, taking promotions that were meant for other people and not even accepting a coffee without some great big sigh. He looks her straight in the eye. 'You need to understand, Miller. Anybody's capable of this murder. Given the right circumstances.'

'No,' she says firmly. 'People, most people, have a moral compass.'

'Compasses break,' he says over the top of his glasses. He's patronising her now. 'And murder gnaws at the soul. Whoever did it, they'll reveal themselves sooner or later. Every killer lets things slip, sooner or later. You know what people are like here ordinarily. Look for the out of the ordinary. Follow your instinct.'

She draws herself up to her full height. 'My *instinct* tells me the Latimers did not kill their son.'

Hardy raises his eyebrows in slow motion, a gesture that manages to be sarcastic, arrogant and dismissive all at once. Ellie boils inside. He's so sure he knows everything about human nature. But Ellie knows *these* humans, *this* family. Hardy might have a string of serious crimes on his CV, but there is more than one type of experience and here, now, Ellie believes that hers counts for more.

Caravan number 3 has seen better days, thinks Hardy; rust has moved in on chipped paintwork. A dreamcatcher – he only knows what it's called because Daisy had one gathering dust in her bedroom – hangs forlornly in the window. This is the residence of one Susan Wright, key-holder to the chalet on the cliff.

At his knock, a dog barks inside, and Hardy recognises the figure even through frosted glass. It's the woman he saw walking her dog the other morning. The woman who all but ran away from him. Gotcha, he thinks, as she opens the door.

The stench of stale cigarette smoke is an assault on his nostrils. He breathes through his mouth and flashes his badge. 'DI Hardy, Wessex Police.'

Her body language is remarkable; she has none. She is motionless and neutral as a dummy. 'What d'you want?'

'The owner of the chalet on Briar Cliff said you clean it. He said he'd phone ahead and let you know to have the keys ready.'

'My phone's dead.' Her accent is the flat London twang they call Estuary English. No matter how long Hardy spends south of the border, to his mind *estuary* will always mean the Firth of Forth.

'I need the keys,' he says. 'Just want a look inside the place.'

'To do with that boy?' She's the first person Hardy's met not to express sorrow or sympathy. 'Show me that ID again.'

Most people have blind faith in his badge but she examines it closely, like she knows what to look for. The slamming door hits the tip of Hardy's nose. She's gone a while and when she returns with the keys, she shoves them into his hand with bad grace.

'I'll have you sign for them. I don't want no trouble if you don't come back.'

He autographs a docket for her; the pen is still poised when the door slams again. He pulls his face away just in time.

Susan Wright stays at the window, her hand on Vince's head. She watches DI Hardy's retreating back, makes sure she sees him get into his car. When the sound of his engine fades to nothing, she goes to a cupboard by the front door and opens it a crack. Inside, a yellow skateboard with a navy blue pattern leans on the diagonal. She looks at it for a long time, then lets the door fall shut.

15

It is the first Sunday since Danny's body was found. In St Andrew's church, the dead in the graveyard outnumber the living inside by a hundred to one. Susan Wright watches through narrowed eyes as Liz Roper is comforted by a friend. Jack Marshall looks determinedly to the altar, where Reverend Paul Coates leans heavily on his pulpit.

'It's at times like this, we question our faith. Why would a benevolent god allow this to happen? I'm sure we're all asking that question after the events of last week.'

Liz's hand rises to the little gold cross around her neck. After the service, the rest of the congregation file out, but she remains in her pew, head bowed, eyes closed. She is there for long enough that when she opens her eyes, the Reverend has changed out of his vestments into simple trousers and a cardigan. He kneels beside her.

'How are you coping?' he asks.

'Oh, it's not about me, is it?' she says with forced cheer. 'It's Beth and Mark I worry about.'

'You're his grandmother. You can't shut it out.'

Her voice drops. 'I know.' She sighs and looks to the leaded lights. 'This helps. It was a good service. Meant a lot to me – and to the others who came.'

Paul rolls his eyes. 'Nineteen people. In a town of fifteen thousand.'

'After the last couple of days. Hardly credit it, can you?'

'I swear, I have done *everything*,' he says wearily. 'I've been into every school and hospital and care home and community centre. I've been to every fête and festival and show. Three years. Even now ... nothing.'

'People never know what they need until it's given to them,' says Liz, taking his hand. 'That's what we need from you. All of us. I'm praying that's why God placed you here. Our challenge is your challenge. Help us.' Paul Coates takes both of Liz's hands in his. They stay like that until she has to pull away and fumble for a tissue. 'There's something I want to ask you. Show you, really,' she says. 'It's outside.'

In the far corner of the churchyard, where the graves are still well-tended, a tall headstone stands under a spreading yew.

GEOFFREY ROPER

1954–2007

Beloved Husband, Dad, Granddad

Gone too soon

The bottom half of the stone is blank.

'We had it left that way for me when we lost him,' says Liz. 'It's all set up so there's room for another grave. I was wondering if we could lay Dan to rest in there? They were thick as thieves, that pair. I know it's silly, but I like the idea of them looking after each other.'

'It's not silly at all,' says Paul. 'I think it's beautiful. Have you talked to Beth about this? The request would need to come from her and Mark.'

Liz blows her nose noisily and shakes her head. 'I didn't want to, not till I'd sounded you out about it first. I thought it might be something I can do for her, take a bit of pressure off her. I know I'm Danny's nan, but I'm still her mum, too.' She starts to cry again. 'But there's nothing anyone can do to help her really, is there? The only thing she wants is the one thing she can never have.'

Ellie and Hardy watch the clifftop car park CCTV footage from the night Danny was killed. The only movement on the grainy screen is the time stamp stripping the seconds away. Time passes with paint-drying slowness and they both jump when, at 1.23 a.m., a car pulls up. It's too dark and blurred to make out the registration but there's no mistaking the figure who gets out. Ellie recognises him before Hardy does. After all, she's known him for over a decade.

'He said he was out on a job,' Ellie whispers. What does this mean? Either Beth knows he was out and she's lying to cover for Mark. Or Beth doesn't know he was out, and Mark is lying to everyone. Adrenalin pumps through Ellie, bringing with it confusion rather than clarity.

On the screen Mark Latimer leans back on the bonnet of his car, arms folded.

'He's waiting for someone,' says Hardy. 'I bet I'm right.'

He peers closely at the screen. Mark stirs, as though he's heard someone approach. Hardy rubs his hands together.

The screen goes black.

'Where's the next tape?'

Ellie checks the evidence bag and finds only a note. 'Apparently they only have one and they record over it, to save money.'

'Bollocks!' Hardy brings his fist down on his desk as this small-town penny-pinching sends Broadchurch down another rung on the ladder of his estimation. Ellie is ashamed of this failure, even though it's nothing to do with her.

There's a knock behind them and Steve Connolly, that phone engineer who's been getting under everyone's feet all day, is in the doorway, his belt full of tools.

'Steve Connolly.' He introduces himself nervously, as though his name is a trigger. 'It's Danny Latimer you're doing, isn't it? It's something to do with water. I've been told it's something to do with water.'

Ellie is close enough to Hardy to feel his temperature rise. 'Told by who?' she asks.

'I have this ... I have this thing, where I get, I get messages. Psychic messages.'

'Ach, for God's sake, who let you in?' says Hardy, pushing back from his desk. He must be half Connolly's weight, but indignation seems to lend him mass. Ellie opens the door to usher Connolly out.

'No, no, no, the thing about the water, that's important.' His hand stretches out in placation. 'I'm supposed to tell you, he was in a boat. He was put in a boat. I don't know why.'

Ellie studies him hard. He doesn't look like her idea of a psychic. No silly hair or flamboyant clothes or runic jewellery. He looks like a phone engineer. It's that, and his admission that he doesn't understand what's happening himself, that's so unnerving.

'Who told you this, where'd you get this from?' she asks.

Connolly blinks at them, like it should have been obvious from his first words. 'Danny.' Ellie can't hide her disgust. 'I don't want this,' he protests. 'It comes to me.'

'Oh, you're a *reluctant* psychic,' says Hardy. He's at his mordant best: almost enjoying himself. Connolly takes the proffered offence.

'You don't want to listen, that's fine,' he says petulantly.

'A child has died,' Hardy roars, his accent strengthening in proportion to the volume. 'And you come in with this self-indulgent *horseshit*.'

The room outside stops buzzing. Frank's at the door, ready to jump in.

'Take him away,' orders Hardy, turning in his chair to face the wall. Frank puts a hand on the small of Connolly's back and guides him out of the corner office. Connolly doesn't resist, but shakes his head. At the threshold, he throws a last riddle over his shoulder.

'She says she forgives you,' he says to Hardy. 'About the pendant.'

Ellie watches as anger blanches Hardy's already pale skin and for a moment she's genuinely worried her boss is about to lose control. He remains rigid, as though he's counting to ten, for longer than he needs to after Connolly has gone.

When finally he snaps into action again, it's as though nothing has happened.

'Right,' he says. 'Back to the real investigation. Let's find out why Mark Latimer lied to us about where he was that night. What now?'

Nish is at the door with a handful of papers.

'Danny's social networking profiles,' he says. 'Fresh from his hard drive.'

'Third of May,' Ellie reads aloud. 'Going to get a lock on my door. Keep all this crap out. Twelfth of May: Dear Dad, remember me? I'm the one you used to play with. Twelfth of May again: I know what he's doing.'

Ellie is at a loss: she never heard Danny talk like this. What could he have meant?

She looks to Hardy for his reaction but he has grabbed his coat and is already leaving in a batwing sweep. She follows him out of the door, dragging her feet. She doesn't want to do this. But doubt has grabbed hold of her and only talking to Mark will shake it loose.

16

Beth keeps the news on television night and day, braced for the moment they show Danny's photograph. She would never admit it to anyone – what would they *think* of her? – but she almost looks forward to it. She waits for that moment like she used to wait for him to come home from school, her heart high in her throat in anticipation of the mundane celebration of his homecoming.

'How are the people who live in Broadchurch coping with events?' asks a reporter off screen.

Beth and Mark both flinch to see Reverend Paul Coates' face fill the screen. 'First and foremost, all our prayers are with the Latimer family.' Beth, remembering their conversation in the supermarket car park, feels a chill of betrayal. Why is Paul doing this? Surely he should have asked her first? 'It's obviously a very worrying time but we all believe the police investigation will uncover what happened. We're a strong community. I hope people who live here know that the Church is here for them, to offer whatever support they need, throughout the coming days, faith or no faith. I know the Latimer family quite well and we'll do everything we can to support them at this time.'

'He doesn't speak for us!' Mark bellows. 'His God left my boy for *dead*.' He punches his palm. 'I'm not going to let him get away with this.'

He slams the front door so hard that it bounces on its hinges and hangs open. The church is only across the field. The camera crew might still be there. Beth screams at Pete to get after him. Now is not time for the world to see what Mark is capable of when he loses his temper. The unwanted memory of his last outburst slams hard into her; the unexpected blood on the knuckles; the remorse seconds later and the way the house was quiet for days afterwards. They were all scared but no one more so than Mark himself, and he hasn't raised so much as a finger since. He had barely raised his voice until Danny died.

Beth turns her attention back to the television, but they have already moved on to the next story and she has missed her chance to see Danny.

Karen White stalks the alleyway that skirts the playing field. She has been here for over an hour but her perseverance pays off when she sees Chloe Latimer, dragging hard on a cigarette as she walks home. Look at her, thinks Karen: she's a baby herself. The cigarette makes her look younger, not sophisticated the way she thinks it does.

Chloe's free hand scrolls through her phone. She's reading, not texting. With luck, she's checking coverage of Danny's death on the web and wondering why there isn't more. That will make Karen's job a lot easier. She reaches into her oversized handbag for the ten-pack of Silk Cut that she always carries for times like this. A shared cigarette, the flint flare of the lighter, is worth an hour on the doorstep.

'Got a light?' she asks.

Chloe turns around and Karen senses the flattery – that she's being treated as an equal by this adult. She offers her a yellow Bic and Karen sparks it.

'Are you Chloe?' The girl's instantly on her guard. 'I'm sorry for what happened to your brother.'

Karen pulls out her second prop from her handbag. It's Danny's toy chimp, rescued from the beach. 'I'm guessing this meant a lot to him,' she says.

Chloe snatches it from her, furious, as Karen knew she would be. 'What're *you* doing with that?'

Karen keeps her voice soft. 'You can't leave it down there. It'll get stolen, end up in the papers, you'll never see it again. Too many vultures.'

Chloe's eyes narrow. 'How d'you know so much?'

'I'm one of them.' Karen grins and is gratified when her smile is returned. 'I work for the *Daily Herald*.'

'We're not talking to the papers.'

'I know. You're right not to.'

They all say that at first. It's a gut reaction and Karen knows better than to take it personally. Look at Sandbrook: both sets of families rejected her at first, but as the case dragged on, Pippa's parents used press attention as a way to process their grief as well as keep the pressure on Hardy, while the other parents pulled up the drawbridge. If that's what the Latimers need, Karen will respect it, but she has to give them the choice. It's too soon to know which way the

Latimers are going to fall. They won't even know themselves yet.

Chloe is watching her intently. Suddenly aware that the cigarette is burning to a stub, Karen pretends to inhale. 'I only came to give you that' – she gestures to the toy – 'to stop others from nicking it. If it was my brother, I wouldn't want strangers having it.'

'Thanks.' Chloe clutches it to her chest. More years fall away from her.

'Can I borrow your phone?' Chloe only hesitates for a second before handing it over: Karen can see that she finds her intriguing.

'I won't call you,' she says, tapping in her own number. 'I won't come to the door. I won't stop you on the way to the shops, like the others are going to. But if you or your family need to speak, or you just need a friend when it's getting a bit much, you call me.' She saves it as A FRIEND before handing the phone back. 'Thanks for the light.'

Karen takes her leave. She knows to quit while she's ahead. Around the corner, she flicks the cigarette away with a grimace of distaste.

It's dusk and the gnats are out in Mark Latimer's garden. DI Hardy, fatally attractive to midges, is tempted to take the interview inside, but Beth is hovering at the window and he needs Mark on his own. The stats are a signpost pointing this way. Most murdered people know their killer: over two-thirds of murdered children are killed by a parent, with fathers more likely to kill than mothers. And Mark Latimer is squirming like a man with plenty to hide.

'Thursday night, the night Danny went missing, where were you?'

'On a call-out? Came through early evening, dunno, half six – this family's whole system had packed in.'

'How long did that take?'

'Most of the night. It was a nightmare boiler. I was there pretty late.' Mark's eyes drop to Hardy's notebook, watching the words go down.

All the while Hardy is assessing Mark. He's tall, with the well-defined muscles of a man who spends all day crouching, pulling and lifting. He could pick *me* up, thinks Hardy. He looks down at the hands and tries to marry these large palms and long fingers to the ligature prints on Danny's neck.

'No. There wasn't a call-out.'

Mark does his best to look mystified. 'What d'you mean?'

'We have CCTV footage of the car park at the top of Briar Cliff. You were there at 1.23 a.m.' Mark looks over his shoulder. Beth's still at the window. He throws her a little-boy smile that's vanished by the time he turns back to Hardy.

'So you're snooping on me now?' he hisses.

'We were checking CCTV in the area. Now, what did you do that night?'

'What, am I a *suspect*?'

'The first thing we do is eliminate people from the investigation. You tell me where you were, who you were with, how long for. I eliminate you from suspicion. It's entirely methodical. You don't tell me those facts, I can't eliminate you. And if I can't eliminate you, you're a person of interest.'

'In the murder of my own son?'

Hardy is damned if he will let Mark play that card.

'I'm sure this is all very straightforward.'

He can see Mark weighing up his options. If that's not panic in his eyes now it soon will be.

'I met a mate. We went off together. They dropped me back at the car park later, then I came home. Three, maybe four in the morning.'

'What's your mate's name?'

Mark's eyes slide to the side. 'Can't remember.'

Sometimes, killing makes people clever. Self-preservation kicks in and the murderer discovers hitherto untapped reserves of resourcefulness and ingenuity. It's almost as though points are added to their IQ. Hardy wonders if Mark was always this thick, or it's grief making him thick, or the whole thing is an elaborate double bluff.

'You can't remember the name of your friend? Where'd you go?'

'I think we had a drink, bite to eat, drive round ...' Something that's almost a smile pulls at his mouth.

'You *think*?' says Hardy. 'It was three days ago.'

'Yeah. And a lot's happened since then.'

Beth's still staring at them attentively, as though trying to lip-read. Hardy steps to one side, so that he's hidden behind Mark.

'And is there any reason you wouldn't want me to know the name of your mate? This is only about who killed Danny. Nothing else.'

Mark rolls his neck. 'It'll come back to me. I'm knackered, I haven't slept, all the stuff on the news, my head's not straight.'

Hardy changes tack. 'When you came in, you went straight to bed. Can your wife confirm when you came back?'

'No, she was asleep,' says Mark.

It's an admission and they both know it. They're getting somewhere. Hardy draws breath for his next question but his phone rings. He paces to the edge of the garden, leaving Mark to wonder.

'Sir, it's El— Miller,' she says. 'I'm at the clifftop hut. We've got a match for Danny's fingerprint up here in blood. We think this is where he was killed, then moved two miles along the coast.' Hardy registers silent approval: Miller is bullet-pointing, the way he likes it. 'SOCO say the place has been meticulously cleaned, but they've also found a set of fingerprints by the sink. I messaged them through to run a match against elimination prints. They belong to Mark Latimer.'

17

Ellie Miller has long perfected the art of getting up without disturbing her family, but this is an early start even by her standards. The sun is up but it's still cold and she pulls on her big orange coat, the one that lets the kids spot her from a hundred paces. Joe has a similar one in royal blue. Mum Coat and Dad Coat, the final surrender of style to parenthood. In the kitchen, she melts inside to see – she was so tired that she missed it last night – that Joe has made her a BLT sandwich for breakfast and two Thermos flasks of tea to kick-start her day.

The clifftop hut is a crime scene now, a cordon flapping between pegs, the entrance tented. Hardy is at the cliff edge, his back to the hut, the wind combing his fringe into a spiky quiff. He's staring at the sea like it's hypnotising him: when he does look at Ellie it is with annoyance, as though she has broken a sacred trance. When she hands him the Thermos he looks utterly baffled.

'It's freezing,' she says. 'Long weekend working, big day ahead. Thought this would help.' Hardy takes it and looks at it without thanks. 'Have you got children?' she asks.

'Why?'

'They must have shit manners.' He doesn't react. She hates this way he has of making her wonder if she has actually spoken at all. Instead, he makes a sudden flailing movement, as though he's tripped over something. It's not the first time she's seen him do this. He's ill at ease on the lumpy turf up here and those shoes, a knackered pair of brogues with the sole peeling away from the leather, aren't doing him any favours.

'You need a good pair of boots.' She studies his feet. 'What size shoes d'you take? Eleven?'

'No thanks,' says Hardy. He cranes forward to look at the beach. 'Makes no sense. Why move him to Harbour Cliff? Why not just throw him off here? Perfectly good cliff for chucking a body over.'

Ellie is appalled. 'Can you not talk about it like that, *please*.' Mentally she retracts her offer.

She chooses to take his silence as apology. In the distant harbour, a handful of fishing boats head out.

'Any boats gone missing recently?' Hardy asks. 'A boat'd leave no tracks.'

It's a good point, and Ellie's pissed off that she didn't think of it herself. 'Moor it on the shore to leave a body, any evidence washed away.'

Hardy nods. 'What time's Mark Latimer coming in?'

'Nine.' Ellie needs him to know he's wrong. Just because she can't *think* of an innocent explanation doesn't mean there *isn't* one. Her head's all over the place and she's tired.

There's probably something really obvious that she's missing. She'll kick herself when the penny drops. 'Sir, he's not in the frame.'

'Look at the evidence in front of you. Stop behaving like you're his bloody solicitor.'

He leaves her there at the edge of the cliff, the wind twisting her hair to dreadlocks.

The sedative they give Beth gets her to sleep but doesn't keep her there. On every waking there are a few beautiful seconds of normality before it all hits her again. If she wakes, and goes back to sleep, four times in one night, that's up to ten seconds' reprieve from the nightmare.

She drags herself groggily to the toilet. Danny is everywhere. In the bathroom, his shampoo is a genie in a bottle. No one else will use it, but the thought of throwing it away is abhorrent. She steps on the scales: she's lost five pounds in as many days. Her ribs and hip bones jut to frame a gently convex belly. When Mark tries the door, she jumps guiltily off the scales.

He's next in, locking the door behind him. They never used to do this. From the landing Beth hears the tap of keys on his phone, the swish of a message being sent and then in reply comes a text alert in Nige's ringtone. What good will he be, hopeless bloody Nige? What can Mark say to him that he can't say to his wife?

She doesn't want to go downstairs. There's always someone *there* now. But she doesn't want to stay up here, either, with Danny's bedroom sucking at her like a dark star. She tiptoes down the stairs, a stranger in her own house.

In the sitting room, Pete empties a postbag on to the table. Some of the envelopes simply say Latimer Family, Broadchurch, but still they have made their way from Newcastle, London, Birmingham, Cardiff and beyond to this little house in Dorset. The kitchen sink is full of flowers and the worktops are piled high with food. Casseroles, pies, cakes and biscuits. They didn't have this much on the buffet at their wedding.

'What do we do with it all?' she says, picking up a jar of home-made jam. It's almost laughable the way people's minds work: *Those poor people with the murdered son, I'm sure a bit of home-made bramble jelly will make it better.*

'I'll take some,' Pete licks his lips. 'Some amazing pies there.' Someone needs to fit this bloke with a ten-second delay between his brain and his mouth. At least this time he realises and has the grace to look embarrassed.

'What happens now?' says Beth, giving him the opportunity to make himself useful. 'We gave them a list of suspects. How far have they got?'

'They'll tell us when they're ready,' says Pete. *Us.* Like this is happening to him, too. Like he's on the inside of it. He turns to Mark. 'You should get going, they're expecting you.'

Chloe says what they're all thinking. 'Why'd they want to talk to you, Dad?'

'Routine, I expect,' says Mark. 'To them, at least.' It's because he had a go at the vicar, that's what it is. Pete got there before Mark could do anything really stupid like throw a punch, but he heard the threats and now they've got him down as a nutter.

Beth watches him go, envious on some level that he's got an excuse to leave the house. She hates being shut up. Mark says she's like a dog, she needs walking twice daily. Back in the bathroom she snaps on rubber gloves and cleans the grouting with a toothbrush, scrubbing until the damp comes away.

Pete gives her half an hour before he's there with a cup of tea. She will wait until he's gone then tip it down the sink. He doesn't go, only hangs around clearing his throat.

'They did ask,' he says eventually. 'The night before Danny was found, you and Chloe were in, watching TV ...'

'We watched a film on Sky, comedy. Ashton Kutcher.' It wasn't even funny but she wishes she had laughed harder now.

'Where was Mark?' She knows what he's trying to do and she's on the defensive. She's not going to make it easy for them to waste time on Mark when they should be looking for the real killer.

'He was out.'

'And he got back ...'

'Dunno. I was asleep.'

'He was working.'

'That's what he said.'

Pete frowns. 'You don't know who for?'

What is the point of this? It's never been part of their routine for Mark to inform Beth where he's working. She's not that interested. It's not that interesting. She resents the way they're turning every little blip in domestic administration into something sinister. She folds her arms. 'No.'

'OK, thanks.'

Beth turns her back on Pete and scrubs until the only dirt left in the bathroom is a ring of dried suds around the base of Danny's shampoo bottle.

The promised extra officers are here at last. Ellie's never seen this many detectives in one station before. Unfamiliar people make coffee in the staff canteen. They need more kettles and one of the new recruits is using Frank's special big mug.

It is hard not to feel intimidated by the influx. Everything has been scaled up. Of course Ellie is gratified that Wessex Police have put their money where their mouths are for once: anything less and she'd be fighting for more. But the swell of voices drives home how much work still lies ahead of them. The case, that she had hoped would be simple and short, is getting bigger, the mountain growing even as they try to climb it. Despite their hard work, they remain stuck in the foothills, and Ellie is exhausted already. She hasn't slept more than four hours since Danny's body was found.

The air-con in CID struggles to cope with the heat generated by the extra bodies. Nish wipes the sweat from his brow, leaving a smear on his cuff. Everyone is tense, waiting for Hardy's briefing.

Ellie pops her head into the boss's office; he is bent over a letter. 'Ready when you are, sir.' Hardy folds the paper into an envelope that he tucks into his inside breast pocket.

'You do it,' he says, his beady eye unblinking. Fear rinses through her. Is he taking the piss? She's never briefed a team on something this big before and he must know it. 'On you go,' he says.

She fights the urge to hide in the toilet and steps out in front of her assembled colleagues. She hates public speaking almost as much as she hates DI Alec Hardy.

'Good morning, everyone.' Her voice sounds reedy in her ears. 'I – um, welcome, I'm Ellie, DS Miller. So we've. Lot to get through, we're already behind because of the weekend and not having resources, which are here now, which are you. So.' She's shaking. Can they tell she's shaking? She clasps her hands in front of her. 'So you know we need to, you know, hit the ground running. Priorities today: house-to-house enquiries, ah, CCTV retrieval, technical data retrieval from phones, and um, alibi follow-ups. On, on top of that, there's a lot of information that's come in we need to sift through. Nish will be the office manager, so if you see him, he'll have actions to give you.'

She finally gets Hardy on his own by the kettle.

'Very inspiring,' he says, reaching for the last mug on the shelf. She slams the cupboard door, sadly missing his fingertips.

'*Don't* do that to me again!' she says. 'What is it, just because I'm not running to arrest Mark Latimer, I get thrown to the lions?'

Hardy dunks what looks suspiciously like a herbal teabag. 'You didn't mention how they can discount Mark Latimer, or your own *exhaustive* list of suspects.' She's about to tell him what she thinks of his constant sarcasm when his next comment disarms her. 'We'll need to interview your son. He should have an appropriate adult with him. Not you, obviously. Latimer's downstairs. We should start.'

*

The interview rooms in Broadchurch police station face dead south. The walls are studded with glass bricks that refract the sun as it crawls from east to west, turning the rooms into giant sundials. An officer who's been there for a while can tell from the angle of the beam what time of day it is.

Right now, an unforgiving morning light is trained hard on Mark Latimer. Dark crescents cup his eyes. He's been crying. Small wonder he's got his movements wrong. Ellie checks that Hardy isn't looking, then gives Mark an encouraging smile. She's confident that they can uncross these wires and have him home again within the hour.

'Sorry about yesterday afternoon,' he says with a strange half-smile. Something twitches in Ellie's subconscious; she's seen that expression somewhere before but can't place it. 'What with everything, I was a bit hazy when you were asking me all those questions.'

'It's more that you tried to lie,' says Hardy.

'I was confused. All the days, blending into one. That boiler I said I'd done, that was Wednesday night. You know what it's like.'

'And on Thursday night, you were with a mate.'

'Yeah.'

'But yesterday you could not remember the name of that mate.'

'It was Nige. Who I work with.'

'OK. You couldn't remember the name of the man you work with all day.'

'It's the shock, doing funny things.' He gives that strange half-smile again and distress slithers through Ellie as she knows where she's seen it before. Danny, at an Easter barbecue a few

115

years ago, swearing blind he hadn't eaten Chloe's Easter egg with chocolate all over his lips. The knowledge that Mark is lying is like a lead weight falling through her.

What the hell could he be hiding? That innocent explanation slips a little further out of reach. 'We'll check with Nige,' she says.

'You go ahead, Ell,' says Mark.

Hardy hands Mark the photograph of the hut on Briar Cliff.

'Ever been there?'

She expects him to study the picture but a glance is all he gives it. 'Did a job there, weekend or two back. Burst pipe. Nicky, who does all the paperwork for us, she'd have the exact date on the invoice.'

'If it's a rental property, who called you out?' says Hardy.

'This woman, can't remember her name. I picked the keys up from her at the caravan park.'

Ellie gives up and lets Hardy take the lead. He's right, she's equal to this.

'Just you, or Nige as well?'

'Just me. Nige was away with his mum.'

Hardy takes a second too long to shuffle the papers in his file.

'Mark, d'you own a boat?' he asks.

'Yeah.'

In the corridor outside, Hardy goes through the list of all the reasons why it's got to be Mark.

'A boat. Prints at the murder scene. And an alibi he made up overnight.'

'You don't know that, sir,' she says, although with less conviction than before. 'We'll look at the boat, talk to Nige and confirm whether Mark did the work at the hut.'

'Ask Pete what Mark told Beth about Thursday night, see if it marries up. And while we check, Mark stays here.' Ellie's stomach tightens around her meagre breakfast. She had hoped that they could get to the bottom of this without putting Beth on high alert.

'D'you understand what it'd do to that family, to this town, if it was Mark?'

'What're you looking for, Miller? An easy answer? The least pain? It won't work like that.'

'I know,' she says miserably. She is beginning to see herself as Hardy does, stubbornly keeping faith in something that might never have been true.

The harbourmaster ferries them past the jetty. A life jacket presses heavily on Hardy's chest, rustling the letter in his breast pocket, as if he needed reminding of its contents.

Miller's got good sea legs – probably bred into her – and the drizzle rolls off her orange coat as she stands on the prow, looking for Mark Latimer's boat. Hardy hates being on the water. The to and fro of the waves is a cruel mockery of the symptoms that plague him. Masts sway dangerously before him. Miller reaches out to throw off the sea-green tarpaulin. The *Old Boiler* – someone's idea of a joke, surely – is painted yellow and, as far as Hardy can tell, in good nick. Bigger than most of the glorified dinghies, this one's got a sort of windscreen roof and a steering thingy. He takes pride in not knowing the right words for them.

117

Miller jumps on board and holds out her hand for him to follow. Hardy refuses. The realisation shoots from nowhere that he can't remember the last time he held a woman's hand. It is unexpectedly, inconveniently, painful.

'Only needs one of us,' he says briskly. 'Minimise the risk of contaminating a crime scene. Know when it was last taken out?'

Miller doesn't answer. She has dropped to her knees at the front of the boat.

'*Shit*,' she says.

Hardy pulls his own focus to where her gaze is fixed. Drops of red liquid have dried to brown. It's blood.

18

'I'll get the coffees this morning,' says Olly. 'My treat, for once.'

Karen appreciates the gesture and, if she's honest, the cash. Her contribution to Broadchurch's economy is growing by the hour, and she still has no idea if Danvers will honour the expenses at the end of it. She needs a lead, and fast.

Olly crosses the road to a nearby cashpoint but returns empty-handed. Karen knows the mortified expression of someone whose card has been declined when she sees it.

'Machine's out of order,' he says, evidently unaware that it's currently delivering a stack of crisp tenners to the next customer. 'Maybe tomorrow.'

Karen pays cash for the drinks, pockets the receipt and together they walk to the harbour.

'I looked at the *Herald*,' says Olly. 'You haven't filed yet.'

She's had time to prepare for this. 'Don't want to, till I've got the full background. I'm thinking about the family. I want to get it right.'

It's important that Olly doesn't realise that Karen needs

him as much as he needs her. She might be the one with a shortcut to the nationals but she needs this local reporter onside to open doors for her. And they might yet be able to exploit his relationship with Detective Sergeant Auntie Ellie. 'So can you help me with that?' she presses. 'Tell me who best to talk to.'

'I suppose,' Olly looks uneasy. 'I know these people. You can't stitch them up.'

'You've read my stuff. You know I show people as they are. I've got no agendas.'

He's still not convinced. 'But . . . Danny *died*.'

Patience doesn't come naturally to Karen, but she tries. 'Listen, Olly. What you do this week will decide your whole career. I know you think I'm being really hard-nosed but opportunities like this don't come along often. It doesn't matter how it happened, or whether you feel comfortable. No one is better placed to do the right thing by the Latimers than you are.' She's almost got him, she can tell. 'I'll pay you. Finder's fees. Proper rates.'

That decides him. 'OK – well, I've got to go into the *Echo* now but shall we compare notes at lunchtime?'

The day stretches out in front of Karen. There's a story hiding somewhere here. It is a point of pride that she puts the clues together faster than Alec Hardy.

Her first port of call is the newsagent. She picks a magazine at random and a Mars bar from the shelf. The man behind the counter has a blank expression that doesn't change even when she turns her fullest smile on him.

'You're Mr Marshall, right? You run the Sea Brigade. Karen White, *Daily Herald*.' She pockets her change and takes her business card from her purse. 'I'm here covering Danny Latimer's death.'

'I don't talk to the press,' says Jack Marshall.

Karen turns her smile up a notch. 'You're a newsagent and you don't talk to the people who make the stuff you sell?'

'I sell 'em. I don't want to be in 'em.'

'Why?' Her cheeks are starting to ache.

'Don't get smart.'

'I'm only trying to find out about Danny. He did a paper round for you, didn't he?'

'Are you going to leave nicely, or do I have to ring the police? I've been courteous.'

She leaves her card anyway. 'If you change your mind?' She correctly predicts its trajectory into the bin. On the way out, she overhears Jack Marshall call her a parasite. She's heard worse.

Outside, her phone buzzes. Work: the seventh call since yesterday. She lets this one go too, and deletes the subsequent voicemail. What can they do? They can't technically pull her from the story, given that she's here without their permission. One more day and she'll have Len Danvers on the phone begging her for a double-page spread on deadline.

She'll turn something up. She always does.

The British summer is living up to its reputation: soft light drizzle has turned to pouring rain. DS Miller wears a ridiculous bright orange coat and carries an umbrella. Hardy gets wet, although his feet, in the new boots Miller gave him, remain bone-dry. She keeps glancing down at the puddles and pulling a smug little face.

Here in the caravan park at the foot of the cliff, a handful of families are determinedly enjoying themselves despite the rain, but the parents keep their children close.

They approach Susan Wright's wretched mobile home. Miller's smile stays plastered on even when Susan greets them with an admonishment for waking the dog up.

'You caught 'em yet?' she says to Hardy. 'There's kids not safe out there.'

At least she won't slow them down with pleasantries. 'Did Mark Latimer fix a burst pipe at the hut on Briar Cliff a few weekends back? He says he got the keys from you.'

'No. We never had a burst pipe up there.'

Beside him, Miller stiffens and he feels another wave of frustration at her refusal to take Latimer seriously as a suspect. The sooner the results on the blood from the boat come back the better.

'When did you last clean up there?'

'Ten days ago. Ain't been nobody in since then.'

'Who else has keys? We're treating it as a possible crime scene.' She has this way of looking at them, like they're the ones under suspicion.

'Me and the owners. That's it.'

'Right.' Hardy snaps his notebook shut. 'We'll send someone along to take elimination prints.'

She doesn't bat an eyelid. 'We finished?'

The door is slammed in their faces before they can reply.

There is one more call to make before they get back to Mark. Miller gives him the lowdown in the car.

'Nige moved back in with his mum, Faye, when his dad died a few years back. They're ever so close. He's worked for

Mark for about three years. Mark trained him up. Nige drives the van. Keeps it parked on his drive.'

Mead View is a couple of blocks away from Spring Close but on a different scale: the bungalows crouch low and the cul-de-sac can't accommodate the car-to-home ratio. Mark's van is parked on a driveway that's not quite big enough for it.

Miller disappears to talk to Faye while Hardy talks to Nige on the driveway.

The bloke's a nervous wreck, his shaved head sheened in sweat. Hardy is on full alert.

'Yeah, I was with Mark pretty much all night,' he says. 'We met up, had a drive, a bite to eat.' He lets out a weird giggle: this poor sod makes Mark look like an accomplished liar.

'See each other a lot socially?'

'On and off.'

'Where'd you meet him that night?'

'Car park by Briar Cliff,' says Nige, almost before Hardy's finished talking. 'It's just convenient.'

Hardy doesn't see anything convenient about a car park up a dirt track in the arse of nowhere.

'What time did you get home?'

'One-ish. Dunno.'

'What were you doing till one?

'Drinking, chatting, bite to eat.' Nige looks miserable.

'Where did you eat?'

'Pub in the Vale. The Fox.'

'What'd you eat?'

Nige's eyes flick up like they're pulling up a pub menu. 'Chips . . . and a pie, steak pie.'

'Lot of places open till one round here?'

'We get lock-ins, at the Fox.'

'So they'll remember you, when we talk to them.'

Miller bursts out of the house. 'Nigel, d'you want to stop pissing about? Your mum says you were in with her, till half ten. That you went out round the corner for last orders. *Not* with Mark.'

A sunbeam cuts the interview room in half: high noon. CDs are stacked on top of a winking digital recorder. Mark Latimer looks at his lap while DI Hardy tells him how it is.

'Since we talked earlier, we've checked up on a couple of things. Number one, the woman who holds the keys to the hut on Briar Cliff has no memory of you fixing a burst pipe.'

'What? That's bollocks! I got the keys off her. She was in a caravan. She had a dog.'

'She says not.'

'Well, she's lying.' He keeps looking at Miller, like she's going to save him.

'Number two,' and this is the big one, 'your alibi is rubbish. Your mate Nige isn't a good liar. Let's not insult each other's intelligence. Your son has been killed, so I'm a bit at a loss as to why you'd mislead us. Point three: we had a look at your boat. And there's bloodstains in it.' He sniffs to fill the dead air. 'Whose blood is in the boat, Mark?'

'Dan's.' He meets Hardy's eyes without apology. 'We took her out weekend before last, that hot spell. Me, Dan and Chloe, fishing about a mile offshore. Caught three bass, we took 'em back and barbecued 'em. Danny was messing about, caught the end of a line in the bottom of his foot.

Gashed it open. He was all hopping around, yelling. Chloe was there, ask her.'

'We will.' Miller is soothing rather than threatening.

'Why are you lying about where you were Thursday night?' says Hardy. 'We can't rule you out until you tell us where you were.'

'How is me being here helping you find Danny's killer? Everything's becoming part of this and it's nothing to do with it.' He brings his hand down hard on the desk.

'Everything matters now,' says Hardy. 'Who did what, who was where. Everything connects and feeds this case. If we don't get the truth, we won't find who killed Danny. And that starts with you.' He folds his arms and sits back.

Indignation pushes Mark's voice up the scale. 'I told you about the hut, and you're saying I'm lying and I'm not!'

'Mark,' says Hardy softly. 'My son dies, I'd tell a police officer everything. I just would. Why did you ask Nigel to give you a false alibi?'

Mark cricks his neck. 'Everything I'm saying is getting twisted. I can't think straight.'

'Mark Latimer, I'm arresting you for obstruction of a murder inquiry.'

'Sir, no, do we really need to—' starts Miller.

'Enough!' barks Hardy, and she stops mid-sentence. 'You do not have to say anything, but it may harm your defence—'

'Is this what you do, Ell?' says Mark.

'Don't make us hold you,' she pleads. 'Tell us the truth.'

'Take his things, Miller.'

The uniforms put him in the cells.

Hardy's alone with Miller in the interview room. He slides the disc from the machine and labels it.

'You think he's blameless now?' he asks her. Surely she can't still be in denial?

'He's in shock,' says Miller feebly.

'His son is dead. Why would he not tell the truth about where he was?'

He waits for her denial, but she can't answer him. Hardy savours the moment. He might be making slow progress on the investigation, but for the first time there's a glimmer of hope that he might make a good copper out of DS Miller.

19

After her fruitless visit to Jack Marshall's paper shop, Karen decides to take Olly with her when she goes to see Nige Carter. It's a smart move: the welcome is warm. 'Olly, all right?' Nige pauses from loading the van with tools – he must be exhausted, covering all of Mark's calls – to shake Karen's hand. He gives her a sweet, slightly gormless smile. He reminds her of an Alsatian puppy, taking up too much space, eager to please, not particularly bright.

'Blimey,' he says. 'Never had so many visitors in a day.'

'Who else has been round?' she asks.

'No one,' he says, suddenly wary. Now he looks Karen up and down properly. She's newly conscious of the formality of her work clothes and wonders if she ought to have dressed down, taken off the tailored jacket, put on a hoody or something. 'Don't think I should be talking to papers.'

'She's all right,' says Olly. 'I'm chaperoning.' Karen allows herself a private smile at the thought of this.

'All right,' says Nige. 'Quick though.'

She opens with flattery. 'Everybody says you're the go-to men in the town. Not rip-off merchants.'

'Soon run out of customers if you did,' smiles Nige. 'We turn up when we say and don't overcharge. Down to Mark.'

'And they're a close family.'

'Oh yeah.' He grins. 'Always off somewhere together. That's Beth, outdoors girl, dragging them up hills whether Mark likes it or not!'

'Compromise, that's what being married's all about,' says Karen, thanking her lucky stars she's single.

'Yeah, well, nothing's perfect,' says Nige, then realises how that sounds in the circumstances. His grin vanishes.

'And you knew Danny well, obviously.'

It's a moment before Nige can speak. 'He'd come out with us sometimes, in the holidays. He liked it, so did the customers, we'd have a laugh. Same when I babysat. I'd take Call of Duty over, we'd sit and shoot away.' He shakes his head in sad bewilderment. 'You go about your day and then you remember he's not here. Listen, I've gotta go. Hey, Olly, how's your mum now?'

The blush from this morning returns to Olly's cheeks.

'Umm, yeah, all right,' he mumbles. It's clear that he doesn't want to talk about it, but Nige is thick-skinned.

'All sorted, is it?'

'Pretty much.' Olly addresses the pavement, looking as though he'd quite like it to swallow him whole.

Mark still isn't back and Beth has cleaned the house from top to bottom. With all the housework done, and unable to stand another second of daytime television, she puts on her coat and is out of the door, ignoring Chloe's demands about where she's off to and Liz's offer to go with her.

She is going mad inside, turning over the night before Danny's murder and wishing now that she had woken up when Mark came in, just so the police would get off their backs. She can see what they're doing: they're trying to drive a wedge between them. It is not only pointless but it's cruel. As if they aren't going through enough. She wants to know that the police are on their side.

It feels good to walk. She takes the shortcut through the field: long grass whispers either side of the path. Walking in the other direction is a thickset man about her own age, body-warmer and gold-framed glasses. As they get close she can tell that he's looking at her the way they did in the supermarket, part sympathy, part voyeurism. What's different about this one is the way he holds steady and even offers her a shy smile. Beth's appreciation at this acknowledgement, this tiny mark of respect, turns to unease as he keeps on staring. She hurries into town and although she doesn't look back, she knows he's still watching her.

It's only half a mile to the tourist office, the place where Beth used to work. Where she still works. It occurs to her she hasn't actually called in her absence and she wonders who did that for her, who is making the arrangements. The machine of her life is ticking over without her effort or consent.

Tourist Information shares premises, and a front door, with the *Broadchurch Echo*. Beth didn't know about this condolence book they'd set up and it's a shock to find Danny is waiting for her at the door, a blown-up picture from last year's sports day. It almost makes her lose her nerve, but she pushes in anyway.

At her entrance the talking stops, laying bare the hum of the machines and the photocopier churning something out in the background. Her colleagues sit in appalled silence as she dumps her bag and sits at her desk.

'Hiya,' she says. 'Can I help anyone? No? Shall I restock the leaflet racks?' Janet gulps at her and stares like she's a freak. And Beth *feels* like a freak. This is the opposite of what she came here for.

Maggie Radcliffe is at her side. 'Sweetheart, what are you *doing*?' she asks. 'You shouldn't be here. You've had a terrible thing happen.'

'I want to be useful,' Beth snaps.

'Let me drop you back home,' says Maggie.

'I'm not going home.' Beth's fervency embarrasses everyone except her. 'I've just come from home. I can't stay in that house.'

'Oh, darling,' says Maggie. 'My heart is breaking for you.'

'I don't need bloody broken hearts!' says Beth. She shakes Maggie off and heads out the fire exit, into the side alleyway. Someone follows her. She doesn't look back to see who it is. One more gentle hand and she'll bite it off. She walks the length of the High Street, cheeks burning, and keeps going until she reaches the bench at the top of the town.

Up there, she lets out all her breath. Getting out of the house has solved nothing. Danny and the loss of him follow her everywhere she goes. If anything, it's worse here. It's not safe to look anywhere. To the left, there's the beach where they found him. Ahead, the sea where he sailed and fished. To her right, the hill where they flew kites. Behind her the town, the school and home. Grief is like a splinter deep in every fingertip; to touch anything is torture.

'Do you mind if I sit here?' says someone.

It's the man from the field earlier. Has he been *following* her? Beth flinches, then realises she doesn't actually care. What's the worst he can do to her? She shrugs and he puts himself gently at the other end of the bench.

'I love this view,' he says. Beth waits for it. One, two, three … 'I'm sorry if it's rude, but I know who you are. I can't imagine what it's like for you. But you'll get through it.'

'And you know, do you?' When she shakes her head, he tilts his to one side in sympathy. It's as though he's parroting her body language.

'Don't take this the wrong way, but I've got a message for you. From Danny.'

It's the cruellest thing anyone's ever said to her, and it's made worse by the way he's got the gall to maintain eye contact.

'Don't you dare,' says Beth. 'Stop speaking to me! Get away from me!'

'I'm not trying to upset you! I just had to tell you! Please!' His words hound Beth back to the house she can't stand to be in.

20

Tom Miller carries his red skateboard into the police station like a security blanket. Hardy says nothing as Joe, the appropriate adult, hands the little one – Alfie? George? – to Ellie for the duration of the interview. He notices the food stains on Joe's top and the rushed, patchy shave. He honestly doesn't know if he envies Joe the time he spends with his children or pities it.

They do the interview that Miller insists they call a *chat* in the family room. Grubby toys that wouldn't entertain a pre-schooler are piled in one corner. The Venetian blinds are pulled flat.

'Just took him to the skate park,' confides Joe as Hardy fiddles with the video camera. 'Thought it'd take the edge off his nerves, you know. But instead the other kids were crowding round him, grilling him about Danny. They think he's got insider knowledge because of who his mum is.' He sighs from his belly. 'I shouldn't have taken him there. I was only trying to do something normal, you know?'

Hardy, checking to make sure Tom is in shot, nods absently. The boy blinks nervously into the lens.

'You last saw Danny when?' Hardy begins. Joe flinches, as though he was expecting a more gentle build-up.

'Before we went on holiday,' says Tom.

'When was that?'

Joe answers for him. 'Three and a half weeks ago. We went on Thursday morning.'

Hardy seethes inwardly. Sometimes the parent is not the most appropriate adult. He saw this when he was interviewing Pippa Gillespie's friends, the protective instinct of the parent overriding everything else. It's actually easier to talk to a kid who's in care: at least a social worker lets him get on with his job.

'Sorry,' says Joe, apparently reading Hardy's mind. He sits back in his seat.

'Three and a half weeks ago,' Tom echoes his father. 'We went on the Thursday morning. The afternoon before, we went to the Lido.'

'Did he have his phone on him?'

'Don't know.' Tom bites the inside of his cheek.

'But Danny *had* a phone.'

Tom nods.

'What did you talk about?'

'Football. Xbox. Usual.'

'What else? Girls?'

'No!' It's the first unguarded response Tom's had. Joe, shifting in his seat, doesn't take his eyes off his son.

'Did he say he was worried about anything?'

'No,' says Tom.

'Did you argue?'

'No!' Again, the word comes too quickly.

'Can you think of anyone who'd want to hurt Danny?' Tom doesn't answer but his eyes triangulate between Hardy, the camera, and his father. 'How'd he get on with his dad?'

Joe, who's been good for the last few questions, now takes a breath in as though he's about to speak, but Hardy shushes him with a look. His mind is racing: whatever Tom's holding back, Joe knows too. He'll have to get Joe on his own if Tom doesn't spill, but it's better coming straight from the boy.

'Anything you say here is *absolutely* confidential.'

Tears rinse the blue of Tom's eyes. 'He said his dad hit him,' he mumbles. 'He gave him a split lip.'

Inwardly, Hardy is cheering. It is the nature of a detective's work that sometimes he will feel elated at the news that a little boy was hit by a grown man. This is such a time.

'So he hit him more than once?' he asks Tom. These things escalate, and not always gradually. There is nothing in Danny's medical records about a split lip, and if Mark had been charged with it they would have picked it up five minutes into this investigation. And neither Beth nor Chloe have said anything about domestic violence. Sometimes, all it takes is for a man to get away with it once for the slope to become slippery.

'I dunno,' says Tom. 'He just said his dad got into bad moods sometimes.'

He breaks down and becomes incoherent. Hardy recognises a witness who has reached his limit.

'OK. Thank you, Tom.'

The video camera is turned off. Miller's waiting outside, praising Tom before handing over the toddler – Charlie? Archie? – and waving her family off with promises of being

134

home for teatime that she must know she won't be able to keep.

Hardy brings her up to speed. 'Tom says that Mark hit Danny. And we know that Pete had to pull Mark off Paul over the weekend.'

Miller looks sadly at a printout in her hand.

'What's that?'

'Nish did a search while you were interviewing Tom,' she says reluctantly. 'Mark's got a record for a pub fight about ten years ago,' she says. 'But—'

'Tell Forensics we need blood analysis on the boat – see how old those stains are. Check Danny Latimer's pathology report for any signs of a gash on the foot. Mark's not going anywhere for now.'

When she's gone, he pulls out the letter one more time. It's in two pages: one, the formalised script of a medical professional, setting out the diagnosis and offering to have him invalided out of the force. The second is a handwritten note from the doctor he's been seeing since it all fell apart. The greeting is fond but the warning is stark: no stress, no pressure, no unnecessary exertion. The language pulls no punches: there is a bomb in his system and he's kicking it harder and harder.

Hardy puts both pages in the shredder. If Jenkinson gets wind of this, it's all over. Destroying the letter can't erase the words from his mind. The brutal sign-off: if he doesn't stop of his own accord, his body will do it for him. And he *will* stop. As soon as he's nailed this killer. He owes it to the Latimers.

He owes it to the Gillespies as well. Thinking about the Sandbrook families is like a blade in his side. But this case

is his penance, and that is the point of punishment. It is supposed to hurt.

I've got a message for you. From Danny. Beth has always been
a cynic but she can't shake this morning's encounter from
her mind. She veers between outrage that someone could
harass a grieving mother and something else. Doubt wrestles
with hope. If there is a one per cent chance that Danny's
spirit is out there, somewhere, sending Beth a message and
wondering why she isn't listening . . . the idea is too big and
frightening for her to cope with. It is too big and frightening
for her to ignore.

Pete enters the living room. His phone is off, but it's
pressed to his chin as though he's thinking deeply. It is the
first time Beth has seen evidence of Pete thinking deeply.
Something is wrong.

'They want you to know Mark's been arrested,' he says.

The carpet turns to sponge beneath Beth's feet.

'*What?*' says Chloe. 'What for?'

'He won't account for his movements the night before
Danny was found. Arrested doesn't mean charged. It's one
step up from being interviewed under caution.'

'So – he's a *suspect?*' Beth is fishing for a contradiction. She
doesn't get one.

Suddenly the chink of Mark's absence cracks wide like a
bursting dam and Beth feels the rising flood return, a repeat of
the panic she felt when she first realised Danny was missing.

'Let's see where we are, once they've finished talking,'
says Pete. 'I'm sure it'll all get sorted.'

Chloe explodes. 'Sorted? My brother's *dead.*' Beth finds

136

herself dragging Chloe by the arm up the stairs and into the bathroom. She bolts the door and takes Chloe's face in her hands. 'From now on, you say nothing in front of Pete,' she says, locking on to her daughter's eyes. 'He's looking at us, all the time. He's not our friend. He's their spy. God knows what they're thinking. I won't have them going through our knicker drawers, thinking the worst of us. We stay tight. Even just you and me, if necessary.'

She realises the impact of her words as Chloe crumples before her.

'You don't think it's Dad.' It kills Beth to do this to Chloe, but this is the last place she can be honest. It's for Chloe's good, possibly her own survival.

'You never really know someone, not even after all this time.' Chloe tries to shake her head but Beth tightens her grip on her jaw. 'We have to be so strong now. You have to be older than you are. 'Cause I don't know where this ends.'

Later, when the fingerprints on her cheeks have faded, Chloe sits up in bed, Big Chimp on her lap, phone in her hand. She frowns at the text message she has spent the last half hour composing.

> If you know where my dad was last Thursday you have to tell the police.
> Important. No one else has to know.

She takes a deep breath and presses send.

21

Olly and Karen are the only people in the bar at the Traders. Tea lights flicker on the table between them as they discuss Jack Marshall.

'What is it then, Sea Brigade?' she asks. She's got a vision of little boys in sailor suits with blue collars.

'Pretty much Scouts with added boats ...' begins Olly, then falls silent. There is an apparition at their table; Maggie Radcliffe, glass in hand.

'Don't mind if I join, do you?' she says, sitting between them. She gives Karen a long look. 'I had your boss on the phone to me. Saying he'd been trying you with no joy. But he had a hunch you'd make contact with the local press. Apparently you've gone AWOL.'

Karen thinks fast: lie to them now and she'll lose them for ever. 'OK, you've got me,' she says, palms up in conciliation. 'I took leave, I'm here off my own bat. You know I used to write crime for the broadsheets? Well, I thought moving to the *Herald* would be a step in the right direction, more readers, but there's no money for reporting, it's all been cut, no specialisms, we all just regurgitate press releases. I should never have moved.'

'But why'd you come here?' asks Olly. 'There can't be any shortage of crime to cover in London.'

She swills her drink around in her glass. In for a penny . . . 'Alec Hardy. I followed him, profiled him, on his last case.' They look blank. 'Sandbrook.'

Maggie claps a hand to her forehead. 'Of *course*,' she says.

'He'd had this amazing career and then he all but vanished after the trial.' It's a relief to say it out loud to someone who she knows will get it. 'Now suddenly he's here. I was in court when it all fell apart. He failed those families. I saw it happen. And I'm worried he's going to do it again here.'

Maggie nods grimly. Karen finishes her gin and tonic so fast that the ice hurts her teeth. 'Same again?'

Becca Fisher is behind the bar but she's lost in the screen of her mobile. Even though there are no other patrons, Karen has to shout twice to get service. With trade so slow, you'd think she'd be falling over herself to look after the few customers she has. What's Becca looking at that's more important than her business?

Liz has gone home, Pete has finally gone off shift and Chloe is asleep in her bedroom, knocked out by a half-dose of her mother's prescription sedative.

Beth is alone for the first time since losing Danny. She eyeballs an uncapped bottle of red. Obviously she knows she shouldn't drink. The flipside of oblivion is the loss of what fragile control she still has. And of course there's the baby to consider. Not that anyone knows yet, not that anyone will judge her. But it's getting dark now, Mark remains in custody and the unanswered questions swarm vaguely in her head. She needs *something*. She pours and drinks. It is strong but not sweet: is it guilt or hormones that sour the grape?

When the doorbell rings, she takes the glass with her to answer it, and there under the porch light is Reverend Paul, the one person in the world who knows she shouldn't be drinking.

'Am I intruding?' he says. His eyes flick from her belly to her hand but he's clever, or kind, enough to hide any judgement. 'Thought I'd see how you were.'

She has to wonder about that. 'How am I? I think, numb.' She waves him into the sitting room. 'I never said thank you. You were nice the other day. Want some wine?'

'No,' he says quickly. 'So. I was thinking about Danny. I know a funeral isn't possible until the police have finished their investigation. But we could hold a memorial service. For his life. A celebration, here. For you. For the town. For Danny.' He's using Danny's name and not talking in euphemism; he isn't scared of her grief and she appreciates it. But is she ready for what he's suggesting? 'There's a wider community, which you're part of. And which loves you, and is hurting with you.' She's getting a bit sick of this, the idea that Danny's death is a community tragedy. She doesn't notice anyone else with a kid in the mortuary. It is the Latimers' loss and no one else's. Sometimes Beth feels that it is hers alone. 'Communal memorial *can* help.' It occurs to

Beth that a memorial service might get everyone off their backs and leave them to grieve in peace.

'Maybe. Let me talk to Mark.' She's not sure he has forgiven Reverend Paul for talking to the reporters the day after it happened, for muscling in on the tragedy. And then there's the God issue.

'How . . . religious would it be?'

'Whatever you like.' It's not the answer she was expecting. 'We can plan it so it reflects who you are, who Danny was.'

The use of the past tense is like opening a vein. 'I just want to feel him close to me. I want to hear his voice. I want to know how he is.'

'He's with God now.'

'Tell God, give me a signal, something, let me know he's OK.' But she knows it doesn't work like that, if it works at all. She wishes she could believe in God if only to rage at him for taking her baby away.

When Paul has gone, Beth wonders if she ought to pray, but she can't find it in herself. What's the point? There's only one thing she wants and she doesn't think God still does miracles. Instead, she spends an hour or so slumped in front of the television, flicking from one news channel to another, her miserable trance broken only by the rattle of the letterbox. She checks the time in the corner of the news: three minutes past ten. The trickle of sympathy cards from well-meaning strangers is constant and this late, it feels intrusive. But in place of the expected stiff white rectangle on the doormat, she finds a folded scrap of paper. She opens it to reveal neat round handwriting.

141

I didn't mean to scare you. Danny wants to contact you. Please call.
STEVE

There's a mobile number carefully printed overleaf.

Beth holds the note in shaking hands, remembering her words to Paul Coates: Tell God, give me a sign. She doesn't believe in this sort of thing. Never has. But what if? What *if*?

22

It is a quarter past ten at night. DS Ellie Miller broke her promise to be home for teatime, then another to make it back for bedtime. Tom says he understands but she doesn't know if he's trying to make it easier for her. Kids do that more than we give them credit for, and lately Tom has been more sensitive to adult emotions than he used to be, maybe because he's on the cusp of them himself. She comforts herself that Fred, at least, won't remember the missed bedtimes and won't feel them as keenly as Tom would have at the same age. When Fred wakes in the night, it's Joe he cries for.

She stumbles down the station steps to reception. Becca Fisher has asked for her by name. Ellie rubs her eyes, glad there are no mirrors around. Becca always has the immaculate, put-together look of a woman who doesn't have kids.

'Chloe Latimer texted me.' Becca looks pained. 'It's about Mark. He was with me, that night, till about one.'

The mystery of the clifftop tryst is solved. Ellie's first reaction is relief. An affair: awful, but better than the scenarios she had begun to imagine. That is swiftly chased by pre-emptive sorrow on Beth's behalf. This will destroy her. From that comes anger, a rushing rage. How dare they?

Ellie wants Becca to say it out loud. 'What were you doing?' She confines her contempt to a sneer, something that can't be quoted and used against her.

'Having sex.' Becca juts her chin, but defiance is quickly replaced by regret. 'I know. Worst decision of my life.'

They bring Mark back out of the cell. After dark, the interview room ceases to act as a sundial. The only light that penetrates is the faint unmoving glow of the street lamps outside, and it feels like time has stopped.

'Why didn't you tell us you were with Becca Fisher on Thursday night?' says Hardy.

'Why d'you think? If this got out . . . '

Hardy lets out a whistle of incredulity. 'You were worried about *gossip*?'

'Not gossip,' says Mark. '*Lives*. My family. Becca's business. If you haven't lived in Broadchurch, you don't understand how these things stick.' He looks to Ellie. 'You can't tell Beth. It was the first time I'd been with anyone else. I've had *chances*, but I never did anything.' Ellie's blood boils on Beth's behalf. What does he want, a medal for all the times he resisted?

'So why now?' says Hardy.

'We're *tired*. I've been married since I was seventeen. There was a chance of something else . . . and I took it.'

'But this is only ever about Danny's killer. Why wouldn't you tell us?'

'Because . . . I'm ashamed. The one time I took it all for

granted, and I lost Danny.' He's broken, a little boy. '*Please* don't tell Beth. This'd finish her off.'

Later, they stand on the balcony outside Hardy's office and watch Mark shuffle off into the night, hands in pockets and kicking at stones. He is clearly in no rush to get home.

It's bad enough that Ellie is sitting on the facts about Hardy and Sandbrook – she still hasn't found the right moment to break it to Beth – but this is far worse. It's not right to know things about your friend's marriage that she doesn't know herself. It distorts the balance of power and Beth is already so helpless. The knowledge weighs Ellie down. She's always been an optimistic person but she is so sad for so much of the time now that she worries the change is permanent.

She calls Joe from her desk. It takes him a few rings to answer and when he does, she can hear the dishwasher running in the background.

'How's Tom?'

Joe sighs. 'He asked whether you thought *he'd* killed Danny.'

Ellie closes her eyes against the thought. 'I hope you told him I don't.'

'Of course! Then he asked why you had to be the police person looking into it.'

'Yeah, well, we're all asking that.' There's a squeak and she pictures him sinking into the sofa, landing on one of Fred's toys. She wishes, for one sharp second, that they could swap places. What wouldn't she give, right now, for his intimate responsibilities, the huge and tiny life of a housewife.

'How's the boss?' asks Joe.

'Same. As if it wasn't hard enough.'

'Smother him with kindness, Ell. Isn't that your usual way?' There's a smile in his voice and she returns it. Feeling better, she goes back to work.

At her desk, she opens the video clip of Hardy's interview with Tom. She watches her little boy talk about Mark hitting Danny. She can see what it costs him to break Danny's trust, even if it is in the pursuit of catching his killer, and she feels a flare of pride in Tom for his loyalty. She presses rewind and watches one more time. 'He gave him a split lip.' The idea of Mark lashing out is sickeningly plausible.

'Tom did well today,' says Hardy over her shoulder. 'He can be in our reconstruction on Thursday night.'

'What?' Ellie is stunned. 'No. I don't want him to. He's just lost his best friend! It could traumatise him for life.'

'Maybe *he* should be allowed to decide that.'

'No! I'm his mum. *I* decide.' It is the one place he can't pull rank. No one, not even Joe, certainly not Alec bloody Hardy, gets to override her here.

'So, your commitment to this investigation stops outside these doors.'

He really does possess a flair for turning positives into negatives. Ellie explodes. 'With respect, sir, move away from me now or I will piss in a cup and throw it at you!'

Hardy shrugs, as if dodging cups of hurled piss is all in a night's work for him. 'Talk to ... what's your husband's name? *Joe.* Talk to him about it. And Tom.'

The mention of Joe's name calms Ellie. What was his advice? Smother Hardy with kindness? Why not? They can hardly go on like this.

'You're invited round to dinner,' she says. 'You don't know many people here and you're living on hotel food.'

'It's not a good idea.'

'Please don't be an arsehole about it. I don't really want to do it either. But it's what people do. They have their bosses round. We won't talk about work.'

In the ensuing silence, Hardy appears to be running the phrase 'we won't talk about work' through some kind of internal translation app. It is evidently a torturous process. 'What *will* we talk about?' he eventually asks. It's a bloody good question. She has no idea. 'Just say yes,' she says through gritted teeth.

Hardy looks cornered. 'Yeah.'

'Thank you. Bloody hell,' says Ellie, and then when he's back in his office, '*Knob*.'

Nige Carter, on the way home from the pub, takes the alleyways home, missing his boss by minutes. He isn't drunk but four pints have given his half-jog, half-walk a fluidity, so he very nearly runs into the figure waiting for him at the cross-junction of alleyways near his cul-de-sac. He puts out his heels to stop, as though he's on roller skates.

Susan Wright blocks his path.

'Don't try and avoid me,' she says. She nods at his house. 'I know where you live. I know what your van looks like.'

'I've told you, I don't want to see you.' There's venom in Nige's voice.

'It's not that simple though, is it?' Susan's monotone doesn't quaver. 'We're *connected* now, you and me. You can't just turn your back on me. You might not like it, but it can't be undone. So we need to work out what we do.'

He leans forward, bearing his gums in a snarl. 'I don't want you near me. You stay away!'

'I'm not going anywhere,' says Susan. Nige turns to sprint the final few yards to his mum's house.

'You can't run from this! We're in this together, whether you like it or not.' She is finally shouting but the wind is in her face, and her words are thrown back at her.

23

Steve Connolly hesitates on Beth's threshold. 'I'm surprised you called.'

Not as surprised as Beth is. She doesn't recognise herself as she invites him in and makes him a cup of tea. It seems ridiculous to fumble their way through small talk when there's something so huge at stake but they do it, awkwardly chatting about what makes a good cuppa. It's reassuring that Steve seems to find it all as weird as she does.

'Why did Danny talk to *you*?' she asks, when the tea is made.

'No, no, he didn't,' says Steve. Beth's dismay must show because immediately he's falling over himself to explain. 'I . . . don't see dead people or . . . I have, like, a spirit guide. She tells me things, about people who have passed over, and over the years most of it has turned out to be true. So I asked her about you guys and she said it was someone, someone close to you. A relative with an R or an S in their name. Maybe a grandparent or someone who played the piano?'

None of it means anything to her. Obviously there's an R

in Latimer, but that's hardly a secret. And no one in either of their families is musical. Hope shrivels and dies in Beth's chest. This is like bad cabaret at a cheap holiday camp. She shakes her head.

'No, OK, wires crossed, that's not a problem.'

She ought to throw him out, but those words what if, what if, keep her going. 'Just . . . tell me the message.' Is this the nervous breakdown? Asking for a message from her dead son? She feels a hysterical, joyless laugh rising up through her and swallows it just in time.

'I should tell you that I don't choose what I'm told,' says Steve. 'Danny wants you to know he's OK. He's being looked after now.' It is not the expected sign: no pet name, no memory, no in-joke, no irrefutable link to her boy. But that's the Danny she loves and misses, a little man, trying to look after his mum. She begins to shake violently at the very idea of it and when she sits on her hands to still them her knees knock instead. 'He says don't look for the person who killed him because it won't help. It won't help. It'll only make *you* upset. Because you know the person who killed him really well. And he says he loves you very much.' He looks steadily at her. 'That's all there is.'

Her second visitor, the second strange man of the night, leaves. And meanwhile, Mark still isn't home. Beth writes down what Steve said. Does it count as madness if you know you're going mad?

She doesn't bother to take a pill before bed. Nothing short of a general anaesthetic will knock her out tonight. But she gets under the duvet anyway and lies there, staring at the clock and waiting for Mark to come home. She wonders whether to tell him what she's been doing with her evening. It's surreal. You left me alone for one night and I had a priest in here *and* a medium. Would Mark see the funny side? She knows it would have been very different if he was here. Paul wouldn't have got past the front door and Steve would've got a broken nose for his trouble.

She keeps this up for a long time, mulling over her own evening so she doesn't have to think about Mark's. But the second she hears the crunch of his key in the door, that changes and the questions she has put off asking herself all evening pull into sharp focus. Why has he lied to me? Why did he lie to the police? What has he told them? Does Ellie know stuff I don't? Who's going to tell me? She lies rigid, listening to Mark kick off his boots, check on Chloe and clean his teeth. Half an hour passes before he slides into bed next to her. He smells of toothpaste and fresh sweat.

'Are you gonna tell me where you were?'

'Not now,' he says.

She rolls on to her elbow. 'Look at me,' she says, flipping on her bedside lamp. He turns his eyes slowly towards her and for the first time in their marriage, Beth has no idea what's going on behind them.

'Did you kill him?' she says. She didn't even know she was thinking it till she said it.

'How can you even say that? Is that what you're thinking? Is that what you see when you look at me? For God's sake, Beth.' He hasn't denied it. Steve Connolly's words ring in her head. It's someone you know really, really well.

Mark storms out of the bedroom, grabbing his phone from the bedside table. On the landing, she hears the click of his

151

buttons and in swift response, a noise she never hears from Mark's phone; not a personalised ringtone but a simple beep, the factory setting for an incoming text. The innocent little electronic noise is an alarm bell for Beth. She sits up in bed as Mark runs down the stairs. By the time she's on the landing, the front door is clicking softly behind him. Through the kitchen window Beth watches him head out across the field towards the High Street. Her trainers are on her feet and she's after him before she knows what she's doing. She is light on her feet and he never looks back, even on the well-lit High Street, even when he makes a sharp right at the Traders and walks down the launch slope to the edge of the harbour.

Becca Fisher emerges from the shadows.

Beth has the sensation of an endless vertical fall, familiar only from nightmares. She presses her back against the side wall and, using the breaking waves to cover her tread, inches closer. She is shrouded in shadow but Mark and Becca are absorbed in each other and wouldn't notice if she came running past in her wedding dress.

'You didn't have to tell them,' says Mark.

'I got you out,' she says. Her hands are on his collar and their hips are pressed together. 'Look, it was a mistake. Last Thursday, all of it. It's timing. We might've had something—'

'We still could,' says Mark. Beth bends double.

'No,' says Becca.

'I lost my boy.' He wilts in her arms. 'Maybe it's some kind of punishment for what we did.' Becca shakes her head and strokes his hair in a gesture of wifely comfort that sends a flare of jealousy up inside Beth. It gets worse. They kiss, and Beth forces herself to watch; she's enjoying this, on some fucked-up level, she realises. This is a new kind of pain and the novelty of it is providing temporary relief from the Danny pain. A change is as good as a rest, isn't that what they say?

They pull away, their fingertips the last point of touch.

'Go home,' says Becca. She heads back to the hotel. Even in heels over cobbles there's a swing to her walk that marks her out as sexy, glamorous, free; all the things Beth will never be again, if she ever was in the first place.

Mark puts up his hood and sits down on the harbour, head in his hands. Beth can't bring herself to confront him. Knowing that she cannot do this tonight, she turns for home: she wants to be back in bed before he knows she was gone.

She passes the police station as the automatic gates slide apart. Ellie Miller inches her car on to the High Street. She hits the brakes when she sees Beth.

'What're you doing out?' she says. 'Come on, let me give you a lift home.'

The inside of Ellie's car is like a bin. Beth has to sweep sweet wrappers from the seat and empty cans clank in the passenger footwell.

'Is he a suspect?' asks Beth, using her feet to stop the cans rolling into each other. 'Have you ruled him out, for definite?'

Ellie twitches in and out of her two roles: friend, policewoman, friend, policewoman. 'It's not that simple—'

'Of course it's that simple!'

A block away from Spring Close, Ellie brakes at a red light

although hers is the only car in sight. 'Me?' she says with a sigh. 'I don't think he did it. Truly, I don't. But . . . there were gaps in his movements, the night Danny died, that he needed to explain and we couldn't let him go until he did.'

'I saw him tonight, with Becca Fisher,' says Beth. 'He doesn't know. Is that what he told you?'

'You have to talk to him,' says Ellie in diplomatic confirmation. Beth's humiliation is complete. Her tears are hot and messy.

'Why is this happening to me?' she wails. 'What did I do? I just want to be the person outside of this, watching from the other side of the road, taking pity on me. I don't want to be in the middle of it. I can't do it, Ell.'

Ellie undoes her seat belt and pulls her in for a hug. Beth's tears roll off Ellie's orange coat. 'I'm sorry, sweetheart, I really am.' They stay like that for a long time, the traffic lights going through their patient cycle on the empty road.

24

Karen White is waiting for Hardy in the hotel bar. 'What time d'you call this?'

'No.' After the way she turned him over last time, he'll never give her more than a single syllable again. Knowing her, she'll even find a way to twist *that*. 'Come on,' she wheedles. 'Five minutes. Couple of quotes. Tell me where you've been, what you've been up to.'

She's like a little mosquito buzzing around, looking for blood. He flaps his hand through the air between them. 'I will *not* let you distract me from the job in hand.'

'You let the Sandbrook families down,' she says from her high horse. 'They still don't have closure, because of you. And I am *not* going to let you do that to another family.'

He is tempted to shove her to one side. He is tempted to tell her the truth about Sandbrook. God knows no other journalist wants it more. But he's powerless on both counts, so he settles for a bitter, 'Get out of my way,' and drags his exhausted body up the stairs. He should pause to breathe at the top of the mezzanine but she's watching him. The push up another flight almost finishes him off, but he counts that as a necessary exertion.

In his room, he takes a shower and falls between the perfect sheets where he achieves precisely thirty-seven minutes of deep and dreamless sleep before his phone rings, jolting him awake. His heart taps a feeble protest on his ribcage. Waking up suddenly is one of the worst things he can do, up there with caffeine, smoking and – ha! – stress.

'Hardy,' he barks into the mouthpiece. It's Bob Daniels. He's down on the beach. There's something Hardy needs to see, now.

As he struggles back into his suit, he notices his hair is still damp. He regrets that shower now, and the ten minutes' sleep it stole from him.

On Harbour Cliff Beach, Danny's shrine is untended. Pinwheels twirl in the breeze, their sails a blur. The candles have all burnt out. A couple of hundred yards out to sea, a boat burns like a beacon, the flames pouring liquid gold on the surface of the sea. Chunks of flaming wood splinter and sizzle into the water.

'No sign of anyone on it,' says Bob.

They can't afford to wait until the tide washes it in.

'Call the coastguard or whoever,' says Hardy. 'I need people out there now, collecting every piece.'

Beth sleeps fitfully, dreaming Danny back to life then waking up to the loss of him again and again. All she thinks about is swapping places with her son. Over and over, she offers up a silent bargain: Let me be taken instead of him.

Let me absorb his pain and his fear. She lists all the things she would endure on Danny's behalf. She'd be raped, she'd have a gang of men on her, she'd be beaten and left for dead if it meant he was safe. The scenarios get harsher and harsher. Beth never knew she had such a vivid imagination.

While she tortures herself, Mark snores loudly beside her. Lying so close to him makes her skin itch. She gets up and opens the curtains. Pale light leaks between the torn flesh of the clouds and there's no point even trying to go back to sleep. There is only one thing for it.

Run.

Her sports bra is tight around tender breasts and the waistband of her running tights is snugger than usual but she fills her bottle and strikes out in the rain, breaking straight into a hard run, no warm-up, no stretching. Her feet take her away from Harbour Cliff Beach, along the concrete esplanade with its ugly railings where the tourists don't go. The rain falls hard and the sea spray cools her.

Running used to empty her mind. Work, kids' stuff, rows with Mark, general stress: there would come a point on any run when she'd become one with her footfall. Today, her body quits before she can reach that state. It's the first time she's been out for a few weeks. She hasn't eaten, she hasn't slept and the pregnancy is slowing her down. After fifty minutes her legs stop cooperating. A full hour has passed by the time she comes panting through the patio door. Ellie and DI Hardy are waiting for her on the sofa.

'Where the hell have you been?' says Mark in the controlling voice he uses on Chloe.

'Running,' she hits back in the stroppy voice Chloe uses

on Mark. 'Am I not allowed to run any more?' She turns to the police. 'I didn't know you were coming.'

'Just bringing you up to date,' says Ellie. 'We've asked Forensics to examine Danny's clothes in greater detail. We're following up on leads from the house-to-house and we've got a number of interviews scheduled today.'

'Now you've stopped messing around with *me*.' Mark folds his arms.

'Don't be a wanker, Mark,' snaps Beth, shocking him into silence. Chloe's eyes saucer; Beth thinks she detects approval in Ellie's.

Hardy cuts the tension. 'We found five hundred pounds cash in Danny's room.'

'What was he doing with that sort of money?' Mark looks to Beth and for a minute they're co-parents again, united in their bewilderment.

'We were hoping you could tell us,' says Hardy.

Beth looks the question at Chloe.

'He never told me about it,' says Chloe.

DI Hardy's face is inscrutable. 'We're holding a public meeting today at the school, to keep the town up to date, answer any questions,' he says. 'You don't need to be there.'

'I'll go, on behalf of all of us,' says Liz, before anyone else can volunteer. Beth recognises the need to stay busy and doesn't challenge it.

'Why isn't there more in the paper about Danny?' Mark wants to know. 'It's like page twelve, couple of paragraphs. Doesn't he matter?'

Hardy frowns. 'Don't judge this investigation by what appears in the press.'

'We were saying, though,' continues Mark, 'if there was more in the papers, it might jog people's memories? What if there's someone out there who saw something but doesn't realise it? If we had more—'

Hardy cuts him off. 'Please, let *us* deal with the media. We have the experience in this.'

He might know his way around the media, but Ellie certainly doesn't. Beth feels a disloyal surge of gratitude that this man is in charge of the investigation. Because right now, it's authority and experience they need and Ellie looks like she's floundering. Really, she would have been brilliant at Pete's job, as a bridge between the family and the detectives. Not that she'd dream of telling Ellie this. It is what it is. But when it comes to finding Danny's killer, Beth knows that everything rides on Detective Inspector Alec Hardy.

SOCO want Hardy down at Harbour Cliff Beach. The tide is out and they've brought the boat in. Miller fields a long phone call as they pick their way over the cobbles.

'Confirmation that we can't trace any of the banknotes from Danny's room,' she reports as they round the jetty. 'They've all been in circulation for ages, can't get anything back on them.'

Hardy strokes his chin. 'Where could Danny have got five hundred pounds from? What about his phone and his skateboard? He was riding that down the street, last moment we saw him. What happened to it?'

'We're still looking at all other CCTV on possible routes but so far, nothing,' she says. 'I've also got the team checking on teachers and teaching assistants at the school.

Classmates, family babysitters. Mark's plumber's mate, Nige.'

A Forensics van is parked up by the water. SOCO Brian and his team are poring over the charred remains of the boat.

'Is this *it*?' Hardy asks.

Brian is affronted. 'On Earth, we say good morning and how're you doing?' he sniffs.

'I've told him,' Miller rolls her eyes. 'Makes no difference.'

'Is it connected to the Latimer death?'

Hardy's question trips Brian into professional mode. 'Traces of accelerant suggest the boat was doused in petrol. I'm finding flecks of glass, fibres of cloth within the wood. If I had to guess, I'd say a lit rag inside a bottle was used to ignite it.' Now his voice has the excited pitch of a geek in his element. 'Molotov cocktail. A *classic*.'

Miller stoops to examine the boat. 'If they took it that far out, at what, 4 a.m., to burn it, how'd they get back?' she says.

'Rear section has marks where an outboard motor might have gone,' says Brian. 'They probably used that to get back on another boat. But look, this might hold the key.' He holds up a fragment of blackened wood. 'Look in the grain. Strands of hair.'

Hardy squints to see a single dark filament caught in a splinter. He feels something approaching pleasure for the first time in months. 'Outstanding, out bloody standing!' he says, clapping Brian on the back. 'Oh, Miller, we've *got* them. Keep going, I want to know as soon as you have confirmation. Come on, Miller, don't hang about.'

As they head for the station, Miller has to trot to keep up with Hardy: Hardy's mouth has to work hard to keep up with his brain. 'A hundred quid says that's the boat they used and those hairs belong to Danny Latimer. They're *panicking*, Miller. Panicking's fantastic, exactly what we want. They're starting to show themselves. I'll tell you what else: they're amateur, they haven't done this before. It's too clumsy, burning it like that, and so soon.'

She doesn't share his euphoria. 'You mean it's somebody here. They were out last night. We could be walking past them now.' She casts wide eyes balefully around the harbour.

'I'm sure of it now,' he says.

The killer's mistake is oxygen to Hardy. He fills his lungs with Broadchurch air and for the first time since his arrival in this shitty little town, it tastes good.

25

For Hardy's second appearance at South Wessex Primary the place is packed to the rafters. They're all the same, these school halls: the climbing frames flush to the wall, adults squatting awkwardly on child-sized chairs. He has a sudden flashback to his first press conference at Sandbrook Juniors and before he can stop himself he's superimposed those faces on the ones before him now. He shakes his head free of the image of Cate and Richard Gillespie and concentrates instead on the residents of Broadchurch.

He takes a silent register of the ones he recognises. Liz Roper, Nige Carter, that vicar who fancies himself as a TV pundit – he'll keep an eye on him – Becca from the hotel, Olly and Maggie and the bad penny herself, Karen White. Incredibly, 'psychic' Steve Connolly has the front to be here. Then there are those two people he cannot read: Susan Wright and Jack Marshall. Do they know each other? They are seated far apart, but that could be for his benefit. DS Miller's there with her family in tow. Hardy watches her watch the crowd.

There's a clamour of questions but he launches immediately into his prepared speech. He is not here to have a conversation on the residents' terms.

'Here's what we're up against. Multiple complex crime scenes, particularly at the beach. Lack of CCTV in key areas. Absence of witnesses seeing Danny the night he sneaked out.' Just in time he remembers what Miller said about firing off lists and slows it down for the civilians. 'We've a lot of information to process. We will get there.'

Susan Wright introduces herself by name. 'I heard you were short-staffed.' The idea seems to please her.

'We have the right resources for an investigation of this size. Next question.'

'I've just come from the pier and there's a bloody great Forensics van parked up there!' shouts a red-faced man with white hair like a dandelion. His words are immediately followed by a chorus of concerned business owners.

'New evidence has come to light overnight and we have to examine it without contamination,' says Hardy evenly.

'Is that the boat that was on fire last night?' This comes from Steve Connolly and there's a mixture of reproach and triumph in his eyes. Hardy suppresses a flare of impatience. It's hardly a stretch, round here, to suggest that a boat was involved.

'You have to understand the work that's going on there,' says Hardy. 'Every grain of sand has to be gone through. Every cigarette butt, stray hair, shard of plastic, fingernail, toenail, piece of skin has to be tested.' Before he can censor the image, a silver pendant swings bright in his mind's eye. 'A crime scene on a beach is one of the most challenging things our officers have to deal with.'

'It's the image you're giving out!' shouts the dandelion. 'We're down 40 per cent on last summer. Nobody's coming. We don't want the name Broadchurch to become a byword for murder like Sandbrook.'

Hardy waits for the explosion but it doesn't come. There's merely a flash of alarm on Miller's face and the three journalists shift in their seats. Karen White looks at him serenely and he has no doubt that his part in the Sandbrook travesty will be front-page news in the *Echo*, and possibly even the nationals, before the week is out. Whatever's making them hang on to it, he hopes it stays that way for the sake of the investigation.

After the meeting, Hardy almost makes it to the car uninterrupted.

'I told you there was a boat.'

'Oh, great, you're just what I need,' Hardy rounds on an indignant Steve Connolly. 'There's hundreds of them around here, you got lucky.'

'Did you look for it? Eh? Does Beth know you didn't follow it up?'

Hardy lays his index finger gently on Connolly's chest.

'How about you heed my very strong advice,' he says in a near-whisper. 'Stay away from her. Do not get involved.'

Connolly shakes his head and walks slowly away. Hardy leans against the car. This is the phase he's been dreading: when a case like this goes on for more than a few days, people get restless. Everyone wants to stick their oar in, develop their own pet theory. Everywhere but in the incident room, opinion begins to overwhelm fact. The media can be worst of all, he thinks, as Olly Stevens and Maggie

Radcliffe march purposefully up. He takes his hand off the car door, resigned to another long conversation.

'Here we go again,' he greets them.

Olly's looking extremely pleased with himself.

'There's something Oliver wants to tell you,' says Maggie.

'We always love hearing from Oliver,' says Hardy. To his dismay, the kid beams; you can't lay the sarcasm on thick enough for these people.

'I found this on Jack Marshall,' he says, producing an envelope from his bag. Inside is a photocopied page of newsprint bearing a decades-old picture of the shopkeeper. 'He was in prison before he came here. He's got a previous conviction for underage sex.'

Karen White watches Olly and Maggie from a distance, relishing DI Hardy's expression when he realises that the press are one step ahead of him. The time feels right to pitch the story to Len Danvers again.

The phone call does not get off to a good start. 'We're chocka with domestic crime at the moment,' he says. 'And I specifically told you not to go.'

'I'm on leave,' she reminds him. 'Len, this is heartland stuff. And the police are struggling. I don't think this'll be done in a day or two.'

'Why will our readers care?' he asks. She knows what he wants to hear and for once she can serve it to him on a plate.

'Model family, two kids. Dad's a plumber, quiet estate, idyllic market town, definition of normal. The mum's very photogenic. English Rose. But ... something might be up with the marriage.'

'Trouble in paradise?' says Len, and she knows that when he talks in headlines he's already made the decision. 'Go on, then. Get me an exclusive with the mum, nice photo and I'll look at it. But you're paying your own hotel bills.'

She exits through the school hall. It's empty now apart from a woman staring forlornly at a basket full of footballs. Karen flips through her mind's index until she locates her: Liz Roper, Danny's grandmother, although she doesn't look nearly old enough.

'How are you coping?' asks Karen. Liz looks up: clearly, she's already used to strangers knowing who she is.

'Me, I'm tough as old boots. It's the others I worry about.'

In voicing her strength Liz has exposed her jugular: no one has thought about her.

'You must miss him,' says Karen, and Liz wells up.

'My Geoff taught him how to kick one of these,' she says, gesturing towards the footballs. 'Two years old and he could dribble a ball from one end of the garden to the next. He was a little *star*.' She wipes her eyes with the back of her hand. 'I promised myself I wouldn't do this. I'm the strong one in all this. I just want them to catch the sod who did it.' She gives Karen a watery smile. 'Sorry, I can't remember your name.' It's the polite cover for someone who has met more new people in the last few days than in the previous decade.

'I'm Karen. I work for the *Herald*.'

Liz recoils, as Karen knew she would. 'We're not talking to the press.'

'I know. But can I say one thing? Be sure you're getting the best advice. I'd hate for Danny to be ignored.'

166

She lets her hand rest briefly on Liz's, then leaves her crying over the pile of scuffed footballs.

Beth pegs washing on the line in the back garden. Boys from Danny's class play kickabout in the playing field. She's battling the urge to vault the fence, run into the melee of boys, grab one – any one – and hold him so tight that she can feel his heart beat. Usually the football pitch is a kids-only zone, but today a handful of parents stand nervous sentinel on the sidelines.

Steve Connolly, chatting to Beth over her fence, attracts concerned glances. One father covertly takes a picture of him on his mobile phone. Everyone's a witness now. Steve doesn't notice; his focus is all on Beth, polite but insistent. 'A few days ago I told the police about evidence they should look for,' he says. 'But they didn't listen and it was burned before they got to it, so it's harder for them to analyse it properly.'

He's talking about the boat they found on fire, he must be. Everyone knows about it. 'Why are you telling me this?'

'Because I can help! I can help.' Steve presses both hands to his chest in an almost priestly gesture. 'But for that to happen I need to be taken seriously, and that's not happening right now.'

Beth doesn't know what to think. She drops her eyes. At the top of the laundry basket is the red dress she was wearing the day she saw Danny lying on the beach. She hangs it out even though she knows she will never wear it again.

'What if you're wrong?'

Steve shakes his head. 'I've got no reason to lie to you.

Beth, I wish, I *wish*, we'd never had cause to meet. But what I have told you is genuine. And you need to convince the police.'

Doubt and hope wrestle inside Beth. The things Steve deals in are too big for her to grasp, just as there is too much grief for her to process. It's not that she doesn't believe in them. It's that she has never, until now, given it much thought. Her old, lovely life had no room for philosophy, and there were no ghosts.

Her life is suddenly all about trusting men she doesn't know. Spilling confidences to the vicar. Depending on DI Hardy. And now this strange, serious man who says he has a line to Danny. She looks him straight in the eye. His return gaze is unflinching.

'OK,' she says.

With trust in her husband betrayed, it is strange men Beth puts her faith in now.

26

Hardy is furious and Ellie mortified. The press pulled up Jack Marshall's previous while CID, still wading through a backlog of actions and checks, had not even thought to prioritise him. She's sickened – physically sickened, she can't finish her lunch – at the thought it might be Jack. This man has been in charge of her son, he's taken all the Sea Brigade camping, zipped them into their sleeping bags, seen them change their clothes.

Jack has been in Broadchurch for so long that he is an honorary local, but of course he wasn't always there: he took over the shop when Ellie was about seven. She remembers it happening now.

It's warm in the interview room but Jack hasn't even taken his coat off. If he's guilty, this is one hell of a poker face.

'Is this about the postman who was arguing with Danny?' he asks.

'No,' says Ellie. 'Though we did talk to him. He says he never had an argument with Danny that day.'

'Load of rubbish. I know what I saw.'

There's a beat while Ellie waits for Hardy to steer the interview. He clears his throat before he speaks. 'Tell us about your conviction for sex with a minor, Jack.'

There's no denial or surprise, only more of the same quiet control. 'So we're into the muck-raking, are we?'

'Just want to establish the facts,' says Hardy. 'You didn't mention it when we spoke.'

'It's nothing to do with Danny.'

'You help with the Sea Brigade. That requires CRB checks, cross-referenced with the sex offenders register.'

Jack is contemptuous. 'I am NOT a sex offender! That conviction was a farce. I'm not on any register.'

'Only because it happened before the register came into being,' says Hardy. 'You should've declared it.'

'What, when I moved into town? Put up a little sign, should I? Ex-convict here. I came here to get away from that. I am *not* what you are insinuating.'

Hardy shuffles the paper in front of him. 'When did you last see Danny Latimer?'

'I've told you, he did his paper round the day before he was found.'

'What about the night of Danny's death, where were you then?'

'In, on my own, reading a book.'

'Anyone vouch for that?' says Hardy, in subtle mockery of the old man's solitude.

'Only the book.' Jack purses his lips. '*Jude the Obscure.* You might not like it: not many pictures.'

Despite the situation, Ellie finds herself biting back a smile.

'We've been told you're a keen amateur photographer, Jack,' says Hardy. 'Took a lot of pictures of the boys in the Sea Brigade.'

Ellie is no longer smiling. Neither is Jack.

'I really do pity you,' he says. 'Seeing depravity in perfectly normal behaviour. I'd hate to be in your mind. Now if you've an accusation or evidence to put to me, let's hear it. Otherwise, let me go back to work.'

He rises from his seat. They have to let him go.

Karen is intrigued: Maggie has summoned her to the inner sanctum of the *Broadchurch Echo*, the editor's office. It's a mess of dusty potted plants and wooden cats, as far from Len Danvers' leather and chrome dominion as can be.

'Still want a desk?' she asks her.

'You've changed your tune.'

Maggie tips the dregs of her mug over a flourishing spider plant. 'Olly would never have gone looking into Jack Marshall if it wasn't for you,' she says. 'And it's better to have you inside the tent pissing out, than outside the tent pissing in, I suppose. But we all muck in. You can start with a round of tea. White, no sugar, for me.'

Karen has little choice but to suck it up. By the time she returns with the tea, Maggie's gone for one of the cigarette breaks she still insists on taking outside the office, sucking hard at the e-cig: old habits die hard. Karen sets the steaming mug down on Maggie's desk and automatically starts to riffle through the printouts Maggie's working on. Topmost is an *Echo* article from three months ago about a Sea Brigade fundraiser: Jack Marshall's there, with a handful of boys in

171

uniform. There's someone else in the picture, too. It's that miserable woman with the dog, although it takes Karen a few seconds to recognise her because in the picture she's smiling. And this, apparently, is Maggie's line of enquiry. She's circled the name ELAINE JONES in the caption with a red pen and scrawled in the margin *Why the name change? Gave her name as Susan Wright at briefing. Chase?*

Karen takes a mental snapshot of the page. She will let Maggie do the legwork here and then, if it becomes relevant, she will take over. It's an interesting sidebar. But it's not the story. Something – experience combined with good old-fashioned gut instinct – tells her it's Jack Marshall they should be looking for.

Back on the floor, Olly's setting up a workstation for her.

'So, have you talked to Jack Marshall?' asks Karen as he does something with Control Alt Delete.

'I thought we'd best leave it to the police.'

Karen sighs inwardly: for all Olly's professed ambition, he still wants spoon-feeding.

'But you've done the work, Olly. And you've got the connection. You were in the Sea Brigade. Don't you want to follow it up? What if it turns out to be him, and you've missed the story?'

Olly is wide-eyed. 'I don't think Maggie'd go near it.'

Karen fights the urge to headbutt the desk.

Steve Connolly, sitting nervously on the edge of Beth's sofa in his overalls, is an unlikely lifeline but she has to offer the police a second chance to grab hold of it. Pete Lawson is making faces behind Steve's back. God knows, Beth understands his cynicism but they can't afford to take a chance. They can't prove what Steve says about getting messages from Danny, but they can't *dis*prove it either. That must count for something. Even he admits he doesn't know why or how it works, and Beth is encouraged by that. She's impressed by things she doesn't understand all the time. Even doctors don't always know how certain drugs work, only that they do. Why should this be any different? She will not be fit to call herself a mother if she ignores Connolly and it turns out he's right. DI Hardy promised he would leave no stone unturned in this investigation. Doesn't this count?

She knows, as soon as Hardy sees her guest, that it's going to be a struggle. He has made up his mind before Connolly opens his mouth.

'This is what you asked us here for?' he asks Beth, and then, to Pete, 'And you're a bloody idiot for letting him in.'

'Just hear him out,' asks Beth. Hardy scowls but shuts up.

Steve addresses the whole room. 'Danny wants people to know he was killed by someone he knew.'

Hardy erupts. 'This is offensive, I'm calling a halt right now—'

'I told you about the boat,' Steve cuts in. 'You didn't listen. And now you've found a boat.'

'Lucky guess,' says Hardy dismissively. He jerks his head in Ellie's direction. 'Tell her.'

Ellie takes both Beth's hands in hers.

'Beth, we checked out Steve's record.' The room begins the now-familiar tilt of shock. 'He's bankrupt, with prior convictions of vehicle theft, petty theft, and conspiracy to defraud.'

173

Steve jumps up. 'That's nothing to do with this!' Instinctively Beth backs away from him, while Hardy advances.

'I don't know whether you're mentally ill, a liar, or someone who believes they're telling the truth,' he spits into Steve's face. 'But I have to find this killer and prove my case in court. I deal in facts and all you've given her is fantasy. You are going to drive very far away from this house now. Final warning. I see you again, I will have you in prison.'

Pete takes Connolly by the arm and marches him out of the house. He is protesting his innocence and sincerity all the while. Beth puts a hand to the wall to steady herself. 'What's he got to gain?' she asks Ellie. 'I've not paid him.'

'In two weeks he talks to the press,' says Ellie. 'Six months, he writes a book: "How I solved the Broadchurch murder". Go into the bookshop in town, have a look, those books are in there.'

That hits home. Beth has seen those books, browsing the shelves back in the days when things weren't so loaded with meaning; she's seen the red-and-black paperbacks by former detectives and psychologists, the killer on the cover and the victims nowhere in sight. She understands with a chill that she doesn't have to give Connolly cash for him to make money off her. Her grief is a commodity and he is a shark. How can anyone be so cynical? How could she have been so stupid?

There is a commotion outside the window as Pete pushes Connolly into the driver's seat of his own van, one hand on his head like he's bundling a suspect into a police car. The women watch through the glass as Connolly sits behind the wheel and throws what can only be described as a tantrum, rocking, shouting and pounding the dashboard with his fists.

Beth turns away from the window, an empty ringing in her head.

27

Hardy and Miller traipse through St Andrew's churchyard where huge yews overhang crooked tombstones. Reverend Paul Coates has been flagged by the house-to-house enquiries as one of the few without an alibi for the night Danny was killed. Miller is wittering excitedly about their forthcoming dinner party, extolling the virtues of her domestic god of a husband. Hardy, still seething from the encounter with Steve Connolly, has tuned out.

'Know this new vicar well?' he asks her. The ground between graves is uneven and he almost turns his ankle in one of the divots.

'No, he's only been here a couple of years. We're not big churchgoers. Midnight Mass . . . Easter, if we remember.'

'And so did Christianity fall.'

'What about you, then, sir? You religious?'

'Yes, I pray nightly that you'll stop asking me questions.'

Coates is waiting for them on the bench at the top of the graveyard, an iPad on his lap. Dog collar aside, he could be dressed for a game of pool in the pub. Hardy can see that

Coates gets a kick out of being more modern than people expect him to be, and that he's longing for them to comment on the iPad, so he makes a point of ignoring it. He isn't wild about clergy in general but there's nothing worse than a trendy vicar. He's probably got an electric guitar mounted on a wall somewhere and synthesisers on the altar.

'How well d'you know the Latimer family?'

Coates puts down his iPad. 'I know Liz, his grandmother, better. She's one of our sidesmen. But I taught the IT club at Danny's school. He was a quick learner, same as Tom.' Miller beams. 'They just get it instinctively. It's more like me keeping up with them.'

Hardy's mind whirrs: now that there are no more choirboys, now that all the kids worship at the altars of Apple and Microsoft, what better way to access little boys? 'Why are you taking the IT club?' asks Hardy.

Coates folds his arms to reply. 'I try to connect with the community in whatever way I can. Besides, I got asked. I think the last teacher to really understand computers had a nervous breakdown.'

'Oh yeah, Mr Broughton!' says Miller. 'He used to sit there and laugh to himself.'

'Yup. I'm one up from the man who sits there giggling to himself.'

'Where were you on the night of Danny's death?' says Hardy to cut through this crap.

'I did talk to the uniformed officers about this … At home, on my own. I live in the house at the bottom of the hill. I was up late, trying to write a sermon. "Trying" being the operative word. I have terrible insomnia. Have had for

177

about the last six or seven years. Can't find anything to cure it. I've tried everything. So I'm often up, wandering. That's my best attempt to deal with it.'

Hardy's gaze wanders as he listens. He notes that from the churchyard he can see the field that backs on to the Latimers' house. Miller's, too, come to think of it.

'But you weren't up wandering on that Thursday night?'

'I don't remember it,' says Coates. 'I mean, I could've gone outside for some fresh air at some point – I often do. But I don't remember it.'

When they're done, Hardy and Miller walk back through the graveyard in glum silence.

'I *hate* what I'm becoming,' she says.

'A good detective?'

'Hardened.'

She has yet to understand that they are one and the same thing.

The RIB boat that takes tourists out for thrill rides is anchored at the top of the jetty. Susan Wright stands at the mooring, handing out flyers to passers-by.

'Broadchurch Blaster! Half-hour ride!' She presses a leaflet into the hand of a strolling mother. 'Next one in fifteen minutes, here you go, love, best fifteen quid you'll ever spend. Kids half price, perfectly safe.'

The woman studies Susan's face and holds her daughter's hand a little tighter. She lets the paper drop into the first litter bin she passes.

The next person to take a leaflet is Maggie Radcliffe.

'Looks good,' she says, holding Susan's gaze. 'Maggie. I edit the *Echo*.'

'Yeah, I saw you at the meeting.'

'You're Susan. Or is it Elaine?' Susan's stare grows colder as Maggie's line of enquiry hots up. 'Only I've got a picture of you with the Sea Brigade boys, under a different name.'

Maggie is triumphant but Susan is unruffled.

'Your people must have wrote it down wrong,' she counters.

'If there's one thing I drill into my team, it's get the names right and spell them correctly.'

The two women remain locked in stalemate while holidaymakers mill around them.

'I don't know what you want, but I'm at work,' says Susan at last. Maggie says nothing, but backs away across the harbour, flyer scrunched tight in her fist, never breaking eye contact.

28

Karen White climbs carefully over the sack of unopened post that sandbags Beth's front door. 'Thanks for saying you'll talk to me.'

Beth nods. She's still not sure. It's Liz who decided they should talk to the press.

'I'm not here to hassle,' says Karen, like she knows what Beth is thinking. 'I've been here since day one and I've left you alone.'

'It's true,' chimes Chloe. 'I left Big Chimp at the beach. She brought it back to me, save it getting nicked.'

'I think this should be getting more coverage,' Karen says. 'But it's a mad summer and there are a lot of stories around right now.'

Beth doesn't like that word. Pheasant poaching, parking fines and celebrity gossip, those are *stories*. This is life and death stuff. *Story* is an insult. It's even worse than *case*.

'So what should we do?' asks Mark.

At Beth's gesture, Karen sits on the sofa, right on the edge of the cushions. She pushes her sleeves up her forearms and leans forward. 'OK, you won't like hearing this, but part of the reason Danny's death isn't getting the attention it deserves is it's not the right profile. If Danny had been a girl, and blonde, and a few years younger, this place would be crawling with reporters by now.' She catches Beth's look of disgust. 'I'm sorry,' she says, and she looks like she means it. 'It's just how it works. Eleven-year-old boys run away from home all the time. I know it's brutal, but the papers only ever reflect what the public latch on to. If you really want more focus on this case, it's down to you, Beth. You tell your story, every mum will respond. If I could have a picture of you and Danny to go with the article, we'd get two pages out of it.'

Two instincts tussle within Beth: the desire to do whatever it takes to get publicity and the feeling that she might as well let them go through her dirty underwear. What will she achieve, putting herself under the spotlight, spilling her guts to a journalist she's only just met? Beth searches her family's faces for guidance but finds her own cluelessness reflected back at her three times. It's her decision: they are merely waiting for it.

'It's the *Herald*, I read the *Herald*,' says Liz, like the newspaper owe her something for her forty-odd years of loyal readership. Beth doesn't know much about the media but even she knows it doesn't work that way. She twists hard at the hem of her dress.

'What if she shows us what she's written, before she sends it in?' asks Chloe.

'I wouldn't normally do that, but maybe this time . . . '

She's making it sound like she's doing them the favour.

Perhaps she is. 'Is that what we want to do?' Beth thinks out loud. 'Shouldn't we clear it with the police?'

'You can absolutely do that,' says Karen, but her body language – leaning away, arms folded – tells a different story. 'I will say that they're very cautious, particularly after Leveson, and DI Hardy especially, because of the Sandbrook connection.'

There's a cold sinking sensation in Beth's throat, like she's swallowed a block of ice. Sandbrook is only famous for one thing. She can see the girls' faces without even trying.

'What's he got to do with Sandbrook?' asks Mark.

'Because he . . . you didn't know?' Karen's composure slips for a second. 'Alec Hardy was the officer in charge of the investigation. I was there. I profiled him on the case. It's his fault it all fell apart in court.'

The chill inside Beth reaches her core. That abruptness she took for ruthless efficiency looks very different now. And they have trusted him. They have trusted him with the most important job in the world. Surely he should have been legally bound to declare it or something? She opens her mouth to speak but it is dry as dust. Nothing comes out.

'How did he get another job?' asks Mark.

'I don't know,' says Karen. 'But one of the reasons I'm here is to make sure he doesn't do it again.'

Something occurs to Beth and she finds her voice. 'Ellie would've told me.'

'I assumed *someone* had,' says Karen. 'I'm sorry. I wouldn't have blurted it if I'd known.'

The chill spreads to Beth's skin. How could Ellie keep something like this from her? Whose side is she on?

The room waits for Beth's answer. She doesn't trust her own judgement any more, that's the problem. Look how far off the mark she was with Steve Connolly and Alec Hardy. With *Ellie*, of all people. Who's to say Karen White will be any different? Then again, what's the alternative? Send her away, refuse to give the interview? There is a ripping sound and Beth looks down to see that she has torn through her skirt.

Karen puts her head on one side. 'I realise I'm biased, but now you know, it's all the more reason to use the press. Because, I'm sorry, Beth, but Alec Hardy isn't exactly rounding up the suspects on his own, is he? The more coverage we get, the more pressure there is on him.'

Put like that, it's easy. Beth's desire to look after Danny has not diminished with his death. If anything, it is stronger now than it has ever been.

There's a photograph on the windowsill, Beth and Danny at the beach last summer, arms around each other's necks. As she slides it from the frame, she knows that she can live with herself if this turns out to be the wrong choice. But she will not be able to live with herself if she does nothing.

The late-afternoon sun paints the Sea Brigade hut a buttery yellow. In the yard, an upturned boat is stacked with child-sized life jackets. Jack Marshall is in his leader's uniform, crested navy tie on a sky-blue shirt, overseeing his little charges erect another shrine to the lost boy. This one has a nautical theme: seashells instead of flowers, laminated drawings. There are photographs of Danny on the beach, Danny in his Sea Brigade uniform, Danny picking litter from sand, Danny holding up a fish, Danny tying knots.

Olly Stevens pauses for a moment in front of these pictures. He shakes his head slowly and rubs at his eyes. Then he clenches his jaw, sets his phone to record and sticks it in his pocket.

'Hi, Mr Marshall,' he says brightly.

'Oliver!' says Jack. 'Come to help?'

'Well, d'you think we could talk inside maybe?'

Jack is on guard. 'No, we can talk here. Can you not see I'm busy? What is it you want?'

'I've come across some information and . . .' Olly guides Jack gently away from the boys. 'Being as we know each other, I thought I should come to you before it gets out.' He takes a deep breath. 'I'm really sorry, there's no good way of asking this. Is it true you've a conviction for underage sex?'

Fear and anger hit Jack's eyes. 'You little *bastard*!'

'I'm not trying to stitch you up—' begins Olly. He doesn't get the chance to finish. Jack, with the speed of a man half his age, grabs him by the collar and pushes him against the railings. The Sea Brigade boys back away, young and out of their depth.

'Who told you?' snarls Jack. 'Was it the police? You're all as bad as each other, gossiping and accusing.'

'I think you should let go of me!' Olly says through the stranglehold. Jack does, and suddenly he's a frail old man again.

'You've known me how long?' he implores. 'When did I ever do anything improper with kids?'

'If we can talk inside . . .' pants Olly.

'So you can trick me into saying something incriminating?'

'How can I incriminate you if you're innocent?'

'Oh, they've trained you to be a clever weasel, haven't they? Get away! Go on!'

Olly knows when he's beaten. He leaves the Sea Brigade hut at a pace halfway between a walk and a jog. Lost in his thoughts, he doesn't notice Nige Carter is parked up nearby, eating chips in the cab of his van. With the window down and the wind in his favour, he has heard every word.

29

Hardy arrives for dinner still in his suit. He's got flowers, a bottle of wine, a box of Matchmakers and the expression of a man facing the gallows.

What the fuck was Ellie thinking, asking him into her home? It's bad enough she has to put up with him all day at work without actually inviting him into the house voluntarily. She looks daggers at Joe. It's his bloody fault, telling her to be kind. Look where it's got them.

'You can come again!' says Joe, relieving Hardy of his burdens.

'I can call you Alec tonight, can't I?' Ellie takes his jacket. 'I can hardly call you "sir"! Here's your dinner, sir!' She feels like a dick. This is definitely Joe's fault.

'I don't like Alec,' says Hardy, following them into the kitchen. 'Never liked Alec. *Alec.*' Even his own name is sour in his mouth. 'Why does everyone have to use first names so much? Like we all work in marketing or something? I mean, if you're looking at the person, if I'm looking at *you*,' and he pauses for effect, his eyes boring into Ellie's soul and out the other side again, 'you know I'm talking to you, I don't need to say your name three times, just 'cause I'm congratulating myself on remembering it to create this, what, false intimacy.'

Ellie is grimly satisfied to watch Joe realising that she has not been exaggerating.

'I'll show you to the dining room.'

Joe's done her proud: candles dotted around the room to hide the dust, a spread of the best Mexican food this side of Guadalajara. It goes unremarked upon.

'How'd you two meet?' says Hardy, in the same tone he uses in the interview room. He's right, thinks Ellie, he's *not* an Alec.

'Through the job,' she says. 'Joe used to be a paramedic.'

'Not any more?' he asks and she braces herself for the judgement.

'Gave it up when Fred came along,' says Joe. 'I was getting a bit jaded anyway. Too much red tape, stuff that stopped us being able to help people, masquerading as Health and Safety.'

Joe's drinking quickly; even if it weren't for his rapidly emptying glass, Ellie would know by the way his accent comes crawling out of the shadows.

'Where you from, originally?' says Hardy.

'Cardiff. Moved down here thirteen years ago for the work. I met Ellie, and the rest is history. You married?'

Hardy swallows. 'Great food. Make this yourself?'

'Self-taught,' says Joe. 'Mexican's my speciality. We should really be having margaritas.'

'No,' says Hardy.

'Not margaritas?'

'Not married. Not any more.' It's the first Ellie's heard of a wife.

'I'm sorry to hear that,' says Joe. 'What was it, pressures of work?'

'Sort of. This job does it to you.'

'Not to us!' says Ellie brightly. She'll be damned if she ends up like Hardy in any respect.

'Any kids?' asks Joe. Red wine has painted an exaggerated smile on his lips.

'I've got a daughter,' says Hardy, to Ellie's astonishment. Joe's got more out of Hardy in five bites of chimichanga than she's managed in over a week. 'She's fifteen. She lives with her mother.'

She tries to imagine Hardy as a father. 'Dad' no more suits him than 'Alec'. As for 'Daddy' . . . forget it.

Hardy swigs his wine. She hopes that Joe will be sensitive enough to put him out of his misery and she feels a rush of love for him when he changes the subject.

'You think you're gonna solve this case?'

Hardy seems almost relieved to be back on the safe neutral ground of murdered children. 'Certain.'

'Good,' says Joe. He pours more wine. Hardy puts his hand over his glass.

'I'm not supposed to—'

'Shuddup and drink.' They've finished the first bottle already – nerves – and by the time Ellie comes back from the kitchen with the second, they're *laughing*. Clearly they've created some private joke in the ten seconds it's taken her to uncork the Pinot. She's annoyed with Joe now. She wanted him to bond with Hardy, but not at her expense.

Later, when he goes to leave, she tries to get him a taxi but he's not having any of it.

'Walk'll be good,' he says. 'See you in the morning. This was nice. Thanks, Miller.'

They manage not to laugh until he's out of earshot.

'I love you, *Miller*,' slurs Joe.

'Don't you start,' she says. 'You and your new bloody little mate.'

Maggie taps away at her computer with a glass of wine to hand and her electronic cigarette resting on her mouse mat. Even Olly has finally admitted exhaustion and gone home, leaving absolute quiet behind. Olly has his own little repertoire of noises. He's always tapping: his pen on the edge of the desk, his fingers over the keyboard or, more likely, on the screen of his phone. He bounces on his chair and makes it squeak. Maggie is always aware of him in the periphery of her hearing. Sometimes he's an irritation, but more often than not he's a comfort, and his absence has put her on edge.

The usual white noise of an August evening is missing, too. There is nobody on the street, no drunken arguments to reassure her that life is still going on as normal outside, not so much as a single footstep. Maggie shudders. Silence has always freaked her out. Give her hustle and bustle over silence any day. It's when it's quiet that the bad stuff happens.

She rises from her desk, links her fingers and stretches her arms above her head. Then she looks over the darkened newsroom. Her domain does not offer its usual comforts. This story has got under her skin in a way that no other has.

Of course child murder is as bad as it gets, but Maggie hasn't got kids so why does she feel such acute fear? Why is she taking it personally? Not even working the Yorkshire Ripper story – which is still, thirty-odd years later, the most savage and gruesome crime she's ever covered – shook her up like this. She's still keeping it together at work, but Lil knows how hard she's taking it.

It's partly because it's happened to Beth, lovely Beth who she saw every day at work. But more than that, it's because it's home. It's because whatever happens – whether they catch the killer or not – Broadchurch will never be the same after this. It has changed already. No one is unaffected, from the small business owners who won't survive this slow summer to the parents who haven't slept since it happened, the single blokes who find themselves suddenly drinking alone in the pub. And then there's the children. Who knows what all of this is doing to the children?

The silence around Maggie builds and grows.

She has worked herself up into a fever of speculation when the telephone on her desk shrills. Maggie rushes to answer it, her pulse fast in her fingertips. It's Lil, asking when she's going to be home. She can't quite hide her disappointment when Maggie tells her it's going to be another late one. She's been dropping hints lately about Maggie taking early retirement. She's been with the same newspaper group for over thirty years, and a bloody good pension awaits her. Maggie has always insisted they'll have to drag her out of the *Broadchurch Echo* kicking and screaming (that's actually happened to a few of her colleagues in the provincial press lately, even generous redundancy not enough to soften the blow of a closing paper). But now, for the first time, alone in a darkened newsroom, Maggie gives retirement serious consideration. She is tired, and she is constantly anxious.

Maybe. But not now. She will see this story through to its conclusion. She takes a sip of her wine and a drag of her fag, palms her dry eyes and returns to the screen. A loud noise, like the bang of a door or something falling, makes her jump in her seat. Creeping out of her office, her eyes are unaccustomed to the relative darkness and she peers into the pitch. Turning on the main lights confirms that she's alone. She smiles to herself, visibly relieved. The lights are flicked off, and she goes back to her computer.

'Why're you so bothered about me?'

Maggie wheels around to see Susan Wright standing in the corner of her office. Small eyes glitter dangerously in an otherwise expressionless face. Maggie's heart hurls itself against her ribs.

'How did you get in here?' Maggie asks, though she knows the answer. She's always had an open-door policy at the *Echo* – the best stories about a community come *from* the community, after all – and too late, she sees the folly of it. There's a murderer on the loose, for Christ's sake. Why wasn't it bolted from top to bottom? She curses her own naivety as she presses herself against the far wall.

Susan takes a step closer. 'You're gonna stop asking questions about me.'

'Why would I do that?' A tremble in Maggie's voice undermines the words.

Susan curls her lip. 'I know about you.'

Maggie might be afraid, but she isn't fazed by this one-size-fits-all threat. There's not that much to know and nothing she's ashamed of. Is that all you've got? she thinks, and she's about to say it when Susan leans forward. Instinctively Maggie recoils from the whiff of stale tobacco. Now Susan's breath is hot in Maggie's ear. 'I know men who would rape you.'

She lets her threat – as convincing as it is unexpected – hang heavy in the air between them for a long time. Images of the Ripper case, never too far from her subconscious, assault Maggie's memory and her breathing turns shallow. Susan doesn't blink. 'And if you start asking questions, or go to the police, they'll come after your *mate* as well.'

Without another word, Susan disappears back into the darkness. Heavy footsteps echo as she crosses the newsroom. The door bangs closed behind her.

Maggie is left shaking and alone. She picks up the phone to call Ellie Miller. She's got Broadchurch CID on speed-dial. It only takes one button but her forefinger quivers above it for nearly a minute and eventually she has to accept that she can't do it. She can't take a chance. Lil knew, when they got together, that late nights, cancelled holidays and a large wine bill were part of the deal, but she didn't ask for any of this.

She drops the receiver back in its cradle and a tear oozes its way out of her eye. Maggie is crying with shame as well as fear. She doesn't recognise herself. It's this bloody story. It has changed her on a deeper level than she realised.

No one and nothing around here will ever be the same again.

*

The wine was a mistake. It's all Hardy can do to put one foot in front of the other. On the High Street a lone figure emerges from the *Broadchurch Echo* office but his vision blurs before he can even determine whether it's a man or a woman. Somehow he makes it through the hotel reception and up the stairs without being intercepted. He's drenched in sweat by the time he crashes into the bedroom and through to the en suite where his medication is.

Vertigo turns the little bathroom into a hall of mirrors, walls seeming to curve and the surfaces to tilt at crazy angles. Vision failing, he feels for the blister pack of pills but it's empty. Where are the spares? Where the fuck are his spare pills? Hardy's last thought, as he gives into gravity, is of the packet in his desk drawer at work. He cracks the back of his head on the bath as he falls. Darkness is instant and total.

30

There is a pure white line of light above Hardy. An angel appears before him, a dazzling aureole edging her golden hair. Then the angel speaks with an Australian accent. 'It's all right,' says Becca Fisher. 'We're getting you to the hospital.' The white light suddenly reveals itself as the neon strip on an ambulance ceiling and Hardy tries to protest. Once they get him into hospital that's it, it's over. They'll take one look at his records and they won't let him out again. But the words won't come, and he goes under again.

When he wakes up, his head throbs violently and there's a sharp pain in the back of his hand where the drip's going in. Becca Fisher is at his bedside: Hardy is suddenly acutely aware that he's naked beneath a hospital gown.

'Nine stitches,' she says, setting aside her newspaper. 'Took quite a crack. How're you going?'

'What am I doing here?' he croaks. 'What're *you* doing here?'

'You passed out. I found you on the bathroom floor. The person in the room under you heard the noise. Luckily.' She holds up his wallet and his heart contracts painfully: she's got it open on the little girl's picture. Suddenly nudity seems like the preferable option. 'This your daughter? She's pretty.' She doesn't give him a chance to answer. 'I was looking for your next of kin. I couldn't find any, so I told them I was your wife. Look, I'm glad you're OK and awake but I have to get back.'

Hardy thinks quickly. If they still think she's his wife, maybe they'll let him go with her. He tries to get out of bed. It's much harder than he imagined. The pain in his head doubles, as though he's left part of his skull behind on the pillow. He stumbles a little and tries to clutch at her hand.

'You can't tell anyone about this. This is my *life*,' he begs. 'Promise. They'll take me off the case. I *need* to finish this case, Becca.'

He's almost surprised to see her give it real consideration. She glances at the newspaper on the bed and whatever she sees seems to make up her mind.

'On one condition: you get some proper medical help. 'Cause next time, someone might not find you.'

'Thank you,' he nods. He'll agree to anything right now. Becca gets up to leave. 'Can I have the paper?'

She hands him her copy of the *Daily Herald* on her way out.

MY DANNY, shouts the front page. EXCLUSIVE INTERVIEW WITH MOTHER OF TRAGIC DORSET BOY. Danny's face beams out. Karen White's picture accompanies her byline, the hack's holy grail. He hopes she's happy with herself.

Hardy opens the paper to find a double-page spread dominated not by Danny's picture but by Beth's, eyelashes batting at the lens. WHO WOULD TAKE MY BEAUTI-FUL BOY FROM ME? she pleads in big block letters.

His eye is drawn to the boxed-off text on the right-hand page and his cracked skull feels like it is going to fall away from his brain.

DANNY: SANDBROOK LINK

There's a ten-line précis of what happened at the trial and a picture of Pippa, in case they all needed reminding.

So this is what Karen White was waiting for: save it all up for one big splash. The gloves are off: the word is out. In a fucked-up way, it's almost a relief. He grudgingly admires Karen White's dedication to the Sandbrook families. She's a pain in his arse, but you can't say she doesn't care. She'd probably make a good copper.

Sometimes a story comes together perfectly. Karen's phone vibrates with messages of congratulation from colleagues, swiftly followed by ill-disguised attempts to steal her contacts. She's doubly glad now she got to Olly Stevens first. His head might be turned by any one of the reporters currently on the 8.03 from Waterloo. To make sure, she invites him to breakfast in the Traders.

'It's great,' he says over his eggs Benedict. 'Captures Beth just right. But you know Maggie's going to be pretty miffed.'

Karen's not so sure. Maggie, like her, has Beth Latimer's best interests at heart and will be well aware that one line in a national like the *Herald* is worth twenty pages in the *Echo*.

'I'll talk to her,' says Karen. 'Beth and Mark were desperate for people to know about the case. Think of the witnesses who might come forward. You'll have to lean on

Ellie, see if you can get an idea of how busy their phones are today.'

There's the usual uncomfortable silence that arises whenever Karen suggests that Ollie exploit his relationship with the DS on the case. 'Well,' he says eventually, 'Hardy certainly isn't going to talk to us now.' But he's smiling. 'So you're the golden girl on your newsdesk, are you?'

'The boss is officially happy,' says Karen. Danvers didn't actually tell her off, which is the next best thing. 'And the rest of the papers are scrambling to catch up in the later editions. But the *Herald* has to own the story now. They're asking what's the follow-up? Who's in the frame? We should talk about Jack Marshall.'

Their phones both beep at the same time. Olly glances at his and his face goes white. 'I've got to go,' he says, pushing back his chair and leaving the remainder of his breakfast untouched.

Karen doesn't have time to wonder what he's up to: she is distracted by the message on her own screen. It's a text from Cate Gillespie:

Saw today's paper. I cried my heart out for that poor mother.
    Thank you for mentioning Pippa; it keeps her memory alive.
    It's so good to know you're still fighting our corner.
    Keep in touch. C x

Olly drives home so quickly that he almost takes the bend into their street on two wheels. He parks a few doors down from his house because the space directly outside is blocked

197

by a huge van, a removals lorry really. Two gigantic men, all in black like nightclub bouncers, are taking the HD television and putting it in the back. He looks over their shoulders and cries in dismay to see his bike and his scooter impounded, along with his entire DVD library. He glances at the car where his laptop lies on the back seat. He knows from last time, and the time before that, that they're not legally allowed to take anything he needs for work. They better not have had the printer.

'Don't be brave, son,' says the taller of the two bailiffs, as though Olly was dancing around him with his fists up. Olly has no intention of being brave; not in that sense, anyway. But it does take courage to ring the only person who might be able to help them out.

'They're here again,' he says when Ellie picks up. 'They've taken my Vespa this time.'

'Oh, Oliver,' she says. 'Is she still in Bournemouth?'

He looks through the net curtains to see a thin figure inside. 'She's here,' he says. 'Ellie, I hate to ask, but is there any way you could—'

'No.' She cuts him dead.

'She's really sorry,' he improvises.

'Is she bollocks,' says Ellie. 'I'm sorry, this is tough love. I'm sorry about your stuff, but I can't keep bailing her out. Not after she—' She stops herself mid-sentence.

'I wish you'd talk to her. You've never fallen out like this before.'

Ellie's tone is uncharacteristically harsh. 'Oliver, I'm in the middle of a murder investigation, and I haven't got any money *left*. I'm sorry, I've got to go.'

The line goes dead.

Olly follows the smaller bailiff back into the house. Lucy is twisting her fingers in the now empty sitting room. Wires dangle from the wall where the television has been taken. She looks helpless as they take the Sky box, but as they unplug the wireless router she springs into life.

'Don't take that!' she says, trying to grab it from the bailiff. 'It's not worth anything! What'll you get for that, couple of quid on eBay?'

Olly prises it from her fingers and hands it to the bailiff.

'Take it,' he says. 'Just fucking take it.'

Once the repo men are gone, he rounds on Lucy.

'For God's sake!' he says. 'You said you'd fixed it!'

'It's a mix-up,' says Lucy. 'They've got it wrong ... oh, don't do that face, you look like your bloody father when you do that.'

For a moment Olly looks as though he's going to hit her. Then the fight goes out of him.

'Mum, when is this going to stop?' he asks. 'Why don't you understand the trouble we're in?'

31

Ellie Miller lies in the dark watching her digital alarm clock chew its way through the numbers. Saturday night turns into Sunday morning. One, two, three, four a.m. come and go. She is exhausted but the unaccustomed stimulant of guilt keeps her awake. She has done the wrong thing by two people she cares about.

One is minor – or, if not minor, then spontaneous at least. Olly caught her off guard but she mustn't let Lucy ruin their relationship too. The way she let Beth down runs deeper. It is unforgivable that she had to find out about Hardy's history from journalists. Now Ellie grills herself remorselessly about exactly why she kept the information back. Was she really waiting to find the right time, or was she just afraid of Beth's face when she told her? It was naivety or cowardice: both are unforgivable. She knows she won't sleep until she's sorted it. She heaves herself on to one side and retrieves her phone from the bedside table. Joe stirs and mumbles beside her so she mutes the keypad and turns down the brightness. She writes to Olly first.

Didn't mean to be snappy. Stress of the case.

I hope you know I'm always here for you, no matter what's going on between me and your mum.

Auntie E. Xx

The one to Beth is harder to write.

I should have told you about the Sandbrook thing and I'm sorry.

I did the wrong thing for the right reasons; I was trying to protect you but I should've been straight with you.

Let's talk soon. Call whenever you want to. Ell. Xx

As soon as she is satisfied, her eyelids grow heavy with the release of a guilty conscience eased. She sets the phone down, the messages waiting patiently to be sent in the morning. The last time she remembers looking at the clock it is 5.14 a.m.

She wakes again at 9.10. It's hot outside and the world is up early. Soft Sunday sounds float through the open bedroom window: birdsong, the kids in the garden, a distant lawnmower. Not that Ellie will get to potter around today. She is due in the station at ten: Beth and Mark are taking part in a press conference that evening and Hardy wants all hands on deck. Ellie hits the send button on last night's apologies, then stands under the shower and tries to wake up.

Joe is on his hands and knees in the sitting room, wiping slug trails from the rug. She runs a hand over the velour of his head, and he reaches up to catch her hand and hold it there for a moment.

'Hey, I was thinking about taking Tom to church this morning,' he says.

'Church?' They don't really do spirituality. 'Why?'

He looks almost shy. 'I don't know. Just ... felt ... the thing. Know what I mean?'

It's funny but she does. 'You take the boys,' she says. 'I'll see if Hardy will give me special dispensation.'

She's used to the boss looking rough but he's taken it to a new level this morning. She circles him slowly and freezes when she sees the back of his head. His hair is matted with blood and are those *stitches*? He didn't have that much to drink last night, surely?

'Jesus, what happened to you? You look terrible, if you don't mind me saying.'

'Slipped in the shower last night,' he says in a tone that closes the conversation. 'Seen the *Herald*?'

'Yeah,' she says. 'I didn't know the Latimers had done that. We had Pete out on backup statements, must've happened then.'

'They've opened the floodgates,' says Hardy. There's resignation where she was expecting fury, as though he'd been anticipating this all along. 'Media officer's been deluged with calls. As you know, we've called a conference for this evening, a family statement. Try and keep as much control as we can. Meantime, I need full background on Jack Marshall, Steve Connolly and Paul Coates. Anyone without alibis goes to the top of our list.'

'I'll get Nish and Frank on it,' says Ellie. 'Can I ask a favour?' she adds, bracing herself for Hardy's rebuttal. 'I was thinking of going to church ...'

'Good idea. Everyone all together. Chance to check on who's behaving normally.'

That wasn't the idea, but never mind.

Ellie picks Joe and the boys up on the way to St Andrew's. It's a beautiful morning; hot and hazy. The bells are ringing and butterflies throng the buddleia at the roadsides. She falls into step behind the Latimers, who are looking fixedly ahead.

There's a wall of photographers, like something outside a courtroom. They're all shouting at Beth like she's Princess Diana.

'Beth! Beth! Over here!'

Beth is a rabbit in the headlights. Mark's doing his best – 'Will you let us through, lads?' – but they're not taking that for an answer. Beth can't take this and she doesn't deserve it. Ellie goes on to autopilot: she's acting like a copper but also as a friend.

'Away, now, or I'll have you all arrested.' She shoves her warrant card up close to the nearest lens.

'We're not breaking the law,' says the ratty little man behind the camera.

'Have a bit of bloody decency,' she says. She puts herself between the family and the photographers. Let them get a picture of her, another angry mum, she doesn't care. It's not her family that's been ripped apart. She lets the Latimers creep past behind her. One photographer raises his camera.

'Lenses down. Or I kick you in the balls. Each one of you.' She turns to Tom. 'You didn't hear me say that.' She turns back to the photographers. 'But I really will.'

'Your mum's awesome,' says Chloe behind her.

'I know,' replies Tom.

Beth looks at Ellie with gratitude. 'Come for lunch today,' she says, as they file into the nave. 'Nige is cooking.'

The olive branch is welcome but unexpected. 'You sure?'

'Like we always do,' says Mark firmly.

Ellie says yes, even though she's supposed to be working. Hardy can't force her to do more overtime – although, knowing him, he'd have her spying on her friends over Sunday lunch.

She has never seen the church so busy, not even for weddings or funerals. When Paul Coates comes out of the vestry in his robes, Ellie starts; she's used to seeing the dog collar but not the whole flowing Gandalf bit. He looks nervy and excited, like a pub singer who suddenly finds himself playing Wembley Stadium.

Becca Fisher's high heels clack on the flagstones; after Beth stares her down, she tucks herself discreetly in the corner.

Jack Marshall genuflects before taking a seat with a good view of the altar. Nige, one row in front of the Latimers, turns around to catch Mark's eye, then looks meaningfully at Jack. They know something, or they think they do. Ellie resolves to have a word with them at lunch. Between Mark's temper and Nige's lack of control, she doesn't like how this could pan out. She thinks about the split lip and the pub fight. She remembers now a football-pitch disagreement that would have turned into a brawl if Joe and Bob hadn't been there to calm Mark down, and recasts that moment in the light of what she has since learned about Mark. If he can lose it over trivial things, what might he be capable of in grief?

All heads turn when Hardy walks in, looking like something that's just crawled out of the graveyard. It's his first public appearance since Karen White's piece in the *Herald*. Someone tuts loudly and an old woman in the next pew actually hisses.

'Didn't know he was religious,' says Joe.

'Didn't know *we* were,' Ellie flashes back.

She was expecting to start with a hymn or a prayer or some incense or something, but Reverend Paul seems to have gone off-script. 'Thank you for coming,' he says as he takes the pulpit. Electric candles glow softly on either side. 'I was thinking how to start. I found this, in Corinthians: "We are pressed on every side by troubles, but we are not crushed. We are perplexed, but not driven to despair. We are hunted down, but never abandoned by God. We are knocked down, but we are not destroyed." As a community, the hardest thing for us is to remember, we have not been abandoned by God. We are not destroyed. Nor will we be.'

Ellie's mobile vibrates in her pocket. She knows it's bad form to use your phone in church but she slides it out as surreptitiously as she can. It's a text from Hardy. In the last few minutes, SOCO have confirmed that the hairs in the boat are Danny's.

32

It's barbecue weather really but Nige wants to cook a Sunday roast, so a roast it will be. The stove is rammed with saucepans, and steam curls around him. Mark pulls the dining table to its fullest extension and brings in the patio chairs. In the garden he uses the hose to rinse down the kids' old high chair they always use for Fred Miller.

Beth lays the table with a rock-heavy heart. This evening, she and Mark are due to make a television appeal for help. What are they thinking, having everyone over, stuffing their faces, drinking wine, pretending everything is normal? She doesn't have to reach deep for the answer. If the house is full of people, she doesn't have to confront Mark about Becca Fisher. Whenever she thinks about it, a scream rises up from her belly, but for the time being she's managed to suppress it. She can feel it now, crouching in the base of her throat, like a tiger waiting to pounce.

'That's quite a spread, Nige!' says Liz. 'You'll make someone a lovely husband one day.'

'They'll have to catch me first, Liz,' says Nige, as if he's beating the girls off with a stick.

The Millers usually burst in through the patio doors waving bottles, but today they ring the front doorbell. It's a nice gesture and Ellie's remorse about hiding DI Hardy's Sandbrook connection from her is plain. Beth is slowly coming round to her explanation that it was done for her own protection, and after the way she had a go at the paparazzi, their friendship is back on its old safe footing. She hugs Ellie hello and holds it for a second longer than usual to emphasise her forgiveness. It's a relief to let the anger go.

After a couple of dropped pans and a bit of swearing, Nige is ready to serve. The Latimers and the Millers squash around the table in a parody of normality. Beth feels like she's watching it all from outside her own body as Nige sits at the head of the table and carves the lamb, smiling goofily at the chorus of appreciation. Everyone's talking a bit too loudly but for Beth the absence of Danny's voice is an echoing silence, as conspicuous as an empty chair. It hurts her ears when Tom speaks, a one-sided prattle about his new Xbox game that Danny will never get to play.

Every time she looks up, Mark is staring at her and if it's not him it's her mum or Ellie. She feels their eyes, worse than the photographers' lenses. She is overcome by the desire to disappear. Not to die – one look at Chloe sends that thought back to the shadows it came from – but to go away for a while. Out of this life and into someone else's.

Still, she eats. Her appetite is coming back in ways that have nothing to do with her. She falls on the lamb and the potatoes: she wants meat, fat, iron and carbs. The parasite is making its presence felt.

Mark's plate is virtually untouched. Joe, topping up the wine glasses, lays a supportive hand on his friend's shoulder and Chloe reaches for her dad's hand and squeezes it. Beth is momentarily shocked out of her own grief and into Mark's. Then anger eclipses her sympathy, and the scream shifts closer to her lips.

The plates are cleared – no one will let her lift a finger – and Tom disappears to the toilet before the apple crumble and custard come out. Beth slips away while the others are passing bowls and spoons around. She is waiting for Tom when he comes out of the downstairs loo.

'All right, sweetheart?' she says. His eyes dart around, looking for help. He can sense what's inside Beth: the need that pours out of her like smoke from an oven.

'Yep,' he says. 'You OK?'

'Can I ask you something? You can say no.' Tom looks suspicious, frightened even and there's no need, it's such a simple and harmless thing she needs from him. 'Can I have a hug?'

Sweet, soft little Tom; she can see him swallow his awkwardness and embarrassment in his desire to make her happy. She opens her arms to him and wraps him tight. He smells all wrong, the wrong fabric conditioner and shampoo and the wrong base note, the wrong hair and skin, but it will do, he's the right size and so warm. 'I miss his hugs,' she says. Tom seems to squirm but even that reminds her of Danny. Just as Tom is beginning to hug her back, the doorbell chimes and he leaps from her arms.

'I'd best get that,' she says. Tom can't get back to the dining table fast enough. Beth can't decide if she feels better or worse.

Jack Marshall is at the door, unexpected but then so is everything now. She waves him into the living room, wondering if he's eaten. He's not exactly the life and soul, but it seems rude not to ask. There is plenty of food left and they can squeeze one more place setting around the table. She's about to ask Jack, but something in the way he's holding himself – perfectly upright – tells her this isn't a social call after all.

When Beth steps aside to reveal their guest, Mark jumps up from his chair, almost upsetting his plate. 'Everything all right?' he asks. His cold manner suggests the opposite. Beth looks to Ellie; she is ashen.

'I found this,' replies Jack, uncurling his palm to reveal a small black box. Beth leans in and then jumps back. It's a phone. Danny's battered old Nokia. 'I heard a beeping coming from the delivery bags. I found this at the bottom. He must've left it on his last round. The battery was going, that's what the beeping was.'

Ellie flies across the room in her haste to retrieve the phone but it's too late: it's gone from Jack's hand to Mark's. She all but snatches it from Mark: he holds it for a fraction too long before releasing it. She wraps it carefully in a paper napkin.

Mark's voice is measured, *too* measured. 'Why've you got this, Jack?'

The old man looks at them all in turn. 'Mark, Beth, they're going to say things about me. And those things aren't true.'

Beth's stomach contracts around the greasy paste in her stomach. What the hell is going on? Ellie doesn't look surprised and neither does Mark. She feels her gorge rise.

'Get him out,' Ellie orders Liz, who is clearly as much out of the loop as Beth is. Still, she does what she's told, gently guiding Jack to the front door.

'Something happened before I was here,' he says over his shoulder. 'And they'll be saying I did it. I'm looking you in the eye, because he was your boy, and I'm telling you I'm not that kind of man.' There's a commotion outside and the now-familiar click of camera shutters starts up. Joe Miller pulls the living-room curtain closed. 'Please believe me,' pleads Jack Marshall, as he steps into the barrage of press. 'Beth. Mark. You have to believe me.'

Before Beth can process what's happened, there's another click and a flash from the opposite direction. All heads turn to look at the back garden, where a photographer on a ladder peers over the back fence. Seconds later, another head appears at his side. They've got the house surrounded.

'*Bastards*,' says Mark, making a run for the back garden, Joe and Nige at his heels. 'Get out!' he roars. 'Go on! Before I smash all that!'

He doesn't get a chance to make good his threats. Joe charges at the fence with the garden hose in his hand. He lets a cannon of water fly over the fence, drenching the photographers. The mood shifts suddenly; the men's laughter is catching: even little Fred is cheering. 'Genius!' says Mark, clapping Joe on the back.

The lightness is short-lived. 'What've we done to ourselves, eh?' says Mark. This, realises Beth, is the consequence of talking to the press. These are the floodgates that Ellie warned them not to open. They issued the invitation themselves.

But floodgates work both ways. Finally, eleven days after Danny was left on the beach, a proper press conference has been called.

It is the first time Beth has been back to South Wessex Primary since that morning. The playing field where she brought his lunchbox, where Beth knew her last few seconds of peace, is sunbleached and empty now. Beth can't bear to look at it, but inside it's worse: this is the school hall where she watched assemblies, nativity plays, end-of-year concerts. She used to perch on these undersized chairs, camera phone in hand, recording Danny's off-key singing. Now she is on stage in a performance no parent should ever have to give, sitting behind a black cloth between her husband and daughter as Pete pins microphones to their collars. Karen White is in the front row. Beth mouths a 'thank you' to her and gets a warm, encouraging smile in return.

'Why do they need all of us?' asks Chloe. She is pale with nerves: her freckles stand out even under thick make-up.

'So people understand how much losing Danny meant to us,' says Mark. 'How strong a family we are.'

His hypocrisy is more than Beth can take. The tiger crouching in her throat will not stand for this, but now is not the time to free the scream. Instead, Beth leans in to her husband and whispers, so quietly that only he can hear her: 'I know about you and Becca Fisher.'

Her words gouge lines on his face, giving her a rush of

sick satisfaction. There's a buzz of feedback as the microphones go live, a storm of flashbulbs, and they're on.

Not much grows in the modest yard behind Jack Marshall's house on the edge of the beach. The paved area is cluttered with boating paraphernalia, frayed ropes and broken machinery. An old metal bin serves as a brazier. Jack watches as the flames lick the air.

A battered cardboard box stands on a warped wooden table. From it Jack takes a pile of photographs and sifts slowly through them. Boys in their swimming trunks. Danny changing out of a wetsuit. Jack with his arms around Tom Miller. These pictures did not make it on to Danny's memorial wall outside the Sea Brigade hut.

In amongst these is another picture which makes Jack catch his breath: with shaking hands he puts it to his lips and kisses it, letting his eyes close for a long time. When at last he opens them, it's to stare at the photograph some more, as if debating what to do with it. Finally he secretes it in his pocket.

The rest of the pictures he throws into the smoking brazier. The glossy paper burns slowly at first, then quickly. Ashy flakes swirl around Jack and settle in sooty deposits on his collar. The picture of Danny with no top on is the last to go, curling at the edges before shrivelling to nothing.

33

It is eleven o'clock on an August night but Broadchurch is a ghost town. No cars pass by. No drinkers spill from the pubs. The restaurants are empty. White fairy lights twinkle on the box trees outside the Traders Hotel but the terrace is deserted.

A lone child stands at the top of the High Street, skateboard under his arm. He's wearing a thin grey T-shirt, black jeans and blue trainers with a yellow flash. He sets down his skateboard, steps on and glides down the dead centre of the empty street. The rumble of plastic wheels on tarmac is the only sound.

But his hair is blond, not brown. This is Tom Miller, not Danny Latimer. And despite the late hour, he is not alone.

A procession of adults follow. Ellie Miller heads the sad little parade, her eyes never leaving Tom. Alec Hardy and a handful of officers watch everyone *but* Tom.

The Latimers are there, distraught but strong, hands held in solidarity.

Nige tags along behind Mark.

Reverend Paul Coates is not far behind, his professional, sombre face on.

Joe Miller pushes a sleeping Fred in his buggy.

Karen White walks alone.

As Tom passes, people emerge from doorways to watch him. Olly Stevens and Maggie Radcliffe stand side by side outside the *Broadchurch Echo*, then fall into step with the others at the rear.

Becca appears in the doorway of the Traders. She catches Mark's eye and a look of sorrow passes between them before they can stop it. Beth notices and drops Mark's hand. Becca lowers her gaze and steps back into the shadows.

Susan Wright and Vince watch from a distance like a witch and her familiar.

Beth turns to Ellie. 'Tell me this'll make a difference,' she begs.

Ellie threads her arm through Beth's. 'I'm sure it will.'

Tom rounds the corner towards the harbour. Union flags and bunting flutter noisily, competing with the sea's roar. Tom hits the cobbles and the clatter of his wheels drowns out everything else. A news crew, their camera balanced on a dolly grip, trundle after him as he passes the chip shop.

Beth blinks away tears. 'I can't bear to think of him, out here alone, this time of night.'

Tom cruises past the newsagent's. Jack Marshall is outside, hair lank around his shoulders and soot dusting his collar. He mutters the Lord's Prayer under his breath. 'And lead us not into temptation,' he murmurs, 'but deliver us from Evil.'

Mark Latimer falls into step with Hardy. 'Do you think it's him?' he asks.

'I'm not speculating about anyone,' says Hardy, but he doesn't take his eyes off the old man.

'You might not be, but everyone else is,' says Mark. 'They'll calm down as soon as you arrest someone.'

At the jetty, Tom skids to a halt. They are now in the territory that CCTV does not cover, and they have re-enacted the last of Danny's known movements. He jumps down from his skateboard and turns to look at his parents, who nod their pride and approval. Tom gives a weak smile of relief.

Jack Marshall's hands are clasped so tightly in prayer that the bones glow through his skin. 'For thine is the kingdom,' he intones, 'the power and the glory, now and for ever. Amen.'

Eleven thirty p.m. and CID is buzzing after the reconstruction. DS Ellie Miller is wide awake. While she was out, Frank put up a list of boats reported missing in the last month. There are no matches; nothing even comes close.

She goes through the next file. More notes from Forensics, and they're hard going. She is the wrong kind of alert: she's too wired to concentrate and it won't go in. If only she had a spare hard drive that she could plug into her brain. She worries that she simply can't retain this much information, that some vital clue will go unnoticed. She takes a deep breath and starts the file again from page one.

They've got the prints back on the phone that Jack Marshall gave them. Something about that phone's been bugging Ellie since she saw it in Jack Marshall's hand, and she realises now, realised when she saw Tom with his phone earlier. She's puzzled because although Mark confirmed that this was Danny's phone, *she* always saw Danny with a smartphone, the same as Tom's. They even got different covers in case they got muddled up.

There's no data to be retrieved from the bog-standard one they've got. No texts, contacts or call logs. It's set to forward all calls and texts to another number – a pay-as-you-go SIM card, turned off so there's no signal. She puts it on the grid anyway. If it turns up they need to be able to move fast. She scoots across the office on her chair to bring Hardy up to date. The wound on the back of his head has been cleaned up, but the rest of him is still a mess. His shirtsleeves have been shoved up to his elbows and sweat patches yellow his armpits.

'Mark's fingerprints were on the phone, but he handled it, I saw him do it, he took it off Jack at the house. And Danny's DNA. And Jack Marshall's, too. Although that tallies with him finding it.'

She can almost see the light bulb ignite over Hardy's head. 'Or Jack *claimed* to find it because he knew his DNA was already on it,' he says. 'Why does a kid his age have two phones? How could he afford this other one?'

'The cash we found in his room?' suggests Ellie.

'Could that money have come from Jack Marshall?' asks Hardy. 'You know him, what do you think?'

Ellie doesn't feel she knows anyone outside her own front door any more.

'He had regular contact with Danny,' she considers, 'but what's his motive? Anyway, Danny was asphyxiated. Jack's frail. I can't see him dragging a body two miles down the coast.'

'Accomplice?' Hardy fires back. 'We don't know there's only one killer. You talk to your son at the end tonight?'

The last thing Ellie wants is to discuss Tom's emotional state with Hardy.

'A bit,' she says. 'He just wanted to get home.'

'He's a good lad,' says Hardy, throwing a file down on to her desk. 'Tell him from me: he did right by Danny.'

To Ellie's shame, her eyes start to well. She can handle the relentless sarcasm and the impatience. But kindness from DI Hardy? It's more than she can bear.

34

Unlike Alec Hardy's investigation room, the *Broadchurch Echo* does not have a clean-desk policy. Karen and Olly, going hard after Jack Marshall, are drowning in paperwork. Every surface is awash with Post-its, web printouts, newspapers and notes spilling from box files. It seems to multiply when they're not looking, as do the dirty mugs that pile up around them.

They are alone in the office. Maggie's ill or something: she's been in a strange mood all day, snappy and vague, forgoing her usual long walk home in favour of getting Lil to come and pick her up in the car. Olly's worried about her but Karen feels liberated; with Maggie gone, she can do things her way.

'Anything interesting?' she asks. Olly rummages noisily through loose pages until he finds a picture of Jack with his arms round a Sea Brigade boy.

'I'm going to dig out the original,' he says, handing it to Karen and taking the photograph she gives him in return. It's a picture of Jack looking angry on the threshold of the Latimer house.

'Wow,' he whistles. 'Where'd you get this?' Karen is gratified by his response. She got the picture exclusive herself, inviting the photographer to her hotel and making an offer on behalf of the *Herald*. When the story made the *News At Ten*, Danvers all but gave her a blank chequebook.

'Why'd he go to their house?' asks Olly.

'*Exactly*,' says Karen. 'OK. Four hundred words on the reconstruction and then, main article, the exclusive, everything you dug up on Jack, especially his previous convictions. Write it up.'

'Me?' Olly looks equally delighted and terrified. 'I've never written for a national.'

'Look at your little face! Of course you. You did the work, you write the article. They can run it under my byline, it'll be our secret.'

She keeps Olly topped up with tea and biscuits, watching surreptitiously over his shoulder as he types. He's making some rookie mistakes – not mentioning Marshall's age until the end of the piece, neglecting to mention how close his house is to the beach – but he's got all the facts, asking questions, there's a clear point of view and nothing's sensationalised. Karen thinks fondly back to her own apprenticeship, learning on the job as seasoned Fleet Street hacks taught her how to be a reporter, line by line. Most of the kids coming up through the newsrooms now don't know how to write an original report. It feels good to hand the old skills on, even if they are on their way out.

She motions for Olly to pull his chair close to hers. She can feel his breath on her cheek as she edits the piece, hard. He's crestfallen at first, but she talks him through the reason for each cut-and-paste and by the end he's grinning with the delight of what she's done to his piece. 'That is brilliant, it's *loads* better. You've smashed it,' he says.

'Shall we press send?'

He hits the button himself, happy as a little kid being allowed to play on his mum's computer.

Karen is more guarded. It's good copy. But that doesn't guarantee it'll make tomorrow's paper. They are still at the mercy of Len Danvers' whim and of course the news itself, which doesn't respect her commitment to this story. Who knows which other stories are creeping up on the inside lane? Karen is losing track of what's happening in the outside world.

She is so lost in thought that she barely registers the small shifting movement at her side. When Olly lunges to kiss her, she recoils in shock rather than distaste.

'Sorry.' Olly is mortified. 'It's just . . . I've been wanting to do that ever since you first walked in.' His olive skin flushes.

'You cheeky bastard!' says Karen, to cover how flattered she is. 'We're working here.'

'Sorry. It was inappropriate.' But there's no denying the tingle his lips left on hers.

'Yeah,' says Karen. 'It was.' A second later, she's kissing him back.

Four hours after the press conference and Beth is already used to seeing her own face, drawn and tear-stained, on the television. Danny is the top story every half-hour. What's weird is how quickly it stops being weird. This is how it should be: this is what he deserves.

When midnight comes and goes, and yawns distort the

screen, Beth and Mark go up to bed. Automatically she turns the bedroom television on, too, volume on low so as not to wake Chloe. If it goes off, they might have to finish the conversation that was cut short by the press conference. Beth wonders now what possessed her to initiate it. Mark takes the remote from her hand and gently mutes the set.

'Are we going to talk about what happened?' He's fidgeting, shuffling his feet and smoothing down his hair. It's a long time – years – since Beth has seen Mark nervous about anything. Despite her anger, there's a reflexive urge to comfort him. She summons the image of him and Becca on the harbour and the urge subsides.

She turns so that she's sitting on the edge of the bed with her back to him. If they're going to have this conversation, she's not sure she can bear to look him in the eye. It's the only way she'll stay strong enough not to break down.

'You mean what you *did*?'

'Yeah.'

The swelling hurt inside her finally bursts. 'OK,' she begins carefully. 'You selfish ... childish ... egotistical ... self-centred *bastard*.' Each word lets a little more air out of the balloon.

'Yeah,' he agrees. Is that all he's got? Rage rises again. She has an unlimited supply of it.

'Two children. *Two. Children.*' She begins to shake. 'Fifteen years of collecting all of everyone's shit and washing it and cleaning it and folding it and tidying it and going back to the start like I'm on a bloody *wheel*. I've had offers too, you know. I could've shagged my way around the King's Arms, for a start.'

'I'm sure you could.'

'But I *didn't*. Because I'm a … I'm a human being, not a bloody animal. Fifteen. Fifteen, I've been with you, since—' He's got no defence, and the humiliating but essential question she's been dreading slips into the silence. 'Do you still fancy me?'

''Course I do!' he says indignantly. It's almost more insulting than the 'no' she was expecting.

'No, *not* of course you do! You had sex with someone else! Why? What don't you get from me? Truthfully.' She stares fixedly ahead. A long pause follows: she can hear Mark weighing up the pros and cons of truth and lies. She can't see his face, but she doesn't need to. She knows him well enough to picture the twisting mouth, the shifting posture.

'Surprise,' he hits her with.

'Wow,' says Beth, vainly trying to mask her hurt with sarcasm. ''Cause I'm not, what, inventive enough? What is it you want, S&M? Role play? Threesomes? Well, I'm sorry, but if I'm dull, it's only because I've never slept with anyone apart from you.'

'It wasn't about you, Beth.' Impatience tinges his words.

'Becca, then.' She spits the name. 'What's so great about her?'

'She was different.' Mark shrugs. 'Not sexier, not prettier. Just … new.' He sweeps his hand across the room. 'This house, this town, the job of mine, that's all my life will ever be and I knew every second of it and every second to come. I just felt trapped, Beth. And that's why I did it. And I wish to God I hadn't.' His voice breaks. 'I wish I could get our old, predictable, beautiful life back, because what I wouldn't give

222

for that right now. But I can't, can I?' He waits for her response but she's too bloody tired. 'I don't want to lose you, Beth. But I think I already have.'

'I'm pregnant,' she says, to her own shock as well as Mark's. He fails to suppress a smile and she's furious with herself.

'Since when?'

She rolls her eyes. It's not like their sex life is so relentless it all blurs into one. 'Ouzo night. First shag in months.'

'You have to keep it.'

'I don't have to do anything you say right now.' Finally something feels good. The moment of triumph is swiftly followed by the sickening realisation that she has only told Mark about the baby for the spiteful pleasure of threatening to take it away from him.

The weather is on its best behaviour this morning. There is just enough breeze to take the sting out of a strong sun, and the sea and the sky compete for the brightest shade of blue.

Up on the clifftop path, Beth is a blur of black-and-red Lycra. She runs too fast for eye contact or condolence, too fast for anyone to notice the subtle convexity of her belly. If she could bring herself to look at Harbour Cliff Beach she would see that the crime scene tents are being dismantled and the cordon removed, restoring the shoreline to its picture-postcard glory.

Down on the harbourside, Reverend Paul Coates looks on as Becca Fisher comes to the end of an interview for local radio. The reporter brought her down to the sea for the sound effects but the waves and the seagulls are proving stiff competition and she is forced to lean in close to the microphone that she's clearly terrified of.

'As you can see,' she says, 'the police tape's coming down, the beaches are fully open, it's a beautiful part of the world, and we hope people won't be put off coming by this tragic but *isolated* event.'

The reporter slips his headphones around his neck to signal that the conversation is over and Becca gives a long exhalation of relief. She turns to Paul. 'Did I sound like a complete arsehole?'

'Not a *complete* one,' he smiles. 'I'm next up, so you'll have some competition.'

'I hate this stuff,' she admits. 'I've never done it before.'

'I do it all the time. Just nobody normally cares except my mum. It's the only time she believes I'm a real priest.'

'That's parents for you,' says Becca. She folds her arms and kicks an imaginary pebble at her feet while the reporter listens to the playback of their conversation.

'You got family here?' says Paul.

'No. Melbourne. Worrying about me. I wish I'd never told them the business was in trouble.'

Paul frowns, as though only now remembering something. 'Wasn't there a guy who used to run the Traders with you?'

'My partner,' she says with a grimace. 'Ex-partner. It ended badly. Well, started badly, middled badly, ended badly. Here's what I've learned: don't buy a hotel with a dickhead.'

Paul smiles. 'Good advice. Paul's letter to the Corinthians says much the same.'

Becca laughs in surprise. 'You're funny. Never met a funny vicar before.'

The researcher motions Paul over to the bench. He rubs his hands together in anticipation before stepping up to the microphone.

The beds at the Traders are very comfortable. Olly Stevens and Karen White, who have had something of a late night, both sleep in well past breakfast.

He wakes first, jumping out of bed like a jack-in-a-box when he realises the time. Karen stirs but her head stays firmly on the pillow while she replays the events of the previous evening in fast-forward. Behind her, she can hear Olly fighting his way into his clothes. Fun as it was, she doesn't want this going public any more than she wants him getting heavy.

'You are going to use the back entrance, aren't you?' she says.

'You really are one dirty girl,' begins Olly, then blushes to realise she was being literal. 'Ah. Got you.' He does up his shirt, the buttons misaligned with their holes so that he has to start again. 'But we had a – a good – I mean, it was nice? It was all right, wasn't it?'

Karen stretches like a cat under the covers. 'You're quite needy, Olly, always wanting affirmation, anyone tell you that?'

'Always grateful for feedback. Happy to give it another go.'

'Maybe,' she says. She needs them to part on a professional note. 'Hey, I was wondering, that boat the police turned up? How would you get out that far? Could you row, do you need a motor?'

He gathers his coat from where it lies puddled by the door, then puts one hand on the doorknob. 'I'll tell you, if you call me later,' he grins, then he's gone. Before she can remind him to use the back door, he returns, the smile vanished and a copy of the *Herald* in his hand.

'This isn't what we wrote,' he says.

Karen doesn't care who sees them together as they sprint to the *Echo* office. She wants to make this call on speakerphone, with Olly and Maggie as her witnesses.

'That's not my article!' she says when Len Danvers picks up. 'You rewrote the whole bloody thing, loaded it against him.'

'Now it's got punch,' he says. The mask of anxiety on Maggie's face flickers briefly into something like amusement.

'But everyone here's going to think *I* wrote it!' Karen can hear the whine and barely recognises herself. What's wrong with her? These people are getting to her. She'll turn into one of them if she stays here any longer. Maybe the small-town mentality is sexually transmitted.

'Don't get too close to the flame,' Danvers crackles over the speakerphone. 'You're ahead of the pack. Keep going.'

When he ends the call, Karen turns to Maggie. 'Before you go off on me, read the piece I sent. It was totally different.' She's surprised how important Maggie's respect has become to her. She needs the real thing, she realises, not just Olly's adulation.

Maggie snorts. 'You got a page-one story but they threw you under the bus,' she says. Clearly she saw this coming from day one. 'The more things change, the more they stay the same. No use feeling sorry for yourself. Get back out there and write something so brilliant, so truthful, that he can't change a word. You owe us that.'

The words hit home hard. Karen isn't used to questioning her own judgement, and it's a horrible feeling. It's not that she thinks Jack Marshall is innocent – far from it – but reluctantly she admits to herself that maybe, in her haste to beat Alec Hardy, she might have jumped the gun. She should have waited until she had something harder, a better source, and then she should have written the piece herself. Even with a hard edit, Olly's article was still loose enough for them to pick apart and knit into this sensationalist shit.

Cheeks blazing, she sits down heavily at her desk and checks her emails for the first time that day. There are forty-five unread messages in her inbox. Even at a glance she can see that most of them are from old contacts – people she hasn't spoken to for years – wanting the inside track on Broadchurch. Karen's misgivings evaporate. The search for Danny Latimer's killer is the hottest story in the country. She has done the right thing by the victim's family. Nothing else matters.

There are no customers in the newsagent's. The only movement in the shop is the soft plastic ripple of the rainbow curtain.

Jack Marshall stands behind the counter, a copy of the

Daily Herald before him, staring down into the terrible mirror of the front page.

I DID NOT KILL YOUR SON
EXCLUSIVE: EX-CON SHOPKEEPER'S PLEA TO DANNY'S PARENTS

His face is blank.

35

Mark's been drinking in the King's Arms since he was four-teen, but tonight when he enters, the place goes as quiet as the saloon in a Western when a stranger comes to town. Just for a second, there's no sound but the fruit machines, then the low rumble of conversation strikes up again. Unable to face the bar, Mark sends Nige up to get the beers in. When he comes back he's got a pint in each hand and a copy of the *Herald* tucked under his arm. He spreads it on the table between them: Jack Marshall eyeballs them from the page.

'He's got a conviction for kiddy-fiddling and they're let-ting him serve ice creams,' he says. 'Mate, who *are* we? We look after things ourselves. If things are wrong, we sort them out. Like with that Neil from the Lion, when we heard he was nicking bikes out of gardens.'

Mark turns the paper over and folds it in half, so that only a small column of football news and the crossword are vis-ible. 'This isn't nicking bikes,' he says. 'Until we have evidence—'

'And what if waiting for evidence means it's too late?'

Nige demands. 'What if it's another kid? Say he has got something to do with this, and we've just let him carry on. How sick are we gonna feel?'

'*Enough!*' Mark erupts. Every head swivels in their direction, then turns away as quickly. Mark speaks in an urgent whisper: 'Stop banging on at me! You think I'm not being eaten up by this? You know *I* can't do nothing! You want to do something, fine.'

Nige lets the paper fall on to his lap and holds his hands up in surrender. 'I'm sorry, mate,' he says. ''Course. I understand.'

'I haven't got a thirst for this,' says Mark, pushing his pint away. 'I'm off home.'

'No worries,' says Nige. 'I'll give you a lift.'

There's a huge toolbag on the passenger seat of Nige's car. When Mark leans to move it, Nige almost sprints to intercept it.

'What've you got in there, anyway?' asks Mark as the bag sags in Nige's hands. 'A kitchen sink? You haven't been taking scrap without permission again, have you, mate? You know we can't afford to piss off the customers.'

'No, no,' says Nige, slinging it into the boot. 'It's only tools. Don't worry. Your business is safe in my hands.'

He holds up the hands in question: they are large, slightly dirty, and calloused.

Mark grins. 'Sooner I get back to work the better.'

Back at home, Nige heaves his bag into the garage, unzips it and pauses for a moment to look at the dirty blanket inside. Slowly, almost reverentially, he removes the blanket and unwraps it to reveal a crossbow.

The weapon is large and heavy. Although it is modern, made of matte black steel, there is something mediaeval about it. Unlike a gun, where the deadly mechanism is hidden on the inside, a crossbow, with its exposed wires and triggers, makes its intentions clear. There is no such thing as a rapid-fire crossbow. Ammunition has to be reloaded before each premeditated shot. You really have to know what you're doing with a crossbow, and self-control is vital. You wouldn't want it to get into the wrong hands.

That evening, Chloe and Dean are in the alleyway that threads around the back of her house, pressed together against the fence. Her face is buried in his T-shirt: his chin rests on the top of her head. A car door slams on the other side of the fence; she does not hear it.

'This is the closest I've ever been to your house,' says Dean. 'I'll get to go inside in about six months at this rate. Your dad ain't that scary, is he?'

'Let's just say it's not a coincidence that my last two boyfriends became my exes within about two hours of my dad finding out.' She flicks a small smile at Dean's chest, then says, 'You been speaking to the others, about Jack?'

'Yeah. I can't believe it. Makes me feel all ...' He gives a theatrical shudder.

'I'm gonna ring around everyone, tell them to boycott the shop,' says Chloe. Dean nods wisely.

'Look, I better go,' he says.

They pull apart only to come together in a long kiss. Chloe's blonde hair dances in the breeze. Dean smooths it down and tucks it behind her ears. She watches him walk the length of the alleyway to the street where the bike is parked up, hugging her arms to her chest, and blows him a kiss before his visor goes down. Then she turns around and walks slap bang into her father.

'In the house,' says Mark. 'Now.'

Chloe obeys immediately, but her mouth is pursed in a mutinous rosebud. In the sitting room, she toys with her phone for security, sliding her fingers absently over the screen. Mark paces up and down, visibly trying to keep his cool.

'Who was that?' he asks her. 'And don't mess me about, 'cause we're way beyond that in this house now.'

Chloe fights anger with truth. 'His name's Dean.' She meets Mark's eyes as he puts his fists on his hips.

'How old is he?'

'Seventeen.' Chloe straightens her back, ready to face the eruption head on.

'And he's going out with a fifteen-year-old!'

'Yes,' she fires back. 'Just like you did with Mum.'

'Don't get smart with me!' shouts Mark, but he hasn't got a leg to stand on and they both know it. He paces faster now, his breathing slow, deliberate and controlled. It doesn't leave much room for talking, and in the end it's Chloe who moves the conversation forward.

'Just ask me, Dad,' she sing-songs, 'I know you're dying to.' She turns her face up to him, hiding nothing. Mark falters for a second. His daughter might be half his age and size, but she's the closest thing he's got to a true sparring partner.

'You having sex with him?'

'Yes,' says Chloe. She can't hide her pride. Mark looks at

the wall as though he wants to punch it. He raises his hand as if to hit her but instead runs it down the back of his hair with laborious self-control. '*And* we use condoms, which is more than you and Mum did.'

Mark turns puce. 'I'm not having you talking to me like this, Chloe.'

Chloe stands up to him now, literally. She points a finger at his chest.

'I got you out of a *police* cell,' she says. Mark frowns in confusion. 'Because I'd seen how you and Becca Fisher were looking at each other. Now you want to talk about that too?'

The shock of being discovered shoves Mark roughly into an armchair. He is not qualified to set one toe on the moral high ground. He lets his head fall into his hands.

In one short conversation their relationship has been bent into a new shape. Chloe, sensing the fragility of the new order, shifts temporarily back into little-girl mode.

'Are you going to tell Mum about me and Dean?' she says in a small voice.

Mark lets out a long breath. 'It'd be better coming from you,' he suggests. 'She'll like it, you confiding in her.'

Chloe shakes her head. 'I will, but not today. She's got enough on her plate right now, what with finding out about you and Becca.'

Mark's mortification deepens. 'How'd you know she knows?'

'Oh, come on, Dad. I'm not deaf. Let's give her a bit of time for that to sink in before we go dropping any more bombshells.' She looks around the house, registering Beth's absence for the first time. 'Where is she, anyway?'

36

A VACANCIES sign hangs in the window of the Traders Hotel. This is unheard of in August. Beth hesitates at the open front door, then walks slowly into reception. A room key hangs on almost every hook. There are no guests in the lobby and no one behind the desk.

Low conversation rumbles from the bar. Beth rounds the doorway to see Becca sharing a table with Reverend Paul Coates. They are poring over open books together, their heads bent so close that they are almost touching. It hasn't taken Becca long to find a new target. Beth, who has come to see Paul as her confidant over the last few days, feels the now-familiar kick of betrayal. She holds her breath the better to eavesdrop.

'So basically you're a year behind the projections, with no sign of an upturn,' says Paul. 'And the bank is demanding a repayment of ten thousand pounds within forty-two days or they repossess.'

Becca blows a blonde curl from her eyes. 'What with the weather, and then *this* . . .'

This, thinks Beth. My son's death. How dare she? A small sound escapes her and Becca looks up. Shame darkens her face.

'Beth! Didn't expect to see you . . .' she begins.

I bet you fucking didn't, thinks Beth as she barges her way behind the bar. The first breakable to hand is an empty pint glass, still warm from the dishwasher. Beth hurls it at the floor where it shatters into diamonds. It feels fantastic. There's a row of highball tumblers at eye-level. Beth quickly establishes a rhythm: grab, smash, grab, smash, grab, smash. The champagne flutes, with their crystal chime at the breaking point, are the most satisfying. She flips the taps on the beer pumps so that the drink pours freely, overflowing the drip trays and flooding the floor. Let Becca's profits drain to nothing. The sooner she's out of Broadchurch, the better.

'For Christ's sake!' explodes Becca when Beth reaches for the spirits. 'That's *enough*!'

Beth stifles a manic laugh. 'Enough? I'm doing your windows next.' A shard of glass, long as a dagger, rests on the bar. Beth could pick it up now, run it across Becca's neck. It's easy to take a life, easy.

'Beth,' says Becca, turning off the cider tap. 'I'm so sorry, it was a mistake.'

'Fucking right, it was!' says Beth, turning the tap back on. '*My* husband. I will nail you to the floor before I let you wreck fifteen years of my life!'

Becca looks helplessly to Paul. 'If we'd known what was going to happen . . .'

'Don't you dare!' shrieks Beth. 'Don't you *dare* bring that into it. Come near my family and I will break your fuckin' *face.*' She is out of control, like she's drunk all the booze she's spilling. She doesn't recognise the way she's speaking.

She feels hands on her upper arms and tries to break free, but Paul's hands are large and his grip is strong. 'All right,' he says, guiding Beth away from the bar. 'We should get some air.'

'D'you know what she did?' says Beth.

'I've got the gist,' he replies.

The fight goes out of Beth as suddenly as it arrived, and she lets him steer her across the sodden carpet, glass crunching under their feet. They turn left out of the Traders: he's walking her home. Beth wonders bitterly whether it's for her protection or Becca's.

There's a sobering breeze on the High Street and Beth starts to come down from the high of destruction.

'Sorry. To you, not to her.' She wants to laugh but the tiny detached part of her that still cares about these things knows how it will look, and she bites it back. 'It felt good, actually. Do you think I'll have to pay her? I'm not paying her, she can whistle for it.'

'Beth . . .' Paul stops her in her tracks. 'Have you thought about seeing a bereavement counsellor?'

Not him too. They've got themselves on some kind of mailing list. Victim Support and the doctor keep writing to them with offers to talk it through. So far she's managed to stash the letters and leaflets in the bookshelves where Mark never goes. 'I don't want to see a counsellor,' she tells him. 'A counsellor will want me to stop being angry. I need my anger. It's all I've got right now.'

Paul doesn't flinch, merely nods to show his understanding. He mirrors her pace as they turn right out of the High

Street. Not for the first time, Beth wonders what's really going through his mind. Is he honestly as non-judgemental as he seems, a forgiving Christian through to the bone? Or is his mind a relentless stream of suppressed criticism? She finds that she doesn't much care, as long as he listens. This priest, a virtual stranger up until a few weeks ago, has become one of the few constants in her life, and in some ways she is more intimate with him than she is with her husband. Thinking about this prompts another confidence.

'Mark knows,' she blurts. 'About the baby. He said I had to keep it.'

He gives the only answer a priest is allowed to. 'I think he's right.'

'Oh well, if the men think that's what's best, let's do it,' Beth deadpans, then grows suddenly shrill. 'I hate it!' Paul's eyes mirror her own shock. It's the first time she's said it out loud, but she's started now and she can't stop. 'This thing, growing inside me. I don't want it. It's not right. Danny should be growing, I'm not done with Danny yet, I didn't finish my job. I want *him*.' Her voice cracks and rises. She doesn't care if anyone overheard her. 'I had one job as his mum. Get him ready for the world, set him up to meet it and be the best he could be. And I failed him. I let him down.'

'No. You didn't. He was taken.'

She turns on him. 'Why? Why did your God create him, and then take him back?'

'I don't know. Some people think He takes those He loves most first.'

'Pretty bloody selfish God. Why am I being punished?'

'I don't know. I wish I did.' At least he's got the grace to

237

look apologetic while he says it. He clears his throat. 'Have you thought any more about a memorial service for Danny? It'd be a service of thanksgiving for his life. The shape of it's completely up to you. We can have music he liked, people can talk about him.'

What Beth really wants is a funeral. A coffin. A goodbye. But that impulse to move, to act, to do something for her son, remains irresistible. Something dormant stirs within her as she realises that she must not let his death overshadow his life. 'OK,' she says. 'I want to do it. Mark'll agree with me.'

Paul looks pleased and then almost sheepish. 'We should think how we announce it. I mean, I'm very happy to go on the local news, give them some quotes, save you the bother.' Beth can't resist a smile. He's not your average vicar, what with the computers and now a hotline to West Country News. 'I've got a feeling this service might end up being quite big. There's going to be media coverage, but also people will want to come. We may spill out from the church. Are you all right with that?'

'Big as possible,' says Beth. Paul's enthusiasm is infectious. She would invite the whole world if she could.

He leaves her at the top of Spring Close, as though he doesn't want Mark to see them together. He doesn't retrace their route over the pavements but cuts across the field. Beth can't tell whether he's going back to his church or back to Becca Fisher.

37

Karen White is no longer the only national newspaper journalist in Broadchurch. The town is crawling with them now, print and television. She knows half of them from years covering the courts, but while the rest of the pack catch up over drinks in the Traders, she's in the inner sanctum of the *Echo* office, jealously guarding her exclusive. This afternoon she got a lead on something that will keep her ahead of the game, but it's a long time now since she took the call and she's starting to get nervous.

Olly wheels his chair across to Karen's desk so that he's virtually sitting in her lap. 'It's late,' he says, placing his hand over hers. 'How about we go back to—'

'No,' says Karen, firmly removing his hand. 'We're waiting for someone.' She doesn't confide her fears that they've had a change of heart.

'Oh?' says Olly. His obvious disappointment is shot through with intrigue.

'Mm-hmm. Two people, actually.'

Right on cue, the door swings wide and a teenage couple

walk hand in hand through the darkened newsroom, crash helmets swinging from their free hands. Olly's eyes saucer in recognition.

'Dean's got something to tell you,' says Chloe Latimer, nodding at the tall, good-looking youth at her side. 'Tell her what you told me.'

Karen looks Dean up and down. The first she heard of his existence was in Chloe's phone call. He's a couple of years older than Chloe. Seventeen at least if he's riding a motorbike. From the corner of her eye, she notices Olly's raised eyebrows and silently wills him to stop. His poker face needs work.

'I was in the Sea Brigade,' says Dean. He has a strong local accent. 'Jack Marshall threw me out.'

'Go on,' says Karen.

'He was always wanting hugs from the boys,' says Dean. 'And he'd love to watch us getting in our trunks when it was hot. That's when he'd go round, putting his arms on our shoulders. I was like, "No thanks, mate. No hugs from me."' He gives a little quiver of revulsion. 'He took against me after that. Kept asking what was wrong with me.'

Karen stifles a whoop. She needs to get this straight. 'This happened more than once, Dean?' she asks.

'*Loads.*' Dean turns to Olly. 'You must've seen it, during your time.'

Olly looks uncomfortable. 'Maybe. A bit,' he admits. 'I didn't think of it like that.'

'I need this corroborated, I can't just take your word for it,' says Karen, but Chloe, media savvy now, is one step ahead of her. She has made a list of names and numbers of boys who were in the Brigade at the same time as Dean. Some of them have got stars beside them.

'They're the ones who've said they agree with Dean, and they'll talk to you,' says Chloe. Karen is momentarily lost for words. 'Everyone knows he did it. Well, everyone apart from my nan, and that's only 'cause he's a Bible-basher like she is. They took my dad in when there's a paedo on the loose. We all know what he's like and the police are doing nothing.'

'Have you been to the police with this?' asks Karen.

Chloe shakes her head. 'You gonna use it?'

Karen looks at the clock, then back at the list. If she and Olly work fast, this will make tomorrow's front page. It will strike a blow for the Latimer family and against Alec Hardy. Thought about in those terms, the decision is easy.

'OK, let's do it,' says Karen. 'People should know. When we're finished here, you need to put this in a statement to the police, OK?'

They hit the phones as soon as Chloe and Dean have gone. One boy after another confirms Dean's statement. Their quotes make perfect copy and Karen knows as the words fill the screen that the *Herald* won't have to change a single one. Some stories sensationalise themselves.

She hits send in time to make tomorrow's first edition. It will be on the presses within the hour, on the vans just the other side of midnight and online not long after that. The other journalists will spend the night playing catch-up.

Ellie walks down her garden path, one hand rooting in her bag for her house keys. The security light is activated as she gets to the porch.

'Bloody hell, you work late.'

If she didn't recognise the voice, Ellie would have screamed. As it is, her heart rate doubles. Lucy steps out from behind a bush, as though Ellie has failed to honour a long-standing appointment to meet in a dark suburban garden after midnight. Shadows rush in to fill the hollows of her cheeks.

'You're back, are you?' says Ellie. She finds the right key and slides it into the lock.

'Are you interested in what I've got to say?'

'Keep your voice down,' hisses Ellie under her breath. They're directly underneath Fred's bedroom. She might miss him, but that doesn't mean she wants to spend quality time with him in the small hours of the morning. 'That depends,' she says. 'Are you willing to give me back the money you stole from my children? Are you willing to seek proper help?'

'How many times?' says Lucy. 'I didn't take your sodding holiday money.' Ellie gives an inward screech of frustration: the repeated denials are almost worse than the original theft. 'And I don't need that sort of help.'

She is lying on both counts but with such conviction that Ellie wonders, not for the first time, if she actually believes herself. Lucy leans in and speaks in a gruff whisper.

'I saw something, Ell. I think you'll want to know. The night Danny Latimer got killed.' Ellie freezes with one foot inside the porch, hope soaring inside her. It doesn't do, with Lucy, to let your desperation show, so she merely raises her eyebrows expectantly.

'I just need a bit of money to stand me up again,' says

Lucy. 'Only nine hundred pounds. A thousand. Lend it to me and I'll tell you.'

Ellie is too disgusted to reply. She closes the door in Lucy's face. Nothing changes. Even with everything that's going on, Lucy only cares about herself. She would even use a boy's death to her own ends. Ellie is ashamed to be her sister.

38

Jack Marshall's infamy has spread. His picture is on the front of all the papers, not just the *Herald*, although Karen White's report, with its headline HUGS FOR THE BOYS is the only one with the right to the word *exclusive*. The paparazzi have his shop surrounded.

Ellie and Hardy stand on the shop floor, blinking in the gentle strobe of flashbulbs. The photographers are silhouetted against the roller blinds, their cameras turning them into alien shadow puppets. They call Jack's name repeatedly, but in very different tones to the ones they used to get Beth's attention at Danny's memorial. This is what a witch-hunt feels like, thinks Ellie.

'I need protection,' begs Jack. 'I'm under siege!'

She asks the questions that protocol demands of her. 'Has anyone threatened you or physically intimidated you?' she says, even as the glass in the window shakes.

'Stay inside,' says Hardy, as though Marshall has a choice. He can't take his eyes off the window either, flinching with every flash. 'With a bit of luck it'll all abate soon enough.' He doesn't sound convinced.

'You're doing this deliberately to see if I'll crack. You've got me marked and nothing I say makes any difference.'

Hardy regains his composure. 'Cooperate with us a bit more, then, and we can clear you of suspicion.'

'You think I haven't heard that before!' snorts the old man. 'Cooperate and we'll make it all right. Next thing, I'm being charged.'

Hardy sighs. 'All I want is to get to the truth of Danny Latimer's death. If you're not involved—'

'I am not involved! I told you, I was in all night. If I'd been out, it'd be on my security cameras.'

Hardy and Ellie look to each other in disbelief, then back to Jack. 'On your *what?*' asks Hardy.

'Security cameras, front and back. Had them installed after a break-in. Cost me a fortune. But my front and back doors are on there. If I'd left, it'd be there.' Jack begins his sentence with the contempt of someone who's stating the obvious, but he falters as he goes on. You see it all the time, people missing something vital because they take it for granted the police see their tiny worlds from the same angle they do. Sometimes literally, in this case.

'Why didn't you mention them before?' Hardy doesn't hide his exasperation.

'I forgot,' admits Jack. 'I was angry. *You* had me all confused.'

His defensiveness lays bare his vulnerability. Ellie sees the chance to ask him about his past again and takes it.

'Why don't you tell us what happened, Jack?' she says, her softness a deliberate contrast to Hardy's severity. Jack's face remains impassive but there is a tiny shift in his posture, a fractional lowering of the shoulders, and when he speaks the relief is clear.

'I was a music teacher. Rowena was a pupil. A *girl*. No boys involved. I'm sure you can fill in the gaps. It was a relationship.'

'And you had sex, how many times?' asks Hardy.

Jack wrinkles his nose in disgust. 'You think I put notches on my bedpost?'

Hardy folds his arms. 'Who told the police?'

'Her father.' Jack's defiant stare suddenly gives way to an unfocused glaze; Ellie shifts into his line of sight, but she can't make him meet her eye again. 'I was made an example of. Served a year. I was lucky to make it out alive. She was fifteen years and eleven months. Four weeks and a day later, nothing would've been amiss. I served my time.'

'Did you ever have contact with the girl after you were released?' asks Ellie.

'I married her.' This catches Ellie off guard, and she consciously steels herself against what might yet turn out to be a sob story. 'The week after I came out of prison. She was seventeen, I was forty.'

Reverend Paul Coates is braving the crowds outside the newsagent's to wait for the police.

'You need to protect him,' he says as Ellie and Hardy shoulder their way through the scrum. 'He's my parishioner. He's scared stiff.'

Hardy looks Paul up and down. His eyes linger on the dog collar like it's a stain. 'You're certain he's innocent, are you?'

Paul is unbowed. 'You're certain he's not?'

'Your concern's noted.'

Ellie follows Hardy back to the nick in a hail of bullet-points. 'What he said doesn't alter the facts,' he says. 'Jack Marshall has a conviction. He's still a suspect. We can't be distracted by his convincing sob story, or this press. We persevere with the evidence. Williams is going over the CCTV as we speak.'

As if on cue, SOCO Brian is waiting for them upstairs.

'Next time you have a crime scene on a beach, call someone else,' he says. 'It's been a bloody nightmare. Layers, moving, shifting, it's impossible. We've eliminated about four hundred separate pieces of evidence as detritus or irrelevant.'

'I prefer relevant,' scowls Hardy. Brian holds up a clear bag containing four cigarette butts.

'All within three feet of one another. Four feet from where the body was found.'

'What makes them special?' says Ellie.

'Timing. If they'd been there more than a couple of hours earlier, they would've been washed away by the high tide. But there's no trace of tidewater on them, so they must've been left there that morning. Around the same time the body was. They're high-tar cigarettes which is quite unusual these days. If they were bought locally, you might be in with a shout of people remembering the purchaser.'

Hardy says what they're all thinking: 'All that way to drop off a body, then stand and smoke. It doesn't make sense.'

When Brian has finished, Hardy retreats to his office. He pulls closed the Venetian blinds then turns out the light, so that only pinstripes of white leak between the slats. There's a sofa in one corner, and he lies awkwardly down on it, long legs dangling over the edge.

He closes his eyes and has his suspects line up in an imaginary identity parade. It's a little technique he's used since day one on the job whenever there's more information coming in than he can process. It served him well in the early stages of Sandbrook and he hopes it will bring him a similar clarity now.

Mark Latimer naturally remains in the frame. Obeying the axiom that the closer to home, the greater the likelihood of guilt, he is a prime suspect. Even with Becca Fisher's testimony, there is still a two-hour gap in his alibi. He hit Danny on one occasion. Correction: he hit Danny on one occasion that they know of.

Jack Marshall is equally plausible, although for very different reasons. A bachelor from out of town with a conviction for sex with a minor who was later persuaded to marry her abuser, suggests that Marshall is a skilled groomer. Just because Danny's body showed no signs of sexual assault doesn't mean that none took place. Experienced abusers know that there's more than one way to molest a child. Experienced criminals of any persuasion know how to make contact without leaving a trace. As leader of the Sea Brigade, Jack Marshall had little boys on tap. He had Danny alone in his shop every morning and the boy's phone in his possession after he died. His house is a stone's throw from the deposition site. He has obstructed the investigation at every opportunity: the longer Hardy thinks about Marshall's forgetfulness, the more convenient it seems.

Reverend Paul Coates takes his place next to Jack. His lack of alibi is a red flag and the church is a minute's walk across the field from the Latimers' house. He had a relationship with Danny and dozens of other boys through the computer club. But it's his eagerness to get his voice on the airwaves and his face on camera that really disturbs Hardy. He's seen this before, the urge the guilty have to perform for the media. It's a kind of sick pride in what they've done, an inability to let their involvement go unacknowledged, no matter how tangentially.

Nige Carter is borderline. Terminally single, by all accounts, he lives with his mum and clings to the Latimer family like a limpet. Next to Mark, Nige was probably the most prominent adult male in Danny's life. He has lied to the police already, ostensibly to protect Mark, and Hardy can't shake the feeling he's still holding something back, something big. Of course, Nige has an alibi, but Hardy is inclined to dismiss it; he has long held that an alibi provided by someone's mother is not worth the paper the statement is written on.

Finally, Hardy thinks long and hard about Steve Connolly. That business about the boat was either a lucky guess or a witness statement, which means Connolly is either a charlatan or withholding evidence. With no confirmation of the latter, Hardy ought to conclude he is the former, and dismiss him. And he will, as soon as he has determined how Connolly knows about Pippa Gillespie's pendant. Late at night, alone in the office, Hardy has searched extensively for a link between Connolly and Sandbrook and found none, either to the case or the place. Until that happens, Connolly remains, if not officially a suspect, then deeply suspicious.

It is times like now, when everyone else has gone home, that he misses Tess the most. He misses the informal debriefing at the end of the day, the final volley of ideas and theories. He has yet to meet a copper so entirely on his own wavelength. Even towards the end, they always had work in common. It was the last thing to go.

Feeling sorry for himself won't get this killer caught. Hardy takes off his glasses, closes his eyes. Mark Latimer, Jack Marshall, Paul Coates, Nigel Carter and Steve Connolly stand shoulder to shoulder in Hardy's imagination. He lets his mind's eye travel along the line-up and they always come to rest on the same man. He massages his temples, wishing that something would bloody happen. It doesn't need to be dramatic. A grain, a single cell, of proof, would do. And soon. Now. His case is slipping away from him.

39

Frank finally gets to the end of Jack Marshall's CCTV footage. There is no sign of Jack leaving or entering his house on the night that Danny was killed. They have examined every angle, but they can't find a blind spot. Ellie turns to Frank.

'He's innocent,' she says in amazement.

While she's dashing off an email to let Hardy know, a call comes through from Bob Daniels. There is what he describes as 'unrest' outside the Sea Brigade hut. Ellie sends her email and runs from the station, Frank at her heels.

The men have gathered on the unmade road outside the hut. The angry mob of villagers wield camera phones, the twenty-first-century equivalent of pitchforks and flaming torches. Ellie recognises these men as individuals – they are school dads, shopkeepers, uncles, blokes from the five-a-side league – but collectively, they are terrifying, loaded with violence, faces twisted in hate. She has never seen anything like this in Broadchurch before. Bob, unusually ill-at-ease in his uniform, looks like he wants to join his mates on the other side of the divide.

Tonight is when the Sea Brigade usually meet, and although Jack has put on his uniform and opened the doors, not a single boy is in attendance. It is a huge misjudgement. What looks, now, to Ellie, like an innocent man refusing to let allegations get the better of him, has been interpreted by the mob as provocation. The men throw accusations like stones. The press, naturally, are loving every second. The angrier the men get, the more the cameras click. A scruffy photographer has his lens virtually up Nige Carter's nose as he snarls threats.

Ellie has called for backup but the first car on the scene is not a police vehicle but her own battered family car and her husband is at the wheel.

'What are you doing here?' she asks Joe. Mark Latimer emerges from the passenger side. A vein pulses on his forehead like a worm trapped under his skin.

'I couldn't stop him,' says Joe. 'And then, I couldn't let him come on his own.' But he is helpless as Mark shoulders his way through the rabble to the front. Ellie's pulse quickens. Where the hell is her backup?

If Mark loses his temper, this lot will be on Jack like hounds on a fox.

'There's no meeting here tonight, Jack,' Nige Carter shouts. A fleck of spittle flies out of his mouth and lands at Jack's feet. 'No boys are coming. We don't feel safe with that.'

'You don't even have kids, Nigel,' says Jack. His tone is one of weariness, almost boredom. He doesn't help himself. Ellie wills him to show some emotion other than arrogance. 'You didn't even get a badge for knots.'

'I can speak for those that do,' counters Nige.

'Not really, Nige,' says Mark Latimer with a quiet control that astonishes Ellie. 'Boys,' he addresses the crowd. 'Stand down, eh?'

If they don't quite fall silent, they at least begin to mumble their abuse rather than shout it.

'You don't need to be involved, mate!' says Nige. 'We're doing this for you!'

'Get back!' Mark raises his voice in a warning shot and this time everyone obeys. Joe puts his palms up in pacification.

'They're saying a lot of stuff about you, Jack.' Mark speaks evenly but a muscle at the side of his mouth is in spasm, his face betraying the exhaustion and the emotions that toil on him.

'I am not what they're calling me,' says Jack. 'And I did not go near your boy.'

'You had Dan's phone.' An upward flick at the end of Mark's statement turns it into a question.

'He left it in the bottom of the delivery bag. I swear.'

'You been to prison though, ain't you? Eh?' says Mark.

Jack straightens his back. 'There was a girl. We had a relationship. She was fifteen, nearly sixteen. The same age as Beth when you met her.' Mark takes a few seconds to swallow and digest this. 'Mark, we married, we had a son together.'

Mark's suspicious again. 'Yeah, where's he now, then? Why aren't they with you?'

'He died, the day after his sixth birthday.' Jack drops his voice so that only those closest can hear. 'Car accident. She was driving. They both went through the windscreen. She survived; he didn't. The grief ripped us apart. So I came here. New start.' His eyes take on that distant look that has frustrated them so much throughout the course of this investigation, but where Ellie previously saw evasion or disconnectedness she now sees a man staring into his own past. 'They're saying I wanted to hug the boys because I'm a paedophile. It was never that. I missed my boy. I missed touching him, holding him. I miss my boy every day. What sort of world is this, Mark, where it's wrong to seek affection? I would never harm Danny. We're the same, Mark. No parent should outlive their child. Your boy, he was a good boy.'

Mark struggles to control his face. Nobody speaks. Waves slap against the harbour wall. Even the cameras hold fire for a few seconds. Finally, the silence is broken by Joe, who takes a tentative step into a lion's den.

'You OK, Mark?'

Mark knuckles away a tear but then answers in a roar. 'Go home, boys!' he shouts so loudly that a nearby seagull takes flight. 'The lot of you. *Now.*'

They retreat and then disperse, but the threats keep coming, angry voices riding the early evening breeze. It's obvious that the temporary ceasefire is for Mark's benefit. The two men look at each other, united in membership of the club every parent dreads joining.

'You're not safe here, Jack. You're dead, mate.' Mark's words are harsh, but his tone is soft. He is passing on the threat rather than making it.

Jack stands his ground. 'This is my home now.'

'People have made up their minds,' says Mark. 'You want to stay safe? Get as far from here as you can.'

He leaves Jack standing proud but pathetic in his Brigade leader's uniform, outside the hut Ellie knows he will never fill again. Jack must know it too, but he is too proud to show it. There is something military about his bearing: ramrod spine, eyes front, shoulders pulled back.

The photographers get one last shot of him, then down their cameras and go to the pub.

The dusk and the drizzle have driven the vigilantes home. Only Nige Carter is still out, his engine idling on the edge of the caravan park. For a long time, he watches the rain obscure caravan number 3 before the wipers reveal it again. Then something inside him propels him out of the van. He is at the caravan in three long strides, beating the door with large fists.

Susan Wright does not look surprised to see him although her welcome is cool: she folds her arms and blocks the doorway.

'Can't live without me?' she scowls.

'I'm not staying.' Nige is virtually running on the spot in his impatience to leave. 'There's things that're happening, I need to see to. So I want you to take that and go.' He holds out a thick A4 envelope. 'Five hundred quid.'

'Is that what I'm worth? You're lucky I've got a sense of humour,' she says, but she doesn't crack a smile. She stares him out, as calm as he is agitated. If her plan is to tip him over the edge, it works. His arms begin to flail.

'See that van?' he shouts. 'I've got a crossbow in that van. I'm not messing around here.'

255

Susan looks at him evenly. 'I don't think you should be saying those sorts of things to me, Nigel. We need to find a way of working this out together.'

Nige knows when he's beaten. He climbs back into the van and slams the door, throwing the envelope down on the passenger seat. He makes a messy three-point turn on the sand and drives off.

Susan stands in her doorway until Vince breaks her trance, winding his way around her legs.

40

Oliver is waiting in reception. Ellie braces herself for a tussle. Either he's after inside knowledge or Lucy's sent him to do her dirty work. She isn't sure she has the energy to fight him on either count. She doesn't even have the energy to walk down the stairs. Waiting for the lift, she is suddenly aware of her body: the gnawing hunger in her belly, the acid tug of too much coffee. She has half a mind, as she descends to the ground floor, to give Olly the scoop on Jack Marshall's alibi right now and let the press exonerate him. They've still got time to make the papers. It's clear that the public pay more heed to the *Echo* or the *Herald* than any statement from the Wessex Police. But she's not convinced that they'd run with it: Jack Marshall's innocence gives the lie to their smear campaign, so they'll probably just bury the story. Dirty old men sell papers; doddery old victims don't. What's more, she hasn't let Hardy know about the CCTV yet, and she wants to do this by the book. By the time the lift doors open, Ellie has made her decision. She will log it all properly tonight and, if Hardy approves, feed it to the press in the morning.

Oliver isn't wearing his wheedling, give-me-a-story expression, so this must be about Lucy. Ellie's heart plummets.

'Your mum can come to me if she wants,' she snaps. 'I'm a bit busy, in case you hadn't noticed.'

Olly clicks his tongue. 'It's nothing to do with her. It's about Danny. Well, it might be. Have you identified that burning boat yet?'

So he *does* want a scoop. 'Oliver, what have I told you about giving you preferential treatment?' She's overcompensating because she came so close to doing just that. 'We'll call a press conference when we've got something to say.'

He is up in arms. 'Would you just hear me out before you go making accusations? It's my dad's boat. She's missing.'

The conversation flips 180 degrees as Ellie realises the implications of this. 'Why didn't you tell me sooner?' she asks, but she should have checked herself. Half of Broadchurch knew about that boat. Half of Broadchurch have taken it out.

'I sort of went off her after Dad left. I don't go on the water from one week to the next these days.'

'I don't suppose you've got a picture, have you?' says Ellie.

Olly scrolls through the camera roll on his phone and comes up with a picture of himself and Tom in the little dinghy, surrounded by tackle. 'This do you?' He attaches it to a text message and puts Ellie's name in the recipient box but he dangles it like a carrot. 'If you find out it was Dad's boat, can I have the story? Don't announce it. Give it to me.'

'You're incredible,' she says.

The chastisement works. Olly hits the right key and seconds later a buzz in Ellie's pocket heralds the picture's arrival in her own phone.

Upstairs, she emails the picture through to SOCO and spends the interim drafting a document for the press office about the new development with Jack Marshall. She emails it through, knowing it won't be read until the morning but satisfied that one more job has been crossed off the list.

Brian comes up to CID to give her the news in person. She has never seen him out of his boiler suit before: he looks odd in normal clothes.

'It's the same boat,' he says. 'I'd bet my mortgage on it.' It's the first positive lead they've had in days. Ellie feels weak with relief. She slumps back in her chair, catching a glimpse of herself in the window as she does. God, she looks like shit: matted hair, no make-up. On her next day off she's going to book herself in for a haircut. Not with Lucy. Somewhere posh. Somewhere they do your nails at the same time. Brian breaks into her reveries of a makeover.

'Listen, d'you fancy a drink one night?'

'Sorry, what?' It takes five seconds for her brain to catch up with the words. 'I'm married, Brian.' She cocks her head towards the picture on her desk: all four Millers, grinning at the camera.

'That's an issue, is it?' He perches on the edge of her desk.

'*Happily* married, Brian.'

'Oh, OK. Fair enough.' He slides off her desk and retreats from the brink of harassment. 'Well, there we go. D'you want anything from the kitchen, cup of tea . . . ?' Somewhere beneath Ellie's indignation is a ridiculous flare of offence that he's willing to give up so easily.

'No,' she says. 'I'm fine.' Brian saunters back to his lab and Ellie puts her face in her hands, trying to process the surreal little interlude. She quickly gives up. Her priority now is to tell Hardy about the boat.

'Something weird,' she pokes her head around his office door. 'We've got an ID on the burned boat. It used to belong to Olly's dad.'

Hardy goggles at her. 'The boat that was used to transport Danny Latimer's body used to belong to your brother-in-law?' There's a world of judgement in his words: of her lax investigation skills, of her family, of her home. Ellie tries to let it roll off her.

'It was left just off the beach with the motor chained up,' she says. 'Olly barely used it any more – bad associations, that's why it took him so long to report it missing.'

'Who knew it was there?'

'Lots of people. It wasn't a secret.'

'See if Forensics can get any other DNA or prints off the shards, match them against all the elimination prints. Call Brian now, get him to prioritise this.' The name triggers a reflex giggle in Ellie. 'What's funny?'

She's got to tell someone, and she doesn't think it would go down very well with Joe.

'He just asked me out,' she confides.

'Brian?' Hardy wears his does-not-compute expression. 'Why would he do that?'

'Thanks very much!'

'You're *married*. Flattering, though.'

'I suppose. But SOCO ... They've had their hands everywhere.' Ellie wrinkles her nose and waggles her fingers.

'Dirty Brian,' says Hardy, with a playful roll of the Rs and a rare smile. Ellie can't remember a moment of genuine good humour between them before: naturally she seizes on it and ruins it.

'Sir, what if we don't get the killer?'

His face shuts down, the joke cancelled. 'We will.'

She takes a deep breath to galvanise herself. 'You didn't on Sandbrook.'

Hardy freezes: no blinking, no breathing. Then he puts down the pen in his hand.

'How long have you been waiting to bring that up?'

Since the day Jenkinson first uttered his name, she thinks, but lets a shrug answer for her. 'That was different,' says Hardy.

'How? It all got hushed up.'

'I didn't want that,' he says softly, although there is no one there to overhear them. 'A mistake was made. A big mistake.'

'By you?'

Hardy seems to shrink in front of her, like the authority has all been drained out of him. 'I don't want to talk about it.'

But Ellie knows she might not get another chance. 'Sir, these are my friends, people I've known all my life. We can't let them down.'

'We won't,' says Hardy. He is looking straight at her but his glasses reflect the computer screen before him, white windows of words and numbers, and Ellie can't see into his eyes.

It's nearly one o'clock in the morning now. Before powering down her computer, Ellie emails Olly a copy of the Jack Marshall press release. It's too late to make the papers, but he can have the online exclusive. It's her way of saying thank you for coming forward about the boat, and for holding back when it might have made things awkward for her. He's a good boy really.

41

Mark and Beth are in bed with the radio on for company.

'Can we not listen to the news?' asks Mark. Beth turns the station over to a music channel, then lies on her back, one arm hooked behind her head, staring at the ceiling. They lie side by side on their backs.

'You know I love you,' he says.

'I know you *say* it. Since you've been caught out.'

Beth listens to the adverts like they're lullabies. When he tries to hold her, she goes rigid. She is so drained by this anger, but she can't let it go. She is frightened of what's on the other side of it.

'Beth, *please.*' She can hear the effort of patience. 'We've only got each other now. Why don't we make an agreement. For tonight. No bickering. No silences. Just ... find something else.'

'Like what?' she says. He's got nothing.

A mindless jingle gives way to soft piano, the opening chords of a song that pierces both their hearts with a single arrow. It was everywhere the year Danny was born. It was playing the first time she felt him kick inside her: it was on the car radio when they drove home from the hospital with him tucked up in the car seat.

This time, when Mark goes to hold her, she lets him. They stay like that for the duration of the song, rocking slowly in time with it. When it's over, Mark reaches for the keepsake box that's been gathering dust on top of their wardrobe for years.

The radio and the lights are on low as Mark and Beth sit on the floor in their nightclothes, spreading the mementoes of their children's earliest days around them.

Mark hands her a tarnished silver heart-shaped locket with two curls of soft baby hair, white-blonde for Chloe and brown for Danny. 'Oh, look,' says Beth. Gingerly she picks up Danny's hospital tag: Male Infant of Elizabeth Latimer, 8lb 2oz. There's a picture of him at two hours old. Here's the first thing he ever wore, the blue-and-white-striped sleepsuit that he seemed to outgrow overnight. Knitted baby booties. Tiny red wellies that he wore on the beach in the winter. His first football boots. She used to hate cleaning mud off the studs with a knife. Now she knows she'll never do it again, she misses it.

She picks up an empty toilet roll tube and wonders why they kept it. Mark holds up a little paper cone and fixes it to one end. 'He was mad about rockets, wasn't he?' Beth sees it for what it is now; it's a model spaceship Danny made at pre-school. She cradles it in her hands. Now she wonders why they didn't keep it on display.

They move on. A shoebox is stuffed with photographs of their first holiday abroad: Spain, 2005. Danny loved every second of the plane journey, even the turbulence.

'Oh my God, Mark!' laughs Beth when she finds a picture of the four of them sitting solemnly at an outdoor table at a tapas restaurant. 'D'you remember that evening?' He joins in her laughter. How could he forget it? They'd ordered paella to get in the local spirit only to find that the prawns not only still had their shells on but eyes and bloody *tentacles*: all four of them had been in hysterics at the sight of it. They left it untouched then went to a neighbouring restaurant to get pizza.

They unearth swimming certificates, stick-man drawings, birthday cards, school reports. She even takes a bittersweet pleasure in a piece of faded card with a shrivelled violet tacked to it, from the time a seven-year-old Danny picked half the flowers from an elderly neighbour's garden as a present for Beth. She made him go round and apologise but she pressed the flowers and kept them. She brushes against a petal and it crumbles to dust under her touch. Her shoulders buckle.

'I lie awake at night thinking, what do we do about his room? We'll have to clear it, with the baby coming and . . .' He's talking through tears now. 'I don't want to. Every time I think the pain's getting less, there's something to deal with.'

It is the first insight Beth has had into what goes on all night on the next pillow. She has been too consumed by her own guilt to register the detail and depth of Mark's. She looks into his brimming eyes and the thaw is instant as she sees her own grief reflected. She understands for the first time that they have been mourning Danny at different paces, two wavy lines on a graph that come in and out of range but rarely touch, taking it in turns to be the strong one, the angry one, the sad one, the quiet one, as though a double dose of the same emotion is more than the family could take. But now, on the floor of Danny's bedroom, amid the rubble of his little life, their discrete lines of grief connect and spark like two currents. Beth is plunged into true intimacy for the first time since it happened and the comfort of knowing her husband understands warms her skin like sunlight.

'I'm drowning here,' he says, giving in to tears.

'This isn't on you,' she says. With one hand resting in Mark's, she turns her attention back to the pressed violet and stares through it until she can see a little boy's soil-covered hands delivering the stolen flowers into her lap and a sad smile tugs at her cheeks. Beth is still light years from being able to give thanks for Danny's life. His death is still too big for that and too close. But for a few minutes there is respite from the present in the past.

Jack Marshall flails awake to the sound of breaking glass. His feet find their slippers in the dark and he reaches into his dressing gown. He pads downstairs to find that a brick has been thrown through his window. Shattered glass is everywhere. He throws open the front door; the vandals have fled but not before spray-painting the word PAEDO on the side of his boat. They've had a go at his car, too, cracks spreading around a hole in the dead centre of the windscreen.

By the time he has finished picking up the worst of the glass from his furniture and carpets, it is two o'clock in the morning. The van carrying the next day's newspapers will be here any minute. There is no point in going back to bed. He sits in his armchair and he waits for the familiar thud of the stack of papers landing outside the newsagent's.

FIRST PICTURES: CHILD-SEX BRIDE OF BROADCHURCH JACK screams the *Mirror*, while the *Mail* has gone with FAMILY PHOTOS THAT HIDE A DARK SECRET.

In the accompanying picture, Jack's hair is still dark: Rowena's is long and blonde and her face still flawless. Between them, Simon puffs out his cheeks, preparing to blow out the candles on the birthday cake before him. There are six flames, one for each year of his life.

There is a strange, dry groan, like the creak of a door that has not been opened for decades, as the old man begins to cry.

He walks slowly through the darkness to Harbour Cliff Beach. The waxing moon is his only witness as he steps out of his slippers close to Danny's shrine then continues barefoot across the sand. He comes to a standstill at the foot of the cliffs.

Water laps at his bare feet; waves throw tiny stones at his toes then drag the sand from under him. From his pocket he takes the one photograph that the press did not get their hands on and that he could not commit to the fire. Bringing it to his lips, he kisses his wife and child goodbye and recites the Lord's Prayer for the last time.

Dawn breaks two hours later to reveal Jack Marshall lying on his back, his arms spread wide as wings. Seaweed writhes around his dressing-gown cord and laces his hair. Waves wash over him, then retreat. White foam traces the outline of his corpse.

PART
TWO

42

Ten days have passed since Harbour Cliff Beach gave up its second body of the summer. Already the newsagent's has been boarded up, an estate agent's hoarding nailed across the door offering the premises for rent. Despite its prime location between the harbour and the beach, there has been no interest. Sand gets everywhere but mud sticks.

Jack Marshall's only public exoneration is a sheet of newsprint taped to the window. In the photograph, which was taken on the last night of his life, he is wearing his Sea Brigade uniform. The accompanying report, written by Oliver Stevens, has a one-word headline: INNOCENT.

It is half past ten in the morning and Karen White has already been up for five hours. Her journey began in London at dawn with a black cab, took in a long train ride and now she's in a minicab, windows wide as they speed along the only road into Broadchurch. They keep loose pace with another minicab, a grey Vauxhall, that left Taunton station at the same time. The passenger is a skinny middle-aged woman in a black hat with an old-fashioned lacy veil. She's too formally dressed to be press. It looks like Karen's the only hack who's bothered to make the journey.

She checks her BlackBerry and thinks about calling Olly. Their last conversation was his panicked small-hours visit to her hotel bedroom. He was almost in tears as he told her that they'd fucked up, that Jack Marshall's alibi had suddenly come good, and even though he should have known better he begged her to stop the story that had already gone to press. She hadn't slept, but skipped town the following morning and steeled herself to ignore Olly's barrage of texts and calls and then, a few days later, his email of the over-emotive piece he'd written for the *Echo* about how Jack Marshall had been hounded to death. Karen tried to get the *Herald* to print a more restrained version of the same story. Danvers, furious at her fuck-up, allowed her a single paragraph on page thirteen. She knew she was lucky even to get that. The story is dead.

In the intervening week and a half, Hardy has come up with no new leads. This means no reporter will touch the story again until there's an arrest at least, probably until someone's been charged.

Her last contact with anyone in Broadchurch was a curt email from Maggie Radcliffe saying that she hoped Karen was pleased with what she'd done. Karen didn't bother to dignify it with a reply. Of all the sanctimonious shit . . . she didn't notice Maggie taking Jack in when it all kicked off. Her precious Broadchurch turned on him happily, *eagerly*, like a bunch of Elizabethans cheering at a public hanging. The bottom line is that there's still a killer walking free and, a month into the investigation, Alec Hardy is no closer to catching him than he was the day after Danny died.

Naturally she has regrets: a man is dead, after all. She is sorry that in putting Broadchurch on the map, she opened the floodgates for the tabloids and the inevitable muck-raking. She's not happy about the way the red-tops went after him. But she did what she had to to bring Danny Latimer's case into the public eye, and she won't be made to feel guilty for that. Maggie should know that already; when Olly grows up a bit, he'll realise it too. But she won't let the blood be on her hands. She – *they* – wrote the best piece they could from the sources they had. At the time, Karen would have bet her mortgage on Marshall's guilt. All the evidence pointed in his direction and the police found nothing to contradict it until it was too late. If Hardy and his team were even halfway competent they would have checked Marshall's house out properly the first time they cautioned him and he would have been dismissed before they had even had a chance to consider him. Checking for CCTV, for fuck's sake: how basic does it get? And when they had exonerated him, they should have put a wire out then and there. They knew that the vigilantes were after him. Karen is sickened that Hardy actually seems to be doing a worse job in Broadchurch than he did in Sandbrook. He needs to be taken off this investigation and replaced with someone competent.

Until that happens, the Latimers won't be getting the coverage, or the justice, they deserve. Karen is still in touch with Beth, just as she is still in touch with Cate Gillespie, and she has promised her one last-ditch attempt to keep

Danny in the public eye. Today she has fought back with the only weapon she knows how to wield. She looks down at the copy of the *Herald* on her lap, a first edition bought from a vendor at Waterloo station. Hardy's bloodshot eyes stare blearily out from the front page. She's pleased with the headline.

The minicab turns into Church Road. Black-clad mourners stream up to St Andrew's. The bells sound one note over and over in an insistent, dolorous toll. The grey Vauxhall pulls up to the kerb in front of them. The passenger climbs slowly out of the back seat and stares up at the steeple through her veil.

Karen White folds the newspaper on her lap and reaches into her purse for the fare. Everyone else is here to bury Jack Marshall. She is here to bury Alec Hardy.

43

As the pews of St Andrew's fill, Hardy slumps alone at his desk, a copy of the *Daily Herald* in front of him. He has been staring at it for so long that the words above his photograph keep blurring, then snapping back into horrifying focus.

TWO BOTCHED CASES
ONE CHILD-KILLER ON THE LOOSE
AN INNOCENT MAN DEAD
IS THIS THE WORST COP IN BRITAIN?

He folds the paper in half and looks helplessly around his office. Thick folders, boxes of documents and bulging files obscure every surface. The black tie that he last wore at Pippa Gillespie's funeral swims across a sea of paper.

Operation Cogden has hit its budget ceiling. As of next week, Jenkinson is pulling back on staffing levels and forensic requests. This is how it goes when a case drags on. The bosses lose confidence and panic about explaining it to the accountants. It's up to Hardy to get as much as he can out of his team in the next few days. He'll break the records for overtime while he still can.

He looks down at his scrawled list of outstanding tasks and tries to prioritise. Miller can chase the forensics from the boat. They need to nail whoever smashed up Marshall's car, double-check the alibis of everyone in the vigilante crew.

Reluctantly, Hardy winds the funeral tie around his neck. Today's *Herald* will draw all the wrong kind of attention his way. But he must be seen to show his respects, and besides, if Danny's killer is at the church, it will be with another death on their conscience. He wants to see who's looking worried.

The Sea Brigade boys form a guard of honour, oars crossed above the heads of the mourners. Hardy, taller than most, has to duck under the improvised tunnel. A few of the boys are crying, but not Tom Miller.

Inside, the church is cool. There is a faint smell of incense. Sunshine illuminates the saints in the glass and the dark rosewood pews are almost full.

When Hardy walks the aisle, Beth Latimer turns as though alerted to his presence. She fixes him with a long, steady look that conveys the irony that whilst she can attend this old man's funeral, she still can't bury her boy. Hardy does not need reminding. He feels the irony. He lives it.

He settles into a pew with a good vantage point and takes a register. That woman with the bright red hair standing next to Olly Stevens must be Miller's prodigal sister. She has the hardened look of an addict. Hardy searches her face for a family resemblance and finds none, but her identity is confirmed when Miller pointedly takes a pew on the other side of the church.

Many of the congregation shuffle around awkwardly, clearly unused to being inside a church. Others look at home here: Liz Roper has a kind of ownership of the place. Maggie Radcliffe arrives arm-in-arm with her partner Lil. They know what's appropriate; they don't gawp in touristy wonder like a lot of the others, although they exchange a look loaded with meaning that Hardy can't interpret as they head up the aisle together. Some churches are still old-fashioned about same-sex couples but he imagines that they appeal to Paul Coates' highly developed sense of political correctness. Maggie turns left towards the front pew, then swerves so quickly that she crashes into Lil, who nearly loses her balance. Lil whispers something in her ear; Maggie shakes her head, then nods it, as if to say she's all right. The two women eventually settle on the far right-hand side of the church.

Hardy cranes to see what has spooked the usually unflappable Maggie. Directly underneath the pulpit sits Susan Wright, wearing a gargoyle scowl.

The congregation sing 'For Those in Peril on the Sea' as the coffin is brought to the altar. On top of the casket is a ship in a bottle and the photograph of Jack that accompanied Olly Stevens' tribute in the *Echo*. Liz Roper cries loudest of all, noisy racking sobs that she manages to subdue by the time the hymn comes to an end.

Hardy folds his arms as Reverend Paul Coates takes the pulpit, his white vestments billowing around him. He doesn't know what he's looking for – signs of anxiety, guilt or evasion, the usual – but what he gets is a man coming to life in front of his audience.

'We're assembled here today to share our grief and to

celebrate the life of Jack Gerald Marshall,' says Coates. 'Blessed are those who mourn, for they will be comforted.' Will they fuck, thinks Hardy.

'Jack Marshall was a good man. As has been made clear since his death, an innocent man. The local newsagent and Sea Brigade master, who kept children secure on land and safe at sea. So how are we here? We let him be smeared and intimidated. We weren't there when he needed us. So today, in celebrating Jack, we also have to admit: some of us failed him.' He trains his gaze on Hardy, so obviously that heads turn in his direction. 'Just as we failed Danny Latimer. The second commandment tells us: "Love thy neighbour as thyself." In this, the darkest of times, we have to be better. If we're not a community of neighbours, we're nothing.'

Hardy hopes his anger isn't showing on his face. Coates knows perfectly well that he was a lone voice of support for Marshall, but by repeatedly using the word 'we', he sides with those who pointed the finger at Jack and cast the stones, creating alliance where really there is none. The crafty bastard. He wonders how the background checks are going on Coates and makes a mental note to prioritise them.

At the end of the service, there's a satellite delay on the congregation's 'Amen' as the heathens hastily tack their prayers on to the tails of those who know the protocol.

Miller joins him on the short walk to the Traders Hotel for the wake.

'So,' he begins, embarrassed by the mascara that dirties her cheeks. 'Keep an—'

'—eye on everyone, say if I see anything out of the ord-inary. I've got it,' she recites.

Hardy bridles: if she would only bloody listen, he wouldn't have to repeat himself.

In the packed bar, he's on high alert. He notices that Paul Coates is about the only other person who doesn't seem to have an alcoholic drink in his hand. To keep control while all about him lose it? He's certainly revelling in the new atten-tion, shaking hands with strangers who thank him for a beautiful service.

'Holding a wake for Jack here,' Coates says to Becca Fisher as she takes his empty glass. 'It's very Christian of you.'

'Which is funny, 'cause I'm a total heathen,' she says with a wink. Their shared laughter suggests a deeper relationship than Hardy was aware of. If he had known the bar was set that low, he might have made a move himself. There's no accounting for taste.

There is a lull in the chatter, a subtle shift in atmosphere that always occurs when the Latimers enter a room. There's an added frisson this time, perceptible, Hardy supposes, only to those who know about Mark's affair with Becca. Beth's head is high as she approaches the bar. 'I'll have a white wine, and a beer for my *husband*,' she says. Becca only nods. Mark looks like he wants to vaporise.

Coates' smooth progress through the crowd has taken him out of the bar and into the atrium. Hardy finds him halfway up the stairs, in earnest conversation with Tom Miller, who's sitting on the top step. An alarm bell sounds in his head and he pushes towards them.

He has barely taken his first step when the image of the

vicar and the boy begins to swim before his eyes. Not now, not here, he thinks. Short of a televised press conference, he can't think of a worse place to have an attack. He tries to apply mind over matter but his vision doubles and his legs buckle. He falls against a table of drinks that crash to the floor. All conversation is silenced: there's a sarcastic cheer and someone makes a jibe about one too many. Hardy, dripping with someone else's beer, steadies himself with immense effort. By the time his focus returns to the stairs, Paul Coates has gone. He looks around for Miller: she's nowhere to be seen, but he hauls himself up the stairs and sits next to Tom. If he picks up on anything that gives him concern, they'll do this properly, by the book.

'Do you get along with Paul?' he asks.

'I suppose.' Tom looks uncomfortable.

'Did Danny get along with him? Did they ever talk in private? Or meet, outside of computer club?'

Tom opens his mouth to speak but Joe Miller joins them, his face set to Protective Parent: whatever Tom was going to say, he won't say it now.

'Just talking,' says Hardy.

'I hope so,' says Joe. 'He's just lost his best friend.'

Tom leaps to his feet. 'I wish everyone would stop saying that! He wasn't my best friend. I hated him. And if you really want to know, I'm glad he's dead.'

Tom bursts into tears and flees the room, shoving his way past a frail-looking woman in a black veiled hat. Joe's anger turns to mortification, red spots appearing high on his cheeks. A second later, he's down the stairs as fast as the crowd will allow, following Tom out of the front door. Hardy is too wrecked to chase after them. He shouldn't have approached Tom. But he hardly goaded him into his outburst. He runs his identity parade through his head. The men stand four abreast now, then he lets his mind's eye drop to take in a little boy's figure.

It's probably the pressure of the case getting to Tom. The pressure of having lost his friend and barely seeing his mother for weeks. Or is it? The way this case is going, Hardy can't afford to rule anything out.

He turns his attention back to Paul Coates.

The journalists have been watching Hardy watch the crowd. Karen White is particularly interested in his interest in Paul Coates. He can't take his eyes off him.

'Look at that,' says Karen to Maggie. 'I think our dog has found a new bone.'

'Paul *Coates?*' says Maggie. 'No . . .'

'You watch,' says Karen. 'He'll go after that vicar now whether he's guilty or not. Once Alec Hardy's got an idea in his head, that's it. He gets so obsessed with one aspect of a case that he gets tunnel vision. He can never see two sides to a story, that's his problem.'

'Hmmm,' says Maggie with a smirk. 'Actually, I know someone else like that.'

Karen looks around the crowd, but she has no idea who Maggie might mean. When she looks back, Paul Coates has disappeared.

On the way to St Andrew's, she passes the veiled woman waiting, presumably for her cab to Taunton, at the bus stop. Shame she's not press: they could have shared a cab back to

Taunton and split the expenses. The woman steps towards her on spindly legs.

'Karen White?' she says. Maybe she *is* press after all. Karen's smile is wide.

'Sorry, do we know each other?'

The woman peels back her veil by way of reply. Karen gives an involuntary gasp. The woman's hair is a sleek blonde chignon but her skin is pitted, countless flecks of shiny pink scar tissue lacerating white flesh. The planes of her face are familiar but fugitive, like Karen's looking at the sister, or the mother, of someone she has met only once. It's hard to tell; she is distorted, like something that has melted and then reset. Karen makes these assessments in seconds, and only then does she notice the fury blazing in the woman's eyes. She tilts her head back. By the time Karen realises what's happening, it's too late: a warm globule of stale saliva lands on her cheek.

'You people *disgust* me,' she says. She is trembling all over.

The grey Vauxhall pulls up at the bus stop. The driver opens the passenger door and Rowena Marshall gets in without a backward glance.

44

People keep telling Beth that time heals. But what happens if time has broken? Some hours pass in a blink: some minutes last for ever. Her mind feels like one of those Salvador Dalí paintings where all the clocks have melted. Since Danny was ripped from her, time has lost its shape. Chloe is in charge of her own teenage life. Even in grief she lives out the long lazy unstructured days of the summer holiday. When Mark goes back to work his life will have a different kind of spontaneity, the rapid response of emergency callouts. But Danny: his life was still hers to shape her own around. The circadian rhythm of school, football, swimming. Breakfast, lunch, tea. These things still defined her day far more than work.

A baby would solve this. A baby would give time shape again, measured out in her own swollen belly and then enslavement to its routines. It would give her a reason to get up in the morning. It would give meaning to the constant waking at night.

*

Ellie wakes up late to find the house empty and a note from Joe saying he's taken the boys to the park. Tom, apparently, has been awake since six. This doesn't feel right. Fred's normally up with the dawn but Tom used to be someone you had to shake awake, pulling the covers off him. He has refused counselling so far but it remains on offer for all Danny's classmates and Ellie wonders if they should ask him again. She barely sees Tom from one day to the next at the moment. She checks the clock: half an hour until she's due in. Five minutes later, she's showered and dressed. Within ten, she's at the skate park, coffee in hand.

Joe is impossible to miss in his Dad Coat. 'Another nine!' he shouts, as Tom rounds the half-pipe. 'Dead heat! Goes to another round.'

He sounds enthusiastic but violet shadows cup his eyes. Ellie has been so overwhelmed by her own exhaustion and concern for Tom that she keeps forgetting it's taking its toll on Joe, too. Since this investigation started, he has had to be both parents at once. She is gratified that, despite this, his face still lights up when he sees her.

'How're *you* doing?' he asks, pulling her in for a hug. 'You were a bit . . . distant, yesterday.'

She buries her face in bright blue nylon. 'I kept looking round the bar at the wake thinking: It's someone here. Why can't I see it? The longer this goes on, the more I start to suspect everyone.'

'Oi!' Joe feigns offence. 'When you say *everyone* . . .'

Ellie grins. '*Nearly* everyone.'

'That's a shame, because I am available for rigorous questioning in our bedroom every evening.' He offers her his

284

wrists. 'And you might want to bring your handcuffs, because I can be quite a troublesome prisoner.'

'I hope you've got a good alibi.'

'My wife, as it happens, in bed next to me, all night. Snoring, I'm afraid.'

'I do not snore. I *exhale*.' They've been having this conversation since the first night they spent together. There's deep consolation in this old familiar script.

'I'll record you one night, then you'll see.'

Joe leans in for a kiss, much to Tom's disgust.

'Dad! Get a room! You're supposed to be scoring!'

Ellie smiles. She kisses Joe, then Fred, goodbye, spares Tom the ordeal in front of his friends, and heads into work smiling, her mood recalibrated.

Hardy's at his desk, glowering over herbal tea and toast. 'Do you know what I did last night, Miller?'

'Dressed up as Lady Gaga?' she asks. He ignores her and she feels the slow puncture of pleasure that her boss's company always evokes.

'I followed our young vicar. I thought, he likes to walk of an evening. I wonder where he walks. Well, yesterday evening, he didn't walk, he drove. To Yeovil. Over the border, darkest Somerset. All that way for a meeting of Alcoholics Anonymous.'

'*Recovering* alcoholic, if he's going to meetings,' corrects Ellie. 'If we're suspecting alcoholics, you'll have to include half this station.' Behind the quip, her gut instinct is denial. There's no way it's Paul Coates. But she notices what she's doing and checks herself in time. She's learning to throw her weight behind every line of enquiry whether it makes her comfortable or not. 'Is it relevant?' she asks.

'Well, he didn't mention it.' Hardy clicks his pen to press home his point. 'Let's redouble our efforts on him while we've still got the resources. I want everything on him. Last parish, old girlfriends, overdue library books and exactly what goes on in that computer class.' He sifts through the files on his desk before lighting on the one he wants.

'Forensics from the boat,' he says. 'What d'you make of that?'

It's hard to read properly under Hardy's eye, and Ellie feels that she's under suspicion because of her family's link to the boat. Still, she tries to block Hardy out and manages to digest the meat of the report. They found Danny's blood, hair and handprints, paint chips that match his skateboard and traces of the cleaning product like the one used on his body. Hardy is still staring at her and she thinks fast.

'So … while they were transporting Danny's body down the coast, the killer was trying to clean any traces they may have left on it. The cleaner's probably from the supplies at the hut, which means none of this was planned. They were panicking.'

Hardy nods his approval: they're on the same wavelength for once. 'What were they doing with Danny's skateboard in the boat?' He drums his fingers on the desk. 'Who had access to it again? I think it's time we asked your little nephew.'

At the *Echo*, Ellie feels self-conscious and gauche: around Oliver it's impossible not to be Auntie Ellie, and she's glad when Hardy takes the reins.

'Who knew it was moored there and when was it last taken out?' he asks.

'Everyone knew,' says Olly. 'Everyone who walked down on that part of the beach, anyway. Last time we took it out was that really hot weekend in March; we went paintballing down the coast, with Tom and Danny.' Ellie does a double take: Tom's never been paintballing. Olly colours slightly. 'Um, Mark asked Joe 'cause he knew you'd say no to Tom using weapons. It ended up being me, Tom, Danny, Nige and Mark. Legendary day. Probably the last day I spent any time with Danny.'

Ellie is still reeling from the knowledge that Joe would go behind her back over something like this. She is temporarily lost for words.

'So all those people knew how the boat was stored, how to unlock it, how to start the motor?' says Hardy. 'Who else?'

'Loads of people. Mum lets people borrow it for cash all the time. Everyone's had a day on it, one time or another. Umm . . . Kev the postman. At least three of Tom's teachers. It's a great day-boat for fishing.' He casts about for more names. 'Oh yeah. And Paul Coates.'

Finally Hardy looks satisfied.

45

It's Mark's first day back at work. Nige can't carry the load for ever, and they need the money. Beth makes him a packed lunch: ham-and-mustard sandwiches, banana, those sodding crisps that she never wanted once she'd got them home from the supermarket and a can of Coke. She wonders, as she presses down the seal on the Tupperware, what happened to Danny's lunchbox. Last she remembers of it was carrying it across the school playing field the day they lost him. There are lots of tiny holes like this in her memory now, trivial things that it nevertheless disturbs her not to remember.

'Will you be all right, back at work?' she asks Mark.

'I'm always all right, me,' he says. There's a pause. 'When do we talk about the baby?'

She shuts him down. 'Not today.'

'You've been saying that for weeks now. We need to plan. One way or the other.'

She's not doing this. Not now. 'Have a good day at work. Send my love to Nige.'

She waves him off to a day of other people's houses, tense

on his behalf. They won't know how to treat him. They'll be embarrassed for him, embarrassed for having problems as trivial as a blocked U-bend or a temperamental boiler when his own life has been torn apart, and they'll overcompensate with biscuits and mindless chatter.

Beth envies Mark the escape. She has put her old employers at the Tourist Information out of their misery and handed in her notice. How can she go back to her old job? Broadchurch has become synonymous with a child murder. The few happy families who haven't cancelled their summer holidays won't want the dead boy's mum giving them directions to the RIB boat.

As if embracing the spirit of new beginnings, Chloe is taking a day trip to Exeter with her friends, an epic bus and train relay that she's been doing since she was fourteen, but it feels bigger and further away than usual today. When Beth drops Chloe at the bus stop, the girls pick up on Beth's nerves as well as Chloe's own desire to get out of Broadchurch.

'We'll look after her, I promise,' says Lara, linking an arm through Chloe's. Lara is Bob Daniels' eldest and she's grown up with Chloe. Beth still has her number in her phone from years ago when she used to pick both girls up from their ballet class.

The concern flows both ways. 'Will you be OK in an empty house?' asks Chloe. Beth nods so she doesn't have to lie outright. She's not going home to an empty house. She loops around the block to cover her tracks, then takes the road out of town, on her way to the meeting that Karen White set up, driving a little too quickly so that her doubts cannot catch up with her.

After two hours in the car, Beth finds herself pushing

open the door of a Little Chef on a quiet A-road in a part of the country she's never been before. She is the first one there. There is still time to back out as she orders an over-priced coffee that she doesn't really want and watches tyres whip drizzle into spray on the road outside.

As the caffeine hits her bloodstream she wishes she had gone for decaf. She's a nervous wreck. When the door opens, she gets a jolt, like she's seen someone famous. Cate Gillespie's face tells her that the recognition is mutual and Beth realises that's her too, now, that grotesque celebrity who can silence a room.

'God, this is weird, right?' she says, as Cate slides into the opposite seat.

'Yeah,' says Cate grimly. 'Listen, I'm sorry for what you're going through.'

She orders a pot of tea. Up close, their differences are obvious. Cate's a few years older than Beth and better-spoken, like she's been to university. She reminds Beth, if she's honest, of those middle-class mothers, the ones who'd moved to Broadchurch from London or wherever, who used to look down on her in the baby groups when Chloe was tiny. Despite this, their bond is fast, deep and true.

'I understand your pain.'

'You're the first person to say that who I've properly believed.'

Cate twists her mouth into a sympathetic smile. There is a vestige of prettiness that suggests she was beautiful before it happened. She still is, in that all her features are still even and her eyes are still bright green and her hair is still glossy, but a disfiguring grief emanates from her.

'D'you get those people,' says Cate, 'who are so desperate to let you know how deeply they feel your pain and you're thinking, "Piss off, you haven't got a clue"?'

'Yes!' says Beth, giddy with the relief of having it articulated for her like this. 'And it's like they stick to you, they won't leave you alone, they're so desperate for you to be grateful.'

'And they haven't got a clue about grief, not real grief, not like this . . . ' Cate waves her hand vaguely at Beth. 'I used to assume that grief was this thing inside that could be fought and vanquished. But it's not. It's an external thing, like a shadow. You can't escape it, you have to live with it. And it never grows smaller, you just come to accept that it's there. I kind of grew fond of it, after a while.' Beth has no idea what her face is doing but Cate suddenly breaks off. 'Is that mad? Am I too bleak, too quick?'

'You're the first person I've met to talk any sense,' says Beth. Even Mark doesn't understand her like this. She feels that she and Cate can say anything to each other. Forget Paul Coates, forget Mark, Ellie, even her mother and Chloe. *This* is the relationship she's been looking for.

'What's it been, five weeks?' asks Cate. 'Marriage still OK?'

Abruptly Beth realises that she *can't* say anything to Cate. The stuff with Mark is too messy, too tawdry for this conversation, it's disrespectful to Danny and Pippa. She swallows hard, then settles for, 'Up and down. You?'

Cate's set face says it all. 'Divorced. Most couples with a murdered child get divorced, you know that, right? You've googled all of this, I presume. Just like I did.' She brings her cup to her lips but doesn't drink from it. 'Karen said you've got DI Hardy in charge.' She leans in close. 'Listen, Beth, that man is *toxic*. They lost evidence, they ballsed up the trial. The man who killed my daughter is still out there because of that man. Do not believe anything he says.'

Beth feels sick. She has no *choice* but to trust Alec Hardy. And this is different to Sandbrook, isn't that what everyone keeps telling her? 'OK, but—'

'God, there's so much I want to tell you,' says Cate, and for the first time it occurs to Beth that this is a kind of therapy session for her as well. The thought is unsettling: she realises that, in a fucked-up sort of way, she wants Cate to maintain the role of authority here. 'But you've probably got questions.'

'Yeah, I have,' says Beth, wondering where to begin. 'My husband's gone back to work—'

'Wow, he didn't waste any time,' says Cate sardonically. 'There's the man for you, has to do things, can't bear to be thinking.'

'And my daughter, she's going to be back at school in a couple of weeks. But I don't want to go back to work, it doesn't feel right.'

'Of course not,' says Cate. Beth is so relieved. Maybe she's got the real answers.

'I just keep feeling, I wish there was a guidebook for this,' she says. 'Because minute to minute, what do I do? What do you do?'

Cate seems to hollow out and Beth feels a corresponding void deep in her own belly. 'I worked for a little bit,' she says flatly. 'But I got these terrible headaches and I couldn't concentrate, let alone do people's accounts. But also that nagging sense of pointlessness. What does it matter if I don't finish this work? The worst has already happened.'

This is not what Beth wants to hear. 'So how do you keep busy, during the day?'

'Honestly?' Beth nods even though she knows she's not going to like it. 'I go to bed. I sleep. Then I wake up and it's still the same so I have a drink. And then another drink. And then I cry. Maybe a couple of hours. And then I watch TV, unless it reminds me of my little girl, which it does, nearly all of the time, in the maddest ways. So I take a sleeping pill.' She picks up on Beth's distress at last. 'Sorry. You probably came looking for answers. I don't have them. My life got stolen that day. The best part of me was killed. And I can't get back from that. Maybe you'll do better than me.'

The conversation dries. Beth's desire to get away from Cate is suddenly as strong as her need to be with her was a few minutes earlier. They have a half-hearted tussle about who should pay for the drinks, solved only when the waitress tells them that the bill has already been taken care of, that it's on the house. Beth doesn't understand at first, but at second glance the waitress has clumped wet lashes and blotched cheeks, and it's obvious what has happened.

'Please,' says Beth, rooting for her purse. 'I can't let you, I can't ...' her voice cracks. What she wants to say is that it feels obscene to accept this hospitality, that it feels like she is profiting somehow from Danny's death, but she can't bring herself to speak so she tries to pay instead. Her fingers shake as she fumbles for coins until Cate's still hand presses lightly down on hers.

'Let them,' she says gently, and nods at the waitress, who scurries off gratefully as though she's been given dispensation. Beth understands that this has happened to Cate before, possibly dozens of times, and that this won't be the last time it happens to her.

They go their separate ways with promises to meet again. Beth has no idea if Cate means hers: she has no idea if she means it herself. The rain is coming down in sheets now, and she sits behind the wheel, unable to drive. She watches Cate pull out of the car park with the feeling that all hope for a normal life is going with her. She had thought that nothing could match the horror of the past. Now she dreads the future.

She checks her phone before driving back to Broadchurch. There are no missed calls but one text message that sends her heart flying to her throat. It's from Lara.

Tell Chlo we hope she's OK. Lara xx

She calls Chloe first to find out what's going on. The phone is turned off. Keep calm, keep calm, thinks Beth as she hits Lara's number. Life isn't that cruel. She manages to keep her panic under control as Lara tells her how Chloe was very quiet the whole way to Taunton and jumped off the train seconds before it pulled out, before the other girls could stop her and without telling them why.

This cannot be happening.

This cannot be happening again.

Alone in a strange car park, miles from home, Beth calls Mark.

46

Maggie Radcliffe and Lil Ryan stand side by side in front of Ellie.

'Hi, Maggie,' says Ellie. 'You better? Olly said you were under the weather.'

You would need to know the couple well to notice the subtle shift that has occurred. It's not that their appearances have changed. Lil is still soft and dark where Maggie is hard and brassy, but right now, Maggie is subdued while Lil's gaze is shot through with steel.

Maggie opens her mouth but nothing comes out. She looks to Lil, who says, 'I'll tell her if you can't.' The two women join hands and Maggie seems to draw strength from Lil's touch.

'I had a visitor,' she begins. 'I was threatened, in the office, by Susan Wright.' Maggie and Lil exhale as one with evident relief at getting the name out. 'The one with the dog who works for the RIB boat? I found out that she'd been using an alias, Elaine Jones, and I called her out on it. She came into the office when I was alone and she said ...' A shudder racks her. 'She said she knew men who would rape me. Us.' She drops her eyes to her lap; clearly, the threat has been a violation in itself.

'Oh my God.' Ellie is horrified. She writes the name ELAINE JONES in capitals on her notepad. 'Maggie, I'm sorry. I'll have uniform go out and talk to her.'

'Only uniform?' says Lil. She's more aggressive, fighting Maggie's corner, than Ellie has ever seen her on her own behalf. 'She made rape threats. She's using an assumed name.'

Any other summer, this would have shot to the top of Ellie's list. It needs to be flagged as a potential hate crime, for a start. But now . . . 'I'm in the middle of a murder investigation.' It comes out snappier than she intended. 'I'm sorry. But you must understand that we have to prioritise the Danny Latimer case. And a visit from the police can be pretty powerful. I'll send them out today.' At this, Maggie looks slightly mollified. Ellie keeps to herself the irony that a routine uniform call-out currently has a better chance of making progress than one more piece of evidence tossed into the swirling black hole that is Operation Cogden. 'You're welcome to follow it up yourself.' Only after Ellie has made the suggestion does she hear it through Maggie's ears. It sounds like she is subcontracting her own job to the press. Perhaps she is. Perhaps that's what it has come to.

'Thanks,' says Maggie sarcastically, but something inside her has shifted and it's a trace of the old Maggie. She leaves with Lil hot on her heels. Ellie puts a call in to uniform, telling them to remain sensitive to the possibility of a homophobic attack. She kicks back on her chair and stares for a while at the white sky outside her window. Middle-aged women making rape threats to each other. What the hell is *happening* to this place?

Maggie goes back to the *Echo* with a sense of purpose for the first time in days. If even Ellie Miller won't take the threat seriously, then she's got no chance with that miserable Scot. He doesn't do hunches, that one. But if she can put evidence in front of him . . .

Maggie has been scared even to research Susan Wright; of course, she doubts that the woman who lives in a caravan and deals in violence has the capability to bug her office, but something closer to superstition has stopped her taking this into her own hands. But not any more. Maggie will not be cowed any longer.

She lines up everything she needs: her trusty old Rolodex, a glass of red, her e-cig and her telephone. There's a determined set to her mouth.

She flips through the Rolodex to familiarise herself with the old names. It needs updating: a couple of these people have given up the game, and a couple more are dead now. But there are still plenty of contacts she can turn to. Mentally, she lists them in order of usefulness, and puts in a call to Mick Oxford, a brilliant hack whose Fleet Street nickname was the Walking Encyclopaedia. 'I didn't die, just moved to Dorset,' she says, when the sound of her voice on the line is met with disbelief. 'I'm looking for anything from your archives on a Susan Wright, cross-reference with the name Elaine Jones. Any time from 1985, give or take a year. There's a bottle of Jameson's in it for you, petal. I'll email you my details. Love to the family.'

With every contact she calls, she can feel her old strength returning. She's ten phone calls in with two dozen more to go when Olly walks in.

'You're back!' he says with a gratifying smile. He is right in more ways than he can possibly know.

'Indeed I am,' she says. 'Should've done this ages ago. Pop your bag down, make yourself useful. Ring these numbers, tell them I'm looking for anything I can get on Susan Wright.'

Olly's eyebrows shoot up. 'That woman with the dog? What's she got to do with any of this?'

She wonders again whether to tell Olly about the threat. She finds that she can't, although for different reasons now. Before, fear kept her mute. Now it's pride. She is ashamed that it has taken her so long to get her act together.

'That's for us to find out,' says Maggie. 'If the police won't look into her, we'll have to do it ourselves.'

Olly picks up the phone to make the first call but is distracted as the fax chirrups into life behind him. He turns around and looks at it in wonder. 'Who still uses a *fax?*'

'All right, child of the future. My old contacts would still be using inkwells if they'd let them.' She pulls the pages off and reads them. 'But I'll tell you what, Mick Oxford knows how to find anything you need. You won't have to go through my Rolodex after all.'

Her smile falters as she reads the grainy fax. The horror story before her gives credence to Susan Wright's threat. Maggie has no doubt now that she knows men who would commit rape, and worse besides. But as well as writing the lines, she knows how to read between them and there is a subtext to this story, a vulnerability that Maggie will not hesitate to exploit.

'This is golden, Olly,' she says *'Golden!'* She gets Olly to drive her to the caravan park. Her new-found bravado only goes so far. With him waiting in the car, Maggie raps hard on the glass front door of number 3. When there is no answer, she tapes something to the door: an envelope with her name on it and the *Broadchurch Echo* masthead crouched in the bottom right-hand corner.

That night, when Lil comes to collect her, Maggie can't stop grinning.

'What are you so happy about?' she asks as Maggie sidles into the passenger seat.

'I've got her,' says Maggie simply.

Lil returns her wide smile and leans over to kiss her on the cheek. 'Welcome home.'

Hardy has put a rocket up the detectives looking into Paul Coates. Miller lists all they've come up with:

'Assistant curate at Dorchester for three years prior to Broadchurch. All fine. Before that, little village in Wiltshire. Spoke to the parish there – also fine, but then I tracked down a parent from the youth group. According to them, he turned up a bit drunk one night and threw a Bible at a boy's head. The boy got taken to A&E. Paul was gently moved on.'

'I think it's time to bring our man of the cloth in for a little chat,' he decides.

They keep it informal at first, leaving the interview room door open and leading with the last time Coates used Olly Stevens' boat.

'I only used it once, probably over a year ago. I thought,

being as I was here now, I should be a bit more, y'know, fishermanly. So I took the boat and a rod and I caught nothing. Got a nice sunburn, though.' His smile is saintly; Hardy prepares to wipe it off his face.

'How long have you been going to Alcoholics Anonymous?'

It works: there's almost a snarl in its place. 'I see. I make a complaint about your failings with Jack Marshall and you come after me.'

Hardy doesn't bite. 'Not at all. Why Yeovil?'

'Because I can have privacy and not bump into parishioners.' Coates' self-possession is slipping by the second. 'Why is this relevant?'

'Were you drinking on the night of Danny's death?'

'I haven't had a drink for four hundred and seventy-three days.' He turns to Ellie. 'Is he always this objectionable?'

'He is excelling himself today.' As much as Hardy would like to think that Miller's siding with the suspect to lull him into a false sense of security, he doubts it. He consults the file before him.

'In your last job, you assaulted a child after you'd been drinking.'

Coates has the resigned intonation of someone who has trotted out an excuse time and again. 'I didn't assault him, it was a joke gone wrong, he was twice my size.'

'You have no alibi for the night of Danny's death.'

'*Why* would I kill him? What possible reason can you dream up for me to murder an eleven-year-old boy?' Hardy doesn't have to dream up reasons. There are as many motives as there are killers.

'You won't mind giving a DNA sample, will you?' he says. 'I'll do the honours, you wait here.'

As he walks off, he hears Coates say to Miller, 'I'm sorry, but he is a knob.'

'I know,' she replies. To Hardy's surprise, this time it stings.

Pulling on the latex gloves sends up a little cloud of powder that settles in drifts over Coates' black shirt. The vicar opens his mouth for the swab as directed. Hardy deliberately asks the first question as he twirls the cotton bud inside the other man's cheek. 'So what, religion took over the booze? Swapped one addiction for another?'

Coates preserves some dignity by waiting until he can speak again.

'You enjoy trying to rile me, don't you? What've you got against me?'

'Honestly?' says Hardy. 'You worry me. You were so eager to get in front of the cameras as soon as this kicked off. Like you wanted to own this for the Church. And you were round at the Latimers', like a fly round shit. I watch this happen every time. A terrible event, and the Church piles in gleefully because suddenly people pay you attention. When for the rest of the year, you're just that building no one goes in.'

'You have no concept of faith, do you?' says Coates. 'I didn't *muscle in*. People turned to me. Straight away. People who wouldn't normally even *think* about religion. They asked me to speak. They asked me to listen. They needed me. And you know why? Because there was a fear that you couldn't address, a gap you couldn't plug. Because all you have is suspicion, and an urge to blame whoever's in closest proximity.' Hardy folds his arms against the tirade. 'Look, you can accuse me, you can take samples, you can belittle who I was in the past. But you don't get to belittle my faith, just because you have none. People need hope right now, and they're certainly not getting it from you.'

He waits for Hardy's reaction like he's expecting some kind of conversion. Hardy keeps his arms folded and his mouth closed. He will not give Coates the satisfaction of knowing how shaken he is.

The words echo in his head for the rest of the afternoon. It is not true that he has no concept of faith. He has *always* believed in evidence and procedure. But where do you go if they fail you, as they are now? What happens then?

If Hardy were a different sort of man, he would pray for a miracle.

47

Beth shaves twenty minutes off the satnav's predicted journey time back to Broadchurch. Mark's explanation, designed to soothe her, has made everything worse. Boyfriend! How could Chloe have a boyfriend and not tell her? How could Mark know and not tell her?

Guilt has been a constant presence since losing Danny, but now she is choked by a new source of the same emotion. She has been so wrapped up in her little boy that she has forgotten about her little girl. She understands why Chloe would hide this boy Dean from Mark – who wants to tell their protective, angry dad they're seeing someone? – but from *her*? She thought they told each other everything.

Mark waits for her on the drive, engine running, passenger door open. 'He lives on a farm past Bredy Hill,' he says as she buckles herself in.

'When were you going to tell me?' She presses the window down as far as it will go.

'She wanted to tell you herself,' says Mark. He's taken his eyes off the road to look at her, and he has to pull sharply to the left to avoid a cyclist. He's driving too fast, hurtling towards a pothole in the road. He crosses it at speed; the car jolts. Instinctively Beth puts her hand on her stomach.

They turn into a winding lane banked by high hedges. Beth bites her tongue, afraid to break his concentration again.

'What's this Dean like then?' she says, when the road widens and straightens. 'Did she meet him at school?'

Mark pulls a face. 'He doesn't go to school. Um, he's seventeen.'

Beth lets rip. 'Brilliant. *Brilliant.* And you're all right with that?'

''Course I'm not bloody all right with it!' Mark roars back, still not slowing down. Finally he puts his foot to the brake and Beth watches the speedometer drop below sixty. 'But I'm not gonna push her away *now*,' says Mark. 'Look, I bet she's with him. I'm sure she's OK.'

'How can you ever say that now?' says Beth. She turns her face to the window as the van crowns Bredy Hill. The early evening sun casts a golden filter over the picture-postcard landscape. Beth barely sees it.

With little warning, Mark swerves into a run-down farmyard cluttered with old threshing machines and a rusting yellow tractor. Sorry-looking cows munch hay in a vast rusting barn. The only new thing is a shiny motorcycle with two crash helmets hanging on the back.

'He's got a bloody motorbike!' says Beth, but Mark shushes her with his hand on her forearm. She follows his gaze to a small outbuilding in the corner of the farmyard; there's movement inside. Mark stays calm on the short walk to the shack, then loses his composure at the last minute, shouting Chloe's name and shouldering the door at the exact second that Beth remembers the kind of thing she and Mark got up to in the middle of the afternoon when they were young, and thinks it might be a good idea to knock.

Whatever Beth was expecting, it wasn't this. The interior of the shack looks like a youth club. There are beanbags, a couple of battered chairs, fairy lights draped from the rafters and a flat-screen TV that's showing a video game. In the centre of the room, Chloe stands wearing a pair of head-phones. Her eyes are closed and she's gently swaying. Dean – good-looking, Beth registers that even in her shock – is frozen with a games controller in his hand. After what seems an eternity, he pulls the plug on Chloe's headphones. Her eyes saucer when she sees her parents.

'Mum! Dad!'

Beth doesn't know whether to slap Chloe or hug her. 'What the *hell* are you doing?'

'Dancing,' says Chloe. 'Dean made me a happy room.'

Dean gets up to take her hand. 'Somewhere she can just shut herself away,' he explains. 'Enjoy herself without feel-ing guilty.' Chloe smiles gratefully up at him. Beth looks at Mark and knows he's thinking the same thing: it's us, fifteen years ago. She is consumed with the most bittersweet feel-ing, like a longed-for kiss on broken skin.

'What happened to your day out with the girls?' asks Beth. Her anger has melted away.

'They were too *nice* to me,' says Chloe. 'Kept asking me if I was OK. Watching what they said to each other. Like I was a freak. I rang Dean. He came and got me from the train

305

station.' Beth tries not to wince at the thought of Chloe on the back of Dean's bike across miles of open countryside. 'I just wanted a break from being sad. I loved Danny, you know I loved him, but I need a break from being the dead boy's sister. It's suffocating me. And I know you can't understand that.'

Beth fights the tears: she doesn't want to embarrass Chloe by crying in front of Dean. She's grateful when Mark speaks for her.

'No,' says Mark. 'We do understand. Don't we?'

Beth nods, swallowing hard.

'Are you keeping the baby?' says Chloe. Beth looks to Mark – if he's told Chloe, she'll kill him – but he shakes his head. 'I heard you fighting about it,' says Chloe patiently, as if she's the parent. 'What you gonna do?'

Beth decides to repay Chloe's honesty. 'We don't know.' She looks around at the soft lights and the music and the sofas and feels ashamed as well as grateful that Dean has been the one to do this for her. 'But first we need to make a happy room for you at home.'

The door of St Andrew's church is always open, but Steve Connolly tiptoes through it with a trespasser's unease. He doesn't know what to do with his hands: they are too big for the pockets on his fleece, so he worries at his zip, then smooths down his hair. He looks around, studying each stained-glass window in turn, moving his lips as he reads the leaded inscriptions. There is a large stone statue of Christ in the transept: Steve touches the hem of its robe, then dips his head awkwardly. He lights a candle but doesn't find any money in his pocket, so he blows it out and places it back on the shelf. He seems eager to please, even though the church is empty. After making two circuits of the nave, he settles in a pew halfway down and bends his head in prayer. It is in this position that Reverend Paul Coates finds him half an hour later. At the sound of footsteps, Steve Connolly's eyes fly open as if a trance has been broken.

'You don't mind me being here, do you?' he says. There is apology in his body language: he is almost bowing. 'I'm not a regular.'

'Of course not,' says Paul. He squares off a pile of hymn books without taking his eyes away from Steve.

'Can I ask you something?' Steve leans forward in his earnestness. 'I know it sounds daft, but ... with God ... do you hear a voice? Does God talk to you?'

'No. Not directly. I just have faith that he'll show me the way.'

'This thing happens to me, and I'm still trying to work it out. I hear a voice, in my head. And it gives me messages. I had a message from Danny, I had to give to Beth Latimer.' He gives a short, bitter laugh. 'See, say it out loud and it sounds bonkers. But the Bible's full of talking angels and that, isn't it?'

'There's a bit of that, yes.' Steve doesn't seem to register the effort it takes Paul to keep a straight face.

'But what I keep wondering is, what if I was wrong? What if the message wasn't from Danny Latimer. What if it was from God? Or ... What if it's not from either of them, Danny or God, and it's just voices in my head?'

Paul sits down next to him. 'Who have you talked to about this?'

'The police. Beth. Now you.'

'What about medical advice?'

Connolly rolls his eyes. 'I reckon we both know where I'd end up, if I went in to a GP talking like this. I thought *you*'d understand.' His obvious disappointment is shot through with accusation. 'I thought we were both people who heard voices that weren't from the living.'

'I'm sorry to let you down,' says Coates patiently. 'Is that why you're in here?'

'No. I came to pray. The voice has stopped. So I'm praying to make it come again. 'Cause they need me: the family, the police. If I could just get another message, I could convince them. I could help them solve it.' His eyes glaze. 'But I'm getting nothing. And it scares me. What if I imagined it in the first place? What if I was wrong? What if I'm a liar? If I don't hear it again, what am I?'

The reverend is uncharacteristically lost for words.

48

The hands on Hardy's office clock stretch out for six and for once CID is emptying on time. Some lucky bastard – one of the quieter DCs whose name Hardy can never remember – is leaving today, and they're off to toast his post-Broadchurch future.

With time running out, Hardy would have kept the lot of them behind but Miller insists that a night in the pub will give the team the morale boost they so desperately need for the final few days' push of overtime. With collective spirits at an all-time low, he has little choice but to accept this. He draws the line at joining them, though. Instead, when Miller bounces up to his door, he gives her forty quid for a round and watches them file out to the pub with a mixture of relief and despair.

When he is sure they have all gone, he pulls out his mobile phone and rests it on the desk in front of him. In some ways he finds it easier to give a death knock or interview murderers than make this call. He is debased by his longing to hear Daisy, her real voice, not the chirpy voicemail greeting. He stares at his handset, willing it to ring out with her caller ID and spare him the rejection. He envisages her picture flashing up on his screen, feeling foolish at the indulgence. She hasn't called him in six months: why would she do it now? If wishing worked, he would talk to her every day.

He speed-dials her before he can stop himself and, with fast-fading hopes, counts the twenty rings before it flips to the recording.

'Hey, it's me,' he begins. Even to his own ears, the attempt at breeziness is unconvincing, but he perseveres. 'Checking in with your voicemail, as usual. Listen, if you do get the chance, give me a ring, it's been a really long time this time. I mean, I know you're busy, home and school and ... all that other stuff you do. But ... I do think of you. Every day. Sorry, not getting soppy, had my warning on that.' He gropes desperately for the right words. 'We could video call, couldn't we? I'd like that. You can be my first video call. Before you forget what I look like. This is Dad, signing off. I love you, darling. *Please*' – the word fractures halfway through – 'give me a ring.'

He sets the phone down on the desk, feeling utterly wretched. Unable to sit still, he makes a tour of the office, switching off printers, replacing the caps on pens and setting files at right angles. When he's completed his circuit he comes to the Operation Cogden whiteboard. Danny's school photograph has begun to curl at one edge. The immutable facts of deposition – time, date, location – are boxed off underneath the picture, but the rest of the whiteboard is a messy, scrawled-upon palimpsest of discounted suspects and off-the-mark theories.

'I can't do this,' Hardy hears himself say, and the words

are followed by an agonising pain, a huge fist squeezing his heart to bursting point. He staggers back until he hits a wall and slides helplessly down it. Hardy assumes his childhood comfort position, knees pulled up to his chest, so close that he can rest his chin there. Experience tells him that he can hold this pose for hours and hours. He remains motionless amid the debris of his investigation until his heart rate returns to its version of normal. By the time he gets up with a low wheeze and a click of the joints, it is dark outside.

49

Tom Miller, alone in his bedroom, can't settle on anything. He has abandoned his book for a magazine, the magazine for his Nintendo DS, but even that can't hold his focus. It is mid-afternoon, that annoying time of day when it's too late to join in anyone's daytime plans and too early to see if they want to meet up after tea, and in any case, no one's really allowed out late any more.

Downstairs, the sounds of the CBeebies channel and the dishwasher being loaded tell him that Fred and Joe are in. With an expression of resignation, he checks the parking space in front of the house for his mother's car. It's empty, but he sees something else that has him spring into life. He clears the stairs quicker than a skateboarder on a ramp, and is out of the front door in seconds. Joe, wiping down the high chair in the kitchen, doesn't register Tom's exit. Only Fred sees him go.

'Paul!' he shouts to the man walking towards the church. 'I need to ask you something!'

Paul Coates' face, set in a grimace, is wearing a smile by the time he turns to face Tom.

'Sure. Go ahead. Unless it's difficult, in which case I'm just going to run away from you.'

Tom grins. 'If someone deletes something from a hard drive, is it gone for ever?' He scratches his nose. 'My dad accidentally deleted something.'

Coates considers Tom for a second. 'No,' he says. 'There are recovery programs. If those don't work, the right tech expert could probably get it back. So no, not totally gone.'

'OK. Thanks,' says Tom, but he looks far from pleased with the answer.

Back in his room, he spends five minutes trawling through the recycle bin of his laptop, shaking his head at the screen and occasionally looking over his shoulder. The noise of the dishwasher can provide cover for a creeping parent. Eventually he slams the lid closed and slides the computer into his camouflage backpack, although he doesn't bother to pack the lead or the mouse.

This time he lets Joe know that he's going out. 'Jayden's going to the arcade,' he says. 'He's waiting at the top of the alley.'

It's the first time Tom's been anywhere on his own since Danny went missing. 'Tell you what, me and Fred'll walk you to the alley,' frowns Joe. Overprotectiveness is the default setting of all the parents in Broadchurch now, even the ones who used to pride themselves on giving their children old-fashioned freedom.

While Joe is getting his coat, Tom quickly and deliberately upends Fred's orange juice all over him, hair, clothes, the lot. Fred wails, more in bewilderment than discomfort. 'I couldn't stop him,' says Tom, when Joe charges in. Fred needs a dunk in the bath and a complete change of clothes.

'I can't leave Jayden on his own,' says Tom.

Joe looks from son to son. Fred screams louder. 'OK, fine,' he says, but he doesn't look happy about it.

At the end of the field, Tom bears left, away from the direction of the amusement arcade and towards Harbour Cliff Beach. Occasionally he adjusts his backpack to test for the reassuring heft of the laptop inside it. Frequently he looks over his shoulder, but whenever he sees someone else – a dog walker, another boy on a bike, a couple out rambling – he puts his head down and walks on. It is clear that he wants to be alone.

He is on the other side of the caravan park, en route to Briar Cliff, by the time he finds seclusion in a grassy dune. He wriggles out of his rucksack and sets it down. He turns slowly in a circle to check he is definitely alone. Then, from his pocket, he retrieves a small claw hammer. He taps it gently on his palm and stoops to unzip his rucksack.

A loud panting noise shocks Tom into dropping the hammer; it misses his foot by an inch and is immediately half-buried in the sand. His fear turns to delight when a large brown dog bounds over the edge of the dune and licks his hand. Tom laughs out loud, and wraps his arm around the dog's neck.

Susan Wright looms into view, a lead in her hand.

'He likes you.' Tom's face is nine-tenths smile as he wraps his arms around Vince's neck.

'He's so nice,' says Tom. 'I'm not allowed a dog. My little brother's allergic.'

314

'You wanna be careful,' says Susan. 'This is near where that boy died.'

Tom buries his face a little deeper into the dog's fur. 'He was my friend.'

'I'm sorry to hear that,' says Susan Wright. She checks for onlookers. The coast is literally clear, the woman, the boy and the dog the only living things in sight. She appears to weigh up a decision. 'Wanna come and feed Vince with me?' She nods to the third caravan back from the beach. 'He'll love you for ever.' Tom hesitates, looking Susan up and down, but is persuaded by Vince, who nuzzles his cheek and paws at his clothes. Tom nods. He appears to have forgotten the hammer sticking out of the sand, and if Susan notices it she does nothing about it. The smile she gives Tom does not reach her eyes.

The cliffs loom high above them, clouds scudding fast behind, giving the impression that the rock face is constantly falling forward but never hitting the ground. When they arrive at the caravan, they find an envelope taped to the glass front door. Susan tears it off, and open, in one movement, reading its contents in seconds. She turns up her nose but otherwise her expression does not change.

She beckons Tom through the door and checks behind her one more time before closing it. No one sees him go in. The curtains are drawn. Inside, there are tatty pine cupboards, messy worktops and no photographs anywhere. It does not look like Susan and Vince have many visitors: she has to clear a space on the cluttered banquette for Tom to sit down. She shows Tom where the dog's food is kept, in a big plastic box underneath the fire extinguisher. When Vince has finished eating, he engages Tom in a game of tug-of-war with an old rope. She watches them in silence before setting down a plate of biscuits.

'You can take him out for a walk any time you like, now you know where we are.' She pushes the biscuits towards Tom and leaves her fingers on the edge of the plate until he takes one. 'Did you really know that boy that died?' she says. 'It can't have been nice for you.'

Tom nods through a mouthful of custard cream. 'My mum's in the police. She's a detective on the case.'

'Is she now?' Susan stands up. She seems to fill the tiny space; she stands before the window and everything darkens a shade. 'Come over here, Tom. I want to show you something. Come on, don't be shy.'

Reluctantly Tom ends his game with the dog and lets Susan put her hand on his shoulder and steer him towards a slim cupboard by the front door that is fastened with a shiny new padlock. She rattles the key in the lock and pulls the door. There, slanted against the wall, is a skateboard whose yellow underside is painted with a distinctive geometric blue pattern.

'It's Danny's,' says Tom. He is bewildered rather than afraid.

'That's right,' Susan is close behind him. 'I've been looking after it. But if you were his friend, I think it's only right that you should have it. Don't you think?'

'Right, I'm not having this,' says Mark. 'We're going out.'

Beth and Chloe look up from the daytime TV show

they've been watching for two hours, although Beth couldn't describe anything that's happened in it.

'Where are we going?' says Chloe.

'It's a surprise,' says Mark. There's a spark in his eye that Beth hasn't seen for a long time. He's up to something, and in a good way. He keeps the mystery going as he marches them towards the seafront. A boy on a skateboard whizzes past on the opposite pavement.

Danny! Hope dances wildly in Beth's chest. She whips around to catch him but it's only Tom Miller – she recognises his camouflage backpack – winding his way along the pavement. The Danny reflex is still strong in her cruel subconscious. Tears prick. She barely looks at her surroundings after that, so it's with horrified surprise that she learns where Mark is taking them.

'Here we are,' he says with a flourish outside the amusement arcade.

'Are you serious?' asks Chloe.

'Trust me.' Mark is well prepared, taking pound coins from a little bag in his pocket. 'Fiver each. Don't spend it all at once. You'll get most value out of the 2p machines.' Beth opens her mouth to protest. 'Trust me,' he repeats.

She wants to, but she can't trust her own judgement these days, let alone anyone else's. Is this appropriate? Or is it deeply fucked-up? What will people think? But Mark and Chloe are already inside and she would rather be with them than out here on her own, tortured by the sight of a little boy with a mop of dark brown hair begging his mum for another go on the dolphin ride. She forces herself in.

Like the rest of the tourist spots this summer, the arcade

317

is half-empty and Beth's grateful for that. There are only a handful of people and nobody they know. She starts off humouring Chloe who is in turn humouring Mark. She is going through the motions: feeding coppers into the cascade machines and watching them fall. But as Chloe and Mark stalk the various piles, taking bets on which one will fall first, a little miracle happens. Chloe starts to have fun and it's infectious. She spends her last pound on an Air Hockey tournament. Beth takes a moment to notice what fun she's having and that's when Chloe slams the puck into the goal. She holds her fingers to her forehead in an L for Loser, laughing. Beth had forgotten how pretty Chloe is when she laughs. She catches Mark's eye and beams over a silent thank you. It's still too soon for a happy room at home, but he's done his best to create that space for her somewhere new.

He draws them both into a bear hug and utters the immortal word, 'Chips.' A few minutes later the three of them sit side by side on the sea wall, lunch on their laps.

'Was that good, or was that good?' asks Mark.

'It was good,' Chloe admits.

'We used to do this all the time, when you were little,' says Mark. 'When it was pissing down with rain. All four of us.' He uses the old number without thinking and it's as if the wind has died down. They sit in silence for a few minutes.

'Danny would've spent it all on the grabbers,' says Chloe.

'And lost,' says Mark.

Beth arrives at her decision suddenly and with such powerful certainty that she is astonished there was ever any room for doubt.

'We'll have to take the baby in, when it's born,' she says into her chips. 'It'll love all that noise and flashing lights.'

In her peripheral vision she can see the smile that passes between Chloe and Mark.

'Yeah,' says Mark. 'We'll have to do that.'

50

The door bangs, heralding Tom's return. 'Dad, come and have a look at this!' he shouts from the porch. Ellie braces herself for a gruesome find; Tom's taste and beachcombing skills have yet to mature. In the spring he brought home a crab shell complete with putrefying insides. She scoops Fred into her arms so that, if it's something gross, Joe will have to deal with it.

But what she sees turns her blood to ice. Her little boy, clearly delighted with himself, has something tucked underneath his arm that Ellie would know anywhere: there are pictures of its blue-and-yellow markings all over the incident room. She could almost draw the pattern from memory.

'It's Danny's skateboard,' says Tom, the look of triumph slowly disappearing from his face in response to his mother's expression.

Joe appears at Ellie's side. 'Mate, what the hell are *you* doing with it?' he asks. He holds out his arms for Fred: Ellie hands him over and then approaches Tom, so carefully that she's almost on tiptoe.

'Put it down, Tom. Put it down, gently, nobody else is going to touch it.' Slowly, he sets it down on the carpet. 'You won't be in trouble if you tell the truth. Where did you get that from?'

'That woman up at the caravan park. She's *nice*.' A stammer undermines his protest. 'She said I could feed her dog.'

Ellie's legs almost give way. Her hands shake as she calls Hardy. She gives him the facts without elaboration, even as she screams at herself inside her head. She can't believe how stupid she's been. How could she have ignored the warning signs? Why didn't she prioritise Maggie's complaint? Of course they've warned Tom against talking to strangers but from day one it's the bad *man* you warn your kids about. When they're lost you tell them to find a mum, and if you can't see a mum you at least make sure it's a lady. But women hurt children too. And Susan Wright chills her more than almost any other woman she's ever met.

'What were you even doing out on your own?' She directs the question at Joe. She'll have his bollocks for this.

'He said he was meeting Jayden,' says Joe as Tom hangs his rucksack on the peg, then smooths his jacket over the top. 'I was going to see him off but there was orange juice everywhere.'

Orange juice? Jesus. Ellie pencils in a row about priorities for later that evening. Right now, she needs to deal with this skateboard.

'Did you carry it or ride it?' she asks Tom.

'Rode it.' The enormity of what he has done is finally beginning to sink in. 'Should I not have?'

She fights the urge to shake her son, and instead just shakes her head.

A squad car pulls up outside and once the skateboard is bagged and stowed in the boot, they turn on the blues and race to the caravan park.

The uniforms already have Susan's trailer surrounded.

Did Danny come here the night he died? The thought of Tom being in this place makes her flesh crawl.

Hardy calls Susan's name and when there's no response, gives the uniforms the go-ahead. The glass door easily gives way and the officers pour in. Susan's not there and neither is the dog, but the fridge and the wardrobe are both full, her purse is on the sideboard and there's a half-eaten bowl of dog food in one corner.

'Get SOCO here,' shouts Hardy. 'We have to find her. She can't be far.'

As they head back to the station in the back of a squad car, they trade increasingly wild theories about where she might have gone. On the High Street they pass a brown dog tied up outside the *Echo* office. Ellie almost doesn't register it, then—

'Shit!' She puts her foot to the floor even though she's not driving. 'Stop! I know where she is.'

'Why would she—' begins Hardy, but she's out of the car, forcing him to catch up with her. The door of the *Echo* is ajar. Ellie hesitates, afraid of what she might find. If Susan has made good on her threat against Maggie she will never forgive herself.

Hardy twitches beside her but follows her silent lead, tiptoeing after her through the newsroom to the back. In a dark messy corner, Maggie, Olly and Susan Wright sit in awkward conference around the meeting table. Ellie can smell the stale tobacco even from here.

'Thank you for popping in, Susan,' Maggie is saying. She sounds like her old, confident self. 'I did a little digging on you. I've got friends in low places, see. Half the local papers in the country are run by my friends. So I know about your husband. And your children. And what was said, but never proved, about you.'

Olly slides a sheet of paper across the desk to Susan. From where she stands, Ellie can tell that it's newsprint but not what it says.

'What do you want from me?' asks Susan mechanically.

'You threatened me and *I* nearly let you get away with it.' Maggie's anger is directed as much at herself as Susan. 'I'm going to tell the police about this.'

'No need,' says Hardy. Olly is astonished to see the detectives. Maggie looks as though she expected nothing less. Susan remains inscrutable.

'Susan Wright. You do not have to say anything but it may harm your defence if you do not mention when questioned something which you later rely on in court. Anything you do say may be given in evidence.'

He radios to the car outside. Doors slam in the street.

'You can have this,' says Maggie. 'I've made copies.'

'Thanks,' is all Ellie can say. It's an Essex paper, nearly two decades old, but Susan Wright is instantly recognisable. There's a one-word headline above her mugshot: MONSTER. A dozen vile words leap out of the text at Ellie. How could they have missed this?

323

Susan doesn't resist arrest but accepts the handcuffs meekly. Once in the street, though, it's a different story.

'Where's my dog?' she yells. 'Who took my dog?'

Ellie stares at the lamppost. Vince has gone, along with his collar and lead. She asks the uniforms if they know anything about it and is met with blank looks. Susan Wright thrashes and cries, demanding to know what's happened to her dog.

Back at the station, they hold Susan Wright in the cell while they cobble together a case. She has gone from being an afterthought to priority number one. They have to wait for her alibi to check out, which means uniform doing house-to-house in the caravan park. They also need to get the files from Essex police to back up the headlines. Nish is on the case.

And even when they've got the police records, Ellie knows from their experience with Jack Marshall that even the facts are of limited use if the suspect won't talk.

All the while, Susan Wright remains mute unless it's on the subject of Vince the dog. She won't tell them why she had the skateboard. They need to find the dog. Where's it gone? Who would *want* it?

Late at night, the children's playground is deserted. Leaves on the trees crackle like static on a radio. Every now and then a strong gust pushes the empty swing and its chains creak.

Mark Latimer's van pulls up in the adjacent car park. A hooded figure gets out, walking boots crunching on the gravel. He takes the crossbow from the passenger seat. He opens the back door. Inside, Vince looks quizzically at his new master.

Nige slips the hood from his head and aims his crossbow at the dog's head. 'What we gonna do with you boy, eh?' he says.

Mark Latimer has left Beth and Chloe sleeping. Beer bottles are stacked like soldiers ready to be recycled. He pulls another from the fridge. He stares at the flickering telly. Then something in him snaps. He throws on a hoody against the cold night, stuffs his feet into walking boots and sets out across the field. The grass is a swathe of green against black. Soon Mark is swallowed by the night.

On the other side of the field, Paul Coates pushes away a glass of orange juice and looks at it as though he wants something stronger. He lets his head fall into his hands. Then, as though he has come to a decision, he is up. Acting quickly, as though he wants to do this before he can change his mind, he covers his dog collar with a hood and pulls walking boots on to his feet. He winds through the unlit gravestones without a single misstep. Here is a man who comes to life after dark.

51

Monster. If Susan Wright is guilty of the things the press accused her of, there is no other word for her. No wonder she gave a false name to the photographer from the *Echo*. Ellie looks at the dossier that Maggie Radcliffe gave her, aware that this is just the stuff that made it into print. God knows what the press held back. She won't know either until the police files come through, but the archives are shut till tomorrow morning and the computer system in a faraway station has crashed, leaving the digital notes trapped in the glitch. Any minute now, says the stressed-out sergeant in Essex. She's been saying that for two hours. At ten o'clock, Ellie calls Joe and tells him to eat without her, to go to bed without her. He says he doesn't mind in a way that conveys the opposite. Everyone involved in the case is talking like this now, saying the right things but letting the subtext leak out in tone and body language where they can't be called out on it. She spares a thought for poor Bob, doing door-to-door looking for Vince the dog, while Lindsey and the kids sit at home forgetting what he looks like.

She passes the time chasing Susan Wright's alibi. A few long-term residents at the caravan park reported seeing her that afternoon and again the next day, although none of them know her by name. 'Her with the dog,' they all say. It occurs to Ellie that Susan leaving home without Vince would be tantamount to a disguise. There was a party held on the site that night, and despite or because of that, no one was paying attention to caravan number 3. Ellie looks at the list of potential alibis: all but two names have been crossed off as negative.

When her desk phone rings, she takes a second to wonder what has come good first: the alibi, the police files or the dog. It is none of those things but the duty sergeant, putting in a call from the front desk that makes the whole investigation shift.

Someone has reported torchlight inside the roped-off crime scene of the clifftop hut. Ellie moves so quickly that the press cuttings on her desk lift in the backdraught. Hardy knows it's something big as soon as he sees her face, and when she tells him what's come through he is frozen for a second before grabbing his jacket and springing into action. 'Don't stand there wittering, Miller,' he says. 'Come on.'

Ellie slings her handbag diagonally across her body, calling backup on the way to the car. While she drives, Hardy phones through the order to trace the call. Ellie's palms are damp on the steering wheel. She has had the feeling for a while now that the solution was going to come out of the blue, and maybe this is it. It doesn't make sense, but then nothing about this investigation does.

They are the first on the scene. She makes the split-second

decision to kill the lights and the engine at the last minute and they roll into the car park invisibly and in near-silence. From here, the hut appears to be in absolute darkness. The police tape flutters and has not been disturbed. *Please* don't say this is a crank call.

The moon dips behind a cloud and they rely on torchlight to pick out their path. Hardy motions for her to take the front of the hut while he inspects the back. Ellie steps up close to the door. Its window panes form a grid of black mirrors. There is no sign of life inside and she resigns herself to the fact that at best this was kids taking the piss and, at worst, they've had the killer here and lost them.

She brings her torch up to the glass to make sure.

The door swings open and hits her in the face. The pain radiates from her nose and dazes her for a few seconds. She recovers her sight in time to see a figure in a hoody pelt past her. She registers only the basics – white, too tall to be a woman, neither thin nor fat – and he's gone.

The noise has brought Hardy around. He takes only a second to check she's all right and then they're racing after the intruder. The beams of their torches are white balls bouncing over the uneven ground. Lumpy turf gives way to coarse sand, then to a dirt track that leads only to one place.

'Suspect heading for boatyard!' Ellie yells into her radio. A crackled reply tells her that a squad car is minutes away. Hardy is not as fast as his long legs would suggest, he's not much faster than she is. The suspect vaults the wire fence into the boatyard with gymnastic ease. By the time Hardy and Ellie complete this move in awkward clambers, their man has disappeared into the maze of shiny hulls.

It's confusing in here. Sound bounces off the boats, distorting Ellie's sense of space.

'I know you're here,' she yells. 'We've got the place surrounded. You can't get out.' She strains for the approaching sirens that will give truth to her bluff, but hears nothing. The only sound is Hardy's laboured breathing somewhere behind her. She puts her torch out and inhales deeply through her nose, as if to sniff the suspect out. He must be close. She treads lightly to minimise the crunch of pebbles under her feet.

Into this near-silence, her telephone rings, giving away her position. 'Bollocks!' says Ellie under her breath. There's barely time to register the number before cutting the call. It's the records on Susan Wright. Of all the timing . . .

She is barged to the floor before she knows what's happening. She puts out a hand to break her fall but there is a loud crack from somewhere on impact. The base of her palm makes sharp contact with dozens of tiny stones and the flesh is lacerated. She lands awkwardly on her other shoulder, rolling over so that her cheek is grazed and she tastes gravel. This time, she doesn't recover instantly; her internal gimbal has been temporarily disabled and the world rocks wildly around her. When she hauls herself back to sitting, a pain zips from her wrist to somewhere deep in her spine. The blue strobe finally arrives. It's down to Hardy now to hold the man until backup comes. 'Sir!' she says, throwing her good arm in the right direction. 'That way!'

Only one set of footsteps receding into the distance. She stumbles into the gangway between boats and is pulled up short to find Hardy flat on his back, torch rolling at his side, bony hands clutching desperately at his chest as he struggles for breath.

There's the slamming of car doors as uniform pour in to the boatyard. Ellie makes an arrow of her torch, pointing after the suspect.

'Get after him!' she screams.

She drops down next to Hardy. His eyes are bulging, a vein pulses on his forehead like a worm under the skin and his tongue hangs uselessly between greying lips.

Behind her, someone radios for an ambulance. 'Don't you fucking dare,' she says, loosening Hardy's collar. A couple of the PCs begin CPR, punching at his chest. Ellie holds Hardy's hand while they wait for the paramedics to arrive. She feels his pulse with her thumb, the gap between beats growing longer as it slows, and slows, until there is barely anything left to feel.

52

Alec Hardy's blood rhythms soundtrack his dreamscape. Images scroll relentlessly past, like a film he is condemned to watch for ever. Pippa Gillespie's face turns into Danny Latimer's. He's wearing her pendant, she's carrying his skateboard. He sees Daisy at a similar age, uniform on, running into his arms after school. This gives way to another little boy, one he's never seen from the outside before, knees up to his chest as the tide rolls away from Harbour Cliff Beach. Then everything turns white.

The senses come back one by one. Touch is first in the form of pain, a sharp sting in the back of his right hand. Smell follows, the unmistakable sweat and disinfectant of a hospital ward. Something bleeps in his left ear. He tastes the stale interior of his own mouth.

The first thing he sees when the room comes into focus is the vertical blinds that hang like undone bandages at the window. A tube whistles oxygen up his nose and an IV drips something into the cannula in the back of his right hand.

And there, slap bang in the middle of his vision is DS Miller, brandishing a bunch of grapes.

'I hoped you might choke on the seeds,' she says, dumping them just out of his reach.

'I'm sensing you're angry with me.' The intended snark is undermined by his delivery: he sounds drugged and slow.

'You nearly died on me! They told me you've been in here before and discharged yourself against their advice. Heart arrhythmia.' Whatever happened to patient confidentiality? Hardy will have someone's guts for garters over this breach. 'They said you've known for eighteen months. You should've *told* me.' Miller visibly relaxes once that's all out of her system, and returns to her default setting. 'Can't they fix you?'

There is no point now in lying. 'They want to put a pacemaker in, but they don't know whether I'll survive the operation. It won't affect the case. I won't let it.'

Miller's not having any of it. 'It already has! We were pursuing a suspect! We lost them because you collapsed! You're a serving police officer, having blackouts. You came here, you took this case on, took that job knowing you weren't up to it.'

She still doesn't get it. This case is bigger than anything he's going through. 'Miller, we're nearly there. That was the killer last night, I'm sure of it.' He's waking up, growing stronger by the second. 'Male, young enough to be that fast, what's that, between late teens and fifty? We've nearly got him. I was thinking who could it have been? It's the right build for Mark, or his plumber's mate, or the vicar even. And where's Steve Connolly – that voices from the dead bloke – these days? Are SOCO up at the clifftop hut?'

Miller is listening despite herself, but she's not convinced.

'We can manage without you.' This strikes at the core of Hardy's worst fear.

'I have to finish this. I can't let the family down.' At the mention of the Latimers, she visibly softens. He exploits her weak spot: his begging is only partly feigned. 'Please, Miller. *Please*. Don't tell the Chief Super. I'll discharge myself. Give me half an hour.'

'I'm going back to work.' Miller slams the ward door on the way out. Hardy allows himself to hope. She is very far from happy with him. But she didn't say no.

When Ellie stands up in front of CID, she remembers the last briefing she gave, winces a little at her unprofessionalism then, and moves on. She hasn't got time for nerves now.

'As you already know, the boss was taken ill last night, during the pursuit. I'm not sure when he'll be back,' she says. There is a domino run of whispers across the team: she talks louder. 'But we just carry on, don't get distracted. SOCO are back up at the hut after last night. Frank, go through our list of people of interest, compare those without alibis, or questionable alibis, on the night of Danny's death, and knock on their doors, find out their movements from last night. The likelihood is the killer was there last night. We were very close. They're rattled and they're going to make more mistakes. OK. So. We have Susan Wright in custody.' She grips the whiteboard marker and gives a gasp of pain. Her hands sting with little cuts and grazes from last night's fall. When finally she got in last night, Joe picked gravel out of her skin with sterilised tweezers and dressed the cut on her elbow. Gingerly holding the marker with her fingertips, she writes SUSAN WRIGHT on the whiteboard and underlines it twice. 'We've connected her to the site where Danny's body was found; the cigarettes she smokes match the ones found at the scene.' She double-checks the notes that were left on her desk. 'But her alibi checks out. The caravan park owner saw her sitting in the window watching TV with her dog when he went off around 1 a.m. We've a match at the hut on Briar Cliff for her prints and DNA, but the owners have already confirmed she cleans there. No matches with any DNA found on Danny's body. So she didn't kill him. But she *knows* something. I'm sure. And most of you know about her husband by now. Those of you who don't, the file's on Nish's desk. It doesn't make pretty reading.' She hears Alec Hardy's rhythms in her own speech: she would hardly be surprised to hear a Scottish accent. 'We're . . . *I'm* continuing to question her, but time's running out before we have to apply for an extension. I know it may sound daft, but we need to find her dog, Vince. He's a chocolate Labrador. Nish has got a picture. The dog is a priority – she's very attached to it, it might help her to talk. Uniform haven't turned anything up so far.' She tries to rally them the only way she has left: 'We still have a duty to the Latimer family and that's the most important thing. All right, that's it for now, thank you.'

Ellie has to hitch her trousers up twice on the short walk to the interview room; her waistband is loose. She hasn't been this slim since before having Fred. It gives her scant joy to realise that she's finally lost her baby weight. The energy she's burning now comes from somewhere beyond food and sleep. Is this how Hardy got ill?

Susan Wright sits morosely next to the duty solicitor. Ellie clears her throat and begins. Without Hardy at her side, she must switch between the roles of good and bad cop on her own.

'Four cigarettes with your DNA all over them were excavated close to where Danny Latimer was found. And you had Danny's skateboard. You gave it to a local boy.'

'Is that what he said?' says Susan, in her usual monotone. '*He* had it and showed it to me, asked me to keep it for him. He's a lying little shit.'

The fury that erupts within Ellie at this has nowhere to go so she swallows it whole. 'There are traces from the skateboard in your cupboard. Your fingerprints are on the board, as are Danny's. You lied to us about Mark Latimer getting the keys to the hut. Now, what were you doing on that beach next to Danny's body? Why did you have Danny's skateboard? Why did we find your cigarettes near his body? Why didn't you bring the skateboard to us?'

'My dog,' says Susan. 'Vince, where's Vince?'

Ellie seizes on this. 'Susan, I've been on this case for a long time now,' she says, no longer bothering to keep the edge out of her voice. 'And I've lost *so much* patience. Now, tell me how you came by the skateboard. Because otherwise I will charge you, you will end up in custody. And if that happens, who knows what'll become of Vince. He could be rounded up, he could be put down.'

Susan's pupils flare in fear and Ellie knows it's worked. 'Tell me what happened.'

Susan's shoulders lower an inch. Her guard has not been dropped, but it's on the way down.

'I was out walking in the middle of the night,' she says. 'Me and Vince, we like it during the night, no one else about. We walk for hours. We was just going out. We have a nap in the afternoons and we go out at three, maybe four in the morning. It's lovely during the night, round here. Up from my caravan, up the hill on to the clifftop. When we got up, I saw it down on the beach. The boy. We went back down. He was all splayed out. The skateboard was next to him. I had a few cigarettes. Stood there for a while. Looking at him. He was beautiful.' Ellie flinches at the thought of anyone seeing beauty in a dead child, and Susan picks up on this. 'I mean, his limbs were all twisted out of place. But his face was at peace.' She holds that word 'peace' for a second too long, like it's too precious and rare to let go easily.

'I don't understand,' says Ellie, 'how you could stand over Danny's body and smoke and then carry on walking your dog?'

'I knew he'd be found,' Susan shrugs, like they're talking about a dumped mattress. 'I didn't want to get involved. You people destroyed my family.'

'Tell me.' It's almost a whisper. 'Help me understand.' She needs to tease this out: it's her hope that one honest confession about her family might propel Susan along to the truth about Danny. When she gets the truth, she won't need her notes to check that the story tallies: this case history is branded on her memory for ever.

Susan starts to nod her head in a slow unconscious movement, more a self-soothing gesture than an assertion of truth. 'We had two girls. My husband was an electrician. He used to have sex with the oldest, but I didn't know.' A note of defiance lifts her flat voice, like she's reiterating the denial for the hundredth time. Maybe she is. 'Then he tried it on with the younger one. Her sister wasn't having that, wanted to protect her little baby sister. So she got herself killed. He told me she'd gone travelling. She'd never said nothing to me. After a while, people started asking questions. Then you lot came. Took the young one into care. Arrested him. He told them I knew, that I was part of it. I didn't know. I never knew. Look at you – same expression they had.'

Her husband, her child, her home. How *could* she not know? Ellie works harder than ever to keep the judgement off her face. 'I'm just listening,' she says.

'They found her body buried in the woods, three miles away, in the end. I was pregnant. Social Services took the baby, said I wasn't a fit mother. Everything I told the police got twisted, thrown back at me. He was convicted. Got life. Hung himself ten months later in his cell.' She clicks her teeth and looks to the ceiling. 'Death. Once it's got its claws into you, it never lets go.' Finally Susan's blank eyes swim and her lip begins to wobble. 'When I was standing on that beach, looking at that boy's body, I kept wondering if my girl looked that peaceful, after he killed her. I don't think she did.'

Something still isn't right. Susan has opened up about her family, but she is still misleading them about Tom – he is no lying little shit, no matter how convenient that might be for her – and Ellie has the sense that she is even now holding something back. Something huge. But she cannot imagine what it might be.

She's lying about Tom. What else is she lying about?

Once again Tom Miller has left the house under the pretence of meeting friends. This time he is underneath a tree in the graveyard at St Andrew's. Checking that no one is watching, he unhooks his camouflage backpack from his shoulders and takes out the laptop. With two hands, he lifts it over his head and brings it down hard on the corner of a tombstone. It buckles but does not break. Tom repeats the process three, four, five times. The screen shatters and letters are thrown from the keyboard to scatter an alphabet in the grass. Tom is red in the face and breathless by the time the casing finally smashes to reveal the circuitry inside. The hard disk catches the light: Tom can't break it with his hands or his feet, so he scrapes it along the mossy stones. He is lost in a reverie of destruction, and it is some time before he notices Reverend Paul Coates watching him from behind a granite angel.

Tom freezes, then clutches the remains of his laptop to his chest. Paul takes a step towards him.

'What's on there, Tom?' He is gentle and controlled. 'Is it about Danny? If there's anything on this computer, you have to tell your mum.'

'Keep your nose out!' Tom holds the disk at arm's length like a shield. 'Or I'll tell them I saw you touching Danny after computer class, and it was wrong, and he told me he'd asked you not to do it but you did.'

Paul steps over the broken shell of the computer towards Tom. 'I would think very carefully about what you just said.'

'What's the matter?' shrills Tom. 'Won't God protect you?'

It's not like him to cheek an authority figure, and he knows he's gone too far. He turns to escape, but Paul knows the terrain better and besides, Tom is only eleven and could never outrun a grown man.

53

Hardy pushes the police station door, the back of his left hand still sticky from the dressing and weeping slightly where he pulled out the IV line. The medics' voices, imploring him not to discharge himself, echo in his head. They will have called Jenkinson, which means he is no longer counting down the days until he is off this case but the hours, possibly even the minutes. The hospital tag is still on his right wrist. He bites through it and spits it into a litter bin in the corridor.

The hum of chatter in CID goes quiet when he enters, and the phones no longer ring off the hook. The effort of crossing the silent room nearly topples him. Everything he's got left goes into breathing slowly in, slowly out. He will not be beaten by this.

Jenkinson's at his door before he's had time to take his jacket off. She enters without knocking. Her face zooms in and out of focus.

'I've referred you to the Chief Medical Officer, first thing tomorrow.' It's better than he thought: a one-day stay of execution.

'I'm not leaving till this is solved.'

'You don't get a choice. As soon as he sees you, you're done, Alec.' She shakes her head. 'Why take this job, if you knew you were this ill?'

'I can still solve this, otherwise . . . why am I still here?' He doesn't just mean in the police station. He must solve this if it kills him. He notes privately that the phrase is no longer a mere figure of speech to him.

Jenkinson leaves him at his desk, where the wasted man-hours of Operation Cogden manifest themselves in towers of futile paperwork. Evidence and procedure have let him down. Desperation circles around him. Alone in his office, DI Hardy has a crisis of faith; he abandons himself to it.

They meet at the cob wall on the far side of Harbour Cliff Beach. It is low tide and the black rocks are exposed. They look like the rotten teeth of a huge sea beast, lying in wait. Clouds overhead threaten rain and a strong wind blows. It feels more like October than August. Now that the holiday season is too far gone to recover, it's as though the sun has decided not to squander itself on Broadchurch. Hardy's coat billows like a sail and he feels as though a strong gust will knock him to the ground.

Steve Connolly, feet planted firmly apart, hands in pockets, looks like not even a hurricane could shift him. Hardy has a sudden vision of how foolish he would look if anyone saw him. Anyone from the station. One of the Latimer family. Christ, imagine if Karen White turned up. It doesn't bear thinking about.

'You were the last person I expected to call,' says Steve.

'Surely nothing's a surprise to you,' says Hardy. Sarcasm is a reflex he can't help.

'That's very funny,' says Steve. 'Never heard that before. What do you want?'

'The Latimer case,' he says, and somewhere deep inside he feels the heavy thud of a man hitting rock bottom. 'I'm running out of time. If you have *anything*, give it to me now.'

Connolly doesn't bother to hide his surprise. 'Well, thank you. It's about time.' To his credit, he doesn't gloat. He looks Hardy square in the eye. 'Look, that message from Danny, about it being close to home. That felt the strongest.'

Hardy shouts to drown out the oncoming wind. 'What does that mean? Close geographically? Family, friends, what?'

'I don't know,' admits Connolly. 'Just don't ignore it.'

'Prove to me you're not a bullshitter.'

Now Connolly's earnestness gives way to indignation. 'I *gave* you something. I said, she forgives you for the pendant.' Hardy fights to swish away the image the word *pendant* invokes: Pippa Gillespie's face in the press photograph. 'I told you, and you pretended to ignore it.'

Hardy is spooked for a second, but then his belief system overrides it. Shysters study body language, that's how they work. It doesn't mean anything that Connolly knew he'd hit a nerve.

'And what does that mean?' he challenges.

'You already know,' says Connolly. 'I can see it. I haven't got a clue what it means, all I get are fragments. And that's what I got off you . . . that, and you've been here before.' It's a casually thrown dart that pierces the bullseye and Hardy

342

can't cover his shock in time. There's no one else alive who knows about his first visit to Broadchurch. 'You have!' Connolly is delighted and angry at the same time. 'You've been here before. I'm right, aren't I?'

Hardy, no longer trusting himself to speak, looks out to sea. There is no warmth on anything today, only shades of blue and grey. Even the sun is ice-white. Suddenly Connolly's eyes on his are too much and he turns to go while he can still walk, leaving Connolly triumphant on the harbour.

When Hardy spots Olly Stevens standing outside the police station, his stomach tightens. He can't deal with the press right now. The feeling clearly isn't mutual though, as when Olly clocks Hardy, he straightens up and clicks a pen out of his breast pocket.

'No,' says Hardy. He cannot think of a question Olly could come up with that would have another answer.

'You must be feeling better, to discharge yourself from hospital.'

How the hell does he ...? For a town so full of secrets, there's fuck-all privacy in this place. Hardy yanks Olly's arm and pulls him away from the station doors.

'Look, I don't want to stitch you up. Genuinely,' says Olly. In his free hand he waves his reporter's notebook like a white flag. Hardy doesn't release his grip but it's weakening by the second, and it must be surprise or some latent respect for the law that stops Olly breaking free.

'So what *do* you want?' asks Hardy.

'An exclusive.'

54

There are still holes in Susan Wright's story and Ellie can only hold her for another few hours before charging her. That's not the end of the world: she can pick and choose from a list of charges, but she would rather get the facts out of her with as little duress as possible. The sun fires a single glass square: it is just after lunchtime.

'So this is what I'm struggling with.' Her words cover the growling of her stomach. 'I know those cliffs. If you're walking your dog, you can't see straight down unless you're right on the edge, you can't have seen Danny's body. The angle's wrong. What you're telling us, it doesn't ring true. Now have another think, otherwise I'm going to charge you with obstructing a murder inquiry.'

Susan is blank. 'I didn't see anything.'

'Like you didn't see what your husband was up to?' The low blow hits home. Susan turns her head slowly away. Ellie cranes across the desk to catch her eye. She's not letting her get away with it this time. 'You were out walking at the time Danny's body was left on the beach. What did you see?'

Susan raises her eyes to the ceiling as if in prayer, although her lips don't move. She seems to find an answer, though, because when she brings her face back down, the defiance has drained from it.

'I wasn't on the cliff, I was on the beach.' The downward inflection gives away Susan's relief. Finally, there's the sense of confession that has been missing so far. 'I saw a boat come in. Little. Like a rowing boat but with a motor on the back.'

Ellie's heart thuds painfully against her ribcage. 'How many people on board?'

'One. One man. Black woolly hat.'

'What did he do?' Ellie's mind is whirring: why, why, what's going on? She's so busy trying to read the subtext of Susan's words that she's in danger of losing the thread.

'He took the boy's body out the boat. Laid it on the beach. Then he got back in the boat and went off west.'

'Did you recognise the person who left Danny's body on the beach?'

Susan starts to nod again. For a long time, it is the only movement in the room. 'Yes, I did,' she says at last. 'He calls himself Nigel. Works with the boy's dad.'

He calls himself Nigel. It's a strange turn of phrase, but Ellie doesn't have time to analyse it. She rewinds the summer, trying to remember ever seeing Susan and Nigel in the same place, let alone in conversation.

'You know Nigel well, then, to recognise him at night, from that distance. When did you last see him?'

'Few weeks ago.' Her voice is thick. 'He came to my caravan. He had a crossbow. He threatened to kill me.'

Ellie wonders what her face looks like because she wasn't

expecting *that*. She would know if Nige had a crossbow. She wonders now if Susan has picked on Nige to distract them from something else. It's no secret that he was close to Danny, and that he's been questioned in the nick before. 'OK. Why did he do that?'

'He didn't like what I was saying.'

'And what *were* you saying?'

'Don't remember.'

She's lost her again. It takes everything Ellie's got not to scream. If Susan realises the extent of her desperation, they might as well give up. 'You don't remember what you said to make a man threaten you with a crossbow?'

'Not really.'

'So Nigel threatens you, for some unknown reason, and you frame him as the killer.'

Susan looks Ellie hard in the eye and speaks with rock-solid conviction. 'It was him carrying that body.'

Ellie checks the clock again. If they can bring Nige in straight away, they'll have just over two hours with both of them under interrogation. Maybe he can shed some light on all this. When you think about what she is, what she is alleged to have done, what is Susan Wright's word worth? Ellie leaves her suspect in the indifferent care of the duty solicitor and slams the interview room door behind her. The hairline crack in Nige's alibi – the quick trip to the pub – now seems to her a potential chasm. He wasn't out of the house long enough to kill Danny, clean his body, steal a boat and dump it on the beach, but he was away for long enough to commit the murder, then go out again once Faye was asleep and cover his tracks. They should have gone after him harder. Ellie rubs the space between her eyebrows where the tension collects. Her skin feels loose around her skull.

She is wondering who to tell first now the boss has gone when she rounds the corner into CID and collides with a wraithlike DI Hardy. He is thinner than ever, and appears to be wearing pale green make-up.

'Sir, what are you—'

He bats away her concern with the back of a scabbed hand. 'I'm seeing the doctor in the morning, Miller.' She doesn't have to ask him what that means. It's over. What does that mean for her? Keep him involved, or get on with it without him? The words are out before she's aware of making the decision. 'There's been a development. Got an eyewitness account. Nige Carter carrying Danny's body out of the boat and laying it on the beach. I don't know how reliable she is, but . . . ' The news has brought a pink glow to Hardy's complexion. He puts in the call for the uniforms to bring Nige Carter in and there's a corresponding heat in his voice.

'Remind me what we know about Nige Carter,' he asks Ellie as they wait.

'He moved back in with his mum when his dad died, five, six years ago,' she says. 'He's part of the furniture at the Latimers', always in and out the house . . . But I don't believe he's capable of Danny's murder.'

'Everyone we've interviewed is capable,' says Hardy. 'Just takes the right circumstances.'

'And there's your view of the world. I don't know how you sleep.'

'Who says I sleep?'

The gates outside squeal open as a police van and a squad car roll into the car park. Ellie and Hardy watch the yard from the window. Nige leaves the van in cuffs. Even from this distance Ellie can see that he's been crying. The first DC who gets out of the car holds an evidence bag up for them to see: Ellie gasps to see a crossbow inside, but is silenced completely when the second car door opens and a female PC is followed by Vince on a rope lead.

'You take Susan, I'll take Nigel,' says Hardy. 'I'll see where he says he was that night. And why the hell he had her dog.'

She wonders if Hardy's aware how much he's sweating. His whole face is glazed with it.

'You sure you're up to questioning, sir? How are you feeling?'

'Spec*tac*ular,' he says. Ellie silently calls him all the names she can think of.

The detectives wait at the end of the corridor while Nige makes his allotted telephone call. He dials the number without having to look it up.

'Mark, mate.' The echo in the station further distorts his breaking voice. 'I want you to hear it from me. Police have taken me in. They think I had something to do with Danny. It's all wrong, this. *You* know that.' It's impossible to tell from Nige's face whether Mark is raging at him or comforting him.

Hardy studies Nige Carter across the table. For the first time he really registers how young Nige is. The shaved head puts years on him but there's something childish about him, with his eagerness to please and his gangly limbs. Hardy remembers the little armoury that uniform retrieved from Nige's garage and wonders if the happy idiot thing is an act. He's kicking himself for not excavating the fault lines in Nige's original statement properly. Susan Wright's testimony, together with the crossbow, has changed everything.

With the clock hard against him, there's no time for preliminaries.

'Run us through where you were the night Danny Latimer was killed.'

Nige gives a dopey, nervous smile. 'We been through this, weeks back. When you had Mark in. I was at home, with Mum, watching telly.'

'What were you watching?'

'Something about baking. Mum loves all that.'

Hardy slides a photograph of Susan Wright across the desk. 'D'you know this woman, Nigel?'

Nige barely looks at it. 'Don't think so.'

'Do you own a dog?'

'Not really.' A muscle in Nige's cheek jumps.

'Not really?' Hardy is scornful. 'What, sometimes you do? There's a dog comes round part-time?'

Nige smiles. 'No.'

'Is this *amusing* to you?'

The smile is switched off like a light. 'I don't own a dog.'

'Why was there a dog in your back garden?'

Nige squirms. 'Someone asked me to look after it for them.'

'The owner. This woman. Susan Wright. Who you said you didn't know.' Nige is looking anywhere but at the photograph. Hardy sighs. 'If you're going to lie, you have to be consistent. Because then there's the alibi for the night of Danny Latimer's death. The one you told us about when we were interviewing Mark. It was good enough then. But not now. Your mum already told us you weren't in all that night. You went out at half ten for last orders. So where were you, Nigel?'

Nige's mouth hangs open but nothing comes out. Hardy decides to switch gears. He brings out the crossbow, sealed in its clear bag.

'This yours?'

He looks shifty but he doesn't deny it. 'Yeah. I keep it in the garage.'

'You played video games with Danny.'

The change of subject has confused him. 'Call of Duty, yeah. Sometimes with him, sometimes with his mate Tom, too.'

'How often were you alone together?'

Nige's eyes widen. 'Dunno. Never thought about it. He was just Mark and Beth's lad. I saw him when I was around.'

Hardy pretends to consult the file in front of him.

'How do you know Susan Wright?' he asks.

'I don't want to talk about her!' Nige's rage must be very close to the surface to rise this quickly. 'You should arrest *her*, have *her* in here for harassment. She's been on at me since the moment she arrived. It must be five months of it now. I can't take it no more! I've told her, leave me alone, but she won't. Not interested about that, are you?'

'What's she harassing you about?' Nigel, evidently spent by his outburst, says nothing. 'Susan Wright has told us she believes you killed Danny Latimer. She says she saw you on the beach, with a boat, dragging Danny's body on to the shore.'

'She's lying!' A spit bubble forms between Nige's lips. 'He's my best mate's boy, why would I do that?'

'Then why's Susan Wright saying otherwise? What's she got to harass you about?'

Nige shrugs almost imperceptibly, as though admitting defeat quietly to himself. His lips work in silent rehearsal. Hardy has seen this tell enough times to know that a confession is seconds away, but even he is stunned when Nige says, 'She reckons she's my mum.'

55

Beth and Mark drive to the hospital in near silence, exchanging half-hearted reassurances that this thing with Nige is a mistake, yet another example of police ineptitude, another black mark against DI Hardy's name. They tell each other that Nige will be out again by the time they get back to Broadchurch. But they aren't convincing each other. How can they, when they can't convince themselves? Suspicion is the first resort for both of them now.

When the hospital comes into view, Beth is thrust into the moment she's been dreading. They haven't been here since Danny was born. She is paralysed.

'I feel disloyal,' she says, hand on the buckle of her seat belt. 'And I don't know if I want to see it. I *want* to want it, but I don't. My heart's still full of Danny. There's no room for another baby.'

'There will be—' begins Mark.

'Mark, stop telling me how I'm going to feel,' she says. ''Cause you have no idea, and *no* ability to understand. Shutting this out is not an option for me. I can't do that boxing things off like you do. I have to carry a life in me. For another six months. Feeding off me, breathing from me, sharing my blood. I can't let Danny go.'

Mark thumbs the line of her cheekbone. 'Don't load it with everything. Just let it be what it is.'

She nods for his benefit. She knows that he's right, but her heart hasn't caught up with her head yet. The longer this goes on, the more she fears that it never will.

White light pulses in the dark room; the monitor hums. The sonographer is brisk as she administers the cold slick of gel on Beth's belly. She prods and probes for what seems like a suspiciously long time. Beth is unexpectedly gripped by the conviction that something is wrong and the equally sudden and certain knowledge that she cannot survive the loss of this baby.

'All's well,' says the sonographer. 'Everything's where it should be. Do you want to look at the screen?'

Beth's instinct is to say no, but Mark says yes for both of them and slowly the monitor is turned their way. She is almost afraid to look at the screen but Mark holds her hand and together they watch in wonder as the monochrome swirl of pixels coalesce into the first picture of their unborn child. The rest of the world – all the shit, all the grief, the relentless distrust – melts away. Beth laughs with delight to see the thin crescent moon of the skull, the zip of the spine. The baby's heart is a cursor, blinking fast and strong.

'It's a fighter, this one,' says the sonographer.

Something swells from nowhere inside Beth, warming her

through from her core. Not happiness: it's too complicated and too soon for that. But the familiar and strange ache of love is unmistakable.

Ellie jumps as the rat-a-tat-tat on the door breaks the tension in the interview room. Hardy beckons her into the corridor.

'Susan Wright says Nigel Carter is her *son*?' she echoes. 'And she's accusing him of murder? What the *hell* is going on between them?' But there's a connection now, two incompatible jigsaw pieces turning out to be a perfect fit when turned upside down.

They go back to their respective interviewees.

When Susan learns that Nigel has blown their secret, Ellie observes something that could almost be happiness.

'That's the first time he's even acknowledged it.' Finally, Susan's face softens and her shoulders drop. 'They took him away from me, when everything happened. Twenty-five years. Then the law changed. You could request contact. It took me eighteen months to find him. The woman who adopted him, she never told him. She hid the contact request letters from him. So I tried tracking him down in other ways. He didn't know anything about being adopted till I told him. That's not right. If I'd known, I wouldn't have done it like that. He reacted badly. He didn't want anything to do with me. He pushed me away, avoided me. Tried to pay me off. When that didn't work, he threatened me with that crossbow.' Ellie used to interpret Susan's monotone as detachment: now she hears the limitless patience of a mother. 'He'll come round. I can wait. Whatever it takes. He's my boy.'

'Does he know about your family?' asks Ellie.

Susan narrows her eyes. 'You don't tell him.' Her voice is low and scraping: it is like a knife to Ellie's throat: if they were alone, Ellie would be terrified. She understands now why Maggie took Susan's threat to heart.

She rubs her eyes. She's so close now to understanding Susan's actions, but one wrong word and she'll clam up again. 'Susan, here's what I'm having trouble with: if you're his mum and you want to be reconciled with him, why tell us you saw him on the beach that night? Because I'm a mum, and whatever my child had done, I'd want to protect him.'

'I *am* protecting him. I told you because ... I'm scared. *For* him. Because it's *not his fault.*' Susan's whole face begins to tremble. 'If he's his father's son, what is he capable of? What might he have done? I can't just let it happen. Not again.'

56

Nige Carter has gone from being a man of few words to complete emotional incontinence. It's all Hardy can do to make out what he's saying, let alone pick out the relevant information. 'It's like everything you thought you knew about yourself isn't true,' Nige sobs. 'That was stupid, threatening her with the crossbow, but with everything that's going on ... She doesn't belong here.'

Hardy is unmoved. Injured doesn't mean innocent. If anything, this gives Nige depth and complexity that they could never have guessed at.

'Nigel, you have to tell me. Where were you the night Danny died?'

Nige wipes his nose with his sleeve. 'That night, I went out, just for a few hours. Up to the estate past Oak Farm. They've been laying down pheasants. I just went and got a couple, that's all. He's got dozens, he doesn't even know.'

'You were nicking *pheasants*?' Hardy can barely believe his ears. Lying to police under caution in a *murder inquiry* because of a bit of low-level poaching? Of all the provincial bollocks he's encountered down here, this takes the crown.

'The butcher in town takes 'em off my hands. Not like I'm gonna make my fortune working with Mark. Mind, I forgot to fill up the van, so I siphoned some diesel out of his tractor. And then I . . . cut the barbed wire, made it look like a break-in.' Hardy recalls his first shout in Broadchurch, the dawn call-out to the top of the cliff, the angry farmer, the severed fence. It gives him no pleasure to know that it's the only crime he's solved since he got here. 'I was nowhere near that beach,' insists Nige. 'Whatever she thought she saw, she didn't.'

Hardy no longer has any idea which, if either of them, is telling the truth. With iron self-control, he says, 'So she's lying?'

'Mate, I don't even know who she is.'

The hand on the clock jumps, closing the gap on another hour.

Hardy needs to play hard as well as fast to cut through what's connected to Danny and what isn't. If that means breaking Nigel to see if anything else is left in him, so be it. He splays his fingertips on top of Susan Wright's files. Essex police have finally come good and they now contain crime scene photographs as well as the press reports. It is harrowing stuff, even for the most detached reader. Hardy's conscience pipes up; it has Miller's voice. He hesitates for a moment; the progress of the second hand overrides his doubts. Nige is a suspect. He was seen with the body. The information in this file has a bearing on the witness accusing him.

'Do you want to know, Nigel? Because in here are

newspaper articles. About her. About her husband. Your family.' Hardy pushes the file gently across the desk. 'Interview paused. 3.02 p.m.'

He closes the door gently behind him, leaving Nige alone with his terrible legacy. Nige doesn't strike Hardy as a fast reader, but the pictures speak for themselves. A long, strangulated howl follows Hardy down the curved concrete corridor.

There's a buzz in CID. Something has changed while Hardy was in with Nige. It's as obvious as painting the walls a new colour. Miller's up by the whiteboard, team all around her. She turns around, looking almost pleased to see him. 'Boss,' she says. 'You've got to hear this. We've traced the number of the call from last night, the one that phoned in to tell us a light was on at the hut. It's Danny's mobile. The missing smartphone. Danny's killer phoned in!'

'Why would they do that?' wonders Hardy. 'Why tell us where they were – and then run? It doesn't make any sense.' He flips to instruction mode. 'Get Nige and Susan released on bail. Have them lodge their passports here and report in every day. No skipping town.'

Miller's jaw falls open. 'You're going to let them out there *together*?'

'I'll cobble together some surveillance, use some of those numpties they drafted in while we've still got them. Maybe Nige and Susan are *both* lying. Let's see what they do when released.'

Miller folds her arms in disapproval. 'Light the blue touchpaper and then retire.'

Hardy draws breath just so he can waste it reminding her

how little time they have left, but is interrupted by the phone on his desk.

'I'm glad it's you,' says Paul Coates, when Hardy picks up. 'Can you come to the church? On your own?'

Hardy's exit isn't what he was hoping for: he watches in horror as his right hand refuses to grip the door handle. It appears to be stroking, rather than gripping, the metal. He tries again: it's like someone else's arm has been grafted on to his shoulder and his body doesn't recognise it. This is a first. He's aware of everyone watching him as he switches sides; his left arm is only marginally stronger but marginal is good enough, and with huge effort he wrenches open the door. Outside, he takes a moment to register the creeping terror of what's happening to him, then sets it aside.

On the walk to St Andrew's Hardy thrusts his hands into his pockets, no longer trusting them. His feet, at least, are obedient, getting him to the church without incident.

The graveyard is filled with birdsong. Paul Coates, in his dog collar and jeans, waits inside the nave. They've crossed swords often enough to dispense with pleasantries, for which Hardy is grateful.

'This is Tom Miller's laptop.' Coates nods at a bundle of black plastic in his lap. 'I caught him smashing it up in the graveyard.'

Hardy struggles to understand. 'What was he trying to get rid of? Why does he do that after his best mate's died?'

'Were they really that close?' says Coates, as though it's only now occurred to him. 'I never saw much evidence of it. I had to break up a fight between them a couple of months before Danny died. Tom was really laying into Danny.'

Hardy remembers Tom's outburst at Jack Marshall's wake and recasts it in the light of this new information. Coates frowns. 'I reported it to both sets of parents. I thought Ellie would've told you.' Hardy shakes his head: he is surprised and unsurprised. If Miller can't even bring herself to take someone like Nige Carter seriously as a suspect, there's no way she can be objective about her precious Tom.

'I should tell you,' says Coates, colouring slightly. 'Tom knows I have this. He threatened to tell you I abused Danny if I handed this over.'

'And did you?'

There isn't a second's hesitation. 'No.'

Hardy takes the bag, feeling the mess of sharp edges inside. 'How long have you had this, then?'

Coates looks at his watch. 'Just over seven hours.'

'That's a long time to hang on to evidence. I suppose someone like you would be able to look through, delete anything that didn't suit you.'

Coates merely rolls his eyes at the insinuation. Hardy is disappointed that he doesn't seem to be able to rile him any more. He decides to quit while he's ahead. He doesn't know as much about computers as Paul Coates, but he knows that there's nowhere to hide on a hard drive. He turns to go, but one final question burns its way out of his mouth.

'How do you keep your faith, with all this going on?'

It's a straight-up question, stripped of sarcasm or goading, and Coates takes it as intended.

'I question what happened.' He offers up empty hands. 'But I have faith in God to resolve it. I believe that's why he sent you here.'

'Hate to let you down, but he didn't send me.'

Coates returns Hardy's sardonic smile. 'That's what he *wants* you to think.'

The package rustles under Hardy's arm as he treads the divots of the graveyard. With his free hand he makes a call to Ruth Clarkson, an IT forensic he knows from way back.

'I need a favour, on the quiet,' he says. 'Things are complicated here. I need you to get something off a hard drive for me. Send whatever you find to my personal email. And it needs to be quick.' He suffers through the phatic expressions of small talk for as long as he can bear, before cutting Ruth off mid-flow: 'Listen, I have to go. People waiting. I appreciate this.'

57

Over dinner, Dean keeps calling Beth Mrs Latimer, which makes her feel like Mark's mum. Everything about the evening is weirdly formal: the candles in the middle of the dining table; that they are at the dining table at all. Beth seems as keen to impress Dean as he is to impress her and she doesn't know why they're all trying so hard, because he's just a normal boy. Not posh, not rough. Just normal. Like them. She knows that the effort he's making is for Chloe and she appreciates it. He's lovely looking, too, and then there's the motorbike. She'd probably have been after him herself at Chloe's age.

After the meal's over, Dean shyly gives Beth a present. 'It's for all of you. For letting me in, and for the future,' he says. She peels the wrapping paper to reveal a cuddly rabbit. 'It's for the new baby.' She can't help it; tears overwhelm her. Dean is mortified.

'I'm sorry,' he stumbles over his apology. 'I didn't mean to upset you.'

Mark speaks for all of them. 'It's all right, mate. It's all a bit muddled in together.'

'Yeah,' says Dean. He drags his fork across a plate he's already cleaned. 'He was a good lad, Dan.' Beth smiles. Sometimes, it's as simple as that, someone who knew Danny remembering him the right way. It means more than all the clumsy condolences, the I'm-sorry-for-your-losses.

'Have you heard any more about Nige?' Beth asks Mark.

'I asked Pete, but he said there was no news.'

'It's not Nige, Dad,' says Chloe. 'Don't go thinking that. It won't be.'

'This is what happens,' says Mark miserably. 'Not just Danny, but the way it's making us look at each other, not trusting anyone. I dunno how we come back from that, even when it's all done.'

When it's all done, thinks Beth. It doesn't feel like they're making any progress at all; in fact, it feels like they're going backwards. How long until they start thinking in terms of *if*?

'Chloe's right,' says Dean. 'It can't be Nige. Him and Dan got on really well. I saw it every time we went out catching animals.' One glance at Mark tells Beth that this is news to him, too. Dean picks up on their shock. 'They'd come up to the farm and we'd go out from there, late evening? Danny said it was OK. Nige said you knew? They both said you knew.'

Mark's face is cold. 'No,' he says. 'We didn't know.'

Nige Carter saunters down Broadchurch High Street with the unhurried pace of an innocent man. Or maybe it's the slow, deliberate gait of someone who knows he's being fol-lowed, because without warning, he darts into a half-hidden alleyway and sprints. He zigzags at speed through the network of footpaths that lace the town together, finally emerging near the caravan park. Hood up, he creeps along the back of the trailers, past the burbling tellies and the boiling pans.

When Susan Wright comes home, a pint of milk dangling from her right forefinger, she finds Nige sitting on her sofa, his arm around Vince's neck.

'I've got a life here,' he snarls at her. 'I've got a *family*.'

'Keep going, boy. Get it all out. God you're the spit of your father.'

'I don't want to hear anything about him.' The words hiss through Nige's clenched teeth.

'He got things wrong,' Susan attempts to soothe him. 'He got confused. But deep down he was a good man. Like you're a good boy. Nigel, you're in trouble, and I understand.'

'You don't understand anything. How could you tell them it was me?'

'Because it was.'

Nige draws a knife. 'If you don't go, within the hour, I will gut this dog while you sleep.' He grins manically through his tears.

Susan studies him. 'If I go, I won't come back. We'll never see each other again. I can do that. I've done it plenty of times.'

Nige stands. 'You contact the police and say you made a mistake. It wasn't me you saw. And then you go.'

They are in deadlock.

'You're the spit of him, Nigel,' says Susan sadly. 'You've got him in you. And it *was* you I saw.'

After Nige has thrown down his knife and gone, Susan

sits for a while in the empty caravan before getting to her feet. With a practised hand she removes the clothes from the hangers and the shoes from the cupboard. She picks up all she needs: bag, shoes, dog food. She moves swiftly and mechanically, pausing only for a second over a battered leather photograph album, which she throws into the suitcase without opening. She has packed so little that there is still room to spare when she zips it up. Vince looks up at her. We're on the move again then, his face seems to say.

'Come on,' she says, attaching the dog's lead to his collar. They are up on the cliff pathway before anyone sees them go.

Two minutes later, the uniformed officer whose job it was to keep track of her pulls up outside caravan number 3 to find the cupboards swept bare and the frosted-glass door swinging open.

By this time, Nige Carter is almost home. He keeps to the alleyways and, rather than be seen in the cul-de-sac, he vaults the fence into his back garden. Faye has dozed off on the sofa in front of *Emmerdale*. With great tenderness, Nige takes the blanket from the back of the sofa and tucks his mother in. He lifts the corner of the net curtain and sweeps the street for police. Seeing nothing, he closes the front door gently behind him. No one stops him as he climbs into the cab of Mark Latimer's van and takes the long straight road out of Broadchurch.

58

Evening is closing in as Alec Hardy heads for the
Broadchurch Echo office. With one more night left as a serving police officer he feels bound to grant the promised
interview now, while his badge is still in his pocket. He
wants to talk while he still counts for something.

No one will miss him from the office: every officer he can
spare is out looking for Susan Wright and Nige Carter, both
of whom appear to have skipped town. Together? Alive?
Hardy has no idea.

Outside the Traders, he perks up at an email on his phone
from Ruth Clarkson but slumps at its content. She's confident she can retrieve the data from Tom Miller's hard drive,
but not until the early hours of tomorrow morning.

Maggie Radcliffe is waiting for him at the door. She leads
him through the dark office to a back room where tall
shelves packed with archive boxes form a coracle about the
size of the interview rooms at Broadchurch nick. Maggie sits
next to Olly Stevens: Hardy takes his place across the table.
An old anglepoise trains an interrogatory light upon him.

'Why were you in hospital?' asks Maggie. When she's not writing, she holds her pen like a cigarette.

'I was pursuing a suspect,' says Hardy. 'There was an incident. I was injured.'

'Can you name the suspect?'

If only I could, thinks Hardy, I wouldn't be here. I'd be hammering on someone's door with a van waiting outside. 'No. I'm sorry,' he says. 'That's all I can give you right now. I know it's not what you want. I promise you'll be the first to hear.'

That seems to satisfy Maggie.

Olly clears his throat. 'The Sandbrook case fell apart at the trial.' Hardy is jolted out of this case and into another. He still hasn't learned to see the S-word coming, even though it lurks around every corner. 'Tell me what went wrong.'

'Channelling your friend Karen White?' says Hardy, more to buy himself time than anything else.

'No. I'm not her,' says Olly firmly. The eager-to-please kid is developing a quiet authority. 'We've seen you here. We know you're doing the best for the family, for the town. And I don't think that was any different on Sandbrook. So what happened? How did it go so wrong? You can't keep it a secret for ever.'

Actually, Hardy *had* intended to keep it a secret for ever. But with his career in its death throes, he hears the siren call of impending relief.

'Ach, maybe you're right,' he hears himself say. 'Maybe it is time.' Maggie and Olly, who are usually in constant communication through scribbled notes and secret glances, have not looked at each other once since he started talking. Sandbrook holds all journalists rapt.

'We had our prime suspect, but all the evidence was circumstantial.' He takes off his glasses to soft-focus the faces opposite him. 'Then, during a search of a car he'd just sold, one of my DSes found the pendant belonging to one of the girls. There were clearly prints on it. It was the smoking gun. My DS was taking the bagged evidence back to HQ. And ... ' He stops without warning, even to himself. He relives this story so often, but the difference between thinking it and saying it out loud, sharing it, is astonishing. He clears his throat. ' ... she stopped off at a hotel on the way, for a drink. And ... her car was broken into.' He can still picture the inside of that car better than the one he drives today. 'Car radio, valuables and her bag were all taken. It was only a quick smash and grab – local kids, probably.'

'And the pendant.' Maggie guesses correctly.

'Yeah. We could never make the case, after that. He's still out there.' Never mind the hours and the effort they put in. One fuck-up and the whole thing boils down into those last four words.

'*Why* did she stop off at a hotel?' asks Olly. The question scratches at Hardy's bones, pricking the marrow. He looks at the shabby office furniture as though for an escape route and thinks seriously that if he's going to have a fatal heart attack then now would be an opportune moment. But the shelves do not part to let him leave, and his heart beats limply on.

'She was having an affair with one of the other DSs on the team,' he says. 'She thought she'd celebrate.'

Maggie falls on the half-truth like a bloodhound. 'But this was all reported at the time. The *Herald* got the story, but they said it was you. Your car. You took the blame.'

'It happened on my watch.'

'But she deceived you.' Maggie couldn't have chosen a more apposite phrase. They're so close to working it out for themselves, he wishes they'd just take a potshot guess and spare him the ordeal. Hardy grits his teeth.

'That detective sergeant. She was my wife. We've got a daughter. I didn't want her knowing that about her mother.'

He's expecting to see triumph on their faces. Now their scoop has a sexy angle. The worst cop in Britain is a cuckold. But Maggie looks mortified on his behalf. 'So you took the blame. For years. The family blame you, and it's not your fault. This is what made you ill, isn't it?'

Hardy's vision blurs again, but this time it's with tears. He tilts his chin upwards, as though he can divert the water back into his eyes, and keeps his head like that until the ceiling comes back into focus. 'Do me a favour. Tell the Gillespie family before you publish, eh? Tell them I haven't given up on Sandbrook and that the case is still open. Then after that, do whatever you like with it. On one condition. You do. Not. Name. That. DS.'

He points at the table, using his forefinger to poke each word home.

59

'*Miller!*'

Ellie jumps to her feet, annoyed by the muscle memory of obedience. One thing she won't miss is being summoned like a soldier. She narrows her eyes across the room at his office. There's still time to piss in that cup.

'Forensics from the hut,' he says, pen tapping at his monitor. 'Boot print in the mud up the hill, match with a print they found inside. Man's, size ten.' He spins his screen. 'What's Nige Carter's shoe size?'

Ellie checks the notes on her desk. 'Ten,' she says with a shiver. 'So what, Susan *did* see Nige?'

The case has blown open again.

'Are we missing something?' says Hardy. 'What if more than one person was involved?' They have asked each other this question a hundred times. They are back to square one after all. Hardy picks up his mug, takes a sip of cold tea and makes a face. 'By the way, your boy and Danny. Did they fall out?'

Ellie is wrong-footed: where the hell is *this* going? 'No . . .'

'Paul Coates, the vicar, says they did. There was a fight. He mentioned it to you.'

'What? No, he didn't!' This is what Hardy does when he's on the back foot, he lashes out and she is sick of being his punchbag. 'Hang on, what're you saying, you think I've been covering for my son?'

'When was the last time Danny came round to your house?'

'It's two in the morning! I don't know!' She barely knows her own name any more. As she struggles to remember, she slowly realises that Danny's visits had been growing fewer and further between. She keeps this to herself until she has time to examine it.

'Can we borrow Tom's computer?' he asks. 'Would you bring it in tomorrow?'

Anything to shut him up. He probably won't even be here tomorrow. 'Fine,' she says. 'Good night.'

Then, on the drive home, it hits her with such force that she finds herself slamming on the brakes. There was that time Tom and Danny fell out at computer club. She'd forgotten it because she thought it was an innocent scrap. It *was* an innocent scrap. She stalls the car, angry that Hardy's poison has infected her. This is what the case is doing to them. Making little boys' fights out to be something they aren't. The sooner they get Tom's computer checked out, the better. She's no techie, but maybe she can have a quick root around in his documents and history, see if there's any cause for concern before she hands it over to IT.

Tom's asleep under his stripy duvet when Ellie gets in. His hair is damp with sweat and his lips slightly parted.

There's a little-boyness to him that she never sees when he's awake any more. How long will he still look like this? He starts secondary school in a couple of weeks. He'll be a teenager soon. She bends to kiss his forehead before beginning a silent search of his bedroom.

The laptop isn't on his desk where she expects it to be. Neither is it under his bed, or in his bag. She tells herself that the cold current of panic travelling up her spine is just a symptom of exhaustion.

In Tom's desk drawer, she finds the mouse and the power cable from his laptop. She's holding it in her hand and wondering if this is significant when the light from the landing is blocked. Joe stands in the doorway, bleary-eyed in pyjamas.

'Ell, it's half two in the morning,' he whispers. 'What are you doing?'

'Where's his computer?'

For a former paramedic, Joe has never had much concept of urgency. 'I'm sorry, I don't know where it is. If we go through his room now, we'll wake him up.'

Reluctantly Ellie follows him into the bedroom and flops on the bed. Still in search mode, she notices the peeling wallpaper and the unpainted plaster that she hasn't seen for months. Joe tries to snuggle into her. 'Do it tomorrow,' he mumbles into her neck. Ellie shoves him so hard he nearly falls off the bed.

'That's your answer to everything! Do it bloody tomorrow!'

'What have *I* done?'

'Yes, what *have* you done? You can't even finish decorating this room! Six months!'

Joe's hurt turns to anger. 'For God's sake. Go to sleep, Ell.' He flicks the light off.

Ellie has never been so tired, but sleep won't come. Where is Tom's computer? Where the hell is it?

It is three o'clock in the morning. Hardy is in his office, refreshing his inbox every minute as if that will make Ruth Clarkson's email arrive sooner. The empty CID is in darkness before him. There is no point in going back to the Traders. There isn't even much point trying to doze on the sofa in the corner. He's got, what, seven hours until he's off the case – off the force – for ever.

The email entitled *Tom Miller Email Transcripts* finally lands in Hardy's inbox at 3.14 a.m.

Hardy clicks it open and reads. He compares it with the data from Danny's laptop. The connection is made, so obvious that he's furious with himself for not seeing it before. There is a brief bright burst of euphoria, swiftly followed by dread.

This is going to break as many hearts as it heals.

For the first time in his career, DI Alec Hardy hopes desperately that he is wrong.

60

Height, weight, eyes, ears, nose. Pulse, temperature, oxygen. Hardy sits passively in the Chief Medical Officer's surgery, staring blankly at the anatomical posters on the opposing wall. The stethoscope slides cold across his chest. His medical file is as thick as a Russian novel. With an expensive pen, the doctor writes the final chapter.

Because he has nowhere else to go, Hardy heads back to the police station, and is half-surprised when his pass card still allows him access. In CID it is business as usual; the team are checking the shoe size of everyone who has been involved, even fleetingly, with the investigation. The list of men with size ten feet is small but growing. Paul Coates. Nige Carter. Steve Connolly. There are only two people left in the frame that they haven't accounted for.

He is working up to the phone call when Jenkinson summons him to her office. 'You're done,' she says. 'Office clear by the end of the day, please.'

Hardy does the calculations: eight more hours. He can still do this.

*

Joe Miller lies on his belly along Tom's bedroom floor, spitting dustballs as he fumbles under the bed. He retrieves a half-made model aeroplane, torn magazines, a shrivelled apple core and half a dozen odd socks, but no computer.

When Tom sees his dad's legs sticking out from under his bed, he can't hide his terror.

'Dad, *out!*' he screams.

Joe wriggles backwards and props himself up on one elbow. 'Mate, where's your laptop? Mum needs it for the investigation.'

'I lost it.' Tom shrinks into himself as a dishevelled Joe gets to his feet. 'Ah, a week back? Maybe longer?'

Joe looks him in the eye. 'Why didn't you tell us?'

'You've both had a lot on your mind.' It sounds feeble, like the excuse it is.

'Don't lie to me, Tom.' Joe puts his hand on Tom's shoulder and searches his face. There is the threat of a threat in his voice. 'Where's the computer?'

Ellie staggers into the station like a zombie. She was kept awake all night by the creeping feeling that Tom *is* hiding something from them. Susan Wright's description of Tom echoes in Ellie's head: *lying little shit.* Despite this, she is confident that he's guilty of something innocent. He's probably lost it, or swapped it, or he's bypassed the parental controls and looked at a website he shouldn't have. Ellie laughs bitterly to herself: it has really come to something when you take comfort in the idea of your child watching Internet pornography.

The suggestion that Tom is somehow involved in

Danny's death is obviously ludicrous. Hardy has finally lost the plot: with so little time left, he is inventing straws for the express purpose of clutching at them. Nige has done a runner, as has Susan Wright, the only person who could put him at the scene, and Hardy is panicking, tying mismatched loose ends together for the sake of it. She glances up at his office: the blinds are open but the light isn't on, meaning he must still be in with the doctor. Ellie wishes she could play the boss at his own game if only to show him how stupid he's being, but she has exhausted every lead she's had. She scrolls through the case files on her computer for confirmation: there isn't a single box unchecked. She rewinds the case in her mind's eye, looking for inspiration.

It occurs to her that there is one interview that was never entered on the system.

Ellie deliberates for a long time whether to pursue it now, then something inside her propels her into action. If it takes the heat off Tom, until they can get to the bottom of what he's hiding, it's worth a shot. She writes a cheque that will eat up all her overtime and puts it in her handbag.

It is the first time in months that Ellie has been to Lucy's house, and it's in a shocking state. It has the bare, temporary appearance of a squat. Lucy doesn't look much better. She's dyed her hair again, a bright bus red presumably intended to make her look young and funky. It puts ten years on her, but her face lights up when Ellie hands over the money.

'Oh, my little baby sis, you never let me down.' She goes to hug Ellie, who remains rigid, hands still in pockets.

'Look, we're running out of time,' she says. 'My boss is on

his way out and I'm scared to death another child is gonna get hurt, so you just tell me what you saw.'

Lucy pockets the cheque, as though afraid Ellie will snatch it away mid-sentence. 'Night of Danny's death, I was up really late. I took a break at around four,' she says. She doesn't have to explain what she was taking a break from: the only question is whether it was the online slot machines, poker or bingo, and Ellie couldn't care less about that. All she wants is the statement. 'I was looking out the window down the road and I saw a man in the distance, dark clothes, bald head under a little black hat, and he was shoving what looked like a bag full of clothes into someone's bin. The bin truck was just coming up the road.'

The description matches Susan Wright's statement. It matches Nige. Ellie puts a hand on the wall to steady herself. Dismissing Lucy has been an unforgivable oversight, possibly a career-ending fuck-up. If Lucy's telling the truth – and Ellie's gut tells her that she is – then Ellie has let Danny and his family down in the worst possible way. With huge effort, Ellie keeps her cool. She tells Lucy to come into the station when she's cleaned herself up, to make it formal and give them a proper description.

Frank stops Ellie on the way in to CID and tells her that Hardy's been given until the end of the day. She finds the boss in his office; he is still there, but only just. His complexion is working its way through a variety of mineral tones: if yesterday was chalk, today he is granite.

'Sir,' she says, shifting her weight from foot to foot. 'I was talking to my sister. She saw a man on the night of Danny's murder, throwing a bag of clothes into a dustbin. She gave me a description: height, build, short hair, possibly bald. It matches Nige.'

Hardy is agog. 'Why's she coming up with this *now*?'

Ellie can't meet his eye. 'I think something jogged her memory.'

Hardy's not as fired up by this statement from Lucy as she thought he would be. The fight has gone out of him already; she's surprised and then disappointed.

'Did you find your boy's computer?' he asks.

Why, after what she's just told him, is he still on about this? 'He says it was stolen.'

'Do you believe him?'

It breaks her heart to say no.

'I called Tom and Joe,' says Hardy. 'They're coming in.'

Ellie gasps. 'When were you going to tell me?'

Before Hardy can justify himself, there's a knock on the door. 'Ellie?' says one of the female PCs. 'There's someone outside wanting to talk.'

Kevin Green is looking haunted on the harbourside. If it weren't for his red T-shirt with the Royal Mail logo, Ellie wouldn't have recognised him. Even now it takes her a while to pinpoint him as the postman Jack Marshall reckoned he saw arguing with Danny at the beginning of the summer. So much has happened since then. His appearance has changed, too: he's lost weight and his previously clean-shaven face is covered by a ragged beard. What can he possibly want now?

'I was lying,' blurts Kevin. 'I *did* have a row with Danny a few weeks before he died. Someone had keyed my van, left this big long line. And he was the only one about that time in the morning. I thought it was him.'

The repercussions of this lie come screaming at Ellie: taking Kevin at his word made a liar of Jack Marshall, for a start. Would they have gone after him so hard if they had believed him on this?

'Why did you lie to us?' She's too tired and sad even to get angry.

'I was a bit panicky,' says Kevin, warming to his confession. 'Boy dies, you get seen having an argument. I thought, he wasn't around to say otherwise. I haven't slept in weeks. It's been giving me merry hell. So I thought I should tell you. Am I in trouble?'

Ellie resists the urge to push Kevin backwards into the harbour. 'What shoe size are you?' she asks resignedly.

'Eleven and a half.' Kevin wears a rabbit-in-the-headlights expression. 'Why?'

Hardy is in the family room with Tom and Joe Miller. A video camera nestles on a tripod and Tom blinks nervously into its lens. Joe is more restrained than in their last interview, although the effort of staying silent leaks into his body language, his left leg jiggling uncontrollably.

'My computer got nicked,' says Tom in answer to the first question. 'At school. I left it in a bag and then it was gone.'

Hardy leans forward, elbows on his knees, hands clasped before him. 'You mustn't lie to me, Tom.'

Tom looks in panic to Joe, who manages to button his lip. Hardy places the bag of smashed-up computer components in front of Tom, who flushes red.

'Paul Coates said you threatened to accuse him of all sorts of shenanigans if he were to give this to us.'

Joe is incredulous. 'You threatened the *vicar?*' Tom darkens further.

'I think you smashed it up because it had your emails with Danny on it,' suggests Hardy. 'Are these your emails?' He pulls out a batch of printouts from his file. Tom recoils from the paper as Joe leans in close to read.

'How did you get those?' Fear thins Tom's voice.

'They're stored on your server. We haven't seen these before because Danny was using a different email address than his home computer. And you're the only person he wrote to from this address. No, no – actually, you and one other person. We think he sent them from his smartphone.' At the mention of the phone, Tom looks relieved. That's one less secret for him to keep. 'Where'd he get that from?'

'He said he'd saved up from his paper round,' says Tom.

'In these emails, Danny's asking you to stay away from him. He says that he doesn't want to see you any more and you're no longer friends. Why was that?'

'He said he had a new friend,' says Tom. 'Someone who understood him better than me.' Hardy registers the wording; it's a strange insight for a pre-teen boy. It has the ring of something parroted from an adult.

'You email back, "I could kill you if I wanted".'

Joe can no longer override his protective instinct. 'For God's sake, it's just kids!' he jumps in. 'It's just boys falling out.'

'I'm talking to your son, Joe. Not you.'

Joe reluctantly sits back in his chair but his outburst has

unnerved Tom. Hardy pushes as hard as he can before the boy clams up completely. 'Did you kill Danny, Tom?'

'*No.*' Tom shakes his head.

'If you're lying to me, there'll be very serious consequences. If you want to tell me that you were involved in Danny's death—'

Now Joe really loses it. 'That's enough! You want to question him like this, we need a solicitor.'

Hardy looks from son to father and makes a judgement.

'Fine. We're done for now. We need a DNA sample. Then you can go.' They stand up to leave. 'Oh, Tom? What's your shoe size?'

Tom blinks at the apparent non sequitur. 'Five.'

Hardy writes it down. 'What about you, Joe?'

'Uh . . . ' says Joe, as if he has to think about it. 'Ten.'

61

DS Ellie Miller doesn't walk any more. She trudges. She drags her exhausted feet from one place to another, hope dimming a little with every step. She takes her time on the walk to Harbour Cliff Beach. She has no idea why DI Hardy has called her down here. It hasn't been a crime scene for weeks now.

She hears the sea like a rumour. The sandstone ripple of the cliffs reaches away from her to the vanishing point. She squints into the sun, on the lookout for Hardy's matchstick-man figure. It's only when she shifts her focus downwards that she finds him. He is sitting on the sand, folded in on himself with his knees drawn up to his chest, halfway to the shoreline. The sun plays upon him, breathing life into him; his skin is golden, his hair almost auburn. Maybe there is hope for him after the police.

'They've caught Nige Carter,' she says. Hardy scrabbles to his feet, brushing sand from his suit. He looks at Ellie as though she's spoken to him in a foreign language. 'Nige Carter?' she repeats. 'They found him hiding out in the hills in Mark Latimer's van. He's back in custody. He's a shoe size ten,' she reminds him.

Her words don't have the impact she was expecting. He's given up, she thinks. He's had enough. Even though he is clearly broken, she envies him. At least freedom is imminent for Hardy. She can't imagine a time when this will no longer be her life. She can barely remember a time when it wasn't.

'I was here before, on this beach,' he says. 'I came here as a kid. We had a tent on some campsite near the cliffs. I tried looking for it when I first came.'

Ellie doesn't know what surprises her most; that he's been here before or that he used to be a little boy. She pictures him in a suit, surly and unshaven, aged eight. '*You* came on holiday to *Broadchurch*?'

He nods. 'Didn't remember it was here till the day I came back. Freaked me out. Those bloody cliffs still the same. I used to sit under them, get away from my parents arguing.' His attention shifts to the horizon. 'They spent days sniping and shouting. The third day in, I sat here, all day, on this beach, right into the night. Thinking, I'm not going to have a family soon. When I got back they were livid. They'd been out looking for me. They didn't think to look on the bloody beach, mind.'

'Did your mum and dad split in the end?'

'No.' Hardy kicks at the rough sand. 'Kept bickering till the day my mum died. Last thing she ever said to me: God will put you in the right place. Even if you don't know it at the time.'

The two detectives face the horizon together, listening to the drag and deposit of shingle in the waves. It's a repetitive, hypnotic sound that brings about an eerie peace deep within Ellie. Broadchurch has always felt like the middle of the world to her. Right now, Harbour Cliff Beach feels like the edge of it.

The lull is shattered by the ring of her telephone. It's Nish. Ellie listens, then cuts the call. She is as adrenalised now as she was peaceful ten seconds ago.

'It's Danny's phone,' she tells Hardy. 'It's back on. They're tracing the signal now.'

Hardy doesn't share her excitement, but nods decisively. 'I want the tracking signal coordinates sent to my phone. You get back and question Nige Carter, get the truth out of him.' The shutters have come down again and it's hard to believe that this is the same man who has just confided in her. 'Go on, go. Go!' he barks. Her trudge has a new impetus behind it as she heads back towards the station. If Nige is in custody, then who's got the phone? Are they looking for two people after all? For the first time in weeks, she feels that the answers to her questions might be within reach.

'Miller!' What now? She turns back, shielding her eyes to see him. They are separated by a tract of sand and the breeze is picking up again. Hardy has to raise his voice. 'You've done good work on this, Miller. Well done.'

It is the first praise he has ever given her. Ellie shivers, as though someone has walked over her grave.

The sun is an old bronze coin, low in the sky.

Hardy walks the length of Broadchurch High Street without looking up from his screen. His progress is tracked by a red pin: Danny's phone by a blue. It is too soon to be precise about the location. That will come as he closes in. For now, the blue pin is merely a triangulation point between three possible locations. He speeds up, noticing as he does that his vision is pin-sharp and his legs strong and obedient. It is as though his illness, recognising the gravity of the moment, has decided to suspend play for a while.

The dull end of the High Street abruptly gives way to nondescript suburbia. Hardy zooms in. He looks up, makes a mental calculation, then turns left into an alleyway. It's the first time he's entered this hidden network of pathways and with none of the landmarks he has come to rely on, he loses his bearings and is temporarily a stranger in Broadchurch once more. A glance down at his phone roots him again. With technology as his guide, he covers the footpath in fifty paces and comes to the playing field. The red pin is almost over-lapping the blue. Hardy stands equidistant between St Andrew's church dead ahead, the Latimer house to the right, and there to the left ...

He puts his handset in his pocket and bears left across the field. With one final alleyway to negotiate, Hardy checks his phone again. Here, in Lime Avenue, the two pins on his screen converge.

The Millers' garden path feels a mile long. The front door is open. Tom and Fred are in the sitting room, laughing at a cartoon. Hardy is pulled up short by the black device in Tom's hand, but it's a TV remote, not a phone. He clears his throat and the boys look up, but he only takes their attention away from the screen for a moment. They are used to seeing policemen in their house. Hardy backs into the hall and con-tinues through the kitchen. The knot in his stomach pulls

385

taut as he walks through the unkempt back garden. The shed door is ajar. Hardy pauses. His bile rises for reasons that have nothing to do with his illness.

It's dark inside the shed and his eyes take a while to adjust. He turns slowly around and takes in the logs drying out, the skateboards in two different sizes, the bikes and the camping equipment. In the middle of this, Joe Miller stands, wearing jeans and a checked shirt, his left arm curled protectively around his body, his right hand holding Danny's phone to his lips in a loose kiss.

'I'm sick of hiding,' he says.

62

It is the dark side of midnight on Thursday, 18 July.

The Miller family are back in Broadchurch after three blissful weeks in Florida. They arrived home four hours ago to a pile-up of post and carpets glistening with slug trails.

Three members of the family are asleep. It was a tough flight and the effort it took to keep the kids awake all the way home from the airport now seems worth it; they have crashed out in their beds, unbathed, teeth unbrushed. Ellie is out cold, the seal broken on the bottle of melatonin pills she bought at Orlando Airport.

Joe Miller is wide awake despite the jet lag. That sick twisted feeling in his guts, absent for three blissful weeks, is back. He told himself, while he was away, that he was ... he hates the word *cured*, as it suggests he's done something wrong, and he hasn't. Well, *they* haven't. It takes, two, after all. But it's the only word that really seems to describe the way he felt on holiday. For the first time since it started, he felt utterly in the moment. His boys were enough. Ellie was enough. They had sex almost every night for the first time since trying for Fred. In Florida, Joe told himself that he was *cured*, but it came back, that longing swirled with shame. It came back on the road into Broadchurch. It came back stronger than ever. The last food he ate was an airline meal six hours ago but his appetite has vanished. He is literally sickening for Danny.

Joe Miller stands for a while on the landing, watching his wife and children sleep, and then at the ping of a text message he's downstairs, feeling in the dark hall for the car keys. His is the only car on the one-track road. Now and then as he skirts close to the cliff edge, there's a wink of moonlight on sea in the distance. Joe drives slowly, trying to order his thoughts. After the initial swoop of relief that Danny will see him again comes doubt. Danny wants this to be the last time. He's been very clear about that. Joe thinks hard. There's no way he can get his hands on any more money – Lucy hasn't been to the house for months, he can't make her his scapegoat again – so if he's going to convince Danny to keep meeting, Joe's going to have to persuade him with words. And if not … well, the thought of this being the last time makes Joe want to weep, but if this is how it's got to end, then they must make this last time count.

He parks the car up at the usual meeting point, the half-made road flanked by high hedgerows, lush and lusty with summer foliage. There is a purity to this place, far from the traffic and CCTV of the town. Joe's stomach clenches at the sight of Danny balanced on his skateboard, in the middle of the lane. The moon shines a spotlight on him. His hair's got a little bit longer in the last few weeks. That top is new. Joe is too overwhelmed to speak, then Danny does a trick on his skateboard, a flip-over that Joe taught him. They both laugh:

the tension is shattered, and Joe knows that it's going to be fine.

'Hiya,' says Danny. The harmless word hits Joe like a bullet: Danny's voice has broken while he was away. It's a hook in Joe's heart, but he doesn't know which way it's pulling him.

They do the final fifty yards to the clifftop hut on foot. Danny moves a rock to get the key out, and they're into the place Joe thinks of as their haven. He takes a moment to appreciate the clean smell of it, the neutral seashell art and the colour scheme, so tasteful you don't even notice it. How could anything that happens here ever be tawdry?

Joe sits on a chair and lets Danny sit on his lap. He is the perfect weight: the perfect size. When he's on his knee, Joe catches their reflection in the window and is pulled up short. The difference between how it looks on the outside and how it feels on the inside is huge, too big to explain even to himself. He closes his eyes against the image and just breathes him in. But something's wrong. Danny's arms are open, loose. He's in Joe's arms but he's slipping away.

'We don't have to stop this,' murmurs Joe. The intended reassurance backfires: Danny moves out of the hug.

'We do.'

'I know I said tonight was the last night but ... we're not doing anything wrong.'

'So why does it have to be a secret?'

Joe winces. He doesn't like this gruff new voice at all. 'People wouldn't understand.' Even as he says this, he knows that the problem is not that people wouldn't under-stand but that they would. Danny knows it too.

'I'm not going to meet you any more.' Joe doesn't recognise this new edge. Danny's got harder, somehow, in the last few weeks. Florida now seems a million years away and Joe finds himself wishing they'd never gone. He shouldn't have left him alone for so long. Three weeks is an age when you're eleven.

'I'm going. Try and stop me.' Anger surges in Joe. Why come all this way just to reject him? There's a cruel streak in Danny that he's only just uncovering. 'I'll tell my dad about this.'

Panic turns up the dial. Mark will kill him. Joe blocks Danny's way, to buy himself just a little bit more time.

'Let's not get silly, eh? What would you say, anyway: we meet and hug? So what?' Joe's been rehearsing the argument for ages. 'You tell your dad, he won't understand. And that'd mean no more Sunday lunches, no kickabouts with both our families.' Danny is unmoved. Joe delves deeper, grasping at the thing that brought them together in the first place. 'It means, next time when your dad hits you – or worse – you're on your own. 'Cause I was there for you, when you needed me. You tell people what we've been doing, no one will understand. They'll think it's wrong and sick, and it's not.' He doesn't know who he's trying to convince any more. 'And it will burn everything down. The whole of our world, the whole of our lives. And it'll be on you. Is that what you want?'

Danny's expression changes. ''Course not,' he says. Thank God. He's got through to him. Joe sinks into the chair, spreads his arms again. Danny runs not towards him, but out of the hut, the door springing behind him.

'Shit. *Danny*!' Danny runs through the dark, panicky, breathless, jagged. At the fence, he catches his hand on some barbed wire. It's a shallow cut but the blood flows fast. 'Danny. Dan!'

The skateboard is at Joe's feet. He picks it up. Danny can't go far without it. When he looks up, Danny has stopped at the rim of the cliff.

'We shouldn't have ever done this.' There's accusation in his huge blue eyes and tears too: he wipes them with the back of a bloody hand. Joe can't stand to see him cry. He can make it all right, if only Danny will let him. Danny squeezes his eyes closed tight. 'If I jump, everything's all right.'

Even in Joe's most paranoid fantasies, things never got this dark, this fast. 'No, mate.' He slows his breath to keep his voice steady; it's an old paramedic trick, a way to avoid freaking out accident victims even when you're panicking inside. 'Don't do that. Come on. I'm sorry, I shouldn't have said those things.' Danny shuffles forward. The tips of his feet are lined up with the edge. Blood trickles down his arm and drips from his fingers.

'Please, Dan, please. Don't be daft.' Joe stretches out his hand. 'Come on. It's all right. We can sort this out. I'm sorry. Let's go back together.'

Their hands are lubricated by the smear of blood on Danny's palm, and Joe cocoons Danny tight in a hug. Relief is a drug in his veins. 'There we go. It's all right. It's all right.'

Back in the hut, Joe turns the key quietly behind Danny's back. He has never locked them in before, but this time is different and it's only until they have come to an understanding. He almost gets away with it but at the last moment there's a loud click as the lock tumbles. Danny whips around in fear. Joe sees the broken trust and knows that it's over. He wants to weep, but he can't, because everything now is damage limitation.

'Promise it'll stay between us. Then you can leave.'

'What, or you'll hurt me?' says Danny. He squares his shoulders, a cocksure gesture that Joe's seen Mark make when wronged in the pub or on the pitch. 'I know what you want from me. You're too scared to ask. Why don't you do it to Tom instead?'

The line that Joe has taken such pains to respect has been crossed. To pollute what they have is one thing, but to bring Tom into it? Joe is not that man.

What he feels is too big to be contained by his own body. He has the sense of watching himself from above as he slams Danny against the wall. 'You need to not say those things, Dan.'

Danny remembers his manners at last. 'Please, get off me, please!' he begs. That's better. Of course, Joe intends to let him go but not until he's said his piece. Danny is struggling, losing it, and he'll never hear what Joe has to say until he calms down. 'I won't have you say that sort of thing about me! I helped you!' Danny starts to flail. Joe bangs his head twice against the wall to shock him into silence. 'We had something between us here! You won't spoil it. You do not spoil it!'

Finally the message gets through: Danny stops fighting and starts listening. He is utterly still.

He is too still.

Joe is horrified to see that the hands he thought were on

Danny's shoulders are around his throat. He freezes with the boy in a stranglehold. Danny's beautiful blue eyes are a maze of red threads. Petechial haemorrhage. Joe has been trained to save lives but the only skill he can draw on now is diagnosis. He knows death when he sees it. To loosen his grip will be to acknowledge what he has done. His hands let go of their own accord. Danny slumps down the wall and Joe has to catch him.

He holds him close and paces the floor of their sanctuary. 'I'm sorry I'm sorry,' he cries into his neck. 'Dan, I'm sorry.' The embrace he was denied in life grows tighter and tighter in death.

Joe falls silent but the word sorry runs on multiple loops in his head, a chorus that becomes a deafening rush in his ears. His mind is both blank and racing at the same time. What the fuck has he done? How has this happened?

For a few minutes, carrying Danny is effortless. Then, as the numbness of shock wears off, Joe's arms begin to ache and reality rushes in, followed by the primal instinct of self-preservation. Gently he lays Danny's body down on the floor and strokes closed the blood-laced eyes.

It is not as though Joe makes a conscious decision to hide what he has done; rather, he finds himself going through the motions of it, wiping down the door handle with his sleeve and checking the cupboard under the sink. There's a big box of cleaning products and a packet of latex gloves. He pulls them on without thinking and it's only when he looks down at the white-gloved hands of a bad magician that he first understands that he intends to cover his tracks.

Danny's life is over, and so in all the ways that count is

Joe's, but do Ellie and the boys deserve to go through hell? Put like that it is not a choice at all but an obligation.

What he is left with now is a hundred tiny choices and each must be right. He spins on his heel in the open night, wondering where to go. He searches the sea for inspiration and it provides. Down on the beach is a line of small boats. One he knows in particular.

He ties plastic bags over his walking boots. He pockets a rag and some household cleaner. On the short walk to his car, he inventories the stuff in the boot. He's glad now he didn't tidy up the car before Florida like Ellie nagged him to. He has to rummage through the jumble of family life – Fred's wellies, a torn luggage tag, a bicycle pump – to find what he's looking for. There's his old gym bag gathering dust under Fred's travel cot. He will need that, but not until later. He fumbles in the dark until at last, wedged into a corner, his fingers close over the cold steel of the bolt cutters, still there from the time Tom forgot the combination on his bike lock and Joe had to cut it free.

Thin clouds scud across the full moon as Joe half-runs, half-falls down the cliff path, Danny's skateboard under his arm. He uses the bolt cutters to snap the chain that tethers Olly's boat and pulls it along the beach, as close to the shoreline as he can.

The next trip to the beach, with Danny warm and limp in his arms, is hard work. Danny's weight throws Joe off balance and he can't see the sand-steps under his feet. By the time he reaches the boat, he is drenched in sweat and his muscles are in spasm. His arms want him to drop Danny, but Joe lays him down in the hull as gently as though he were sleeping.

Danny's bleeding hand brushes against the side of the boat: Joe wipes it clean. The skateboard goes in next. Joe pushes the boat out into the water and they're off, the outboard motor churning the black sea to foam.

He waits until they are a mile offshore to look down. Danny's gone, he tells himself. Do what you have to. This isn't Danny. Not any more. His stomach clenches like a fist as he starts the clean-up operation, spraying Danny's skin with the cleaner and then wiping him down. When he has scrubbed every inch of Danny's skin, he hauls the body to the side of the boat. He lets go, preparing himself for the splash but it does not come and he realises that he is still holding Danny. It's as though his hands are glued to the boy.

He can't do this. He can't do this. He can't do it to Danny. He deserves better than to be dumped at sea. Mark and Beth deserve better. Joe drops the body to the floor of the boat. He looks behind him; the water has carried them a mile or so along the coast: the lights of the town and the amber cliffs call them home.

Joe starts the motor again and heads for Harbour Cliff Beach. There he places Danny gently, respectfully, on his back in the middle of the beach. He lays the skateboard parallel, hoping that one day, Mark and Beth will work out that this last gesture was done out of love.

There is no time for him to cry over the body but as he gets back into the boat and retraces his route, it strikes him how vulnerable Danny looks. He recognises the thought as irrational, grotesque, but he can't help hoping that the tide will be kind. He keeps his gaze trained on the beach until the outline of Danny's body is absorbed into the liquid dark.

It has gone one o'clock by the time Joe gets back into the hut and the next hour passes in a blur of activity. He puts on new gloves, ties new bags around his feet, and cleans the hut from top to bottom, wiping down surfaces, vacuuming the chair where they sat, the sofa where Danny lay, washing the walls and mopping the floor. The incantation *sorry sorry sorry* is replaced by *shit shit shit*. Joe works manically, his goal the aseptic cleanliness of an operating theatre.

When he's satisfied, he strips completely, shivering naked in the moonlight before putting everything he's been wearing inside a bin liner along with the latex gloves and his boot coverings. In his sports bag is a tracksuit: it's soft against his skin, a tender touch that he doesn't deserve. There's a black wool hat tucked in a side pocket that must have been there since last winter. He pulls it down over his ears. There is still more to do.

On the drive back into Broadchurch, the incriminating bin liner crackles on the passenger seat. Joe knows that the refuse collection starts at Lucy's end of town the hour before dawn, and throws the lot into a communal bin behind some garages.

It is four o'clock in the morning when Joe gets back to Lime Avenue. The full force of his exhaustion suddenly hits him. Gravity doubles its force and he wants nothing more than to lie down. First he must wash, to rid himself of traces of Danny and because he feels toxic, like he'll poison the whole house. He turns the shower as hot as he can take it, then a little higher still. After ten minutes under the water he still feels filthy, so he stands before the bathroom mirror and scours his face and hands with a nail brush. 'Come on,' he tells his reflection. 'You can do this, you can do this, you have to do this. It's gonna be all right.'

When he crawls into bed, Ellie readjusts herself but doesn't wake from her stupor. Behind her, Joe balls himself into the foetal position. His scream is an absence of sound, a wordless cry that goes on and on. A small detached part of him observes and diagnoses the full nervous breakdown as it happens. He feels the searing clutches of an army of devils, come to drag him irretrievably into hell.

63

Hardy studies his suspect across the table. Joe Miller's clothes have been taken away and he's in a police-issue white paper suit that crinkles when he moves. There is a wedding-ring tan line on his left hand. He does not look like a child killer. They don't always.

'I was in love with him,' says Joe. There is bewilderment and apology in his tone but something else that grates with Hardy, a helplessness, as though this is something that has happened to him rather than a crime he has perpetrated.

'When did this start?' Hardy asks.

'About nine months ago,' says Joe. 'Mark had given Danny a split lip. They'd had a big row. Danny came round to ours, to see Tom, didn't know where else to go to. I fixed him up. We talked.'

'Then what?'

'He'd come round and play with Tom and he'd always find me. We'd have a chat. He told me he couldn't talk to his dad like that. Then he took up the skateboard and he asked me to teach him like I'd taught Tom. That's when we started meeting up, just the two of us, once a week or so. Skate park, when it was quiet. Country lanes that were good for skateboarding. It was only lessons.'

'Did you tell Ellie?' Hardy holds his breath for the answer. The rest of this investigation hinges on what DS Miller knew. Joe breathes a rueful little laugh and shakes his head. 'I wanted something that was *mine*,' he bleats. 'I gave up my job to look after Fred. Ellie has her job and Tom does his own thing, but Danny . . . I felt like he needed me.'

'Where did she think you were?'

'Gym. Running. Cycling. Pub.' Joe's lies are a strike against Miller's judgement but ultimately in her favour.

'Did you ever touch him?'

'I didn't *interfere* with him.' Joe almost vomits the word. 'That's not what we did. All I ever asked was for him to hold me. That's all. There was no abuse. Not then, not ever.'

No, thinks Hardy. You killed him before that happened. He keeps the thought to himself and ploughs on through his list of questions.

'Standing up, sitting down? Clothed, naked?'

'On a chair,' says Joe, appalled. '*Clothed.*'

'How long did the hugs last?'

'Why does it matter?'

'Everything matters. I need to have the facts, Joe. I need to understand.'

'If I can't understand it, why should you?' bursts Joe. The plea seems genuine, but Hardy's not taking anything at face value. Joe has had a long time to replay this murder, long enough to reframe his intentions even to himself.

'Did you give Danny presents?'

Joe's face twists at the question. 'Mobile phone, beginning of the year. I told him not to show Mark and Beth. And I gave him five hundred in cash the day before we went to Florida. It was part of our spending money. Ellie assumed Lucy had taken it and ... ' shame blooms on his cheeks, 'I didn't correct her. She was livid.'

'Why'd you give Danny that money, Joe?'

'I wanted him to love me,' says Joe pathetically. 'I knew he wanted to stop, I thought it'd make the difference.'

'If he wanted to stop, why was he at the hut that night?'

Joe can hardly get the words out. 'I said it'd be the last time.'

Hardy orders his thoughts. Each answer throws up a dozen new questions and it's hard to prioritise. For now, he must keep it broad. The detail will come.

'The boat,' he begins. 'Why burn it so much later?'

'I didn't have time on the night,' he says. 'But I knew you'd find it if I left it any longer. I had to sneak out while Ellie was on duty, and the kids were asleep. I had to leave them by themselves. I was terrified something would happen to them ... ' Joe trails off as the irony slams home.

Hardy moves on. 'So today, you turn on the phone deliberately. But two nights ago, why call from the hut?'

'I couldn't take any more.' His eyes plead for understanding. 'I caused Jack's death too. I knew you'd check the number. I thought it'd just be you. To confess. Ellie said she was tied to the desk all night.' At the second mention of his wife's name, Joe finally breaks down. 'Does she know?'

'No,' says Hardy.

'I can't tell her,' he snivels. 'You have to tell her.'

Hardy is no longer able to hide his contempt. It bubbles under his skin and he's very close to losing his cool when there's a knock on the door.

'Alec?'

It's the Chief Super. Hardy suspends the interview.

They look at each other in sorrow, their last encounter forgotten. Jenkinson's pink eyes and nose strip her of her rank, peeling her back to the human behind the badge. 'The boys are with Pete Lawson,' she says. 'Ellie's still in interview room Two with Nige Carter. She's going round in circles. We can't stall her for ever. D'you want me to break the news?'

'No,' says Hardy. 'He's my suspect. She deserves to hear it from me.'

He waits until Jenkinson's court shoes are an echo in the corridor, then interrupts Miller's interview without knocking. She whips around in disbelief.

'Sir, d'you mind?' She's hoarse. 'I'm in the middle of – for the sake of the tape, DI Hardy has just—'

'Interview ended one thirty-three p.m.,' says Hardy, shutting down the machine. 'Take him away,' he says to the PC on duty. Nige looks suspicious rather than relieved, as though this is a ploy to confuse him further.

'He's my suspect!' says Miller as Nige is led away.

Hardy sits in the chair Nige has vacated. It is unpleasantly warm. 'It's not him,' he says.

Miller draws her eyebrows together in doubt. 'How d'you know?'

Hardy draws on his twenty years' experience as a police officer: every interview, every confrontation, all the training.

It is not nearly enough. 'I have to ask you a couple of things. Where were you on the night of Danny's death?'

'What?' She's almost amused.

'Just – I'll explain – just – we need to keep this simple.' He palms the air downwards in a calming gesture, intended to soothe himself as much as her. 'I'll ask questions, you give me the answers.'

She laughs out loud now. 'What, you think it was me?'

He can't soften the blow but he can prepare her for it. 'Please, Ellie.'

Laughter is abruptly replaced by alarm. Her pupils blow black and huge. 'Don't call me Ellie,' she says.

'Tell me where you were the night Danny Latimer died.'

Her mind is working furiously, he can see that. Is she on the right track, or is she thinking about Tom? 'At home. We'd just got back from Florida.' Impatience briefly trumps her fear; she's said this before.

'So that night, what did you do? Unpack? Get ready for work?'

'I went to bed. I get terrible jet lag, so I have these pills and they knock me out.' Hardy needs to cut to the chase: any longer and he'll start to patronise her, and that's the last thing he wants.

'Did you notice Joe come to bed?'

'No.' Fear loosens her lower lip: it trembles like a child's. 'Tell me what's happening.' Hardy stands up and brings his chair around the table so that he's sitting next to her. 'What're you doing, why you coming round here?'

He makes sure he keeps eye contact. 'It was Joe.' Miller

throws her head from side to side as if to shake his words free. 'Joe killed Danny Latimer.'

'No he didn't. What the fuck?' She bucks backwards, her chair scraping across the floor. 'No, he didn't. He wouldn't.' Hardy watches in horror as her face falls apart. Lines he has never seen crack the panes of her cheeks and forehead. He needs to counter this emotion with fact: the merciless equivalent of a slap to a hysterical face.

'We have him in custody.'

'Who's got the boys?' she says in panic.

'Pete,' says Hardy.

She gets to her feet only to double over. She staggers into the corner of the room and retches. Hardy identifies the contents of her stomach – tuna sandwich, baked beans – as they reverse up her throat. Thin yellow liquid splashes his shoes and trousers but he stoops to comfort her, his hand resting uselessly on her arm. She's falling down a bottomless hole and neither he nor anyone else can catch her. He wants to help her, but he's never been any good at saying the right thing. For a moment, he thinks about telling Miller about Tess, that he knows what it's like to be betrayed by your spouse. As soon as the thought is formed, he understands that he can't insult her with the comparison. After a minute or so, Miller's gagging noises are replaced by racking sobs.

'I'm sorry,' says Hardy. The word has endless applications. Sorry it took so long. Sorry it's him. Sorry it's you.

'But ... no ... Susan Wright.' Miller is agitated by hope. 'Lucy. They *saw* Nige.'

'They saw Joe,' says Hardy evenly. 'Same build, facial

similarities, bald head beneath the hat. They thought it was Nige, but it was Joe.'

'No. Not Joe. Not. It's not Joe. *Please*. You're wrong.' She presses her cheek against the smooth concrete wall of the cell. The porous surface soaks up her tears like a sponge.

'I'm not,' says Hardy.

'The boat,' she says, hope punching through the despair. 'I was working when the boat was set alight. He wouldn't have left the kids.'

'He's confessed to that too.'

Miller's tears stop like the tap has been turned off. She wipes a slick of snot with the side of her hand.

'I want to see him.'

64

There are twenty paces between interview rooms 1 and 2 in Broadchurch police station. Ellie walks on rubber legs, counting every step. Too soon she arrives at the door she's touched a million times. Now it feels like a portal to another world. She lets her fingertips rest on the wood for a second.

'You don't touch him,' warns Hardy at her shoulder. 'You don't do anything that might jeopardise a conviction.'

'What am I gonna do? He's bigger than me, there are cameras everywhere.'

Joe, ridiculous in his white boiler suit and canvas shoes, leaps to his feet at their entrance. A beast rears up inside Ellie at the sight of him; she is a wolf in a woman's costume.

'Sit down,' she growls. He obeys. 'Is it true?' His inability to answer is the confirmation she needs. It is only anger that keeps her on her feet. Only the buzz of the CCTV cameras in the corner and the presence of Hardy keep her from lashing out.

'I never touched Tom or Fred,' says Joe. 'I never touched Danny. Ell, I've always loved you—'

'He was *eleven*!' Her shriek cuts him dead.

'I can't explain it . . . ' he sobs, tilting his face up to her like one of the boys. He actually expects her to comfort him. 'Can I see Tom?'

At this crass demand, the wolf rips through to the surface. Ellie lunges at Joe, knocking him off his chair. He curls up on the floor. Her first kick gets him in the balls, then she alternates between the head and the ribs. The aftermath of every beating she's ever seen comes back to her so she knows exactly where to aim to cause him maximum pain. She doesn't recognise the noises that come tearing out from a place inside she never guessed existed. It only lasts a few seconds: Hardy shouts for help and two PCs burst into the interview room to pull her off her worthless sick fuck of a husband. Their hands are on her arms when she brings her toes hard against his kidneys. Hardy steers her into the corridor and closes the door on Joe. The rage subsides as rapidly as it came. By the time she's back in Hardy's office, a strange, deep calm has descended and she concerns herself now with practicalities.

'If there's anything you need me to do on the paperwork or stuff I've been following up, my desk is a mess.'

'It's fine,' soothes Hardy in the low hush of a father reading a bedtime story. His tenderness is more than Ellie can bear. She longs for the old world order, the sarcasm and the sparring and the knowledge that she could put up with his shit at work because she always had her family to go home to.

'We've booked you a family room at the hotel by the roundabout,' he continues softly. 'Pete'll meet you there with Tom and Fred. You can pick some stuff up on the way. Don't talk to anyone. Shut the curtains, lock the door, don't answer the phone to anyone who isn't me. Do you understand?' She can only nod. 'Your car's outside now. I'll see you soon.'

Ellie has to walk through CID to get her coat and bag. She risks a glance around the office and sees not accusation but pain on the faces of her fellow officers, her friends. The framed family photograph on her desk has been rebranded with lies. She flips it face-down. As DS Ellie Miller leaves CID for the last time, there's the sound of a woman weeping.

The police cordon has isolated the Millers' house from the rest of Lime Avenue. Squad cars parked horizontally across the street make a roadblock. Her neighbours regard her with fear and accusation. Ellie remembers with a jolt how sure she was that Susan Wright must have known what her husband was up to. Now it seems that that weird, wretched woman is the only person in the world who might understand a little of what she's going through.

Brian is in the hallway in his boiler suit, mask looped around his neck. He's got Joe's blue Dad Coat in an evidence bag. In a trance, Ellie accepts the forensic shoe covers and gloves.

'I'll accompany you round while you get your stuff,' says Brian. 'I'm so sorry, Ellie.'

In the sitting room, she picks up a couple of DVDs for the hotel. A fat black slug sits on the centre of the carpet. She brings the ball of her foot down hard on it; glistening white innards shoot out like ointment from a tube. Upstairs, she chooses the boys' clothes with care but stuffs items from her own wardrobe into a suitcase at random.

In the porch, she looks back into her shabby home: the half-painted walls, the kids' toys, the books and the music and the photographs. She tries to remember it the way she left it that morning, when it was a haven, a place of happiness, but it's already too late for that.

In London, Karen White is heading north across Blackfriars Bridge in a taxi when DI Hardy calls her mobile. It's a bad connection and the distortion makes him sound more robotic than ever.

'You, mate, are a bastard,' she greets him. 'I've had Olly Stevens on the phone. You gave the Sandbrook story to him.'

'We have Danny Latimer's killer.'

Instantly Karen forgets about the story she was chasing. 'Who is it?'

'We'll be making a statement in three hours. Nobody else will have advance warning. If you're down here, you'll have first access.'

'Thanks,' she says. 'But why'd you call me?' The phone goes dead. Karen looks in her handbag; there's an unopened packet of Marlboro Lights, a fully charged iPad and her purse. Good enough. She knocks on the glass partition. 'Waterloo, please.'

The cab makes an illegal U-turn and re-crosses the river.

65

Hardy gathers the Operation Cogden team in front of the whiteboard. He still doesn't know them all by name: he used to rely on Miller for that sort of thing.

'At 5 p.m., I will tell the family,' he says. 'I'll then make a short statement to the media. And then we all need to be on hand. This information is going to run a crack through this community. Nish is distributing a list of responsibilities for individuals and groups. You all know DS Miller. She has been removed from the case and put on leave with full pay. There is *no suggestion* she knew.' He draws a line with his finger in the air. 'There is *no suggestion* she covered anything up. You're her colleagues and friends. This is unthinkable for her. She'll need you. She'll need all of us.'

There are no raised eyebrows, nothing to hint that anyone suspects Miller's guilt or complicity. But Hardy's next speech will have a very different audience.

Mark Latimer lets him into the house with no sense of occasion. Visits from the police are routine here now and the family wear their pain like old clothes. They have waited so long that they have stopped being ready. When he asks them to sit down, they do so without anticipation, lined up on the sofa in the same order as the day he and Miller confirmed the news: Beth, Mark, Chloe, Liz. Hardy perches on the edge of a dining chair.

'We've charged someone with Danny's murder,' he says.

'Oh God,' says Beth. Her hands cup her belly, then her mouth. 'I don't want to know,' she says, turning her face away.

'No, no, that's good,' says Mark.

'Is it someone we know?' says Beth.

'It's Joe Miller.' Four faces wear the same stunned expression; for a few seconds they are frozen in shock.

'Oh my God.' Chloe looks to her parents.

'It can't be,' says Liz. 'They only live across the field.'

Beth begins to rock back and forth. Mark drops his head to his knees, linking his hands behind his neck.

'He's confessed,' says Hardy. 'He and Danny had been meeting secretly for a few months.'

Mark flips. The women on the sofa shrink backwards as he kicks over the coffee table. The whole house shivers as he throws a chair against the wall. Beth, Chloe and Liz are screaming at him to stop, but he's gone, the front door slamming so hard that Danny's picture leaps from the wall. Beth darts to pick it up: her fingertips trace the contours of his face before she hangs it again. She turns around slowly.

'*Ellie.*' It's an accusation.

'She didn't know,' says Hardy, but he can see she doesn't believe him.

*

The hotel on the edge of town is part of a chain; simple, functional, anonymous. Ellie places a sleeping Fred on to one of the two double beds. She has a sudden picture of Joe carrying a tiny Fred in a sling and is momentarily convinced, 110 per cent sure, she would bet her life, that Joe is innocent. Her good, kind man, her doting dad, he is incapable of killing a child. Then she pictures his face as she last saw it and knows it is true. She tucks Fred under the shiny counterpane and hopes that he is young enough to forget what he and Joe used to mean to each other.

'This is nice,' she says to Tom, drawing the chintzy curtains against the view of the car park. 'It's an adventure. You hungry? We could get chips. Sit on the bed, watch telly, eat chips out the packet ... '

Tom isn't fooled for a second.

'There's something you need to know.' Ellie pats the bed and Tom sits next to her. She feels like a surgeon about to operate without anaesthetic.

'They've, we've, found out who killed Danny. And ... ' She digs her fingernails into her palm. 'Sweetheart, it was your dad.'

'*No.*' She watches Tom repeat the process she began in the police station. 'He wouldn't do that. He *didn't.*' His denial tears at her heart.

'He did.' She is crying already. 'And I don't know why and it's nothing we did and I can't explain it and I am so sorry, you should not have to go through this. But I am here with you and I will never leave you and I'm sorry. Tom, I have to ask you.' Bile floods her mouth; she swallows it. 'Did your dad ever touch you, or do anything you felt uncomfortable with?'

411

'No! Mum, he's not like that.' Tom's disgust is unfeigned. 'I promise, I'd tell you. He didn't, ever.'

'OK. Thank you.' She pulls him closer: their tears mingle. 'Tom, why did you send Danny those threatening emails?'

'He said he didn't want to be my friend any more. Said he had a new friend. I was angry.' He screws his face up as the connection is finally made. 'That was Dad, wasn't it?'

A storm tide of anger surges inside Ellie. They worked so hard to raise Tom happy, independent, and enthusiastic. And now, with one blow, Joe has undermined all of it. All the bloody flash cards and home cooking and storybooks and co-sleeping in the world can't insure against something like this.

'Yes, love.' She kisses the top of his head. 'You know I love you.'

'More than chocolate?' If she can give the correct response to his call, then that at least will be normal. She forces a smile.

'More than chocolate.'

'I don't understand. Why would he kill Danny?'

Make it stop, thinks Ellie, *please* make it stop. 'I don't know, sweetheart. I don't understand either and I really wish I did.'

Tom cries into her shoulder while Ellie rocks him. On the other bed, Fred turns over in his sleep. The knife has gone in: it is up to her to minimise the scar tissue. Silently she dedicates the rest of her life to getting her boys through this. The three of them are on their own now.

There is a night-before-Christmas hush on Broadchurch High Street. Blinds and shutters are pulled down and the signs in shop windows are turned to CLOSED.

The local media are out in force for the briefing; they stand at the foot of the police station steps, taking light readings for their cameras and checking the batteries on their phones. Karen White is the only national journalist, press or broadcast. When she sees Hardy she gets a shock: his bones protrude through his skin and his eyes look loose in their deep-grey sockets.

'A thirty-eight-year-old man from Broadchurch has today been charged with the murder of Daniel Latimer,' he addresses the camera. 'Danny's family have been informed and ask for privacy at this time. I would ask for all members of the media not to do anything that would prejudice the suspect's right to a fair trial. This investigation has affected the whole of the local community. Few people have been left untouched. As Senior Investigating Officer, I would respectfully ask that the town is now left alone to come to terms with what took place here. The privacy of everyone concerned should be respected. There will be no further statements. We are not looking for anyone else in relation to the crime. This has been a delicate and complex investigation and it has left its mark on a close-knit town. Now is the time for Broadchurch to be left to grieve and heal, away from the spotlight.'

He does not take questions.

Karen White falls into step with Maggie Radcliffe on the way back to the *Echo*.

'Someone local,' says Karen. 'Any idea who?'

'I want to know but at the same time I can't bear to,' replies Maggie.

In the newsroom, Olly is overseeing the layout of the front page, shifting text around the screen, increasing the size of the headline – DANNY KILLER CAUGHT – and pulling Danny's photo to the centre of the page. There's a new confidence and decisiveness in Olly that kindles in Karen something nearer to maternal pride than to desire. She gets close enough to read. Under the sub-head LOCAL MAN CHARGED are four perfect paragraphs of concise, objective reporting. She looks up to congratulate him, but he's on the other side of the room. His mother is in the doorway, her face sallow against her bright hair. They are too far away for Karen to hear or lip-read, but whatever she says has Olly back at his desk within seconds, gathering up his wallet, keys and phone.

'Family emergency,' he mutters. He throws his jacket on and he's gone.

Karen and Maggie exchange bewildered looks. What kind of family emergency could take Olly away from the biggest story of his career? Lucy looked stricken but not ill. Something to do with his dad?

The penny drops for both of them at the same time.

A thirty-eight-year-old man has been arrested.

Uncle Joe.

Maggie sits down hard in her seat. 'Christ,' she says. Karen breaks the seal on her packet of cigarettes and offers one to Maggie. After a second's hesitation, she takes one for herself.

Karen can hear Danvers' voice as clearly as if he were standing next to her. The wife is the story. Find the wife and get her to talk.

66

Mark Latimer runs as if pursued, or pursuing. His is not the measured, purposeful stride of Beth in her running gear but a flailing, directionless lope. Only when he arrives at the Harbour Cliff Beach does he understand that this was his destination all along. He finds a deserted stretch among the rock pools and stops dead.

The sky is orange streaked with sooty black clouds, a fireball stretched across the sky. Mark rages, shaking his fist at the freak sunset. '*Why?*' he asks over and over, although if there was anyone to hear him the word would not be intelligible. It comes out in an animal howl. He throws stone after stone into the choppy sea until his arm is sore. Anger flows out of him hard and fast but doesn't diminish. When the stones are gone and there is only shingle and sand left, Mark drops to his knees and weeps. Salt water soaks his jeans and shoes.

He should go home to Beth. She needs him. Chloe needs him. But the thought of being back in that women's world of talk and comfort repulses him. He needs to act. He makes a phone call to Bob Daniels, the only friend he has left on the force, saying he's on his way to the station. He ends the call before Bob can ask why. It is a warm evening and his jeans dry quickly, a salty tidemark snaking around his calves.

On the harbourside, he stands a distance away from the station entrance and the abstract horror of it takes shape; Danny's killer is somewhere in that round building.

Bob is waiting for him on the steps. A slap on the upper arm substitutes for a hug. 'Jesus, Mark,' he says. '*Joe*. I still can't believe it.'

He shakes his head in anger and something else too: the subtext is clear: I didn't think he had it in him. Mark knows they're both thinking it.

'I gotta see him,' says Mark. 'I need him to look me in the eye.'

What he's asking would mean instant dismissal, and Bob's got a family to support. Mark knows this. But he can't help himself.

'*Mate*.' The word is freighted with twenty years of history: every pint they've shared and every game of football they've played. The kids, the wives, the *lives*. 'For Danny.'

Bob throws a quick glance behind him. 'Go round the back,' he says, shaking his head in disbelief at his own action. 'I can buzz you in through the side door. Nobody can know about this or I'm *fucked*.'

It is the greatest thing another man has ever done for Mark. He hopes his face conveys his gratitude because he doesn't trust himself to say it. The door Bob opens leads straight down into the cells by way of a long, pale yellow corridor with a sour, antiseptic smell. Mark gives brief consideration to the logistics of getting him in here. How has Bob done it? Turned the cameras off? Neutralised an alarm system?

'He's in number 3,' says Bob, sliding open a gate. '*Two minutes.*'

It is the only occupied cell. Mark lets the viewing panel fall open with a clang.

Joe Miller sits on the narrow bed in his white boiler suit. He looks tiny. Partly it's a trick of perspective, framed by the hatch, but he is also somehow reduced. He is so much less than the man Mark thought he was, a pathetic little eunuch.

Mark's face is a dark-red growling monster in widescreen. 'You were our friend,' he says. 'You were in our *house*.'

'I'm so sorry.' Joe raises his palms. A line from the post-mortem comes rushing back to Mark: Danny was facing his attacker. This blank egg was the last face his boy ever saw. The thought nearly sends Mark falling to the floor. 'I'm so sorry,' Joe bleats.

Mark's cheeks run wet with tears and spittle. 'You not man enough to kill your own boy? You had to take mine.'

'It was an accident,' says Joe. 'I put him on the beach so you'd know. I could have left him at sea.'

This is at the limit of what Mark can take. 'Have you *heard* yourself?'

'He only came to me in the first place because you were no sort of father to him. Because you hit him.'

'Don't you use me as a fucking excuse!' Mark feels something in his throat tear with the force of his words. 'It was only ever *once*. And I'll suffer for that my whole life now.' Joe is crying too. How dare he? 'You did things to him, didn't you? I know they're saying you didn't, but you must've.'

'I swear, I never did,' Joe beseeches. 'I only ever cared for him. You have to believe that.'

Mark pushes his face against the door, metal digging into his flesh. 'I thought I'd hate you, Joe.' He spits the words. 'But now I see you here, you're not even worth that. I pity you. Because you're nothing.'

Mark slams the viewing panel closed before Joe can see that he's lying. He does hate Joe; hate isn't a strong enough word for the ball of dark energy in his chest, firing violent impulses along his body. He is glad of the thick cell door, not for Joe's sake but for Beth's and Chloe's and the new baby's. Given the chance, he would kick the life out of Joe Miller.

It's dark and wet outside now. Ellie and Tom race raindrops down the windowpane while she waits for the call to come from Hardy. She doesn't know if she still has a right to know what's happening. What is she now, a witness?

A hammering on the door makes them both jump and Fred murmur in his sleep.

'It's Lucy.' Ellie slides back the bolt and lets her in. Everything is stripped away, the arguments and the money and the lies, because family is where you go when there is nowhere and nothing else left. They hug for a long time and then, without being told, Lucy understands that Ellie needs to go.

'Take as long as you need,' she says, helping Ellie into her orange coat like a child.

As she hits the edge of town she wishes she'd worn something less recognisable. The Mum Coat marks her out like

418

a buoy in the harbour. She puts her head down and travels via the back alleyways. Even so, someone sees her crossing the road near the *Echo*, and it's the last person in the world she needs to see right now.

'DS Miller,' says Karen White. Ellie's legs flex beneath her as if to run away and she looks up and down the street for a photographer, but it looks like Karen is alone. 'I'm sorry,' she says, and Ellie can't work out if she's expressing sympathy or apologising for the ambush. 'They're all going to be after your side of the story.' This is more like it. Ellie braces herself for the barely veiled blackmail: give me an exclusive and I'll look after you. What Karen actually says takes Ellie's breath away: 'Don't talk to anyone.' She steps back into the shadows before Ellie has time fully to recognise the favour, let alone thank her for it.

She keeps trudging, sticking to the paths and minor roads. Her eyes stay on her feet. There is no need to look up. She could walk this town blindfold. She could draw a map from memory and name every street.

At the edge of the playing field, she stops. The church is in darkness but lights blaze in every room of her own house: she can see the indistinct figures of the SOCO team and recoils to imagine them rooting through her kitchen, her wardrobe, her life.

Slowly, Ellie turns her head towards Spring Close. There is no movement there: only Beth, framed in her bedroom window, hands on the sill. Ellie puts her head in her hands and when she looks up again, Beth has gone. A chink of light expands and contracts to show Beth's back door opening. It is the least Ellie can do to meet her halfway. The two old friends walk slowly towards each other. There is so much Ellie wants to say to her, but she will give Beth the first word. She is braced for tears, rage, violence.

She gets silence. They stand opposite each other for a long time. Finally Beth moves her head from side to side, slowly, deliberately, almost sarcastically.

'How could you not know?'

As she walks back towards her house, Ellie howls inside. Beth's reaction is a barometer for the rest of the community. It is nearly a relief to know that she has to go. Miraculously, her voice holds steady during a quick call to a whispering Lucy. Tom is finally asleep, an arm curled protectively around Fred. She retraces her steps back through the alleyways, cutting into the High Street at the Traders, and makes it up the stairs to Hardy's room without anyone seeing her.

He sits on the bed while she slumps opposite him in a tub chair, still in her orange coat.

'I want to kill him.' She's not ashamed of it; it's almost a point of pride. 'Help me understand,' she says, deferring to Hardy's experience. 'Because I can't. Do you believe him? Do you think it's possible? He says he was in love. How could he, how could any adult be in love with an eleven-year-old boy? Is he a paedophile? The pathologist found no evidence of abuse on Danny, and I asked Tom and he said Joe never touched him. So what does that make him?'

Hardy takes his glasses off. 'Just because he didn't abuse either boy, doesn't mean he wouldn't have gone on to,' he says in his new, soft, good-cop way.

'Doesn't mean he would've, either.' She hears her own desperation.

'We'll never be sure.' His voice is heavy with sorrow. 'Maybe he was romanticising, in order to justify what he felt. Or maybe that's as it was. I don't have those answers. People are unknowable. And ... you can never really know what's in someone else's heart.'

'I should've seen it.'

'How?'

'I'm a bloody detective! Miller, such a brilliant copper, the murderer was lying next to her.' For the first time it hits her that Hardy knew before she did. How long has she been making a fool of herself? 'When did you suspect?'

'Last day or so,' he says. 'It always had to be someone close. There was the description. Who could it be if it wasn't Nige? The way Joe behaved when Tom was interviewed. And then Danny's email account on the missing phone. It only had two contacts. Tom ... and Joe.'

Ellie's humiliation is complete. 'All along, you said don't trust.'

Hardy lets all the air out of his lungs. 'I *really* wanted to be wrong.'

67

They let Beth have her boy back in the first week in September. Danny should be starting Year 7, scuffling off to South Wessex Secondary in an oversized blazer. Instead, Beth is bringing his Manchester City football kit to the undertaker near St Andrew's church.

They return the next day: Beth, Mark, Chloe and Danny, this family of four for the very last time. Outside the Chapel of Rest, Beth holds Mark's hand so tight that he winces in pain. She has seen a dead body before – she was at her dad's bedside when he passed away – but that was fresh death and a long time coming. This is different.

But once through the door, the nerves melt away, replaced by a weird sense of elation. Danny! They've done something clever to him, to make him look – if not sleeping, then not the horror-film corpse of her imagination. The light-blue football top used to bring out his eyes, but they are closed now, his lashes thick and dark on his cheek. As if by prior agreement, they each spend a minute with Danny alone, whispering in his cold ear. Mark goes first, then Chloe; Beth does not eavesdrop on the others' private goodbyes. Chloe has brought Big Chimp along in her bag. She keeps it together as she tucks the worn toy into Danny's arms. 'Night-night, Dan-Dan,' she says, with grown-up tenderness that tears Beth apart. Then Chloe turns around and half-collapses into Mark's arms. 'I can't leave him alone, Dad. I can't do it.' Mark is crying as he leads her outside into the fresh air, and Beth and Danny are together alone.

She lifts the blanket and counts his fingers, the way she did when he was a newborn, and keeps hold of his right hand as she lowers her face to his. 'I love you, baby,' she says. His skin is marble against her lips. 'I am so sorry. I love you, and I miss you so much.'

She stays like that, sobbing apologies over the coffin, for an hour. Mark takes Chloe home to Liz and Dean and comes back again, sensitively prising her away, telling her that it's time for the parlour to close for the day. Before she leaves, Beth runs her fingers through Danny's hair and dishevels it, so that he looks like himself. It is the last thing she will ever do for him and it is pathetically small.

On the morning of the funeral, she puts on a new dress and does her hair and make-up with care. She has muted hopes for the service. Everyone keeps telling her that today will be painful but good for her. They use words like therapeutic and cathartic. This day, fantasised about for so long, doesn't feel real now it's here. Mark in his black suit looks like an actor playing a part. That man in the top hat, standing solemnly at the door is like something out of a history book.

Beth is dragged mercilessly back into the present when

she sees the hearse. There is too much space around the undersized coffin. Danny's name is spelled out in white chrysanthemums and there's a tiny floral tribute in the shape of a football, sky blue and white. Her make-up is gone by the time she takes her place next to Mark in the mourners' car.

The cortège rolls slowly down the High Street: a child could outpace it on a skateboard. They pass the Traders, the tourist office and the *Echo*. Pete had warned them that there might be a few dozen well-wishers on the route – press interest is such that they have had to make the church service invitation-only – but nothing prepares the Latimers for what they see. Hundreds of people have lined the pavements to wave Danny off on his final journey. There are people Beth has known by sight all her life and faces she has never seen before. Pensioners, teens and mums with buggies have interrupted their day to stand in silent respect. For the first time since it happened, Beth is able to take solace in the support of strangers.

At the corner of St Andrew's Lane, Steve Connolly stands in his technician's overalls, his hands clasped in front of him. He is unafraid to meet Beth's eye. The way he looks at her – sad, sorry, sincere – makes something twitch in Beth's chest. Her faith is restored, if not in Steve Connolly's psychic powers, then in his integrity. Is he mad? She envies him, if so. She envies him his world of spirits and voices and signs. All this time they've spent in church and she hasn't had so much as a sunbeam through a window to suggest that Danny's spirit lives on. She turns her head, the better to read Steve, but his head is dipped in deference and then the car turns the bend and he is out of sight.

It seems that everyone has sent flowers. Lilies trumpet their arrival at the church gate and the sickly sweet smell turns September back into high summer. In a dark corner of the churchyard, Beth's father's grave is open and waiting for Danny. Far from giving her comfort, it only layers one loss over another.

Inside, the congregation is a sea of shaking shoulders.

The coffin is borne to the altar by Nige Carter, Bob Daniels, Pete Lawson and Dean. Miss Sherez, Danny's old teacher, lights a single candle and places it next to Danny's school photograph.

Tom Miller is a few rows back, tucked between Olly and Lucy Stevens. With a conscious effort of will, Beth forces herself not to look at him. She doesn't want Tom there, but unlike Ellie he can't, and mustn't, be held responsible for what Joe did. She finds room in a corner of her heart for this boy, Danny's friend, and what he must be going through.

Paul Coates wears a purple stole over white vestments. His is the only dry eye in the house. 'The Bible says: "Let all bitterness and wrath and anger and clamour and slander be put away from you, along with all malice. Be kind to one another, tender-hearted, forgiving one another as God in Christ forgave you."' Doubt ripples his brow. 'Is that possible for us, here, after what we've been through? I don't know. But we have a responsibility to ourselves, and to our God, to try.'

In the front pew, Beth cries loud and hard. Her skin stings with the tears that spill and spill from a bottomless well. There is no therapy here. No catharsis. Only the horrific dawning knowledge that she is no more ready to say good-bye to Danny than she was the morning she saw him on the beach. She will never be ready to say goodbye.

Karen White sips white wine from a plastic glass and looks around the wake. Mark and Beth have done Danny proud. There's a gazebo in the back garden, and they've opened up the gate so that the party spills into the playing field. Kids run in and out unsupervised, giving Karen a glimpse of what it was like in Broadchurch before the murder. It is as though the Pied Piper has given the town back its children.

All the children but one. Karen blots her leaking tear ducts with a paper napkin. Today, people are talking in terms of Danny's life rather than his death. She feels that she is getting to know him properly at last.

In the front room, a looping video of him playing football has Mark and Nige hypnotised.

'You never thought it was me, did you, mate?' says Nige. 'Not really.'

'How could I have ever thought that?' Mark replies too quickly. Karen sees what Nige cannot. Of course Mark suspected Nige, just as Beth suspected Mark, just as everyone suspected everyone except Joe Miller.

Ellie is prominent by her absence. Every journalist in town is after her, but so far no one has got to her. Olly is so protective he won't even discuss her: the police have hidden her well. Karen is aware that Danvers would sack her if he knew that she had the fish on a hook but tossed it back. But she's not interested in that story. It's Beth she's here for: not for what she can get, but to show support. Karen intends to leave after she has said a few words of condolence, but Beth is trailing a watery smile behind a plate of sausage rolls. People queue to talk to her.

Karen refills her glass – the wine is from a box, and it's starting to go warm – and stands under the gazebo where Olly and Maggie are chatting quietly, composure regained after the messy tears they both cried in church.

'It'll be weird for you, going back to covering the parish council meetings after this,' Karen says to Olly. He shuffles awkwardly.

'Actually, I've been offered a job with the *Herald*,' he says.

Maggie just about covers her disappointment with congratulations. Karen is less inclined to mince her words.

'Are you mad?' she says. 'You'll be earning, what, ten grand to rewrite agency stories? If you want to learn the craft, you'd be better off staying here. You'll learn more from Maggie in a week than you will in a year on the *Herald*.'

'That's what I told Len Danvers,' grins Olly. 'It didn't feel right. Thought I'd stay here a bit longer.'

Maggie throws her arms around Olly in delight. Karen reckons she's dodged a bullet there. Life is long, and who knows whether their paths will cross in the future, but right now she's not sure that their working relationship, let alone their physical one, would relocate too well to London.

She takes another sip of her drink. Over the rim of her tumbler, she spies the one she's been waiting for.

Alec Hardy is on indefinite leave while he waits for Wessex Police to decide his professional fate. A life of leisure does not suit him. He looks a little healthier, as though he is at death's garden gate rather than its door, but socially he is floundering. Standing in a corner of the garden on his own, he has no small talk. He is still dressed like a detective, in his blue suit and grey tie, and he's still watching the room like one too, staring intently at everyone. He can't help himself: not just because that's what he's trained to do, but because there is no other way he knows how to be. Karen finds herself in the unimaginable position of feeling sorry for him. Not so sorry that she's going to let him off the hook, though.

'Why didn't you give me Sandbrook?'

'You made my life hell,' he says.

'*You* didn't tell the truth,' she shoots back.

'I couldn't. You want easy answers, scapegoats and bogeymen. The world's more grey.'

Karen is insulted, then bewildered. 'Then why tip me off about the announcement?'

'Because you fought for the families at Sandbrook,' says Hardy. 'It was the right thing to do.'

He puts down his empty cup and walks over to talk to Pete. Karen is fuming. He always has to have the last word. She hasn't finished with him yet.

'Karen.' Beth is at her shoulder. Her face is beginning to plump and glow with the pregnancy but the skin around her eyes is tidemarked with salt that settles in the fine lines and emphasises them. She looks very young and very old at once.

'Keep in touch, won't you?'

Karen wants to howl; as if she would ever leave any of her families alone. She wants to hug Beth, but she looks fragile, as if one more embrace might snap her, and settles for a brief hand on her arm.

'Of course I will,' she says. 'And I hope you know you can call if you ever need anything ... Advice, or even someone to talk to.'

Beth nods. She doesn't have to say thank you. 'Will you come tonight? We're lighting the beacon for Danny.'

Karen's eyes fill again. 'I'll be there.'

The temperature drops as the sun dips over the roof. She looks around for Alec Hardy, but he has gone.

EPILOGUE

It is the night of Danny Miller's funeral. The tide is out and the beach and cliffs are washed pale by moonlight. Hardy and Miller, the jetsam of the investigation, have washed up at the cob wall on the far side of the harbour. They sit at opposite ends of a bench, arms folded, their backs to the sand.

'What will you do?' he asks her.

'Go somewhere else,' says the woman who has never lived anywhere but Broadchurch. 'Give the kids a new start. How could I walk down the High Street now? What about you?'

Hardy puffs out his gaunt cheeks. 'I'm done. Medicalled out.'

'Look at us,' says Ellie with a miserable little smile. 'The Former Detectives' Club.'

They stay side by side and stare at nothing. Behind them, a single golden light flares into life and moves slowly along the seafront.

It has begun.

*

There is a beacon at the top of Harbour Cliff, an old-fashioned metal basket on a mast. It is a relic of the days when fires were lit to warn of an incoming invasion. For a long time now it has served as a landmark for ramblers and a climbing frame for local children, but tonight, kindling and firewood fill the empty nest. Danny's family gather around it: Mark and Beth, Liz and Chloe, and Dean, who holds a flaming torch in his left hand.

Paul Coates leads a group of Broadchurch residents to Harbour Cliff Beach. Becca Fisher, Nige and Faye Carter, Maggie Radcliffe and Lil, Karen White, Olly Stevens and Tom Miller follow the icy-blue beam of Paul's flashlight across the sand. They gather at a pyramid bonfire set yards from where Danny's body was found. One after another they plunge waxed sticks into the pyre and let the flames take hold.

When all the torches are lit, Paul Coates points his electric torch at the top of the cliff and gives the Latimers their cue. Then he turns and flashes the same light at the opposite coast.

'Wrong direction,' says Becca Fisher, gesturing to the clifftop where the Latimers stand. 'You were right the first time.'

Paul gives an enigmatic, satisfied smile. 'Wait and see,' he says.

At the cold wink of the flashlight, Dean hands the flaming torch to Mark, who touches it gently to the beacon's base. The family listen to the woof and crackle as the flames take, hypnotised by the dancing gold.

431

The smoke punishes Beth's dry eyes. The adrenalin of the day is beginning to recede, an exhausted disappointment slowly moving in to take its place. The longed-for feeling of release remains elusive and tomorrow is a looming void. On the beach below, another torch bursts into life every second: from this height, they look like so many lit matches. She burrows into Mark's chest: his lungs work quickly against her cheek.

'Look!' says Chloe, pointing to the other side of the harbour. Another bonfire has sprung up on the opposite cliff. Seconds later, there's another beyond the curve of the bay. And then another. The beacons are *all* being lit for Danny. The family turn as one individual to follow the ancient relay of flame.

'They're everywhere,' Liz whispers in awe. 'How did everyone know?'

The lights continue to multiply. Dozens of bonfires blaze amber, as far inland as the eye can see. Down on the jetty, candles are being lit one from the other. Pinpricks of white mark the shape of the concrete path snaking out into the sea. Out to sea, the fishermen light flares on their boats. It looks as though the stars have fallen into the sea.

Beth turns slowly, looking at the vast cradle the community has made for them. A gust blows from nowhere, sending a cascade of orange sparks across the black. When they clear, she sees Danny standing on the clifftop. They look at each other through the filter of the flames. Danny returns Beth's nervous smile and she has the sensation of something sweet, like warm honey, pouring into her, soothing her from within.

She blinks again and Danny is gone before she can run to

him, but that's OK. She gets it now. The trick is not to let Danny go. The trick is to keep him with her. The fight isn't over and she will not let Joe Miller win. Her job as Danny's mother is not over.

Some lights can never be put out. He will shine through her. He will *shine*.

READING GROUP NOTES

Given the dramatic revelations within the novel, do you think it's ever possible to truly know the person you're married to?

Discuss the difference between watching the Broadchurch TV cast act out their emotions and reading in more detail about those same interior thought-processes in the novel. Did this change the way that you perceived any of the characters?

Should the press have been more restrained in their treatment of Jack Marshall, or were they simply acting on the best information available to them at the time?

Do you think DI Alec Hardy should have taken the blame for what happened at Sandbrook, given the negative impact it's had on his health?

In the novel, Tom Miller keeps a big secret from the adults in his life. Do you think children are usually this good at keeping secrets?

Who were your favourite and least favourite characters in the novel and did this differ to the TV series?

Did you guess who Danny's killer was (in either the TV series or the novel)? Did any of the other plot twists take you by surprise?

What do you think will happen in the second series of Broadchurch the TV show?